Silvana

Cover painting: 'Wildwood' by Emma Panting http://www.emmapanting.com/

Map by Karen Nolan http://www.karennolandesign.ie

Published 2013
by CP Books

ISBN 978-0-473-26402-4

The Copy Press Printed by The Copy Press, Nelson, New Zealand. www.copypress.co.nz

Silvana
The Greening

BELINDA MELLOR

For Peter

Once heard, the song of a Silvana can never be forgotten....

Masgor took the empty beaker from Fabiom's hand. "I would not have you getting ideas. For every man who wins such a wife there are three destroyed in the attempt. Those fortunate few who are chosen have not just the song, but the singer, for the rest of their days. The rest, well — they say the loss is too much for any man to bear."

Part
One

Chapter One

Branches arced over Fabiom's head and the limbs of each tree grasped those of the next, to form a canopy that seemingly went on forever. Wildwood: unbroken, unending. Here he was safe.

The last light of day gilded the leaves of autumns past, so that he trod a golden path between the burnished trunks of ash and elm supporting the living canopy above him.

He was not going home.

Evening chorus rang out from amid the branches. The daytime birds of the wildwood prepared for night, calling their final farewell to the sun and a warning to their neighbours that all territorial disputes would resume at first light.

The little boy tried to impersonate the chaffinch, as his Uncle Tarison had taught him, "*chip chip chip, cherry-erry-erry*." And the stream running alongside the path chuckled and gurgled, as if in amusement at his efforts.

The stream could laugh at him, he did not object to that.

As he knelt to take a drink, a shrill voice shattered the tranquillity of the woods, silencing the birds.

"I see him! I see him!"

Fabiom took one, startled look, scrambled to his feet and ran as fast as he could, regardless of the briars that tore at his clothes and skin, or the nettles that burnt as he hurried past. He knew where he was going, where he would *really* be safe.

"Nimo, you idiot! You scared him. We could have grabbed him while he was on his knees. Now we'll never find him."

"I don't know what you're fussing about, Khime. He'll go home soon enough. It's getting dark. He's not going to want to stay here much longer." Nimo, fourteen and the older of the two brothers by almost two years, looked around and shuddered. "I certainly don't."

"Oh, right. So we just go back and tell Lord Tawr that his four-year-old son is lost somewhere in the middle of the wildwood, but we're sure he'll come home soon?"

For a moment Nimo poked distractedly at a hole in a tree with a stick, then he grinned. "Not quite. We'll tell him that Fabiom said he wanted to show us something deep in the woods and then he ran off and left us to find our own way back – that's why we're so late. We'll be all surprised that he isn't already home, laughing at us."

Khime snorted. "We might get away with it, *if* he doesn't decide to tell Tawr or Vida what really happened. He's such a pathetic little mouse."

"Yes he is, isn't he?" Nimo guffawed. "It was so funny when you put him in that basket and put the lid on it and he couldn't work out how to open it again." He threw his stick at a chaffinch above his head, and missed. "Maybe we shouldn't have pretended to be wild pigs coming to get him though."

He looked at his brother for a long moment until the two of them doubled up with laughter.

"Oh, yes, we should!" Khime spluttered. "Whatever Herbis does to us for it, it'll have been worth it just to have seen the look on Fabiom's face."

4

Belinda Mellor

Fabiom stopped running. Short, useless breaths burnt his throat, while his chest longed for air. Blood oozed from his knee where he had tripped over a root and fallen. He wanted his mother, but he would not go home, not while Lord Herbis and his two horrid brothers were still there.

Fabiom had not wanted to play with them. But when Herbis asked Fabiom's parents to show him around Deepvale's silk mills, the two boys offered to look after him while the adults went off. They promised to take good care of him.

"Watch that he stays in the gardens," Tawr had warned them. "He's a terror for going off into the woods on his own."

At four, Fabiom was far too young to recognise the look of malicious glee that passed between the brothers at that moment.

"Ooh, Fabiom. You mustn't go into the woods. A Silvana might see you. Out she'd come from her tree and swallow you up!" Nimo tried, as soon as the adults were out of hearing.

Fabiom laughed. "Silvanii don't swallow people," he told the older boy disdainfully.

"Her roots and branches would wind around you though, and you'd be trapped, stuck fast in her tree, deep in the woods, where no one could hear you cry for help," Khime elaborated.

Fabiom giggled at that. "Don't you know anything about the Silvanii?" he asked. "They won't hurt you unless you hurt them. They're nice. They sing and they dance."

"And they take your mind and you go mad, mad, mad!" Khime looked at the little boy, who was still laughing. "D'you know where they dance, Fabiom? Bet you don't. Bet you'd be too scared to go there even if you did."

"No I wouldn't." Fabiom smiled innocently. He would not tell them that he knew exactly where the Silvanii danced. That was his secret; his and Tawr's. Not even his mother knew he had persuaded that information from his father.

Earlier that summer, after days of pleading, Tawr had finally brought him to the Dancing Glade. Twice since then he had gone there on his own, despite strict instructions about staying in the gardens. It was easy to find, once you knew the way: all you had to do was follow the stream. So how had he got lost?

The unending canopy no longer looked so friendly. It really did seem as if the wildwood went on and on, that there was nothing else in the world besides. Fabiom sniffed, near to tears. Somewhere near here was a wide grassy glade, encircled by trees, with a stream running through. It *did* exist, just as his father's hold-house existed and Deepvale and all the towns and villages and holdings beyond.

Standing there, lost in the evening gloom, surrounded by towering trees, he was beginning to wonder if that was true.

A tawny owl drifted past on silent wings. Fabiom smiled despite his predicament. He was not really afraid of the woods, even in the dark. There was nothing about the wildwood of Deepvale he did not love; except perhaps the nettles, he decided, as he rubbed his elbow with plantain leaves. The brambles he forgave, despite the damage they inflicted. Soon he would be able to enjoy their sweet berries; that was worth a few scratches.

'*Fabiom —*'

The crushed leaves fell from his hand.

'*Fabiom —*'

The voice was enticing, sweet and kind; leading him away from the path, over grassy hillocks and through dense bracken.

'*Fabiom —*'

He followed without hesitation, until he came out into a small grove of well spaced ash trees. Between the trees, the gently undulating ground was sprinkled with violets and anemones growing in profusion.

Though he was uncertain whether he had really heard the voice calling his name, or just imagined it, Fabiom was in no doubt the giggling he heard now was real enough. His mother had told him stories of the merry

Belinda Mellor

and mischievous woodmaids, denizens of holly and hazel, whitethorn and rowan, and other small trees of the wildwood.

And they had led him here.

Awed, he stood staring at the ash trees towering above him. At least one of them had to be Silvanan. Why else would there be woodmaids here?

"I would have brought some flowers if I'd known," he whispered.

Laughter like dry leaves in the breeze greeted his words. Fabiom paid the woodmaids no heed. He would be safe here, that was certain; and the roots of one of the huge trees formed a circle, like arms, where he could sleep. He was hungry and sore, but most of all he was tired. With a whispered word of thanks to the Silvana of his tree, he curled up in the woody hollow and fell asleep almost at once.

Dreams came in the night. He was in a dark, tight space, not even sure which way was up. There was no way out. His body jerked and he cried aloud. Suddenly he was out of the basket and running, but they were chasing him, catching up, trying to put the basket over his head again. He glanced over his shoulder as he fled. They had heads like wild pigs, with tusks and fierce red eyes, and through their piggy mouths, with squeals and grunts, they called his name. A branch lay across his path; too late he saw it and tripped. Triumphant squealing bore down upon him…. And then silence.

He had not heard her sing to him but, from that moment, only soft and gentle sleep was his. And the song remained in his mind – for the rest of his life.

He awoke as dawn touched the grove. For a moment, he thought he was in his own bed, he was so warm and snug under a thick blanket – of moss and leaves. He sat up, gazing around in wonder. When he stood, he saw the grass was dew-damp and yet he felt perfectly dry. Laughing, he wrapped his arms as far around the trunk of the ash tree as he could reach.

"Thank you," he said, planting a kiss on the rough, furrowed bark. "I've got to go now but I'll come back, I promise."

After that, he had no trouble finding the Dancing Glade; he simply followed the rippling laughter of the woodmaids. His father was already there.

Tawr wept as he scooped his son into his arms and hugged him against his chest. "I should be very cross with you," Deepvale's Lord Holder whispered fiercely.

"They frightened me." Fabiom's big blue eyes filled with tears. "Have they gone away yet?"

"I didn't think anything out here *could* frighten you. But whatever it was is gone, I'm sure," Tawr said reassuringly.

"Back to Windwood?"

Tawr let him down to the ground and knelt before him so that their faces were level. "Nimo and Khime. Is that who scared you, Fabiom?"

Fabiom nodded.

Tawr's brow creased, his jaw tightened, then he brushed his hand over his son's dark curls and grinned. "Don't you worry about them. I think a day cleaning out silk worm trays should keep them from any more mischief, don't you?"

"Smelly silk worms," Fabiom chortled as his father stood and swung him up onto his shoulders.

And laughter, like leaves in the wind, echoed him.

Belinda Mellor

Part
Two

Chapter One

Six amber beads clattered hollowly over the bright mosaic tiles as Vida yanked the string from her neck.

"Would you have me dress in green too?" she demanded.

Tawr, Lord Holder of Deepvale, opened his mouth to reply, and then closed it again.

Cross-legged on the floor, Fabiom glanced up at his parents, before returning his attention to the pile of goose feathers and the arrows he was fletching. He was distracted a moment later as a bright gem came to rest beside his knee. As he picked it up he saw a tiny fern, trapped forever inside the golden sphere.

"I thought you would like it," Tawr eventually said, his voice carefully controlled.

"At sixteen, at his age, perhaps!" She threw the words towards Fabiom, who wished he had chosen another place, rather than the courtyard colonnade, to augment his arrow collection.

"Vida —"

"I'm sorry I'm not as young as you would obviously like. But I don't see how bedecking myself in amber is going to help. If you wanted a wife who wouldn't age you should have offered yourself to the Silvanii when you were seventeen."

"Why do you do this? You always do this! We have just taken inventory of the last Silvanan tree to fall. We have removed all the amber. I brought you six of the most perfect pieces to wear because they were too beautiful to be kept locked away. I'm not implying anything; I am just trying to give my wife a gift!"

Summoned by the house-steward, one of Vida's handmaidens scuttled around, picking up the beads, each worth enough to feed, clothe and house a family for a year. With five collected, the woman looked around anxiously. The amber felt warm on his palm, and Fabiom was sorry to hand it over.

Taut as a bow string, Vida stormed into her dayroom, slamming the door behind her. Fabiom glanced up again but took no further notice, though as his father walked by he made a point of turning away so as not to see the pain on Tawr's face.

"Shouldn't you be at your studies?" Tawr inquired.

Fabiom had no choice but to look at his father then. Tawr's expression was composed, a mask.

"Masgor said he'd be late today. His brother is unwell and Masgor must visit him." He gazed out through the marble columns of the inner colonnade, wide blue eyes narrowing against the brightness of the spring morning. From where he sat on the mosaic tiled floor – deep yellow and red and palest cream to reflect the amber, wine and silk that sustained the holding – he could see his mother in her room across the courtyard. In a moment or two she would return, ready to let fly her arrows of jealousy. Fabiom put his work aside and rose to his feet.

"But I think I should go now, Father," he said quietly.

The hold-house of the Lord of Deepvale was set atop a wide hill, some way outside the town. Between the two, a well-made road ran down the hill and then alongside the River Swan. It was a pleasant walk in all but the most inclement weather. And never was it more welcome. Beside the river, the air was cool and refreshing, filled with the scent of wild thyme and lemon balm. Fabiom took deep breaths and felt himself relax. For once he did not have to hurry towards his destination as he did not expect his tutor for some while.

He contemplated going into town and attending the day's court hearing, though the notion held little appeal, but decided instead that he would wait in Masgor's garden. On the tail of that decision came a regret that he had not thought to bring his newest collection of poetry: *Ice Songs*, an early Spring Festival gift from his mother. Briefly he considered returning to the house to fetch it then dismissed that notion faster than he had the thought about attending court. Instead he decided to amuse himself by seeing how much he could recall, even though he had read it only once.

"*In those far Northern lands of … lands of – of frost and snow where no sunlight ever reaches, where starlight….*" He paused. "Oh, yes. *Starlight brightens the ice crystals and sea foam. There the Lady dwells – alone. She who….*" In frustration, he kicked a stone, and winced, remembering too late that he had opted for sandals rather than boots. "*She whose light is brightest….*" It would take him three readings to be word perfect.

He stopped talking to himself when he neared the outskirts of the town where, from the top of a gentle rise, he could see the municipal centre of Deepvale spread out below him, and, beyond that, shimmering on the horizon, the ocean. A clatter of hooves and a cheery greeting from a fruit-seller on her way to the market soon interrupted his reverie and he accepted a ride, and a pomegranate.

There were few in the holding who did not know him on sight and, as the donkey trotted along the road, the woman asked after his parents and his own wellbeing with as much interest as if she were talking of her own kin.

When they came to the crossroads, Fabiom thanked the woman and hopped off the donkey-cart. With a wave, she turned towards the town centre while he went the other way. Soon the open vista was lost to his sight.

This area, where his tutor had his home and school, was mainly residential – consisting of large houses, each with a good-sized garden. It was a quiet, peaceful place, and few people were about. Those who were, greeted him amiably.

Here the streets were wide and lined with lindens. Fabiom walked in and out of the trees, brushing each with his hand, and tried not to think of what might be happening at home; he would rather look forward to the next archery competition, possibly the last official one he would take part in. Such events were for boys only, and he would be celebrating his coming to manhood before the year was out.

Masgor's other students, eight at present, were attending the court hearing in the municipal buildings, a procedure with which Fabiom was far too familiar. As Holder of Deepvale, his father was a senior magistrate, and frequently took Fabiom along to watch and listen; quizzing him afterwards on what had happened and, more recently, asking his opinion on the rulings that should be handed down. Consequently, he could have been excused from his studies today. However, there was a private matter he hoped to discuss with Masgor and the occasion of an individual tutorial seemed an apposite opportunity.

Despite his dawdling, he was soon alongside the high white walls that enclosed Masgor's garden. Their surface was crumbling and tiny pieces of plaster flaked away under his exploring fingers. He wondered if Masgor knew, or even cared.

The wall ended in a pair of huge and fantastically wrought iron gates. They were closed but unbolted, and Fabiom let himself into the courtyard, glad of the stillness and solitude the place afforded. The sound of running water drew him to the far corner where gushing streams overflowed from the

Belinda Mellor

three inner bowls of a marble fountain, catching the light, toying with it, releasing it in a rainbow of spray.

Fabiom propped himself against the rim of an outer bowl, trailing his hand through the still water, breaking up the mirrored images of magnolias and mimosas and the garden's other exotic trees and shrubs. When he gazed upon the rippling surface he saw his own image made grotesque by the shifting liquid. It occurred to him to wonder if that was how his mother saw herself each morning when she looked at a reflection that, in her eyes, was no longer as beautiful as it once had been.

Fabiom wished he could help her. To him she was as lovely as ever, with her flawless olive skin and thick ebony hair that rippled to her waist in soft waves. She was tall too – though Fabiom had outreached her in the past year and now was barely a hand shorter than his father – and she was beautiful. Yet she could not like the face she saw in her mirror and could not believe that Tawr cared for it any more than she, for when she looked at her husband she saw a man who had fallen in love with the girl she had been. In her misery she imagined he must have found another, younger love. Fabiom knew this for she screamed her accusations around the house; barbed words that cut and tore and left wounds that could not be healed – words which goaded his once patient father to furious rejoinders. Fabiom hated it; feared he would begin to hate his parents – strove against that. But what he truly feared was the possibility that in twenty or thirty years he might be in his father's place, watching love crumble away.

When such thoughts gripped him, he would go out through the walled gardens and across the narrow stone bridge that spanned the River Swan; on into the woods – where ash and elm trees grew in profusion, where the songs of the Silvanii could almost be heard by one who had the patience to listen.

Fabiom cared to listen. He had grown up just that short walk from the wood. He had played there all his childhood days, daring to go into the deepest groves, daring even to climb high into the branches of the trees.

And since the age of four, when – scared and lost – he had taken refuge in a hollow formed by the roots of one of the ash trees, he had a tree he thought of as his own.

When he went to the woods for solace, it was to that same ash tree he invariably wandered, to sit with his back against the sun-warmed trunk and let his frustrations seep away into the cool earth; sit and listen for the almost-heard music of the Silvanii.

The trees in Masgor's garden were more colourful than those of the wildwood yet they held none of the same fascination for Fabiom. Nevertheless, a slight movement in the leaves of the jasmine overhanging the fountain caught his attention and brought him back to the present. The mantis consuming her mate was oblivious of his scrutiny or his censure. Fabiom had raised his hand to knock the callous creature into the water, when Masgor's voice stopped him.

"That is what they do. It's nature's way."

"It's horrible!"

"Perhaps," Masgor said with a shrug, then chuckled. "Saves any domestic disharmony though, don't you think?"

Fabiom's shoulders hunched and he could think of no reply.

The tutor nodded, his smile gone. "Shall we go inside?"

As Masgor dipped his hands into the ornate basin beyond the door, he seemed weary, the lines about his mouth taut.

"I trust your brother is a little better," Fabiom ventured.

Masgor harrumphed. "We're neither of us getting any younger, sad to say."

As he dried his own hands, Fabiom studied the short, upright man across the basin. It was odd. He had never really considered Masgor to be any age. He just was. Yet Masgor had tutored Fabiom's own father and uncle. Maybe the pewter-grey hair had once been another colour, though it was hard to imagine.

Belinda Mellor

They went through to the study where Masgor signalled to his pupil to be seated before excusing himself. Fabiom opened a copy of the history he had been studying, *Chronicles of Lincius, Prince of Morene*.

"Did you enjoy it?" Masgor, returning, inquired.

Fabiom grimaced.

"Not too well," Masgor guessed. "Nevertheless it is instructive. No?"

"Yes," Fabiom agreed, wondering if the moment had come to broach the matter on his mind yet not able to judge Masgor's mood well enough.

"You have a question," the tutor guessed. "Out with it, lad!"

Fabiom grinned, his earlier discomfiture forgotten. "I do," he admitted, "about Lincius's wife. She was a Silvana. Ever young, ever lovely. Was she happy, do you think? Were *they* happy?"

Masgor rubbed his chin and regarded his pupil sternly. "You are rather young to be considering marriage, Fabiom."

"I said nothing of the sort," Fabiom protested. "Though I am coming to an age when I might…."

"Yes, nearly seventeen. A significant anniversary." Masgor nodded. "Tell me then: why do you ask, if not for your own sake? It is hardly a question pertinent to the study of politics or history."

"It's not important – I just wondered."

Something in his voice made Masgor relent. "I should imagine they were happy enough. I've rarely heard of a man who won a Tree Lady for bride who was not content. As for the Silvanii themselves, it seems to be their nature to be cheerful, for the most part; if you exclude those who haunt yew trees and the like."

Fabiom scowled. "Yes, we will exclude those."

Masgor poured himself a beaker of water, and another for Fabiom. "I've had many pupils over the years, Fabiom, and I can't remember a single one who has asked me that question: were they happy?" He shook his head, obviously highly amused, though Fabiom could not fathom what the jest was. "Don't misunderstand me. There's hardly been one who, at some point, didn't ask about the Silvanii – it's just that usually the questions are more along the lines of: are they really as desirable as men say? Or: are they as enticing, as seductive? Or: do I, perhaps, have a copy of that most infamous book that their mothers would not approve of?"

"*Rhyton's Woodland Musings*," Fabiom said without thinking, then coloured as Masgor's brows rose.

"Have you read it?"

There was a challenge in Masgor's eyes which Fabiom could not resist. He took a steadying breath and focused on a small spider spinning in the corner of the window:

"Which dance is fairer to behold –
The branches of your tree bending to the rhythm of the breeze
or your limbs, as lithe,
moving to the rhythm of our love?
For all that you are is beauteous to me.
I am enthralled,
and ever will be, until my dying breath.
To lie with you,
entwined;
your breath
flower sweet,
Your –"

"Yes, thank you," Masgor interrupted. "No wonder you didn't feel the need to ask any of those more basic questions. Does your father know you've read it?"

"No," Fabiom admitted. "I chanced upon it. We have an extensive library at home."

The one fault Tawr would not tolerate was dishonesty, a lesson Fabiom had learnt very early in life. But, while he would not lie, he saw no need to elaborate. As a result, he decided not to inform his tutor that, not only did their library contain a copy of *Rhyton's Woodland Musings*, it was a rare, lavishly illustrated edition.

Trying to clear his head of suddenly remembered images, Fabiom held his glass up towards the window and watched the sunbow of refracted light that danced across the bookshelves. "These past pupils – did any of them go beyond asking questions?"

"Go seeking a Silvanan bride, you mean?" Masgor hesitated, then nodded. "Yes, there was one. He was a year or so older than your father, as I recall."

"What happened to him?"

"He survived the night. But he was dead within the half-year." Masgor took the now-empty beaker from Fabiom's hand. "So I would not have you getting ideas. For every man who wins such a wife there are three destroyed in the attempt. Once heard, the song of a Silvana can never be forgotten; those fortunate few who are chosen have not just the song, but the singer, for the rest of their days. The rest, well – they say the loss is too much for any man to bear. If you have studied the first chapters of the *Chronicles* properly, Prince Lincius's early exploits should have led you to expect that he would make the attempt; his talents and charisma made it unsurprising he should succeed. He was an extraordinary individual."

"That I know," Fabiom agreed quietly.

Indeed, he knew many stories of the Silvanii, of the suitors who had come, of those who had succeeded and the many more who had failed and had wandered lost, or insane, or mute for the rest of their days. He knew of the Silvanii's hypnotic dances and mesmerising songs, of their mourning when one of their trees fell and of their fury when one was cut. And although he could not be sure, he thought he knew which were their trees.

'His' ash tree was Silvanan. That he did know. He had sensed her presence on the first occasion he had gone to the grove where the tree grew, child though he was at the time. Sometimes he brought a wreath of greenery to hang in the branches as an acknowledgement of her presence. Indeed, he talked to her all the time – about everything. He trusted she did not object to his familiarity. On other occasions he brought woven strands of reeds to drape about the remains of the two Silvanan trees that had fallen in the woods in his lifetime, the amber from which, gifted generations ago to the first holder, helped sustain the holding. He treated them all with respect yet he did not fear them. As heir to the holding of Deepvale he would have to live with them all his life. He knew their ways as he had been taught, and he knew the kindnesses he must show them if they were to live in harmony. Yet, in one sense he knew nothing: he had never met a Silvana.

After Fabiom left his tutor's residence he strolled into the town centre, stopping for a few moments near the fish market to watch a fire dancer and then moving on, down a twisting side street towards the municipal centre, pausing to listen to an itinerant philosopher at the corner of the main square. Throughout the town, already festooned with spring greenery in honour of the season, entertainers were gathering for the forthcoming Festival, two days hence.

Fabiom knew every twist and turn, every pale yellow stone building, every statue and fountain of the haphazard town, which had been built and developed over many years in proportion to the holding's wealth and prestige. He had no particular purpose as he wandered, though he hoped to meet someone who might find him a distraction for the remainder of the day.

By chance he met Masgor's other students coming out of the court. Among them, a wiry young man with a mop of brown hair. Nalio was a year older than Fabiom and his closest friend.

"Did I miss anything?" Fabiom asked, with little expectation that he had.

"As a matter of fact, you did!" Nalio's eyes were bright with excitement. "A silk mercer was brought before the court. His goat-cart had overturned

Belinda Mellor

as he set out for Southernport, and when some other traders stopped to aid him they discovered a bag of amber hidden among his silks. Several dozen small pieces, for which he had no licence."

"What?" Fabiom demanded.

"It's true. And he's a local man, apparently," Nalio insisted.

"Who was sitting?" Fabiom began to regret that he had not gone along.

"Your Uncle Tarison. He was not impressed with the mercer's defence that he had no idea what was in the package. You should have been there, Fabiom! You should have seen him squirm!"

Fabiom sighed and pulled a wry face. "Ah, but he was just a pawn, wasn't he? Whoever's behind this outrage will be, at best, annoyed at having lost such a valuable cargo."

Nalio was not so easily disheartened. "Better than that, surely? If it's one of those petty, would-be rulers of Gerik that Masgor insists on telling us about, trying to fund their particular cause, today's events might have seen the end of their quest for power."

"Maybe," Fabiom allowed. "Let's hope it had something to do with Gerik anyway."

"It must have!" Nalio was genuinely shocked. "No one in Morene could be behind something like that. It's bad enough that a local trader was involved at all. Selling amber, possibly. Collecting it! Never."

In his mind, Fabiom could see the amber necklace his mother had rejected that morning.

"*Their tears flow like gold, from a well of deep sorrow.*
Our own are mere water, and dried are forgotten,
While tears of gold linger and last and endure,
Forever and then one day more, and one more." he recited.

Nalio snorted derisively. "Well, it's good to know Deepvale is in capable hands. The heir to the holding can quote at length from the most obscure poetry. But, can he remember the date of the last uprising in Gerik, or the name of the last Gerish ambassador to Morene? No, he cannot."

"Yes, he can," Fabiom muttered. "After the rollicking I got from Masgor yesterday, those two facts are inscribed on my mind for all time, believe me."

"Daydreaming again, Fabiom!" Nalio mimicked their tutor perfectly. He flung his arm around Fabiom's shoulders. "Never mind, you only got a rap across the knuckles. Our friend in today's trial had his silk trading licence revoked, so he's lost his livelihood, *and* he was fined *and* the court imposed two years' extra service on him. Hard service at that, in the claypits."

"Tarison made an example of him then. Good. It's only a pity there are no marble quarries in Deepvale. I believe they're the favoured destination for serious criminals in some of the other holdings."

"Oh ho!" Nalio stepped away from him. "I'll have to watch myself. You're bound to be made a magistrate as soon as you've done your official service, if not before."

Fabiom shrugged. "It depends on whether I impress the Assembly with my knowledge of poetry, or appal them with my historical inexactitudes. Anyway, what are you planning to do that will land you before the court? Poison any of your patients who don't pay you promptly?"

Nalio laughed. "First I have to acquire some patients. I still haven't heard if I've been accepted into the school of apothecary. Anyway, I'm not sure there's room in my head for the name of one more herb with healing qualities –"

"That's only because your head is too full of thoughts of the pretty daughter of a certain sculptor of this town," Fabiom retorted.

"True. Still I'll have to earn my physician's sash and ring if I hope to woo Eifa."

Fabiom shook his head. "Who would have guessed that when we went along to Strabo's studio we'd have come away with so much more than just an ornament for my mother?"

"She looked so pretty, didn't she, posing as a woodmaid? She just stood there, unmoving."

"So did you. Thirteen years old, and smitten. Remind me – what were the first words her father said to you?"

Nalio chuckled at the memory. "Close your mouth, boy." Suddenly he became serious. "Is it true, do you think, Fabiom? Is amber really Silvanii's tears?"

"So I believe," Fabiom replied. "It's said they weep when their sisters fall, or if their own tree is damaged." He grinned. "I found a piece once, about four years ago, in the woods near the house. Just a tiny piece, but so perfect."

"You never told me! What did you do with it?"

"I brought it home to give it to my mother. I thought she would like it."

"And?"

"She told me to put it back where I found it."

"Hmm, wise, I'd imagine."

"Maybe. At the time I presumed she said so because she was afraid they'd be angry, but now I wonder. Either way, she was probably right and I shouldn't have taken it."

They had been strolling aimlessly until, as realisation dawned, Nalio stopped.

"You still have it, don't you?"

The felt pouch pinned inside Fabiom's tunic weighed almost nothing yet he could never forget it was there. "I'll put it back, one day." He wandered over to a nearby fountain set beneath a natural spring and sat on the parapet, watching the bustle of the town.

Nalio followed and cupped his hands beneath the flow of clear water. "So you still go there, to the woods?"

Fabiom twisted a plaited bronze ring around on his middle finger. "Things are not so easy at home. The wildwood is peaceful. And beautiful. I go there to write my own poetry. Sometimes I imagine I can hear the Silvanii singing; as if – if I could just listen a bit harder, or in a different way, I could *really* hear them."

Nalio groaned. "Masgor's right, you are a daydreamer! Follow that path, Fabiom, and there's nothing in my father's medicine chest that'll be able to help you!"

Fabiom arrived home to discover his father and Kilm, their estate manager, waiting for him, ready to go hunting. Yesterday they had taken two roe bucks and a wild goat. That evening they were going after smaller game, not Fabiom's favoured sport, but enjoyable nevertheless.

"You could have gone on without me," he said as he tested his bow. "You know I won't be much help. You put up some wild ducks and I'll hit one of them. By the time I've notched a second arrow, the rest will have flown away. Accuracy I can do; not speed."

"Then we'll go for geese," Kilm said with a laugh. "They're slower. You'll likely hit two, and there's more to eat on a goose than a duck."

"You're quicker than you were," Tawr added, running the fletching of his own arrows through his fingers. "You need the practice, that's all. You never know – one day it might be important. Don't choose not to do something just because it doesn't come easily to you."

By the time they returned with their catch, the sky was a furled bolt of ebony silk, shot with strands of silver. They had five brace of rabbits, of which Fabiom could claim one, and a dozen geese, only two of which he had brought down.

As every year, on the eve of Spring Festival, Tawr and Vida threw a party for all their workers and their families – those from the silk mill and farm, along with the house servants. From early morning, the game brought home over the past few days turned on spits. The tantalising aromas mingled with those coming from the kitchen, where cheese and herb pastries, spiced breads, and honeyed fruits were being prepared. By mid-day there were tender slivers of meat ready to be cut off, wine flowing and songs being struck up. The music and dancing would go on late into the night.

During the afternoon, two couples among their workers came to ask for Tawr and Vida's blessing on their betrothals; three others brought new babies for their lord and lady to lay their hands upon. Fabiom handed out gifts to the young couples and the new parents – silk, wine and a thumbnail-sized piece of amber from fallen Silvanan trees for each.

There was one piece of amber set aside, for the baby it honoured had only arrived the night before. Vida and Fabiom would visit and bring gifts as soon as Festival was done. For now, the amber waited on the stand set beside the servery. Distracted from his intention of getting some meat, Fabiom watched the flame from the nearest bonfire shine in its golden depths; there was no gem or precious metal that could compare.

"Alluring, eh?" Kilm remarked, passing him a piece of saffron bread and a chunk of venison. "It's a generous gift. There can't be an unlimited supply. It's little wonder your father is held in high esteem; not many holders would give away such treasure."

"Thank you." Fabiom nodded towards the food. "Did you hear there was a large consignment of illegal amber apprehended?"

"Yes, your father was saying." Kilm held the piece of amber up so that it caught the light from the bonfire. "It grieves me to imagine where it came from, or how it was acquired. Hopefully it was old, just being moved. Even so, once it came from a living tree. It breaks my heart to imagine men deliberately cutting a Silvana's tree. You're the one studying Treelaw – what would be the penalty for such a crime?"

Fabiom frowned, considering. "Exile, at least. Death, if there was real intention; neither applied immediately, or mercifully."

Kilm rubbed the smooth stuff between his finger and thumb and shook his head. "Which is why we hold our neighbours in Gerik in such low esteem, of course; and why Prince Ravik makes sure to send all sons of holders there for at least part of their service, to see for themselves what can happen to a land where there is no penalty for such crimes."

"Thank you for that reminder," Fabiom muttered. "I can hardly wait. A country with no trees."

"Not really *you*, I agree, but you'll appreciate Deepvale all the more afterwards."

Kilm's nine-year-old son, Calbrin, came across the terrace, carefully carrying an amphora of weak wine.

Smiling proudly at his boy, Kilm accepted a refill and filled a beaker for Fabiom. "Enough of such talk! This is a festival of beginnings – of births and betrothals and plants growing. It is time to celebrate!"

"Indeed it is," Fabiom agreed as his parents swept past in a lively dance; Vida laughed as Tawr lifted her high and spun her around.

Chapter Two

Over the next few months, as the rows between his parents became more frequent and acrimonious, Fabiom spent less and less time at home.

On one rather dismal late-summer morning a message came from Ravik, the Ruling Prince of Morene, addressed to Tawr. Despite the weather, Fabiom went out, not waiting to discover its purport. It was enough to know that his mother objected to whatever it said.

On his return from the mulberry orchards, earlier than he would have chosen had it not been for the damp and the wind, Fabiom found Ramus, the house-steward, packing Tawr's bags.

"Your father is leaving for Gerik," Ramus said with a slight shudder. "Awful place – they say nothing grows there at all."

Before Fabiom could reply, his mother hurried over to him.

"You stop him going! He might listen to you. He won't listen to me!"

"Me? What can I say to him?"

"I don't know, Fabiom. I wish I did. Please, dear one, try. Just try. For me."

"Fine," Fabiom sighed, and went to find his father, who was in the library.

Unlike Vida, Tawr was in good spirits, though he echoed Ramus's view of Gerik. "Grim place. Still, this could be the turning point. Who knows? This treaty business has been dragging on for far too many years."

"Must you go?" Fabiom flopped down on the settle, throwing his legs over the armrest; looking not at his father but the ceiling of the room, seeing faces in the leaves painted there. Most of them looked cross.

"You'll break that one of these days," Tawr said cheerfully. "Your mother wouldn't like that."

"Mother doesn't like anything much these days," Fabiom muttered, which earned him a mildly reproving look from his father though no argument.

"Be nice to her while I'm away. Be kind," Tawr said. "I know it's been hard on you, and I'm sorry. I truly am. But don't blame your mother. It's not her fault. And in answer to your question – yes – I must go. Prince Ravik has asked me to help negotiate the next stage in the treaty with Gerik. And I trust you've learnt enough from Masgor to realise how, for years, that has been the cause of contention between these two lands. It is a great honour, and vital work for the sake of Morene." He picked up a book, put it back, then chose another. "I'll need this."

Fabiom reached for the book Tawr had discarded: *The Settlement Histories – from Cylanus to Lincius*.

"I was thinking about Mother, earlier. With her gold-brown skin and her beauty, and being tall and slender – when she was my age she must have looked almost like a Silvana. Well, like the pictures, anyway." He waved a hand towards the shelves where, amongst the books of poetry and Treelaw, horticulture and histories, there were collections of drawings. "Apart from her hair, of course. I'm not sure what native trees would have bark that colour – other than...."

"Don't say it," Tawr warned.

"I wasn't. I didn't mean that!" He sighed. "I meant, that if people commented; if she was praised for her looks and compared to the Silvanii,

Belinda Mellor

maybe growing older – and knowing that the Silvanii never do – could be harder for her than for plainer women."

"Very astute. And you may be right – up to a point." Tawr chuckled. "And, if you are, there's little you or I can do about it. Perhaps it's no harm that I'm going away for a while. It might be easier for us after a separation." He tousled his son's hair. "My only regret, Fabiom, is that I had planned to take you to Fairwater before the weather turned; just the two of us again – now that you are older. When I come back we'll go. There, that's a promise. Else we could go for your seventeenth birth anniversary – how would that be? All of us. It might cheer your mother up! We could celebrate in the marble city – and you could meet Prince Ravik properly." He paused. "Unless, that is, you have other plans for your coming to manhood and would rather be here?"

Fabiom sat up. "Are you suggesting what I think you are?"

His father shrugged. "Suggesting? No, not suggesting. But you do have a real affinity with the woods – it wouldn't be unreasonable. If you were to set your heart on such a venture I would not dissuade you; your mother, of course, would hate the very idea."

Fabiom was totally nonplussed. "I never considered, not seriously.... Well, of course I have, I mean, I've thought.... Who hasn't?"

"I'm surprised to hear you say so. On the eve of your seventh birth anniversary you told me that you only had ten years to wait. As I recall, you slept outside in the garden that night to 'get the feeling'."

"I was a child, then. I had no notion of the danger."

Tawr frowned and Fabiom fancied he looked disappointed.

"And I had no real notion of duty," Fabiom added.

"Duty? As an only son, an only child? Tell me, Fabiom, what would you be afraid of most, if you did present yourself?"

"Of letting you down, of course. Of letting Deepvale down."

"I think these are your mother's arguments."

"I realised I was being selfish. I have a privileged life. There's a price for that. I understand." Fabiom stared out of the window at the woods beyond and swallowed hard.

"Definitely your mother's arguments."

"Maybe. Listening to Mother occasionally is probably no bad thing."

"True," Tawr allowed. "But if you had a sibling, would that change anything?"

Fabiom glanced up at his father. "Everything. But I don't – do I?"

Tawr laughed. "Sadly, no. Nevertheless, I do, and *he* has a son. The line of Laurrus is safe. That is one concern you should put aside."

Fabiom sat up straight. "You give me leave?" An incredible feeling of hope welled up inside him, a feeling that caught his breath and left him reeling.

"I do. Whatever you decide I will give you my blessing, so long as your decision is made for the right reasons. As lord of Deepvale, I'm pleased you are prepared to put the holding above your personal desire but, as your father, your happiness is everything to me."

"Thank you." At last Fabiom managed a deep breath. "I can't deny that I dream all the time of meeting a Silvana. I've been trying not to, but the nearer I get to my birth anniversary, the harder it is not to think of how it would be to win such a wife."

Tawr chose another book to add to the growing pile. "I know you, Fabiom. I can't imagine anything else satisfying you. Why else do you think I agreed to even consider your betrothal to Herbis of Windwood's daughter? It was easy to say yes when I never thought for a moment that you would be available."

Fabiom frowned. "Yes, about that…."

Tawr held up his hand. "Not now. I promise I'll explain one day. The only thing you need to be concerned about is this quest. As soon as I get back we'll go over everything. I want you to have this chance, but I won't pretend the thought of you presenting yourself doesn't scare me." He rested his hands on Fabiom's shoulders and kissed the top of his head.

Belinda Mellor

"Have you ever known anyone who succeeded?" Fabiom asked, relaxing into his father's comforting grip.

"Not yet."

Fabiom recalled what Masgor had told him about the one student of his who had tried – and failed. "But you knew someone who tried."

"There was one boy, Icrates was his name. He was a bully, as I well recall. He had matured early and he revelled in his strength, and manliness, as he saw it. And he was arrogant. As a result, he wasn't popular with several fathers of young women in the town. It seems he thought even the Silvanii would find him irresistible. They didn't. He came home all right, but he'd lost his reason."

Fabiom turned to look up at his father. "How did he die?"

Tawr looked surprised.

"Masgor told me he did," Fabiom said.

"Ah. Well, it's true. He drowned. Apparently he would go wandering at night. Fell in the river. They found him several days after he went missing." He paused and looked at his son, searchingly. "He was the exact opposite of the sort of man who could win a Silvana's heart; and as different from you as it's possible to be – which is why I don't think you should concern yourself over such events. I truly feel that if anyone could persuade a Silvana from her tree it would be you, Fabiom."

"Thank you," Fabiom managed, realising the magnitude of his father's praise.

"Well?" Vida demanded, as Fabiom left the library and walked, distracted, towards his own room.

"Pardon?"

"Did you dissuade him?"

Fabiom shook his head, more to clear his mind than to tell her 'no'. Gathering his thoughts he managed, "He is determined; he says it is vital and an honour."

"I see. Thank you."

For the rest of the day she remained silent, finally taking to her room long before nightfall and bolting the door. It was not until the following morning, after Tawr had set off for Southernport where a vessel of the prince's fleet awaited him, that Fabiom fully understood the cause of her anger. He knew his father had long since served his time with the prince, so there was no compulsion on him to go. It had been a request not a summons that had been delivered. The alacrity with which the Lord Holder of Deepvale had departed to the cursed land of Gerik was sure indication to his wife that his only concern was to be away from her. His assertion, "It's what I do best!" had left her unmoved. Nevertheless, Fabiom hoped that, in his father's absence, his mother would relax and the house would seem more like a home.

His hopes were soon dashed. What she could no longer say to her husband, Vida said to her son – when he was there, which, despite unseasonable winds and torrential rains, was as rarely as possible.

One evening, driven home by the weather, he tried to talk to her while she sat at her weaving. He found it easier if he played music, so the silences did not seem so heavy and he could try to lighten the mood with chords that were sweeter than her words.

"I don't like that tune. Play another."

Fabiom picked out some notes on the lyre: a line from one tune, a refrain from another, and eventually she glanced up from her threads and smiled. And so he settled for a fishing song from Minnow Lake, the adjacent holding, and Vida's birthplace.

"Do you miss living beside the water and seeing the boats?" he asked her, remembering early childhood visits to his maternal grandparents' house on the shores of the great lake; the delicious pomegranates growing in profusion in the garden, that he would pick away at, one seed at a time; the fishing boats hauling in their catch and the little fish being smoked over the aromatic woodfires. He had enjoyed those visits, though he was

Belinda Mellor

always glad to come back and see the great woods of Deepvale standing, safe and comforting.

"Not really," Vida admitted. "I never cared to be out on the water, nor in it. I was not a strong swimmer. Yet I did like the sunrises over the lake. The colours were so beautiful."

"Yes." Fabiom concentrated on the complicated refrain of the song for a while and then glanced up. "I remember, you used to dress in those colours. They suited you."

"Your father liked them. When we first met –"

She paused and he was instantly wary, unable to read her expression. She fingered the deep wine silk of her gown, and her shawl of green and gold; the colours of Deepvale. "Those days are gone."

He had heard the story, many times. How Tawr had gone with his parents to Minnow Lake to meet his intended bride, how, feeling really nervous, he had taken himself for a walk to the shore as the sun rose and had seen "this vision" as he always described it: a young woman dressed in pink and mauve and palest blue, walking towards him, away from the lake which was bathed in those exact hues, so that he could barely distinguish her from the water. They had not spoken but he had gone to the house of his intended, convinced that he could not marry the girl he was about to meet, that he had fallen in love. And in she walked.

Fabiom wondered if he could persuade her to tell the story again. But before he could frame the request her mouth tightened at her own memories and she said, "Play something else."

He sighed quietly and changed to a song from their own holding, played at the wine harvest. Vida turned her attention back to her loom.

"Sometimes I wonder if he ever really loved me."

Fabiom stared at her, his hands stilled. One final, discordant note, hung in the air.

Vida reached to the small side table and picked up a statuette. It was a holly woodmaid, her dress painted in berry-red, and her hair dark brown and wild. The model had been the sculptor's young daughter, and the hair and colourings based on the artist Telmas's renowned frescoes in the palace in Fairwater.

"*She* wouldn't worry about such things." Vida's voice was quiet. "Look at her – carefree in her eternal youth. Nothing to do but dance and sing and play."

"You used to tell me such stories about woodmaids," Fabiom said, thinking to cheer her with easier memories. The ornament she held had been a gift from him. It was beautiful, but that was not why he had commissioned it. He had been twelve when he asked the holding's foremost sculptor to make something special for his mother and he worked hard to pay for it, pulling out old vines for his uncle in Valehead, scouring the big dye vats in the silk mill and pruning the mulberry trees at end-of-season on their own estate. "I loved those stories. I still do." In those days, when it was very cold outside or raining too hard and he grew restless at being confined indoors, she would sit on the floor of his room and tell him wondrous tales. "Do you remember the one about the boy who wanted to become a master dyer?"

Vida stroked the berry-hued dress of the statuette and, to Fabiom's delight, said, "I do. How did it start? Ah yes, I remember." She closed her eyes. "There once was a boy who desired to become a master dyer. Not content with the colours his parents and grandparents could make from saffron, madder, lichens and ivy, he took more pleasure in the shades he could produce with the bark, leaves and roots of trees, and their flowers and berries. But, in his ambition to become renowned, he paid little heed to what harm he did to the trees as he stripped them of their branches and bark. Over time, his search for new dyes led him deeper and deeper into the woods, until, eventually, he chanced upon a Dancing Glade.

"It was the day of the Greening, when the Silvanii and woodmaids gather to celebrate the first buds opening and, although he could not see them clearly, the boy caught glimpses of the most wonderful colours as the Tree Ladies danced and moved in that place, as if a rainbow had been snatched

Belinda Mellor

from the sky and was being blown among the trees by a gusting breeze." Vida stopped speaking and sat, looking at the ornament in her hands.

When it became apparent she had no intention of continuing the story, Fabiom picked up where she had paused:

"The boy ran after the dancers, grabbing and grasping, but his hands closed on nothing, so he began calling out, crying and pleading and disturbing the festivities, until a holly woodmaid gave him a drink that allowed him to hear and see them, although as if in a dream.

"'This is Festival, and at Festival it is traditional to exchange gifts,' the woodmaid told the young dyer. 'The gift we desire is that you no longer take anything from living trees, but only what you find on the ground beneath. Promise this, and we will grant whatever you ask of us.'

"The boy agreed eagerly, knowing what he would ask for in return – and thinking there was no way she would know whether he kept his promise or not.

"'What gift would you have?' the woodmaid asked, to which the boy replied, 'I would have every colour of the rainbow in my dye vats whenever I dye.' And he pictured bolts of cloth that began in red and moved through the spectrum to purple; cloth that would make him famous the world over.

"The woodmaid laughed. 'Every colour? Every time? Are you certain?'

"He told her he was and off he went home, thinking of the fame that would soon be his.

"And, ever after, regardless what he put in the dye vats, he could never make red or blue or yellow, or any shade in between; the only colour he could make was earth brown – the colour you get when you mix all the others together." Fabiom paused, smiling at the memory. "You used that story to teach me how to mix colours, to make violet and green and orange and all the other shades, as well as what plants give us the colours we dye with. But all I really wanted to know was what was in the drink the Tree Ladies gave the dyer, that allowed him to see and hear them. I still wonder."

Deliberately, Vida opened her hand, and the statuette fell to the floor.

She sat, staring at it, the right arm broken off, the face ruined. And as she stared at the broken ornament, Fabiom stared at her. Eventually, she raised her eyes to his and there was nothing there that looked like regret, or sorrow, or shame.

"It's time you grew up," she told him, and stood and walked out of the room, leaving him alone.

The statuette was ruined beyond mending. Fabiom waited in the day room for his mother to return and then, when she did not come, walked, distracted, around the house in the shelter of the colonnade.

Eventually he went inside and took refuge in his father's study where he took down the bound collection of coloured drawings of Silvanii and their attendant woodmaids. He usually turned to the Silvanan trees that grew in their own holding; Ash first, then Beech, Elm, Oak and Chestnut. This time he opened the book nearer to the back. The image of the yew Silvana was one he had rarely studied, though she was beautiful – with her golden skin and black hair. The original artist, Telmas of Rushford, had been the grandson of a Poplar Silvana, by all accounts. As a result, he had probably had more contact with other Silvanii than most. The rest he made up – basing his impressions on the fact that the Tree Ladies, whether Silvana or woodmaid, differed from each other much as their trees differed, and each favoured her own tree, with skintone that reflected the heartwood, eyes that mirrored the leaves, and hair the colour of her tree's bark. Telmas had painted the lips of the Yew Silvana pale, like death; though Fabiom fancied they would be bright red, the colour of yew berries. He suspected that Telmas, like himself, was guessing. Either way, he was almost surprised that the picture bore no resemblance to his mother, other than the night-black hair.

"You are both poisonous," he said in quiet fury.

Belinda Mellor

Chapter Three

Not a month after Tawr's departure, Fabiom returned home from the silk mill – where he had been helping Kilm sort purchase orders – to be met by the sound of wailing.

Not stopping to rinse his hands, he dashed through the heart room, following the noise. In the day room beyond, the velvet drapes were hanging in tatters and a shattered amphora of crimson wine was seeping across the woven rugs. His mother was not there.

Ramus, the house-steward, came hurrying in. He looked far older than his fifty years; his hands shook and his face was grey with distress.

"Is my father home?" Fabiom asked in confusion. "Surely they're not –"

"Master Fabiom. I couldn't find you. I've sent people all over – to your tutor, and the town, even the woods. I couldn't find you."

"I was at the mill, Ramus. What's happened? Where's my mother? Is she all right? Are *you* all right?"

Ramus, usually so composed, reached out towards Fabiom and then drew back without touching him. He looked around urgently, but no one was there to help him.

Fabiom moved towards him, and grasped his arms. "Tell me. Whatever it is. Just tell me."

"Your father … his ship … lost … Prince Ravik sent word … lost … all lost."

Tears were falling from Ramus's eyes and the words came out as sobs. For a long moment they stood, each holding the other's arms, and Fabiom could not have said who was supporting whom. Around them, the world spun. Nothing made any sense.

Ramus managed to compose himself at last. "Go to your mother, boy. She's beside herself with grief. She'll not be comforted by any other."

"It's a mistake," Fabiom assured Vida as he sat down beside her on her couch where she lay weeping, her face buried in a pile of slashed cushions, her wails muffled. "It has to be. They'll find him. He'll come home and everything will be – different."

He had this vision – for a sweet, brief moment – his father found and returned to them, his mother so relieved that the fights and rows of the past few years were forgotten. The three of them back to being the family they once were.

Vida sat up and stared at him, almost as if she did not recognise who he was.

"He's gone. He left me. I knew he would leave me, and now he has." She tore at her hair.

"No," Fabiom insisted, grabbing her wrists, pulling her hands away from her head, holding on to them so tightly that her fingers twitched and she released the lustrous, ebony strands she had ripped out. "No. He's got to come home. He *will* come home."

A hand rested briefly on his shoulder. Fabiom started. He had not heard anyone approach.

"I'll give her a draught to help her sleep." Namenn, Vida's physician, had arrived, summoned by Ramus. "And, if there's anything I can do for you –"

Belinda Mellor

"No." Fabiom stood and moved away to let the physician take his place next to his mother on her couch. "I don't need anything. There's nothing to worry about."

He needed to think, and he knew where he wanted to be. The woods beckoned.

"Can you stay with her a while, Physician Namenn? I won't be gone long."

"No – don't leave me, Fabiom!" Vida's voice rang after him as he tried to go.

He stayed.

Prince Ravik's deputation, having broken the news and paid their respects to Vida, went from the hold-house to the holding's municipal centre. From there, word was immediately sent to Tarison, Fabiom's paternal uncle, at his home in Valehead, the most northern part of the holding: the ship carrying the ambassadors to Gerik had foundered. All her passengers were lost.

The following morning, notice of Tawr's demise and Tarison's own vicarial role as Deepvale's curator was posted throughout Deepvale's public places. Horror and disbelief mingled with sorrow. Shops and businesses closed, dark-leaved ferns were strewn in the streets and garlands of bitter herbs hung in doorways as Deepvale lapsed into deep mourning.

Two days later, to Fabiom's relief, Tarison came to the hold-house.

Tarison was four years Tawr's junior. Tall, though not quite as tall as his older brother; with the strong arms and chest of a seasoned bowman; the same dark, walnut brown hair; the same blue eyes. Kind eyes – filled with a sadness that told Fabiom his father was never coming home – full of far too much sympathy and concern. Fabiom could hold in his grief and pain no longer. Those strong arms held Fabiom as the heartbreak washed over him; that strong chest, holding a broken heart of its own, accepted the punishment of Fabiom's pounding fists. And then, when the storm abated, Tarison relaxed his hold and took a half step back.

"I'm here. For however long you need me."

That evening, Fabiom finally managed to escape the house.

In a grove deep in the wildwood, he sat propped against the diamond-patterned bark of a huge ash tree; in his hands a small bunch of winged seedpods that had spiralled into his lap some hours before. The light had gone from dusk to fully dark and he was exhausted, both from grief and lack of proper sleep. He had told her everything, though he imagined she already knew – the Silvanii would know when the holder of their land was gone. She would have known long before he did.

"It's my fault. If I had done what Mother asked of me; if I had dissuaded him from going away…. It's my fault he's dead." There were no more tears; just that terrible realisation.

Finally, spent, he slept. As every time he had fallen asleep in the last three days, he dreamt he was drowning. Flailing, he cried out, gasping for breaths that drew no air, lungs aching.

And, as in an almost-forgotten dream that was more real than anything else in his life, she sang to him again. The same song as once, many years before, a song of comfort and rest, a song of healing that banished fear, and wove around his heart, and remained.

The messenger who came from the hold-house, searching for Fabiom, had alerted Masgor to the idea that something was seriously amiss, though the notion that Tawr was gone did not occur to the tutor. Even after the rumours began to circulate, brought to his ears by the house-boy, he dismissed them as nonsense. Not until the following morning, when he received a note

Belinda Mellor

from Fabiom asking that he should be excused for a few days, did he allow himself to accept the possibility.

'*Word has come to us that my father has been lost at sea....*' he read, weighing the phrase, wondering if Fabiom did not quite believe it either.

The note was unemotional and businesslike, and wrenched Masgor's heart. Nevertheless, he waited three days before going to the hold-house. When he did, Fabiom was so obviously pleased to see him that Masgor regretted he had not gone there sooner.

"I thought not to intrude on your time with your family," Masgor apologised as he rinsed his hands in the tall stone basin in the heart room and accepted the towel Fabiom passed him.

For the first time Fabiom noticed the fine tracery of lines on his tutor's face, and how the close-cropped, pewter-grey hair clearly indicated advancing years. With his sudden perception of the mortality of those closest to him, Fabiom felt himself age, as if childhood and youth had been stripped away from him in one stormy sea, one upturned keel.

"I am truly sorry about your father." Masgor regarded his pupil with sympathy. "And you – a boy thrust suddenly into manhood, bearing a man's burden of responsibility. You are very young and still have a lot to learn, yet there is much about you that reminds me of Tawr. As the philosopher Merites says: 'The son will grow to fill the father's place'."

"I hope so," Fabiom said, unconvinced. "You received my note? I could not come to your house. There have been so many people coming and going and my mother is distraught. I could not leave her."

"Of course," Masgor said. "You come back whenever you want, Fabiom – if you are able. It may well be that your days of leisure and study are behind you now. There will be many responsibilities you have to shoulder: your family estate with its silk mill and vineyards; besides preparation for your formal recognition as holder. Of course, I will assist you with the latter in any way I can. But I shouldn't keep you from Lady Vida, if she needs you –"

Fabiom opened the east door, that led to the day room. "No, please stay awhile, if you have time. Her physician – Namenn – is with her; and my uncle is attending to some urgent court business. I would appreciate the company."

As Fabiom walked through the woods that evening, he knew Masgor was right: everything had changed now. His father may have released him from the duty of heir, but now that Tawr was dead, Deepvale had to be his first and only concern.

For four years, the tiny piece of amber he had found had been kept in a pouch inside his tunic. Now he took it out and placed it carefully on a rock beside the water, at the edge of the Dancing Glade. That was easier than the second task he had set himself.

It was almost dark by the time he arrived at his final destination. He paused at the edge of the ash grove, as if seeing it for the first time, before making his way towards the trees at the heart.

"I had hoped to hear your voice," he whispered, leaning his face against the bark. "Whatever the cost, I would have counted it worthwhile. But I cannot risk leaving Deepvale without a holder. I have to try to take his place, to whatever extent of my ability."

There was a sound – as of a sigh. A breeze moved through the mighty branches. The ash tree whispered, the song of the leaves alluring in its own right.

"I cannot stay. Tomorrow we have a funeral service for my father. There are things to prepare. I just needed to come here. To tell you."

In truth, that was not what he had gone to the grove to say. He had intended to tell her he would never visit again. A final and proper goodbye.

"Fool!" he berated himself, even as he stepped off the bridge into the garden. He might have turned around and gone back, but he saw a glow from within the house and, concerned Tarison was waiting for him,

Belinda Mellor

continued onwards. He promised himself he would go tomorrow. And then, no more.

He knew he would have to stay away, that the woods were his no longer. The thought of being there, yet knowing he would never meet her, was unbearable. He would go to her grove one last time, to say farewell. And then he would do his duty as holder. In time, he would visit the Dancing Glade, but during daylight, and only briefly. On the day he was confirmed as Deepvale's lord, he would bring flowers and place them in that sacred site; the place he had imagined sleeping on his seventeenth birth eve.

The funeral service for Tawr was harrowing, more so for there being no body to burn, no ashes to scatter in the wildwood where the remains of generations of his forebears had mingled with the decaying leaves and fallen trees.

The funeral wound its way through the town, the keening and lamentation growing ever louder as people joined the procession. Branches were strewn beneath their feet, wine poured out on the road as they passed by, but all they had to burn upon his pyre were a few symbols of their beloved holder: his finest cloak, a lock of his hair, a favourite kidskin belt and his letter of appointment as Holder of Deepvale, sealed by Prince Darseus fifteen years before. Tawr had been twenty-nine; he always claimed he had been too young.

The procession eventually came to a halt in the public square, where a dais had been set up for the family and the holding's dignitaries. There, gifts were offered in Tawr's memory: food and small treasures that would swell the holding's coffers and would keep the needy fed and clothed, the old and infirm comforted, the orphan or friendless stranger from destitution. There were songs offered, and orations. Tarison spoke eloquently, as did a number of Deepvale's senior councillors, and representatives from various professions, guilds and trades.

Suddenly and completely unexpectedly, Vida said. "You must speak, Fabiom,"

"No!" Fabiom looked to his uncle urgently.

"Vida, he doesn't have to. Have pity," Tarison hissed.

"For goodness' sake! You've won awards for talking about nothing. Say something about your father. Anything."

Having little choice, Fabiom rose to his feet and stepped towards the front of the dais. He wiped his hands on his tunic, willing himself to keep some sort of dignity while he did this. If it was so important to his mother, then he would speak; it was the least he could do for her.

It was true, he had spoken in public many times. He had, as his mother pointed out, won prizes for doing so; a prodigious memory and a poetic mindset had stood him in good stead for several years now. But it had never *mattered*. Winning was never important. He enjoyed the hunt; if he got the prize it was a bonus. This was so much more. He wanted to flee to the woods, but they were no longer his. He would find no more comfort there.

And then he saw a woman he half recognised. She was middle-aged, unassuming, unremarkable. Recognition dawned – the fruit seller who occasionally gave him a ride if she passed him walking to his lessons. She touched her heart and nodded her head. He saw the tears on her cheeks and knew they were as much for him as for his father. Beside her, another woman – he did not know her – she held a child in her arms and another close by her side and the look in her eyes embraced him as if he too were one of her children. And the old man beside her, reaching his hands out....

These people were not going to judge him. If he faltered or stumbled over his words they would not think less of him. He closed his eyes briefly, took a steadying breath and began to speak.

Belinda Mellor

He could not have said how long he spoke for: childhood recollections, nostalgic nonsense, Tawr's fairness, his fierce protectiveness, love for his holding, passion for his family. At first he spoke hesitantly, soon he was lost in his memories and his voice steadied. Even when the tears began to flow he managed to continue. "That you will miss him, eases my loss, that you loved him is a salve to my pain. Thank you, for – all of this, your gifts, your words, your music. He will not be forgotten. In all of us, he will live on."

He stepped back. Wordlessly, Vida took his hand and pulled him towards her. She kissed his cheek. When she released him, Tarison stood and embraced him.

"You have their hearts; make sure you keep them. And your father…" He swallowed hard. "He would be proud of you – as I am. You have honoured his memory."

The following morning, Fabiom bid farewell to his uncle. He would have pressed Tarison to stay except that he had learnt why he had come alone, without his wife: Marid had been confined to her bed. At dawn a messenger had come to say she had lost her unborn child. It was not the first time, that much Fabiom knew, though it was not spoken of openly.

Heart sick, though no longer only for his own loss, Fabiom once again took the well-known path to the ash grove. He brought a garland of olive, laurel and flower-laden japonica, his final gift.

"You have given me so much: shelter, solace, inspiration – and I am ever grateful. I will not forget." He draped the garland over the lowest boughs of her tree then dragged his forearm across his eyes, wiping away unbidden tears, before resting his hands on the trunk one last time. "As much as anything, I would have liked to learn your name."

A narrow beam of sunlight pierced the shadows and an unexpected brightness flared in the hollow formed by the great tree's roots. Curious, Fabiom knelt, barely breathing as he realised what he was looking at: a palm-sized piece of flawless amber nestled amid fallen leaves where once he had slept. In awe, he brushed it with his fingertips but did not disturb it. And then, bewildered, he scrambled to his feet and left.

That night, Fabiom did not sleep. Instead he wrote poetry that became more and more disjointed as the night wore on and exhaustion claimed him. All the while, one thought kept recurring: *if she wept, how can I not try?*

Chapter Four

On most days, when Namenn the physician came to visit Vida, his son Nalio accompanied him. Often, Fabiom and Nalio took bows and went hunting; other days, if neither family had need for meat, they would shoot at targets in the garden. Fabiom appreciated his friend's patient company.

On the tenth day, while Namenn was with Vida, Fabiom suggested they leave their bows and arrows behind. He was ready to talk.

Together they walked across the garden to the stone bridge that spanned the river. It was easier to face his loss with the water flowing away beneath his feet; like life, like tears. Nalio listened while Fabiom vented his anger and frustration. As misery gave way to remembered moments of happiness, Nalio added a few fond memories of his own. As Fabiom's friend, he had known Tawr most of his life and spent many hours in Deepvale's hold-house and the lord holder's company.

"Do you remember when he caught us in the garden with handfuls of yew berries? We can't have been more than five and six. You had already put some in your mouth. He got them away from us and then didn't know whether to wallop us or hug us!"

Fabiom smiled. "As I recall, he did both – with equal force. Then he got an axe and cut the tree down and burnt it."

The storms of the preceding month had blown themselves out and it was a pleasant day. A breeze stripped some of the leaves from the trees and blew them towards the pair. On impulse, Fabiom crossed the bridge, leading them into the woods beyond.

Nalio knew the great woods of Deepvale well enough, though not intimately. It was some years since he had been there with Fabiom. They had been children then, playing wild games, running and climbing. Never before had he observed Fabiom's ease amid the tangled ways, his knowledge of the winding paths or the casual awareness with which his friend touched a branch here, a trunk there. They walked on.

"Talk to me, Fabiom," Nalio said at last.

"I have made a decision," Fabiom said, half reluctant to reveal his intention yet wanting, needing, to share his thoughts with someone. He was well aware that if he did not take this opportunity there might never be another.

Nalio stayed silent, waiting for him to continue.

"It's fifteen days to my seventeenth birth anniversary." He looked at Nalio meaningfully and indeed there was little need for him to say more.

Nalio almost laughed. "Sleep in the woods? You are joking? You're not joking, are you? Fabiom – you can't. How can you even think of trying to win a Silvana now?"

"Now? It's not as if there's any other chance. It's fifteen days from today or not at all."

"My advice? Choose *not at all.*"

"I can't. Truly, Nalio, I can't. I tried –"

"What do you mean, you tried?"

"I came here to the woods to say farewell, to accept I had to live in the world of men and take up the responsibilities my father left me. Instead I found another piece of amber, and the words would not come.

Belinda Mellor

"That night, I tried to imagine my life if I didn't at least make the attempt, and I couldn't – I couldn't imagine *anything*."

"You risk much. Only son of a high house. Heir to a grand holding and a deal of responsibility."

"I know all that," Fabiom replied rather shortly, challenging Nalio to tell him something he did not already know.

Nalio did not oblige. "May I ask why? I mean, I know we all daydream about doing such a thing; I certainly did, even after I met Eifa. I doubt there's a boy who hasn't. But fantasising about wedding a Silvana and actually presenting yourself in the woods on your seventeenth birth eve are two very different things. And that difference is what makes most of us forego the imagined delights of being in the arms of a Tree Lady – for the sake of our continued sanity, or our life, for that matter."

Fabiom had never told his friend of the quarrels that had preceded his father's doomed departure for Gerik, though he thought Nalio must have guessed something was amiss from things said, and left unsaid. There in the enveloping sanctuary of the woods he found himself able to speak at last of the fear and anger, the accusations and dreadful silences that had marred his home life for the past few years. He spoke also of his love for the woods and the life therein, though Nalio did not need to be told of that. He could see it for himself.

"I'm as much at home here as within the walls of the hold-house," Fabiom finished, plucking a handful of swollen, glistening berries from the tangle of brambles nearby. He handed half to Nalio who shook his head, though not in rejection of the fruit which he accepted and enjoyed.

"Not all women are like your mother," Nalio said gently. "Surely you see that?"

"Of course. But those who are not find other things to be discontent about." He could think of many exceptions to his damning generalisation, not that he would admit as much and undermine his argument and possibly his resolve.

Nalio chuckled. "So jaundiced, so young! I wouldn't want my sweet Eifa to hear you speak so. But these are just excuses, ways of justifying your intentions, surely?"

Fabiom shrugged. "Possibly." He turned away and studied the swirls in the bark of a nearby hazel tree. "Oh, it's not women only. All of us are the same. I can't change who I am, so I must choose carefully who I spend my life with." As he said so, the image of his parents fighting came to him, very real and very frightening.

"Maybe something happened between them," Nalio suggested. "They used to be happy. *You* used to be happy. I'm no expert, but I don't think married couples normally fall out like that – without cause. It really doesn't seem a good enough reason to do what you're proposing."

"Maybe." Fabiom took a deep breath, and let it out slowly. He should be having this conversation with Tawr. His father should be walking beside him through the wildwood. He pictured them going together to the one Silvanan tree Fabiom knew of. Tawr would have said something to her, put his son's case or asked her to be merciful. Fabiom stopped walking to place his hand against the trunk of a young ash tree, drawing strength, fighting back tears.

Nalio's voice cut into his thoughts, "Was there not talk of a betrothal? The daughter of some hold lord on the coast – Westwood. No, not Westwood – what's it called?"

"Windwood. And it was just talk. This is what I want. I have to try, don't I?"

"But what if you're not accepted?" Nalio asked, concern in his voice despite his efforts to sound nonchalant.

Fabiom looked up at the intertwined branches of elm and beech, ash and chestnut above his head and then glanced at his companion. "If not one Silvana here thinks me worthy, then such a judgment is probably valid and my demise will be no great loss." He spoke lightly, though he did not feel as easy about the prospect as he tried to sound.

Belinda Mellor

Nalio did not reply.

They walked on for a while in silence, only the sound of their feet on the dry leaves and the occasional chuckle of small birds breaking the stillness until Nalio asked, "You know the form?"

Fabiom did, detail by detail.

Just fifteen days to his birth anniversary: his coming to manhood and his inheritance. He had looked forward to the first for much of that last year, never guessing that the second would be thrust upon him at the same time, that his father would not be there as he took on his adult responsibilities in the community and in Prince Ravik's service.

The prince had sent a long letter of condolence. Tawr had served him, and also his father, faithfully and had been well respected and well liked. Ravik wrote that he looked forward to making Fabiom's acquaintance properly; he also promised he would not call upon Fabiom's services for some years.

Fifteen days. His mother was so wrapped in her loss and her anger that she did not remember. That was some consolation. The last thing Fabiom wanted was a grand celebration and a feast that would be certain to raise some awkward questions as to why he was not eating. In the last couple of days Vida had ceased to insist that he spent every moment with her, though she did not like him to be away long. He returned to his studies with Masgor, as much for the company as anything.

For the last two days of his adolescence Fabiom fasted, drinking only water, eating nothing. He was concerned that his mother ate little more, though the fact that she missed so many meals suited his purpose very well.

Time passed slowly.

Each day, after his lessons, he went to the silk mill for a while, though production was all but stopped while the holding mourned, and no one expected him to be there. In the evenings he fashioned himself a new longbow out of a split bough of shade-grown elm as his father had shown him, stringing it with silk prepared with beeswax from the neighbouring holding of Alderbridge.

He had been just a little boy when they bent almond and cherry saplings to fire reed arrows at woven targets set amid the lavender and the rose bushes in the garden, until Vida shooed them out for the sake of her fruit trees and her flowers. Later, they made bows out of branches hewn from elm trees growing at the edge of the wildwood, and arrows from seasoned wych hazel which they straightened over the fires in the silk mill. Tawr had patiently taught him all these things. They had set the shafts with barbed flint heads and fine silk lines and gone off fishing. Fabiom remembered the first fish he had caught, the pride on Tawr's face, his own elation. His mother had cooked the fish herself and the three of them had shared it.

There was only one thing his father had been unable to teach him, and that was Tawr's own special trick of hitting two flying targets at once. Time and again Fabiom watched his father shoot at woven discs being catapulted into the air and pierce two with a single arrow – three on one memorable occasion. Over the years, with unfailing patience, Tawr tried to pass the knack on: "It's in the timing. You fire too soon. Wait."

"I'll miss them all if I wait."

"You won't. Trust me. Trust yourself."

Fabiom sighed as he tested the new bow, firing several arrows close to the heart of a distant target. It would do, for now. When he was twelve, thirteen at most, Tawr had brought him to watch a master bowyer at work and told him that he could choose any bow he wanted. Both his father and the bowyer wanted him to have the fine yew bow with silver nocks that had just been completed before their eyes but something about the feel of it had displeased him and he chose instead an ash-backed elm bow, nocked with polished horn. He had loved the feel of it in his hands and it had served him well, earning him accolades, awards and praise as he proved himself almost invincible in accuracy competitions thereafter. That was all past now. The bow was no longer tall enough for him and Tawr was gone.

As the afternoon of his birth eve waned, Fabiom asked for a bath to be drawn and, having bathed, he dressed carefully in the plainest clothes he possessed. The freshly laundered cloth was stiff and unyielding and the straps of his sandals dug into his ankles where he had pulled them too tight. He went and sat on the parapet of the balcony beyond his room, gazing out across the garden towards the woods, though they appeared just as an uncertain darkness against the fading light of the day. He loosened the biting sandal thongs and leant his head back against the cold stone of the balustrade. A fox coughed in the distance as if to say 'soon, soon'. Fabiom stood, his left wrist white where he had been grasping it unrelentingly with his right hand. He knew he must relax, believe in himself. The fox called again, a lonely sound. It was not easy.

As he passed through his room he glanced once at the knife belt thrown on the counterpane. He would have no need of a knife nor of any adornments tonight. So thinking, he pulled off his rings and armbands and left them beside the belt. Finally, he dragged a comb through his unruly dark curls. There was nothing else to do. He was as ready as he would ever be, and dusk had fallen.

Ramus was tending pot-plants in the conservatory that served as an entrance vestibule. He nodded to Fabiom pleasantly before commenting, "We have a touch of greenfly it seems."

Fabiom presumed he was referring to the plants. "Is my mother in her room, Ramus?" he inquired, surreptitiously plucking a crimson bloom from a hanging orchid.

"Yes, Master Fabiom, Lady Vida retired some while ago."

The house-steward passed no comment on the flower, neither did he address Fabiom as Lord; that title was not Fabiom's until the morrow. As it was, Fabiom doubted that Ramus or any of the servants realised that it was tomorrow he reached seventeen years. Then again, maybe he would not.

"I'm going out," he said, relieved his mother was not up and about. "No one need wait up. You may lock the doors." And he strode out before Ramus could question him.

He walked purposefully across the garden yet his steps faltered as he reached the stone bridge. The sky was almost black and only a few faint stars managed to break through the cover of cloud. It was not so late but the day had been overcast and night had come early. The wind snatched at his cloak. Fabiom shivered and pulled the garment closer about his body. It was too cold to stand still on the exposed bridge and he would not turn back, so he walked on.

Halfway down the wide swath that led into the heart of the woods was a track to the right. Fabiom needed no light to find the turning. Soon the path branched again and narrowed and he took the left fork. Soft-leaved twigs from low hanging branches brushed his face, touches like soft caresses, causing his concentration to lapse and his feet to wander from the narrow path to where brambles caught at the bare skin of his legs, reminding him of the dangers the night held. He put such thoughts aside and walked on, ducking under branches, climbing over root boles until, with one more left turn, he arrived at the Dancing Glade.

The soft churring of a nightjar on the wing echoed strangely in that open space, and the unmistakable voice of the stream, babbling and chuckling as it ran through the woods and traversed the glade, guided Fabiom to the gently sloping bank. He knelt to wash, gasping as he rinsed his face and arms in the chilling waters, then fumbled with his sandal straps, his fingers almost numb with the cold.

"I hope you were right about me, Father," he whispered to the night. Then, leaving the orchid beside his sandals on the bank, he went back to the centre of the glade. It was time. He was ready. He lay down, his cloak

Belinda Mellor

close about him, and rested his head on one arm. Even as he was thinking it would be impossible to sleep, slumber overcame him.

Night deepened. Still he slept.

On the edge of his dreaming, on the edge of his hearing, voices were raised in song. Laughter ran like the waters of the river.

Fabiom stirred but he did not awake.

"*A handsome one, and daring, is he not?*" a sweet voice asked, followed by light laughter.

"*Or foolish?*" suggested another.

"*I wonder which.*"

Fabiom could hear the voices clearly, as if he were awake, yet he could not move. He moaned slightly, eliciting more tinkling laughter.

"*He is comely, though there is little flesh on him.*"

"*Maybe he is lost, just coincidence today is his birth eve.*"

Singing, sweet singing. Fabiom relaxed. He could listen to such music forever.

"*Casandrina, stop that! You will send him mad.*"

"*No, I will not do so. See, he smiles. He likes my singing. He likes my tree. He has climbed in its branches often enough.*"

Even asleep, Fabiom could feel tendrils of fear brushing his mind, that vanished as the voice sang on.

"*He meant no harm,*" a new voice said hurriedly. Did he hear concern?

"*No, he meant no harm.*" She had to stop singing to speak and he was almost sorry, though he should have been glad at her reply.

"*What now?*" another asked. So many voices, he could not say how many nor easily tell them apart, except the one singing. Was she the Silvana of his favourite ash tree?

"*He is lord of the hold-house beyond, holder of all Deepvale. He knows us. If he cannot stay there one might come who cares nothing about our fate.*"

"*Yes. We must spare him.*"

Whoever agreed it was not the singer, Casandrina, the only name he had heard so far. She did not agree. She only laughed and sang on.

"*Stop, Casandrina! I would claim….*"

"*No, Gracillia. I will not forget how he slept beneath my tree, how often he came there and made it his own. I will not forget.*"

Fabiom could do nothing. He wanted to ask pardon. He had meant no offence.

"*I shall sing to him.*"

He was glad. Foolish! Wake up! Yet he could not.

"*I shall sing to him for the rest of his life –*"

"*No! I shall not step back so easily, Casandrina. You have all heard me. I claim him and I shall have my way – at whatever cost.*"

"*Gracillia!*"

"*Do not sound so shocked, Narilina. You once stood against your sisters for a human – and endured.*"

"*I had my way, it is true,*" the Silvana accepted. "*Nevertheless, I would ask you – both – to desist from this path. It is more than your own wellbeing you risk.*"

There was a lengthy silence, during which Fabiom felt he was being scrutinised. He knew for certain there was only one voice he longed to hear again. Yet when at last she spoke, her words were not what he wanted to hear:

"*Not so easily will I walk away – yet if I were to let you take him, it would be for his sake; not for yours, Gracillia, and most certainly not for my own.*" Her tone conveyed anger and sorrow in equal measure.

Fabiom's heart ached with a sudden loss. Somehow he managed to whisper one word, "No." He feared it was not enough, that they would not understand what he was saying no to. In that, he was mistaken.

There was a sudden cry of anger, swiftly followed by another. Sounds as if of a rising wind filled the Dancing Glade. Fear washed over him: he was in mortal danger where he was, lying helpless amid the maelstrom of fury he had unleashed.

Must wake, must – wake. He could not be the cause of her being hurt. He could endure anything but that.

Belinda Mellor

"Casandrina."

His voice was barely louder than a falling leaf touching the forest floor and yet it cut through all the other, awful sounds until utter silence fell.

"*Enough.*"

"*It is resolved.*"

He did not recognise the voices. What he did know was that the presence in the glade was less, the Silvanii were leaving, peace restored. As they departed, their voices swirled around him, gently, like blessings. Fear leached away from him into the earth as the deep sleep that he had been fighting overwhelmed him and he knew no more until …

… the morning sun filtered through the branches of the ash tree. Fabiom blinked and sat up, rubbing stiff limbs. He was not in the Dancing Glade nor anywhere near it.

Relief and joy flooded through him in equal measure. Above him, his beloved ash tree rose, more beautiful to him than ever. Leaning his face against the deeply etched bark he sighed and murmured, "Sing to me." But all he could hear was the voice of the wind as it moved softly among the winged seeds and few remaining leaves, chanting a lullaby. He resisted the urge to sleep again and stood. His sandals were nowhere to be seen. He smiled as he laid his hands gently on the trunk, then, though he longed to stay, he turned and started for home.

Six more nights, and this next part was unclear. His research had prepared him well for his birth eve; what followed was shrouded in mystery. Yet, despite the uncertaintly, he sang and laughed as he made his way home.

Behind him, a sudden gust of wind caught a crimson orchid lying amid the branches of the ash tree and sent it spiralling to the earth.

Chapter Five

"**Master** Fabiom!"

Fabiom followed Ramus's appalled gaze to his bare feet, dirty from the walk through wood and garden, bloodied from a sharp rock he had trodden on.

"Good morning, Ramus. Is my mother awake yet?" he asked, ignoring the matter of his appearance.

"Not yet. Shall I have one of the servants draw you a bath?"

Fabiom nodded. "Yes, thank you."

"And breakfast?" Ramus persisted.

"No, not breakfast."

When Fabiom came to undress for his bath he realised that it had not been just the state of his feet that had amazed Ramus. His clothes were grass-stained and his hair had moss in it. He smiled at his reflection. *Happy birth anniversary*, he said to himself.

Even though his birth anniversary passed unremarked by the rest of the household, after the events of the night, Fabiom was certain nothing could mar his good mood. Nevertheless, he was growing seriously hungry. Two days of fasting he could endure, three was getting beyond uncomfortable, especially when the cook began baking and the house gradually filled with the aroma of hot bread. Fabiom had never had to go without food before, his life so far had not prepared him for such deprivation. He wondered how he would manage for five days more, whether fasting for so long was even possible. Certainly sitting indoors inhaling the scent of freshly baked bread and spiced pastries was not the answer.

He took himself off into the garden, to breathe instead the sweet fragrance of autumnal blooms. His mother was there, cutting dead flowers from her scented rose bushes. Fabiom wished she would cut some of the buds instead and bring them indoors, though it was no use saying so. She had no interest in live things yet.

"Shall we build a new hold-house?"

Her question took him by surprise.

"No," he said after a pause. "Where?"

"Anywhere. I don't think I can go on living here."

"But...." *Be careful*, he warned himself. "The holders of Deepvale have always lived here. We belong here." It was a statement. He thought it wiser to make a statement than to express his feelings, which at that moment bordered on panic.

"That is of little matter," she countered. "This house is not as old as the holding. There was a house on this site before this one was built, a house like this could be built on another site. What do buildings matter?"

"But the mulberry coppices. We can't move those and they are our livelihood."

Vida put down her pruning knife and turned her full attention to her son.

"They will be tended, as they are now. We have an excellent manager in Kilm. You have shown scant interest in silk production before now. I suspect your absence from the estate would be of little matter." She paused, then said, "You do realise, I presume, the significance of silk to this holding – to this land?"

He gave a short, mirthless laugh. "Yes, Mother, of course I do."

She brushed a hand across her gown. "There is no country in the world, save Morene, where silk is made. And in Morene, Deepvale's silk is among the best and the most sought after."

"I know that," he said shortly. "I learnt that lesson when I was little more than an infant. Do you think me so ignorant?"

"There's no need to be rude, Fabiom. I sometimes wonder, that's all. You are always so engrossed in what you consider important that I fear you have failed to realise what does matter."

"I'm sorry," he said, though not sounding particularly contrite. "And you're right, I do have a lot to learn. But how our ancestors learnt the secrets of sericulture from the Silvanii is something I do know."

He imagined a Silvana directing their own silk production; that would certainly make the process far more interesting, he decided.

"Indeed," she allowed, begrudgingly. "However, that was a long time ago. We have learnt to manage well enough without … them, since those days."

I haven't, Fabiom thought, *I couldn't. And they are here – how could I live anywhere else?*

"The woods," he said. "Would you move away from them?"

She regarded him sternly. "You think too much of the woods, when you should be listening to the litigations in the courtroom, inquiring after the latest discussions of the Assembly, studying in the library. Maybe we should be nearer the centre of Deepvale. You might do such things then, as you ought. Yes, I think that would be best."

She had turned away from him, gone back to withered flowers, pruning and trimming; her mind on her plans for a different future.

Fabiom would not argue, not yet. He stood for a moment, brow creased, jaw set. She would have recognised his father in him had she seen his expression, but she did not look up. He left her and walked away.

Years before, a small tributary of the river had been diverted through the garden, persuaded to become a pond and planted with lilies and flag irises.

Belinda Mellor

It lay beneath a shady bank decked in ferns and mosses which thrived in such sunless, moist places. Out of sight of his mother, Fabiom collected an armful of water foliage and of hart's tongue, stag horn and the softer, wispier varieties of ferns, whose names he had never learnt. He wove them all into a bright garland and, humming quietly as he did so, felt his mood lift. There would be time enough to worry about everything else later, just now he had to concentrate on his Silvana. He hid the garland on a stone which jutted out beneath the bridge and went back towards the house as a fine mist of rain blew over the garden.

As the seventeenth anniversary of his birth drew to a close the rain was falling in grey swathes.

"I'm going out again," he told Ramus.

"Very well, Master Fabiom."

Fabiom had no intention of reminding the house-steward that his title should have been amended. Any interference in his plans now could be disastrous.

He was wet through when he reached the grove where Casandrina's ash tree grew. The wind moaned rather than sang in the branches and he struggled to drape the garland around some of the lower boughs of the huge tree. Despite his elation, he found it hard to think of anything except how hungry he felt. With an effort, he put such thoughts aside and lay down in the hollow that had once sheltered him in his childhood. Then he had been smaller, now he was just uncomfortable, cold, hungry … and asleep.

He thought she came to him, or that he heard her voice, yet when he awoke he had no memory of the night, no memory of her presence or her voice. Maybe it had only been a dream and she had changed her mind, had not come to him. Yet, even as he was thinking so, something brushed against his neck. It was the fern garland and it was draped about his shoulders. He replaced it among the branches, almost laughing with relief. She had not deserted him.

61

"Maybe I could have my sandals back," he suggested.

Though the rain had stopped in the night, the woodland tracks were still sodden. Fabiom sneezed and shivered. He longed for a warm bath, dry clothes and … he stopped himself from actually naming his favourite foods.

A bath was already drawn for him when he arrived home. Deep and steaming, the surface was iridescent with whorls and eddies of plant oils that eased cramped muscles and relaxed the mind. Fabiom lay there a long while, until the water began to cool, then dressed in warm clothes and dozed in front of a blazing hearth.

He awoke with a start, disorientated, shivering – the fabric of his tunic clinging to his skin, damp with perspiration. His throat felt like fire. He heated some water to drink and allowed himself nothing else. It rained again and he leant his head against the window embrasure, indulging in a rare moment of self-pity. The sky lowered over the garden and the woods beyond, obscuring his view and his resolve.

In an attempt to keep his mind occupied, and to convince his mother that it was not necessary to live actually within the municipal centre to keep abreast of events in and affecting the holding, and because he knew in truth she was right, he took himself to his father's study.

Before Tawr's death, the study had been Fabiom's favourite room in the house. The walls were lined with shelves and silk hangings in equal part. Books, scrolls and ledgers vied for space on the large desk and three smaller tables. Three chairs, an old settle and a deep window seat afforded a variety of opportunities to relax, study or work. Normally, Fabiom favoured the window seat, for the study, like his bedroom, looked out towards the woods. But today he sat down behind his father's desk and attempted to make sense of the daily reports from the silk mills, the court, the municipal council – all of which Ramus had arranged in order. He had to learn and understand and know. It was his place, his responsibility, now that Tawr was gone. He had barely begun when a wave of desolation and loss washed over him and he buried his face in his hands.

Belinda Mellor

A memory came to him, so clear it might have been yesterday, though in truth it was four years ago, almost to the day: the first time he had faced down a wild pig alone, when Tawr had lowered his own bow and stepped back. "I know you can do this." His father's voice was as clear in his mind as if he were in the room.

Fabiom sat up straight and took a deep breath. Unconsciously, he rubbed the finger-length scar on his left thigh. His mother had not been too thrilled with either of them that day, though they had feasted well. "I won't let you down," he promised.

He spent the remainder of the day poring over service quotas; who of Deepvale's nearly two-hundred thousand population owed two years' service that year and, of those, who would stay in the holding to boost their militia, to work at the docks, or as clerks and archivists in the municipal offices; and who he would send to Fairwater to fulfill his obligation to the prince. After two days fasting, he found it hard to concentrate, and had to read most lists two, even three times before the details sank in. Despite the difficulty in focussing, it occurred to him that his father had prepared him well; he understood what he was looking at, knew what he had to do.

By evening the rain had cleared and the sky had lifted.

When he reached the grove he spent some time really studying the ash tree, wondering at its – at her – otherness; wondering in what ways she was aware of him, whether she was watching him even now. The enormity of what he was attempting, and the extent of his ignorance, threatened to overwhelm him – until he saw the amber, oozing from two deep slashes along one of the main branches of the tree. All other worries fled from his mind. Horror and anger warred in him. He began to reach his hand out, before pulling back at the last moment. Unsure of what to do, but unwilling to do nothing, he finally and fearfully laid his hand over the damaged bark. Slowly, the amber congealed and hardened into two perfect pieces, each only a little smaller than the piece still nestled by the roots. With great care, Fabiom placed them in a fork of the tree.

His uncertainty about the path he had chosen was gone and he felt calm, though quite poorly, as he settled as well as he was able onto the ground.

As he lay beneath the tree on a mattress of fallen leaves, gazing upwards at the autumn stars shining between the widely spread branches, half asleep, half awake, the sound of singing came to him. It seeped into his stiff muscles, soothed his aching head. He fought against the summons to sleep deeply, not wanting to let go of the voice. It fell silent. He tried to stir but sleep held him too firmly for that.

"*Will you kill yourself before the sevennight is over?*" She was laughing at him. "*I would rather you did not do so. It would be such a waste.*"

He slept, she sang. Maybe it was the other way around. He could not be sure.

"Nalio! Pay attention, you're becoming as bad as Fabiom. Where is he anyway?" Before Masgor could say any more, he was distracted by the arrival of a note from Deepvale's hold-house, in Ramus's hand, asking that Fabiom might be excused from his studies. Masgor scanned the brief missive and then threw it on the fire.

"It looks like we shall not be having the pleasure of Fabiom's company today," he commented then turned to a map of Morene he had pinned to the wall. "Grand holdings and minor holdings – Nalio, tell us please, the main produce of the six grand holdings of Morene."

Nalio stared at the tutor blankly.

"You could start with Deepvale," Masgor prompted.

Nalio swallowed. "Sir, may I have a word with you? In private."

Belinda Mellor

In the afternoon Masgor came to the hold-house. Ramus showed him into the day room, where Fabiom was trying to study a document on proposed amendments to Treelaw that had arrived from Fairwater that morning.

"I was in need of a walk," Masgor explained. "Shouldn't you be in bed?"

Fabiom admitted that he probably ought to be but he did not want his mother fussing.

Masgor looked at him intently, then let out a slow breath. "I have to tell you, I am pleased to see that you *are* sick, strange though that may sound."

Clearly confused, Fabiom frowned and shook his head.

"Nalio was concerned that 'unwell', as in the note I received earlier, meant something else, something more dire. Though he was distressed at breaking a confidence, his anxiety overrode the promises he apparently made to you some days ago –"

"Oh." Fabiom chewed his lower lip.

"For myself, I am somewhat confused. According to your friend, you have reached the seventeenth anniversary of your birth. Your father is dead, and yet no mention has been made of you assuming any of your duties as Lord Holder. Is Nalio mistaken, or has there been some terrible oversight?"

Reluctantly, Fabiom rose from his couch beside the hearth and went over to the door leading to his mother's quarters. Taking care to make no sound, he shut the door then returned to his place.

"Nalio is not mistaken. About anything. I will celebrate a little late, that's all."

"You.... You went to the woods!" Masgor managed to keep his voice low, despite his amazement. "And here you are to tell the tale! I am pleased for you, Fabiom, more than I can say."

"I have not succeeded yet," Fabiom said, more to himself than to Masgor.

Rummaging about beneath his walking cloak, Masgor eventually brought out a small package which he handed to Fabiom. "I will tell you, I assumed Nalio was wrong, about everything. But, in case he was right about your birth anniversary, I took the precaution of bringing something to mark the occasion."

Inside the simple parchment wrapping was a rare volume of the poet Mahov's *Songs of the Fairwater*. Fabiom stared at the book, then at his tutor, his delight evident in his eyes.

Masgor nodded, satisfied. "I'm glad to see I made the right choice. I thought you'd like it."

"Oh, I do. Thank you. This has made me feel better already. Now, if only I wasn't so hungry."

Masgor frowned. "Can you not eat? If I feel unwell I rarely do anything but over-indulge." He snorted at Fabiom's bemused expression. "You're not still fasting!"

"Of course."

"There's no need! Only before the night in the Dancing Glade. Fabiom, Nalio said you told him you knew what to do."

"I thought –"

"I doubt that," Masgor interrupted. "Get yourself something to eat."

A servant was summoned and soon brought some simple fare, as Fabiom requested. Though when it came to eating he was not as hungry as he expected to be and his raw throat did little to help.

"I still don't understand why you have not celebrated your birth anniversary. Of course you have to focus on the woods and your Silvana. Nevertheless, you should have been formally recognised – you should at least have received your father's rings."

Fabiom swallowed and turned away.

"It's not your choice," Masgor told him gently. "It's your duty."

"It's not that. Of course I have to. And I shall. It's just – my mother. She doesn't know. She isn't.... It's something about the fact that Silvanii never age. She seems to resent that. When she finds out what I've done, she's not going to be well pleased with me – whether I succeed or fail."

Masgor chuckled. "However put out Lady Vida is, I suspect she will be

Belinda Mellor

relieved you still have your mind intact. Had you not considered that your coming of age means you don't need anyone's permission?"

"I do need to keep the peace though," Fabiom said. "I'm seventeen years old. Deepvale is a prosperous and strategically important holding; I'd like it to remain so. I am nowhere near ready to take up the responsibility alone. I need Mother's help, and Tarison's, and yours, and many other people's." He toyed with a piece of honeyed bread for a moment, before adding, "Anyway – I couldn't start an argument with her. She is still too hurt. Had she become upset, I don't know if I could have gone against her. She's cried enough. I decided there would be time for both reconciliation and celebrations when – if – I brought my bride home." He laughed self-consciously as he said so.

"Your bride – indeed. So tell me about her," Masgor suggested, his own curiosity getting the better of him. Fabiom smiled wistfully and pushed his plate aside.

"There's little to tell, so far. She sings of mornings and quiet places and the promise of spring. She laughs like water laughs, and moves lightly so that I am not certain that she is there at all or only wish it." He grinned at Masgor and shook his head. "In other words I can tell you nothing. Yet if I was never to hear her voice again –" He paused and briefly closed his eyes. "It would haunt me forever."

"Very poetic." Masgor took a pomegranate from the dish on the table and cut it in half. He handed Fabiom the fruit and a platter of cheese.

"Eat!" he instructed.

"Yes, I suppose I'd better." Despite his poor appetite he felt revived by the food, more able to face the walk and the cold hours that lay before him.

"No wonder she laughed at me," he said.

"You're not going out again? At this time!"

"Mother." Fabiom smiled to hide his confusion. He could not refute her suggestion, standing as he was at the door with boots on his feet and a cloak thrown over his shoulder. "I thought you'd gone to bed."

"I had a headache, I needed some fresh air. I'm not sure about the company you keep these days, Fabiom, out all the time. What of your studies and your responsibilities?"

"I know my responsibilities, Mother, and I do not neglect my studies. I just have to go out for a while. I'll see you in the morning. I – I hope you feel better soon."

He left before she could object further, still he was ill at ease.

As he walked through the evening gloom he wondered what he could do to aid his plans. At last an idea occurred to him.

Chapter Six

With Tawr gone and adulthood attained, Fabiom's days of study should have been over. However, the following morning he put the suggestion to Masgor that he might stay with the tutor for the next three days – and nights – should his mother ask. Fortunately, Masgor was willing to provide him with an alibi, making good use of the time Fabiom spent at his house for extra tuition. Once he was recognised as Holder, Fabiom's duties would preclude him from long hours of study, much as he would have liked to have continued for a further year or so. Besides, he owed the Ruling Prince two years of service, and he understood enough of the current political situation to guess that he would be called upon soon enough, especially if the treaty with Gerik was not ratified.

It was the history of the two lands that Masgor insisted he study in much detail. If he was to be of any use to Prince Ravik, and if he was to secure a good position in the prince's service, he needed more than skill in archery and oratory, he needed to acquire knowledge.

"Knowledge is power, Fabiom," Masgor would tell him at least once a day. Fabiom knew that was true but when it came to books he was far more interested in poetry than history.

Masgor was kind to him during that period, after a fashion. He contrived to bring the Silvanii into every lesson. Despite their aversion to man's politics and schemings, the indigenous dwellers of Morene and Gerik still featured very strongly in those lands' history.

"As we can see on these maps, Prince Lincius moved his capital from Southernport to Fairwater when he won Sulmarita as his wife. Her home was among the beech groves beside the river, so there he built his city."

With a smooth length of willow, which he was not adverse to using to refocus his students' wandering minds, the tutor pointed out the two cities: Fairwater, two days nearer to Deepvale; Southernport, four days by donkeycart. Fabiom had never been to the southernmost of Morene's holdings, the last place his father had seen. He realised he would have to go there one day.

"Moving away from Southernport was going to prove an advantage to Lincius's descendants, was it not? Keeping the capitals of Gerik and Morene a mere day's journey apart, across the Straits, would have been courting trouble."

The tip of the willow stick moved down to the island lying directly south of Morene, to the city-port half-way along its north shore.

"As it was, Gerik was soon to have no fixed capital, but Westmouth is still a mighty port and much trade passes through there. Gerik imports produce from many lands."

Fabiom wondered about Gerik, whether it was true that absolutely nothing grew there but rank grass and moss, that the dying Silvanii had cursed the land, blighting the soil and the water. There were stories of buildings made out of nothing but the timber from Silvanan trees, of amber being used to raise one family to power and topple another. That was in the past. Now they had nothing of worth but some copper and a little iron.

"Fabiom, will you please pay attention." Masgor's weary voice brought him back to the moment, the book open in front of him and the charts on the tutor's walls.

Nalio chuckled quietly and shook his head in mock despair when Fabiom glanced over at him with a sheepish grin.

"You're a dreamer, boy," Masgor had scolded him the very first day he had gone for tuition, three years since. The other students had sniggered, heads bowed over their books. These days, Masgor was still saying the same thing, Fabiom's latest exploits only serving to reinforce that belief. The others still laughed; Fabiom took no offence.

"To continue –" Masgor tapped the charts with his pointer. "You must understand that what Gerik lacks is stability. And *unstable* means what, Nalio?"

"Unstable means dangerous," Nalio recited, quoting one of Masgor's favourite phrases. Lyon, a new student that year, raised his hand. "I don't understand Gerik's claims on Morene, why they won't sign any treaty unless we agree to give them tribute. No one in Gerik or *from* Gerik ever had anything to do with Morene directly."

Masgor turned to Fabiom, "Perhaps you'd like to enlighten us regarding that matter, Fabiom. I would like to think that by this stage in your education you do at least know the answer to that."

Fabiom stood and turned to face his fellow students. Out of the corner of his eye he saw Masgor nod for him to speak. He wet his lips and began, "Eight generations erst, Prince Cylanus, the first Ruling Prince of Gerik and Morene, died childless. Before he passed away he divided his domain between his two nephews, the sons of his twin younger brothers. Prince Lensen, who was the son of the first born twin, remained in Gerik, it being the larger and more accessible of the two lands. Starven, the son of the younger twin, was gifted Morene, which was then wild, wooded and undeveloped. Gerik claims the two lands were one principality under Cylanus and should be jointly ruled again."

"That's ridiculous!" Lyon interrupted, then subsided under the force of Masgor's glare.

Fabiom was unperturbed. "There is no evidence that Cylanus ever set foot on Morene and he was wise enough to realise that he merely ruled those people who lived in the towns and settlements he established, hence he did not style himself 'king' as rulers do in other countries.

"In due course, Prince Lensen of Gerik sired one son and two daughters. However, the son died childless and, though the daughters had issue, they themselves both died young, leaving infants who could command neither power nor title. In the era of uncertainty that followed, the ruling family was destroyed. Claims and counter claims were made but none that could be verified or upheld." He paused, looked around at his audience to make certain he had all their attention and concluded, "Morene's rebuttal of Gerik's demands are therefore twofold: no ruler of Gerik ever laid actual claim to Morene and, as the sole, true descendant of Prince Cylanus, Ravik, the current Ruling Prince of Morene, has a more righteous claim on Gerik than any in Gerik could ever have on Morene."

"Good," Masgor allowed. "Just try to remember the details, such as some dates for instance. We know you can talk."

Fabiom grinned and resumed his seat. Masgor was an expert on Gerish history. Fabiom knew he had spent most of his service and some time beyond as an advisor to Ravik's father, Darseus, the previous Ruling Prince. The problem was, he expected his students to be as enthusiastic about the subject as he. Fabiom would have been perfectly happy if Gerik did not exist, while Masgor wanted to see things happen there, really happen. If it was not for his ailing brother, the only family Masgor had, he might well have removed to Fairwater permanently long before now. Fabiom was certain the tutor would still like to be part of the treaty process.

Nalio elbowed him as Masgor cleared his throat, and, dutifully, Fabiom turned over another leaf of his book.

Two more days passed, filled with names and dates, power struggles, conflicts and uneasy truces; two nights of haunting music and laughter, sweet dreams and uncomfortable sleep. And while the prize that might soon be his was uppermost in his thoughts, Fabiom could not help but wish he had been born in the summertime.

One more night, just one more. During that last day, thoughts of warm rooms and well padded mattresses deserted him. He had but one desire and only one concern – that his plans should proceed, unhindered.

The morning passed in a long discussion about the rights of Gerik regarding the Straits of Morena, and the need for a reciprocal harbouring clause in the treaty. As often, Masgor had a number of visitors besides his current students and, as the day was pleasant, they took their midday meal in the garden. The discussion continued, though Fabiom said little. Besides his preoccupation with his personal life, he could not help thinking – whenever that treacherous water was mentioned – of his father being lost there. His mind wandered to something Tawr had told him as they walked together through the great woods: "Once the last Silvanan trees had been felled, every other tree died. It must be ninety years since a tree grew in Gerik."

A voice from the present brought him back from the past. "Fabiom!"

It was not one of those seated at the table calling his attention back to the conversation, but his mother, who was walking briskly along Masgor's portico. One more night, surely nothing could go wrong now.

He excused himself from the gathering and went to meet her.

"I thought you would have come home before today. Your uncle and aunt are on their way to the house. You should have been home. It is your place now, now…."

"Now that Father is dead," he said, and immediately regretted his tone. "I shall come immediately." He had no choice.

Fabiom greeted their visitors in the heart room.

"This is a pleasant surprise," he told them, not entirely untruthfully. He grabbed his seven-year-old cousin into a bear hug that lifted the laughing youngster well off the ground. It would have been still more pleasant if they had come tomorrow, he reflected.

"You must think us terribly remiss. Of course we would have come sooner, if Yan had not fallen ill." his uncle apologised as he washed his hands.

Fabiom released his young cousin and tousled his hair. "And you are well now?"

Breathless, Yan could only nod in reply.

"Good, that's good."

They went through to the day room and Vida sent for some wine.

"I thought this was a casual visit," she said, perplexed by her brother-in-marriage's tone.

"My only nephew coming to manhood and his father's estate. Hardly casual!"

Fabiom groaned inwardly. Though his mother had neglected his birth anniversary he should never have expected that Tarison would do so. Vida's hand flew to her face.

"Fabiom! I'm so sorry."

"It doesn't matter, Mother, you had too much else to deal with, and I'm in no hurry to take on everything I must, believe me."

"But that's not the issue! Fabiom! What were you thinking? You should have said something."

Too quietly to be overheard by the others, Tarison whispered, "She does have a point, you know."

She promised to make it up to him, a party maybe; would he like a party?

He could think of nothing he would like less, though he did not say so. If she wanted to give him a party he would accept it gracefully, though he thought it likely she would change her mind when she discovered what he had done.

Marid took Fabiom aside. "I am sorry I was not able to be here for you, dear one."

"Hush. I'm only sorry for the circumstances that prevented you." He bent and kissed her cheek. "It has been such a sad time."

"It has. But this is a day to mark a brighter future. And I have something

Belinda Mellor

for you that I think you will appreciate." Her eyes sparkled mischievously. "I hope your mother doesn't object."

As was the custom, his uncle and aunt had brought him gifts, symbolic of his changed status. From Tarison he received a new bow which, like his outgrown one, was crafted from ash and elm combined, though this one was notched with silver instead of horn. Fabiom recognised the same bowyer's mark and he was delighted with the gift. His uncle also gave him a dozen arrows, tipped with jasper and fletched with golden eagle wing feathers.

"They're not for pig hunting," Tarison told him firmly.

"Indeed not," Fabiom agreed. "Though I reckon I could hit anything I wanted with these. Anybody want to challenge me?"

That gift was given solemnly, but then there was much giggling and jesting as they all went outside to see what Marid had brought him. It was something Fabiom had long coveted: a small and rare white donkey from her herd, that he instantly named 'Wish'. They went back inside then, for even the seven-year-old Yan had a present for him. Yan's gift was a decorated pot with a year-old olive tree he had grown himself. Fabiom only wished he could fully appreciate the joy of the occasion. Besides the gifts, they brought him advice, as was inevitable. Fabiom took both with courtesy: the gifts were generous and the advice was sound, yet all the while he was fretting as to how he would escape from the house that night.

After the visitors had refreshed themselves and rested from their journey and Vida had remonstrated with Fabiom, privately, for saying nothing when she forgot his birth anniversary, they went for a walk around the gardens.

"Is the river flooding?" Tarison asked.

Vida shook her head. "It is high though. Hopefully it will stay contained. I go to see every day, though I have not been today."

"Let's go right now then," Yan suggested.

Amused at his eagerness, they passed through the gate to stand upon the bridge and watch the swollen river as it gushed down the vale.

"The river's fine. Can we walk in the woods now?" Yan asked, gazing across to the far side.

"Later, maybe," Vida replied, with little enthusiasm.

As Tarison looked towards the dark shades of the woods' edge, secret and brooding, a half smile touched his mouth.

"So, you were not tempted to spend your birth eve in the Dancing Glade?" he asked Fabiom casually. "I always thought you would, somehow. I think I might have done so myself, had I not been sent to Fairwater to recover from some vile illness that was going around at the time." He grinned apologetically at Marid as he said so, though she was not so easily offended.

She laughed. "He would have done, I'm certain, the way he talks of the woods. Fortunately for me he was safely out of harm's way when he was turning seventeen. Not that I was even aware of his existence at that time."

Yan looked from his father to his mother, then at Fabiom – who was studying a piece of smooth stone in the parapet of the bridge and wondering what he was supposed to say.

He could not lie, so he had no option but to tell the truth.

"Fabiom would not…." Vida began.

How could she be so certain? he wondered. *How could she be so wrong?* "I did."

They all stared at him. He expected his mother to speak first but when she did it was only to utter his name in disbelief.

Marid was enthralled. "What happened?"

He shook his head. "I wasn't in the Dancing Glade when I awoke. So that part went well. But tonight is –"

"The seventh since your birth eve," Tarison realised.

"Yes. Tonight I meet her and I guess it will be settled, one way or the other."

At that, Vida slammed her hands down onto the parapet. "It *is* settled! You will not go back there!"

"No," Tarison intervened. "Even if that were his choice, it is too dangerous. The consequences would be dire. A Silvana would not take kindly to rejection."

"She might destroy him, my only son. How can you stand there and say 'go on'?"

"He does not need our permission or approval."

Fabiom remained silent. Tarison spoke truly: no one could actually stop him.

"And if you succeed?" Vida spoke now to Fabiom. "Do you think I will live with a, with a, with *her* in this house? If you do, you are very very wrong."

"Vida, don't say so," Marid implored, but Fabiom only bowed his head briefly in acceptance. He had feared as much.

"Then I will build another house if I must, for myself or for you, whichever you prefer. I cannot turn back now."

"So, your first action as Lord of Deepvale will be to antagonise another holder?" Vida said.

Fabiom was confused at the sudden change of direction the conversation had taken.

"As far as Herbis of Windwood is concerned, you and his daughter are to be married three years from now." His mother's explanation did little to help.

"I thought it was just talk. Nothing was arranged, was it?"

Marid glanced at Tarison and then away. Fabiom caught the exchange and wondered at it.

"Marid, I know Dala is your niece – I mean no offence to your family," he said.

"Of course not." Marid seemed unusually at a loss for words – glancing between her husband, Vida and Fabiom. "I never.... Dala's a lovely girl, but you should marry for love." She smiled at Tarison as she said so.

"Love! You think he's going to the woods for *love*?" Vida's voice was high pitched. "We all know about that sort of 'love'. Tawr...."

Tarison put his hand on her arm. "Vida, please." His voice was reasonable but his hand was firm. Her eyes widened as his grip tightened.

She pulled her arm free and gathered her cloak around her. "Herbis will be offended. That's all I'm saying – and Fabiom has enough to learn and cope with without having to protect our borders from a righteously affronted holder and his militia. Are you ready to deal with that, Fabiom? If you fail in your woodland endeavour you will be witless; if you succeed – will you even care if your holding stands or falls? I am not certain marriage to a Silvana leaves a man any more of his wits than failure."

"The greatest princes and holders in history have been wed to Silvanii," Tarison said. "As for Herbis –" He took a deep breath. "Legally, Fabiom is in the clear: a vow to a Silvana overrides all other laws. He had every right to present himself and his doing so nullifies any contract of betrothal."

"And Dala is only sixteen," Marid pointed out. "It's not as if she's been waiting, unmarried. They haven't even seen each other in what – two years?"

Fabiom thought back to that time. Dala had challenged him to an archery competition and he had thought to let her win, only to discover she needed no help at all. He had fought hard to beat her and she revelled in the fierce competition. In truth, had he not set his heart on the path he had, he probably could have been happy enough with a girl with such spirit. Then he frowned. "I have no recollection of any discussion of a betrothal at that visit. I did not make any promise to her, nor she to me."

"No," Vida agreed. "It didn't happen then."

"When then?"

"You were very young."

"How young?" Fabiom was suspicious.

"Nine."

"Nine? I don't remember meeting her then."

"You didn't," Tarison admitted.

Belinda Mellor

"I thought for a moment you were going to say I was four. I remember Herbis and his family visiting. He had his younger brothers, Nimo and Khime, with him."

"I'm surprised you remember that," Vida said.

"Oh, I'll never forget. They were the two most obnoxious boys I've ever met."

"Indeed." Marid tried to hide a smile and another look passed between her and Tarison.

"You were nine, Dala was eight, and the promises were made on your behalf." Vida sighed. "It was – expedient – at the time."

Fabiom gazed across the river, towards the wildwood. "I intend to be a good holder, and a good husband. Whatever promises I make I will keep. By going to the Dancing Glade, I made a promise. I will not break it. You cannot ask that of me." He turned his gaze onto his mother.

They returned to the hold-house in silence until, just before they reached the door, Yan tugged at Fabiom's tunic.

Fabiom crouched down as Yan whispered. "What type of tree?"

"An ash," he replied, just as quietly.

Yan grinned. "I can't wait to meet her. Do you think she'll like me?"

"I think she'll like you very much." He glanced up; the others had gone inside. "Right now, I need to make a flower garland for her. Will you help me? But we'd better hurry – I'm in enough trouble as it is."

By the time Fabiom and Yan went in, a fine meal had been laid out in the dining room, but appetites were poor. Vida tried once more to dissuade Fabiom and when he would not be moved she went to her room and locked the door.

Fabiom leant his head against the frame as Tarison tried to talk to her through the closed door. Silence was the only answer forthcoming.

"A scene that is rather too evocative of the last years of your parents' marriage. Come away, Fabiom." Marid put a comforting arm around his waist and guided him back to the day room, where Yan was waiting, playing with a set of wooden shapes that had been Fabiom's.

Marid was chief among the exceptions Fabiom had refused to think of when expressing his views of women to Nalio. He had just turned nine years when his uncle surprised the whole family with the news that he was marrying the then eighteen-year-old Marid, fourteen years younger than he, whom he had known for scarcely two months. However, while other relatives, including Tawr and Vida, tried to persuade the couple to reconsider, Fabiom had been delighted. From the moment he met her, he adored Marid, and had never found reason to feel any differently. As he had hoped, and contrary to most others' expectations, Tarison and Marid had lived happily together since; their total contentment marred only by their unfulfilled wish for a daughter, a sister for Yan.

In the day room, Fabiom poured three beakers of wine before sitting on the floor at his aunt's feet.

"Marid, about Dala –"

"Really, dear one, I am very fond of Dala, though I don't see her as often as I would like. But the last thing I would want for either of you is to be forced into a marriage you didn't choose."

Tarison gave up on Vida and joined the others in the day room where, lulled by quiet talk of the Silvanii and the wildwood, Yan soon fell asleep on a couch.

"Tell us about your encounter with Nimo and Khime when you were four," Tarison suggested, after Fabiom had recounted every detail of his night in the Dancing Glade.

Fabiom was still curious about what his uncle and aunt knew of his apparent betrothal. He was convinced there was something more to the story than he was aware of but had enough to contend with and let it go. He took a mouthful of the rich wine and savoured the taste, not so much the memory.

Belinda Mellor

"Apparently, they were supposed to be looking after me. I vaguely remember they tried to frighten me with words. They thought they could scare me with suggestions of what the Silvanii might do to me."

Marid laughed quietly at that.

"When that failed, they put me in a basket, turned it upside down so I couldn't get out and pretended to be wild pigs coming to get me. Eventually, they rolled the basket right way over, grunting and squealing as they did so. I crawled out and ran away. They chased me through the woods then went home without me. I remember that part clearly – it was the most frightening experience I've ever had."

"More frightening than going to the Dancing Glade on your birth eve?" Tarison wondered.

Fabiom leant back against the arm of the settle, his hands behind his head. "As far as I could see, nothing good could come out of the situation I was in, trapped in that basket. On my birth eve there was a chance, albeit a slight one, that my fondest wish might come true. So yes, on balance, the basket was the scariest thing that ever happened to me." He sat forward again, ducking his head. "I used to have nightmares about it for several years afterwards. I still dream about it sometimes."

"I can imagine," Marid murmured. "I can think of nothing worse than being trapped and tormented by either of those two."

Fabiom had the impression it was not merely a platitude she was voicing.

Tarison leant across and ruffled his hair. "Just don't start dreaming about Herbis marching on your borders, demanding you marry his daughter."

Fabiom twisted around and looked up at his uncle.

"Am I putting Deepvale at risk?"

"You cannot think like that now. You need to be focussed. Any doubt in your heart and you risk more than your holdership."

"It's not an easy thing to ignore –"

Fabiom left early for his tryst, apologising awkwardly to his uncle and aunt who both hugged and kissed him, Marid with tears in her eyes that she tried to hide.

Ramus, the house-steward, having apologised numerous times for letting Fabiom's birth date escape his mind, bid him success and called him Lord, as was Fabiom's due. He handed over the satchel that Fabiom had requested.

Fabiom neither saw the twinkle in the steward's eyes nor heard the softly voiced, "Your father would be proud of you," that followed him as he went towards the outbuildings to collect the garland of flowers he and Yan had left there earlier.

As he crossed the bridge, Fabiom tightened the straps of his satchel containing fruits, fresh bread and ewe's milk. There was indeed no turning back now.

Chapter Seven

Entering the grove, Fabiom perceived a different quality to the air, though he put that down to his own fevered imagination. The evening was clear, stars peered through gaps in the leafy canopy, scents of flowers and trodden grasses mingled in the air. He willed himself to relax, to think only of what lay before him. His thoughts kept returning to the house, to the uncomfortable silence and the broken platter that had marked his mother's exit. He knew he must not brood on such things, he surely had enough to concern him here. Marid had embraced him as if she might never see him again, then his uncle had walked with him to the boundary of the garden, promising, "I will take care of your mother."

Fabiom realised that could mean any number of things. He chose to believe it to mean that Tarison would try to talk her round.

He nearly tripped over his sandals as he leant across a root bole to drape his flower garland amid the branches. So, she had heard him. The sandals were damp with the rains and dews of the last seven days. He moved them aside and sat down with his back against the trunk. He would not sleep tonight. Awake he would meet the Silvana whose tree he had woken beneath on his birth day morn; awake he would win her heart and hand, or lose himself. Exactly what would happen, he had no idea. There was no mention of first meetings in anything he had read.

As he waited, he let his mind drift back to the *Chronicles of Lincius* and other accounts of heroes and their Silvanan brides. He did not account himself so brave, yet, as his father had realised, it seemed natural to him that he would have chosen this path. This night would be a testing, if he had read the stories aright. What tests? He wondered. Tests of the heart maybe.

"I think your sandals are spoilt."

Fabiom leapt to his feet, "My lady!"

"I do sincerely hope so."

Unutterably beautiful, adorned in green silk and strings of amber beads, she had simply appeared in the grove beside her tree and now she was staring at him, seemingly waiting. He had no idea what for.

Nothing could have prepared him for this moment when he would be actually looking into her eyes. He had never seen such eyes, green as spring leaves, deep as the roots of her tree, eyes that held him, confused him. He tried to swallow; his mouth was dry.

"I brought you flowers."

"So I see."

She was as tall as he, her eyes on a level with his. She did not move, just stood looking into his eyes, into his soul. At last, he managed to tear his fascinated gaze away from her face and turn to take the garland from the branches of the tree. He offered it to her. She remained motionless, yet the hint of a smile touched the corners of her mouth and so he laid the flower string around her neck. The scent of jasmine and daphne filled the air as the flowers were disturbed and her hair, as pale as her tree bark, brushed like silk across his hands. His breath caught in his chest.

"Thank you, Lord Fabiom." She adjusted the garland and, as she did so, her stole slipped down her left arm. Two angry cuts showed dark against her pale golden-brown skin.

Belinda Mellor

"You – you are hurt." Cautiously he reached out and touched the cruel marks. "That night, I heard, I don't know.… Were these on my account?"

"It is of no matter," she told him, her voice melodious. "They will fade soon. You, I hope, will stay."

"I will stay," he promised. Whatever happened now he was enthralled. There was no turning back, no leaving. "Will you sing?" He had not meant to ask but the memory of her singing filled his mind.

"I have promised to."

"For the rest of my life," he agreed, wondering how long that might be. She seemed to be waiting still, waiting for him to say something. He felt rather foolish. "Casandrina –"

At the sound of her name she lifted the flowers from her neck and laid the garland across his shoulders, letting her fingers brush down the line of his jaw as she did so.

"I always hoped you would come," she told him, laughing then. "Ever since the night you hid beneath the branches of my tree, I believed you would."

And that was it. There were no tests. Indeed, she laughed at the very idea.

"If there were, you passed them long ago," she assured him. "I have loved you forever. If anything, I was the one at risk – had you a change of heart. I have spent the past seven days transforming; there is no going back for me now."

She bound him to her with cords woven of silk and songs woven of love, his hands to her hands, his body to her body, his heart to her heart, his soul to her soul. Together they planted a seed from her tree; hope for the future.

Days passed as in a dream. Lost in the woods, lost in her touch and her voice, memories blurred and mingled. Songs surrounded him like the stars at night, music as gentle and insistent as her caresses. This was a time he would never forget, yet never fully recall, a waking time that seemed like a dream, and dreams that seemed more real than any time in his life that had gone before.

She taught him about love and showed him the secret places of the woodland, where the wild mulberries grew and the woodmaids spun silk and where the Silvanii danced among the trees. She sang him songs that whispered of a golden future and revealed to him his own capacity for contentment. It would have been so easy to stay forever, feasting on the sweet berries and ripe nuts, mushrooms and good herbs she brought him, sleeping in her embrace, warm beneath a blanket of bracken fronds.

He awoke under a whispering canopy of autumn leaves. Morning was all but passed. It was the eighth day, perhaps the ninth, he could not be certain. A voice in his mind said, *I am truly happy*, and with that he knew it was time to go home, to take her home.

"Casandrina?"

She was not asleep. He thought maybe she never actually slept, though at night she would lie quietly in his arms and rest.

At the sound of her name she raised her head from his chest and smiled knowingly, as if she had been waiting for him to come to this decision which, though unspoken, she could read in his eyes.

"Will I be welcome?"

It was the first time he had heard any uncertainty in her voice or seen the glimmer of doubt that clouded her bright gaze. *This* was her world, all she had ever known. He wished he could say that everyone would feel as he did about her but he could see his mother's face as clearly as if she was standing before him there in the grove and he knew it was not so.

"My mother did not wish me to do what I have done," he admitted.

"She was afraid for you? That is understandable."

"No. Not just for that reason." He moved so that he sat facing her, took her hands and held them tightly. "You are so beautiful; too beautiful for her to be glad for me. I think she will be jealous of you."

Belinda Mellor

"I see."

He was afraid that she would leave him, refuse to go with him. "Casandrina – I'll stay here, we don't have to go. Please, I couldn't bear...."

A lingering kiss silenced his misgivings. Then she smiled wistfully.

"Of course you cannot stay here. You have to go back, as you well know. And I will go with you and be with you, always." She removed a small twig from his hair, smiling and shaking her head. "You look like a forester; no lord holder at all. What would your people say if they could see you now?"

"They would say I was the most fortunate man in Deepvale, for that is the truth," he replied as he pulled her close to him and held her, breathing in the perfume of her skin, feeling the silken touch of her hair against his face. "The most fortunate man in all Morene."

"Tell me about your house," she suggested.

"House?"

"Yes, your hold-house. The place you are going to take me very soon. The place that will be our home."

He sighed and released her. "Ah, that house."

He let go of her altogether and reached around her for a length of dry stick that was lying close by. Seeing his intent, she cleared a section of the leaf-strewn earth and left him a drawing surface of smooth soil.

"It's a fine building, of pale cream stone from one of the Northern holdings, built around a courtyard," he explained, drawing some lines to show her the shape. "The front faces towards the road that leads to the municipal centre of Deepvale – the town – while the two sides and the back look out onto the gardens." With that he drew some more lines, dividing the outline into rooms as best he could. "This is the main living part," he explained. "The rooms at either end are about the same size; this one to the left is for eating and on the other side we have the family room, which is used mostly in the evenings. The smaller room in the middle is for receiving guests –"

"The heart room," she supplied. "With – I know – four doors, one facing each of the winds; two hearths, east and west; and a tall basin for ablutions."

"Yes," he agreed, surprised. "Yes, the heart room."

He looked at her for a moment until she urged, "Go on."

"Where was I? Ah, the heart room, which opens out through the north door onto a courtyard in the middle of the house." He divided the middle rectangle into four and brushed away the centre mark. "This is the courtyard. It has a covered walkway all the way around. Off of this, behind the family room, is my mother's day room – she likes to do weaving there – and this is her maid's room beside it. Behind those is a guest room, the old nursery."

"And on the other side of the courtyard?" Casandrina asked, her expression childlike with the wonder of this unknown world he was showing her.

"Well this would be Ramus's room – he's our house-steward. And the room behind that, facing towards the woods, that's mine." He frowned then.

"Is something wrong, Fabiom? Tell me about your room."

"Nothing's wrong. It's just that I've realised it has none of the comforts a lady's room should have. I'm sorry, I should have thought of this before, I did nothing to prepare." He spread his hands helplessly.

She laughed. "Should I mind? We will prepare *our* room together. I think I shall enjoy that. Though perhaps your mother will not be pleased if we make changes?"

"No." He sighed. "Probably not. Nevertheless she will have to accept it." He chewed the end of his drawing stick for a moment. "Anyway, here are the main bedrooms, each of those is really a suite of two proper rooms," he indicated the part on his sketch. "And that's almost it, except –"

"So, this must be the washing room," she finished for him, touching the square he had drawn in the middle of the bedrooms, opposite the heart room. "With a bath and maybe another tall basin?"

"You have come up to the house! I didn't think you could."

"I have not. Yet, I am not the first of my kind to choose to leave the wildwood. You have your stories about us; did you not think that we would

Belinda Mellor

have stories about you?" Her laughter rang like silver bells and he laughed with her, though he had to admit that such thoughts had never crossed his mind and he found them slightly unnerving. Her laughter was merrier still when he said so.

"I know more." She paused in thought, her head tilted to one side. "Yes. All holders of Morene build their houses on hills, and they like colonnade walkways, is 'colonnade' the right word?"

"Colonnade, yes."

"Colonnade walkways around the outer walls, for shade in the summer and protection from the winter. You see, I know all sorts of things. However, there are many things I do not know, things you must teach me."

"I will teach you gladly, anything you want to know – later. For this moment I would rather learn from you." With that he leant across his sketch to steal a kiss, smudging the picture as he did so.

"You are not done," she reminded him, repairing his picture and pretending to ignore his advances. "You have a room for preparing food."

"Yes," he agreed with a resigned sigh. "The kitchen, that's here." He drew a narrow extension at the front of the house onto the dining area and an identical one onto the family room, leaving the heart room recessed. "On this side is a library and a study. And in front of the heart room we have erected a glass room, a conservatory, where Ramus grows orchids and other rare flowers. The house faces south and it's very warm in there."

"So you go through this flower room to enter the house? I like that."

"Yes, it's very pleasant. I hope you *will* like it, all of it. I want you to be happy, Casandrina."

"I *shall* be," she assured him. "So let us start our life there. Take me to your house, Fabiom. Your house on the hill."

A jay swooped across the track in front of them and was gone again in a flash of blue wings. Fabiom pushed his way through the bracken that was claiming the rarely-used footpath back for the wildwood, while behind him Casandrina moved silently so that he wanted to keep looking around to be certain that she was with him. She began to sing softly, reassuringly; still, he was glad when the path widened and she could walk beside him.

The trees thinned, more birds sang and, in a deep gully, a narrow stream hurtled over black rocks on its way to join the River Swan. For a while they walked beside the gully until they came to a fork in the path that led to the edge of the woods and on to the house. As they turned away from the stream a sudden movement and a glimpse of bright blue, the colour of the jay's wing, someway along the other path, caught their attention. Fabiom glanced at Casandrina, who knew the ways of every creature that inhabited the woodland. She shook her head, clearly puzzled. For a moment they both stood, watching and waiting expectantly, then vigilance dissolved into laughter as their quarry revealed itself as a child wrapped in a blue woollen cape.

"Yan!" Fabiom exclaimed. "Whatever are you doing here? Are you alone?"

Yan regarded Casandrina curiously for a moment, until she held out her hand to him, then he came to her, smiling as if he had always known her.

"They're looking for you." He glanced briefly at Fabiom who nodded, unsurprised, then looked up again at Casandrina, laughing as the ends of her loose hair tickled his face. She brushed it over her shoulders, out of the way.

"I brought you a flower," he remembered, handing her the gold lily he had been clutching. "Ramus said you would like flowers."

Fabiom thought he must have misheard. "*Ramus* said – but he didn't know – are you sure?"

"Yes. And Masgor came to the house. He said you would be all right, that we needn't look for you, but this morning Aunt Vida said we had waited long enough, so we all came searching. But I believed Masgor. That's why I brought the flower."

"Thank you, Yan." Casandrina turned to Fabiom, "Could I have wished for a kinder welcome?"

Belinda Mellor

"Yan!" Tarison's voice echoed strident in the quiet woodland. "Yan!"

"Papa, I found them, I found them," the child declared as they came out onto the pathway where Tarison stood scanning the maze of trees and clearings.

Tarison whirled around at the sound of Yan's voice, then stood motionless, staring.

Fabiom smiled self-consciously. "Uncle, permit me to introduce Casandrina, my wife. Casandrina, my Uncle Tarison, Yan's father, and caretaker of Deepvale since my father's death."

Tarison composed himself to incline his head towards Casandrina, "My lady, welcome," and answer his nephew, "No longer caretaker, Fabiom. Deepvale is your responsibility now. You are a boy no more."

Chapter Eight

Vida met them in the courtyard. They had gone through the conservatory, where Ramus bowed to Casandrina and presented her with one of his finest orchids; on into the heart room, where Casandrina watched and imitated Fabiom's actions as he rinsed and dried his hands. The two side doors, the ones that led into the living quarters of the house, were closed. Only the north door remained open. As they walked through, Fabiom wondered at it, wondered why his mother and aunt waited outdoors and not in the day room.

Fabiom swallowed. "Mother, Aunt Marid, this is Casandrina. She is of an ash tree."

Vida looked Casandrina up and down. "She is very beautiful, I trust you are satisfied."

Marid's sharply indrawn breath was audible, and the only sound until Vida added,

"Now, if you will excuse me. I need to make certain my belongings are packed properly." She strode away, towards her room.

"Casi, I'm so sorry –"

Belinda Mellor

"It is of no matter," Casandrina assured him. "Lady Vida?"

Vida stopped and looked back, her expression wary.

"Fabiom tells me that the gardens here are lovely, and they are your own design and under your care. I would very much like to see them. Would you show them to me?"

For a moment Vida stood, irresolute. "It's beginning to rain."

Casandrina glanced upwards. "Nevertheless –"

"Very well."

Drizzle became rain. Fabiom stood with his uncle and aunt in the shelter of the portico until Vida returned and disappeared into the house. She was alone. Fabiom glanced at Tarison, unsure whether to find his wife or go after his mother. Tarison shrugged.

"I'll speak to Vida," Marid offered.

Fabiom found Casandrina in the orchard, gazing beyond the garden towards the wildwood. A tiny, emerald green spider was weaving a web across her palm, between her fingers and thumb.

"I tried. I asked her to stay." She turned to face him. "I think she is very angry."

"Then maybe it's for the best if she goes to Valehead with Tarison and Marid, at least for a while."

Without disturbing the silk or the spinner, Casandrina relocated the web to some twigs on a nearby persimmon tree. "You do not mean that." She rested her hands on his chest.

Suddenly her expression softened. Over his shoulder Fabiom saw Yan bounding towards them, followed by the white donkey.

"Why is everyone cross?" Yan asked and then, without waiting for a reply, told them, "Aunt Vida has ordered her maids to pack all her things. She says she's coming home with us and we're going right now. Mama and Papa want to stay here though."

"She's leaving immediately?" Fabiom queried. "Are you certain?"

"Uh huh. Look, a green woodpecker." Yan pointed to the bird perched on a peach tree nearby. "You must know all about birds," he said to Casandrina.

"Indeed, I do. Do you like birds, Yan?"

"Yes, and I collect feathers." He looked at the bird and then at Casandrina. "If he pecked your tree, would it hurt?"

"I think it would; very much. But he would not do so."

"Why not?"

"Because I would ask him not to."

At the boy's uncertain look, she raised her hand and, in perfect imitation of the woodpecker's ringing laugh, called the bird to her. "Fabiom, go. Speak to your mother. I will wait here with Yan."

Leaving them with the woodpecker, Fabiom headed towards the house. He glanced back, wincing against a sudden tightness in his neck. Casandrina was holding Yan's wrist with her free hand and passing the bird onto his finger.

Squaring his shoulders, and gritting his teeth at the consequent spasm, Fabiom went through the kitchen and out across the courtyard to his mother's room on the far side. He rotated his head each way, attempting to ease cramped muscles.

The door to his mother's room was ajar. He pushed it wider. Almost everything small enough to be carried had been packed away and the shelves and presses were all but empty.

"You didn't even invite her into the house! You always taught me how important hospitality is, how to receive guests –"

"But she's not a guest, is she?"

"No," he agreed. "She's not. Even more reason to make her welcome –"

Vida passed a coloured glass bottle of perfume and a hand mirror to one of her maids. "Wrap these well. They are precious and I would not have them broken."

"Mother, what are you doing?"

94

Vida merely looked at him.

"This is your home. You belong here." He began to take robes, stoles and other garments out of the nearest wicker hamper and place them on her bed.

She grabbed an armful of the clothes and threw them back in. "Maybe you should have considered that before you defied me. At least now I understand why you deceived me and said nothing about your birth anniversary."

"Deceived you!" Fabiom choked back a laugh. "My mother forgets my birth anniversary and it's *my* fault." He took a deep breath. "I'm sorry. I'm sorry about everything. But, Mama, please. I always wanted this. You know it. And now – why can't you be happy for me? At least stay a while, get to know her. Give her a chance; that's all I'm asking."

Vida's hands clenched around the thin silk undergarment still in her hands. "You don't need me. You have made that quite clear. You have your beautiful wife. That was what you wanted, wasn't it?"

"Yes, Casandrina is beautiful. And I would be lying if I pretended her beauty doesn't delight me. But she is so much more, and everything else is far more important."

"And she can give you but one son. Did you think of that? And not only that, you must wait seventeen years for that child. What if something should befall you meanwhile? You, with no siblings and one cousin only of your father's line – Marid will never carry to term again. Should ill befall Yan also, what happens then to the line of Laurrus? Does Deepvale wait fifty years, a hundred, for your Silvanan daughter to *maybe* take a husband and birth an heir?"

For a moment Fabiom was distracted, *my daughter*; he had not considered that aspect of his marriage. Then Vida's goading pricked and returned him to the present. "I am well, as is Yan. Do not dismiss us both in such haste."

"Well, it's done now. You made your choice. And I have made mine. I'm going to Valehead. Today. Now, if you will excuse me, I think I am ready –"

The woodpecker had flown back to the wildwood. A dozen crates and hampers were piled up on four donkey carts; another two carts stood empty, ready for passengers.

"Don't worry," Marid tried to reassure both Fabiom and Casandrina. "We'll talk to her, I'm sure she'll come around." She touched Casandrina's hand. "I'm glad you are Fabiom's wife. I hope we shall see you often." Then she kissed Fabiom's cheek. "You know where we are."

After they had gone, Fabiom stood alone in the conservatory, staring unseeing at the riot of flowers growing there. This time yesterday he had not a single worry or concern: they had walked deep into the wildwood, far beyond anywhere he had been on his own, when she hid behind a huge chestnut tree. She called to him, her voice dancing about so that he did not know where she was. Laughing, he searched for her, catching a glimpse of long, golden limbs or flowing green silk as she darted away here and there. He caught her at last beneath a young elm and fell, breathless, onto the mossy bank, pulling her down with him. 'A boy no more,' that was exactly how he had felt yesterday, lying with her there in the shelter of the woods.

That was yesterday. Today Tarison's words mocked him, as he found himself responsible for both a home and a holding for which he was not prepared. His head ached, his neck hurt. The house was quiet. Never before had he realised how many sounds accompanied a normal day. He did not know where Casandrina was. Everyone else had gone. Everyone. He could not believe that his mother had taken the entire household, not just her personal servants but the cook, the housemaids, even the gardeners. And Ramus. That was the hardest loss. The house-steward had been a part of Fabiom's life since before memory stirred. Marid had argued with her over it, claiming they had servants enough at Valehead, that Vida needed only her handmaidens, which had only made Vida more determined, so Marid had relented.

Fabiom had no notion how to run the house, and it was quite obvious that Casandrina would have no more idea than he.

Belinda Mellor

"Lord Fabiom."

Fabiom turned. "Ramus?"

"Lady Vida requested that I give you this, to mark your coming to manhood. It was your father's, I believe."

The ring Ramus held out to him was formed of a bronze and silver band twisted together and set with chalcedony. It had indeed been Tawr's, and Tawr's father's before him, back through the generations to the very day Deepvale had become a holding.

"I thought it had been lost with my father –" Fabiom said, remembering that awful day. "Prince Starven himself gave this to Lord Laurrus, my many times great grandfather, along with the holdership of Deepvale."

"Indeed. And your father, like all the lords of Deepvale before him, never wore it away from the holding."

Fabiom slipped the band onto the first finger of his left hand. "I, too, will take care of it, Ramus. Thank you."

Caring for a ring was a simpler task than caring for the holding it symbolised. Now was probably not the time to dwell on that.

"Some supper for you and your lady?" the house-steward offered. "I have made up the unused suite of rooms, I trust that is acceptable. It would seem most appropriate now that you are a married man."

"Yes. But, Ramus, what are you doing here?"

The steward smiled. "Your lady mother has been a good mistress to me, Lord Fabiom, but this house has always been my home. My father was steward here before me. I have known you all your life and, if I may say so, I expect that you will have continued need of my services." His eyes twinkled with merriment. "To think I'd see the day there was a Tree Lady here in this house. I am more than happy for you, Lord Fabiom. Yet not too surprised. If ever a lad was going to win himself such a wife, it was yourself."

Fabiom felt the relief like a tangible thing. "You knew all along, didn't you?"

Ramus gave a half-shrug.

"Thank you, Ramus. Thank you for everything. We'll sort out some new house-staff first thing tomorrow. And yes, supper would be welcome, I think."

Casandrina had returned to the garden. Fabiom found her, breaking off faded rose-heads in the rain.

"Don't do that." He rested his hands on her waist, his head against hers. "If you must be out here getting wet, at least pick some fresh blooms."

"I am sorry," she whispered.

"For taking off some dead flowers? Don't be silly, it's not important. It's just something my mother did constantly, and it bothered me."

She let the withered blooms fall to the earth. "No, Fabiom, not for the roses."

"I know." He turned her to face him, then pulled her close against his body.

"We'll manage. And Mother will see she is being foolish. All will be well." He stepped back from her a pace, smiling, trying to reassure her. "Ramus stayed. He's getting supper for us even now. He knew; he knew all along." Fabiom looked at his lovely wife and shook his head. Her soaked dress clung about her and her hair hung limp, darkened by the rain. "Look at you." He pushed stray strands of hair from her face and kissed her gently.

She lifted her face to the falling rain. "Being wet has never troubled me before now." She sighed. "Ah, indeed I have much to learn."

"We both do," he agreed. "Come inside now. This is your home. We'll pick some flowers tomorrow."

She placed both hands around the back of his neck and immediately her eyes widened. "Oh, my poor love. That must hurt. You are stressed." Her fingers kneaded the knotted muscles and he closed his eyes, grimacing but pressing into her touch nevertheless.

As each knot, each burr, each tightened tendon eased beneath her touch,

Belinda Mellor

Fabiom felt his mood lighten. Her breath, and hint of a song, caressed his ear. The rain slanted down.

"There. That is better."

A smile curved Fabiom's mouth. "Indeed, it is. Let's go indoors. We need to get you out of those wet clothes –"

Fabiom awoke very late the next morning, turned to reach for Casandrina and found the bed empty. Girlish laughter echoed in the room. He sat up, blinking. The laughter intensified.

At that moment, the door opened. "Out!" Casandrina ordered, and three slight figures fled, giggling, from behind a dressing screen.

"I brought you some hot pear juice. You slept well." She ran her fingers through his hair as she climbed up beside him on the bed.

"Who was that?"

"Some of my woodmaids. They like you. They want to stay with us here. They can help Ramus."

Fabiom considered everything he knew about woodmaids, the attendants of the Silvanii. Nothing he had ever heard or read led him to believe that Ramus would greatly benefit from their assistance.

"Of course they can stay." She would undoubtedly want them nearby. "Nevertheless should we not get in some people who would be used to domestic work, as well?"

Casandrina shook her head. "They are very willing. Ramus can teach them. It will be good, you shall see."

As Fabiom told Marid twelve days later, when he went to Valehead to see his mother, Ramus *had* taught them, after a fashion, and they were all getting by.

They were lounging on the patio beside a fountain, enjoying a lunch of tuna with quails' eggs and pine nuts. It was just the two of them; Vida had gone into Deepvale with Tarison early that morning and Marid was unsure when to expect them home.

"This is good," Fabiom said around a mouthful of succulent fish. "I think it's three days since I had a real meal. Not that I'm going hungry, far from it!" He helped himself to a piece of soft bread. "We eat at any time, and rarely proper meals unless Ramus insists. It's chaos. There are animals everywhere, orphaned, injured, or just attracted by free food and warmth. And plants - Ramus thinks he's dreaming. The woodmaids adore him and keep bringing him tiny and apparently extremely rare orchids that make him almost swoon with joy. Somehow, despite the creatures and the flora, they manage to keep everything very clean but they move everything. I can find nothing where I expect it to be, except in the study – from which they are banished."

"And you are loving every moment."

"I am."

"I'm not so sure your mother would, though."

Fabiom lay back against a pile of cushions and gazed up at the almost cloudless sky. "I know. That thought has occurred to me."

Though the sky was bright, summer was long gone and the wind blew chill. Marid pulled a length of bright fabric around her shoulders. "Maybe I was overly optimistic, thinking we should eat outside."

"We can go in," Fabiom suggested. "Actually, Marid, I'm pleased I found you alone. I wanted to ask you something –"

"Indoors then, where we can talk in more comfort. Ah, perhaps not, I hear your mother and uncle."

"– about my supposed betrothal to your niece," Fabiom said to himself as she went to organise the remains of the meal to be brought into the house.

Winter came and went. Fabiom had been certain the situation with his mother would be resolved with the arrival of spring, yet, despite his frequent visits to Tarison's country house, Vida remained adamant. As it was, when she told him that she had no intention of ever returning – that Tarison had promised her a home for life – he was almost glad. He knew she would

Belinda Mellor

not care for the lifestyle she would find if she did return. For himself, he was perfectly content with the life he led, even if he was almost constantly bemused by the woodmaids' domestic efforts.

Shortly after they celebrated the Greening, the Silvanan festival of new life and growth, Fabiom received a summons to Fairwater to be recognised as Deepvale's Lord Holder by Ravik, Ruling Prince of Morene. He would be away for eight days.

It was strange to take off his father's ring, even after such a short time, though he was confident that Tarison would care for it, along with any official matters that arose while he was away.

"Surely you will not go alone," Tarison said. "I would gladly come with you, except I think that I must stay here in your absence."

"I know." Fabiom sighed. "I cannot leave the holding untended, and who else could I trust?" He recalled his father's last, unfulfilled promise that they should visit the city together. "Yet I would have valued your support."

"Support? You are nervous?" Tarison chuckled, not waiting for an answer. "Of course you are. But Ravik is a good man. And facing the Assembly is not as daunting as you may think."

"Nevertheless – I know no one there. If all goes well, it would be nice to have someone to share that with. And if I make a total fool of myself and the prince refuses to grant me Deepvale, it would be good to have company under those circumstances, too."

Tarison burst out laughing. "I think that highly unlikely. I don't suppose…. No, you could hardly ask your wife to travel so far from home."

For a moment, Fabiom did not reply. "To be honest, I'm not sure how I will stand to travel so far from *her*," he said eventually. "But no, you're right. I can't ask her to come with me. I doubt if she could bear it, let alone enjoy the experience. That distance from her tree would be dreadful for her." He laughed ruefully. "I suppose there has to be some downside to being married to a Silvana, otherwise it would be totally unfair to everyone else." He considered for a moment. "I wonder if Masgor would care to accompany me?"

Chapter Nine

Magor was ready long before Fabiom, and at the hold-house by sunrise. They planned to leave after breakfast. Ramus had packed everything he thought Fabiom could possibly want, and more besides: food hampers, wine carafes, blankets and warm clothes, as well as the gifts Fabiom and Casandrina had selected for him to present to the prince. The woodmaids also brought things they thought he might need, some of which he could not even identify and others which, they told him, were so he would not forget them while he was away.

"A rowan seedling – thank you, Kir'h. And Zin'h – what's that?"

"It's spider gossamer, silly. In case you cut yourself." The whitethorn woodmaid pirouetted, her pale hair fanning around her, almost as fine and flyaway as her gift.

A pouch made of beaten bark was thrust into his hands by a darker, sturdier woodmaid. "I've brought you truffles, and nuts from my hazel tree, and an oak gall."

"Thank you, Nek'h. The hazelnuts are lovely. But do I need an oak gall? Truly?"

"You said yesterday they were very useful. I heard you." Nek'h tossed her wild mane of hair while, in the donkey cart, Masgor pretended a coughing fit.

"You're right, I did. However, I certainly can't take the hedgehog, even if it is still hibernating. I'll be back before it wakes up, I promise. Casi, please –"

Laughing, she shooed her woodmaids away.

Even his mother had sent him a gift – a tunic made from fabric she had woven herself in pale yellow silk, bordered with a complex sky-blue and charcoal geometric motif. The gift pleased him immensely – as much for its being given as for what it was, although it was a beautiful garment indeed.

Everything was loaded into the donkey cart. It was time to go.

"I don't want to leave you –"

Casandrina held him close for a long moment. "I have no gift for you but this," she whispered, and she sang to him so softly that only he heard. The ache in his heart eased and his spirits lifted.

"Keep my song with you, my beloved. And return to me as soon as you may."

Twice as a boy Fabiom had gone to Fairwater with his father, the last time four years ago, when Ravik ascended to the throne after the death of his father, Prince Darseus. Well he remembered the wide streets, the bustling life, the visitors from distant lands, and the imposing buildings of white and grey marble.

It would have been overwhelming had Masgor not been there with him: bearded men, with half-length tunics and wrapped legs, spoke to one another in foreign tongues; women, whose already pale faces were lightened further, chattered in incomprehensible accents; street-vendors offered charms and trinkets against previously unimagined dangers; and, on every corner, criers announced entertainments and pleasures to be had.

They spent the morning of the first day wandering the main streets, admiring the architecture, and getting their bearings. In the early afternoon, Fabiom attended one of the several theatres, where a new tragedy by an upcoming playwright was being performed. Afterwards, to banish the gloom – though the play had been inspired and perfectly executed – he bathed in the magnificent public pools. First almost numbingly cold, then hot and then cool. Tiled and mosaiced by skilled artisans, the pools were housed in a massive building set into the side of the hill from which numerous springs poured out their clear waters. Refreshed, he took some time to leave the busy city and walk in the wild beech woods, where once, many generations ago, Prince Lincius had won his wife, the Silvana Sulmarita. Even with the leaves barely breaking through, it was a beautiful place, yet he could not stay long; it was easier to be away from Casandrina in the city than in the woods.

Late that evening, he met up with Masgor again and they took a meal in a splendid dining house where each knee-high table was made from a different timber and the cushions and couches were all of natural hues: the golds, greens and reds of the capital's beech woods through all the seasons. There they sampled wines from foreign lands, and foods Fabiom had never encountered before.

Masgor had spent the afternoon in the city's library and had also caught up with some old acquaintances. He was in very good form.

"So, tomorrow you meet Prince Ravik. You will like him. He has an easy way about him and a quick wit."

"So I've heard. Father always spoke well of him. I met him briefly at his inauguration. He won't remember. He met every holder and their relations that day, as well as hundreds of others." Fabiom considered the wooden skewer in his hand somewhat apprehensively. "Do I like snails?"

"They're more or less tasteless. The sauce, on the other hand, is excellent. Perhaps you would prefer the lobster. Now tomorrow you must ask the prince about the Silvanii frescoes. He may let you see them. They are in the palace proper, unfortunately, so not open to public view."

"Telmas's frescoes? In truth, I would like to see those, very much. Yet I don't think I could ask him. Perhaps another time. And you? Do you have plans for the morrow?" He turned the lobster over. "How do you eat this?"

"However you can; it's worth the effort." Masgor twisted a claw off the crustacean and cracked it with ease born of experience, passing the tender flesh across the table. "Yes indeed, I do have plans. I have been away from the city for far too long. So many people to renew acquaintances with, and there is a visiting philosopher I am eager to engage in dialogue."

Fabiom shook his head in amusement. "I trust you shall not be too busy to attend the formal ceremonies the day after."

Masgor chuckled. "Nothing will keep me away. Don't you worry, my boy. You're not nervous are you?"

"Yes."

"You'll be fine." Masgor raised his cup, toasting him with a pale yellow wine from the distant land of Malandel. "I have complete faith in you. You are both clever *and* intelligent, a rare combination. You'll do well. Just don't do anything rash."

The next morning, after another lonely night, Fabiom was up early. He made his way to the palace, which sat gleaming in the early morning sun, high on the hill overlooking the estuary.

The huge double doors were open and his letter of commission gained him an immediate escort through the ornate entrance hall into the heart room.

In essence, the room was much like the heart room in his own hold-house: simple lines, white walls, four doors, two hearths. The large basin at the centre was of red marble, polished to reveal dozens of fossilised seashells. It was supported by a limb of a beech tree – Sulmarita's tree – which had fallen a hundred and four years after Prince Lincius's passing. Fabiom shivered as he rinsed his hands, though not from the chill of the water.

106

As soon as he indicated he was ready, he was shown into the prince's reception room.

"Fabiom of Deepvale! We meet again." Ravik, Ruling Prince of Morene, though not a tall man, was imposing. Fair of complexion, with rich, copper-brown hair, Ravik strode forward, his right hand outstretched to grasp his visitor's before Fabiom could even think of making a more formal gesture.

"I'm surprised you remember me, my prince." Fabiom returned the firm grip, earning a nod of approval.

"In truth, I *was* somewhat distracted that day," Ravik admitted. "But, I do." He chuckled. "And now it's your turn. I hope you won't be as nervous as I was when you are presented to the Assembly." Ravik clapped him on the shoulder. "They're benign, mostly; clever though. For certain they keep me on my toes."

Fabiom swallowed. "I've been preparing as well as I'm able. I have no idea what to expect, of course."

"They'll talk to you, that's all. Though there's a feeling that some holders are becoming lax with regard to Treelaw, so they'll be keen to know you're on top of that, and care about your woodlands as much as the other aspects of your duties. Otherwise, they'll just talk about general aspects of holdership. Really they want to find out what sort of a man you are. Then they make their recommendation. The final decision as to whether you are ready is mine. Some might hold your age against you, but I can hardly do that. I was twenty when I was thrown into this position. If ever a man wasn't ready, it was me. But come through and relax."

The inner room was rather like its master: elegant yet comfortable. On a sideboard, a selection of fine food was laid out, along with a choice of exquisite wines. Ravik poured the wine himself, bidding Fabiom help himself to food as he did so. "The artichokes are particularly good."

Fabiom glanced at the artichokes. Like the prince, he was partial to them. Winter was barely over and they were the first of the year, so were particularly tempting. Nevertheless he opted for a date stuffed with almond paste instead, thinking it far easier to eat in front of a man he was hoping to impress.

"Sit, now. Tell me about yourself, though I feel I know you already. I knew your father well, of course; he was a good man, and wise. He was very proud of you. He spoke of you often and very fondly."

"Thank you, my prince." Fabiom paused, then admitted, "I miss him, and I feel very young to be in the position I find myself. Yet all is well in the holding and my Uncle Tarison is there to guide me."

"I know Tarison — an honest and fair man as ever there was. And your mother, I trust she is well and is able to help you?"

Fabiom hesitated again. "My mother took my father's death very hard. She left the hold-house some months ago. But she is well."

"So you are alone?" Ravik asked, concern evident in his tone.

"No, my lord. I am married."

"Really? You're one up on me then. And seven years my junior! You will have to tell me the secret of finding a good wife. I'm under a certain amount of pressure from both family and the Assembly to move things on in that area of my life. I presume you brought your lady to Fairwater."

Fabiom looked beyond the prince to a silk wall-hanging of dancing woodmaids in a beech wood.

"I'm afraid not, my lord. She does not travel easily."

Ravik had noted where Fabiom's gaze had gone. "You're not long turned seventeen. You would not have taken a wife while you were mourning your father unless…. Could it be? Your wife — she is not a Silvana?"

Fabiom nodded. "She is of an ash tree. Her name is Casandrina."

"Ash. I see. Your wedding, this would have been a half-year since. No, not quite. But close."

"Yes." Fabiom wondered at Ravik's tone.

"Is it widely known in Deepvale?" The prince was frowning.

"Well, no. With the time of mourning for my father barely begun, we did not celebrate publicly. So hardly anybody —"

Belinda Mellor

"Good. Keep it that way."

Fabiom was taken aback. "My lord, you disapprove?"

"No! Of course I don't disapprove, quite the contrary. It's three generations since a holder was wed to a Silvana; that was in Stormglen, I believe. It's long overdue. But whenever *any* man succeeds there is a rash of attempts by others less prepared, nearly all of which are doomed. And you are not just any man. Think of the young men in Deepvale who might want to emulate you. Do you truly want their fate on your conscience? My father asked every man in your position to be as discreet as possible, I intend to do the same. Most lead very private lives anyway." He laughed. "I say 'most' as if there were many. You are only the ninth that I am aware of, and the first since my reign began. I could wish that more would do so – for the right reasons – and that less would think to copy them who would not otherwise have considered that path."

"I had not thought of that," Fabiom admitted. "I – we – will be discreet." He reached inside the neck of his tunic. "My wife did ask me to give you this. Maybe now would be the time, as we are in private."

The piece of amber was half the size of his palm. Trapped within it was a single ash leaf. As he looked at it, a wave of longing surged through Fabiom and for a moment all he could think was how much he missed Casandrina.

"Fabiom? Is everything well with you?"

"Forgive me, my lord." Fabiom looked up and smiled self-consciously. "It occurred to me how a rejected man would lose his mind – once he knew … once he had heard…." Shaking his head, he offered the amber to the prince. "This is from her tree."

Ravik studied the nugget carefully, turning it every way, so that it caught the light. "It's perfect. Thank you. I will treasure this. And thank your lady. Tell me, Fabiom, have you heard of the artist Telmas?"

The frescoes were situated deep within the palace and were everything Fabiom had expected, and more. They covered the walls of a rectangular room, in the centre of which was a great table. Light poured in from a dozen windows set very high and angled so all that was visible through them was sky.

"I had no idea they were life-size," Fabiom said in awe, finding it hard to raise his voice much above a whisper. "And there are more than I was aware of. How many?"

"Twenty-seven," Ravik replied, his own voice low. "Each one a different Silvana or woodmaid. This is the oldest part of the palace, and, sadly, not much used. As a small boy I used to come here and sit and talk to them." He chuckled at the memory. "Especially when my sisters were being particularly tiresome. I learnt a lot about the trees of Morene here. The ash is over there." He swept his hand to the right. "And the table is made from the trunk of Sulmarita's tree."

"Thank you for letting me see all of this." Fabiom rested a hand on the creamy brown and finely grained table top. "I must admit, I find the table disconcerting."

"I'm not surprised. At least here in Morene we only make furniture from our Silvanan trees when they fall, unlike our neighbours in Gerik."

Fabiom stared at the prince, looking and not seeing anything that might suggest Ravik was exaggerating. "In truth?"

"Did you not know?"

"I knew they murdered their Silvanii for amber; and were indifferent to what trees they felled for timber. But I – I suppose I never considered what that really meant."

Fabiom recalled what Kilm had told him at the last Greening Festival. "You will want me to go there on service."

"Yes, I'm afraid so."

Fabiom nodded. "I'm beginning to understand: some things must be seen, whether evil, like Gerik, or good, like this room."

Ravik looked around. "I should make more use of this space. It is too precious to keep closed up."

Belinda Mellor

Shortly before midday, along with his host, Fabiom enjoyed a second visit to the vast, heated bathhouses that were part of Fairwater's fame, and that he had been too young to use on his previous sojourns in the city. In the afternoon, after an excellent lunch aboard the prince's ship in the estuary, he attended an athletics competition in the city stadium as Ravik's guest. After several running races and trials of strength, an archery demonstration began: a dozen archers, in perfect unison, aimed and shot at small, distant targets. Every arrow hit home and five hit the bullseye. The crowd cheered. Fabiom shifted in his seat, flexing his fingers unconsciously.

"Is something the matter, Fabiom?"

"No, my lord!"

Ravik looked at him sideways. "Yet you seem a little unsettled. If this entertainment is not to your taste, please say so. Fairwater has many diversions. You are only with us a short while, it would be a pity to waste your time at something you were not enjoying."

Fabiom laughed self-consciously. "On the contrary – archery could never bore me. The truth is, I am not used to merely being a spectator. There are some truly excellent bowmen down there."

"And you would like to test your skills against theirs, perhaps?" Ravik guessed.

"Oh yes," Fabiom agreed. "I would."

"These are my top archers, members of an elite unit. Each has fought hard to earn his place. Are you that good?"

Fabiom inclined his head. "Good enough, I'd wager."

"Would you indeed? You are a man of many surprises."

The prince summoned an attendant and, after a brief, whispered conversation, the man hurried away, to speak with an officer standing by the targets.

The officer glanced towards the prince and his guest and nodded enthusiastically.

"You'd better be as good as you say, my friend," Ravik said, with a rather wicked grin.

Fabiom wondered what he had let himself in for and what, exactly, Ravik had in mind. There was no backing down now, not that he wanted to: his hands were itching to get around a good bow and to prove himself against such archers.

"Please, come with me, my lord." An attendant had been sent to escort Fabiom down to the arena. They arrived at a small tent, inside which were two dozen bows of varying heights and woods. "If you would care to select a bow, sir."

Fabiom glanced around until he saw a rack with bows of a suitable height. What to choose? He picked out a couple and tested them, replacing them and moving on until he came to one that felt almost familiar. It was elm backed with ash and it bent under his hands exactly as he knew it should.

"This will suit me very well," he said.

As he left the tent he was met by the man whom he had earlier seen standing by the targets.

"Lord Fabiom. I am glad you can join us. I am Philon of Alderbridge, commander of the palace guard – and currently bow-master to his Highness. We start off with standard targets, as you have observed. After that, things get a little trickier. The lads like to display their prowess. Are you happy with that?"

"As you wish," Fabiom said. "This is a demonstration? It's not a competition?"

"No," the bow-master said, though in such a way as to suggest that 'no' might well mean 'yes', or something very close to it.

Fabiom raised his brows.

"It's not a competition – officially," the bow-master confirmed, "although pride is at stake, and whoever performs best does earn a certain degree of kudos, you understand."

"Naturally," Fabiom agreed. "That does not concern me."

Belinda Mellor

"No, no, of course not." Philon rubbed his hands together. "You see that young man over there. That's Septan of Riverplain, my best archer. I have a small wager with Prince Ravik from time to time on various competitive events: athletics and the like. I am well ahead, if you see what I mean. The prince suggested that we might have a wager here today. He has named you as his champion. Septan is mine."

Fabiom drew a sharp breath. "But the prince has never seen me shoot!"

"No matter. It's purely for fun. Our wagers are small, mostly a matter of jest. And yet I do believe his Highness is somewhat irked by my success. He is looking to you to put him back in the race."

"So, no pressure then," Fabiom said, strapping a leather bracer to his left arm and watching the archer Philon had named as Septan flex his bow, while Masgor's warning, "*Just don't do anything rash*," echoed in his mind.

Grinning broadly, Philon handed Fabiom a quiver of arrows. "Pressure? No. None at all."

Septan was good, very good. For the next demonstration, two dozen parchment scrolls had been suspended from a still-leafless apple tree and were dancing in the chill breeze; Septan's arrow sent the topmost scroll spinning wildly on its thread. The crowd cheered, Philon grinned; Fabiom applauded along with the other archers.

So, the prince was betting on him, literally. Well, why not please him? Though Fabiom was not normally inclined to show off, this was probably the time to make an exception. The arrow would have to fly true to hit such a minute target and to do that it would have to spin – fast. Had he had the time, Fabiom could have fletched an arrow to do what he wanted but he did not have that luxury here. Instead he shaped the fletching on his chosen arrow with dampened fingertips and hoped that would suffice. Taking a deep breath, he sighted the same scroll Septan had hit, adjusted upwards ever so slightly, and, at the moment the breeze stilled, let fly. His arrow cut straight though the fine silken thread and the scroll fluttered to the ground. There was a moment of silence from the crowd and then a huge cheer. Briefly, Fabiom closed his eyes, and allowed himself to breathe again – had he missed his mark he would have hit nothing.

He wondered if this would be a good time to quit. He could go back to his seat with honour intact, and not risk making a fool of himself – except there was the matter of Ravik's wager. Should the Prince have to forfeit because Fabiom was afraid to look the fool, that would not give Ravik the best impression of him. He suddenly realised that his elevation depended on more than the performance he gave before the Assembly tomorrow. He had to finish what he had begun here. With that thought, he wiped his hands on his tunic, almost as nervous as he had been before the night of his seventeenth birth eve for, like then, there was no turning back.

From under the seating tiers at the far side of the arena, a catapult was wheeled out. Fabiom felt his stomach twist. *Please, no.*

The demonstration saw the archers shooting at straw discs as they were catapulted skywards. Septan's arrow flew straight through the centre of the first discus launched into the air, his second took down another and his third clipped a disc's edge and sent it tumbling into the crowd. A young woman rose from her seat holding her trophy aloft and Septan bowed theatrically, to more cheers. As a second and then a third archer released three arrows in rapid succession, Fabiom knew he stood no chance; in the time the discs were airborne he would be able to loose two, no more. And he was not even certain of that.

So far, by piercing two and clipping one, Septan had been the most accurate. Fabiom flexed his shoulders and rolled his head on his neck. This was not the time to be over-tense. He was resigned. If he concentrated he might score two accurate hits. It would not win, but no matter. Should he release a third arrow in the time allowed – wherever it flew – that would level the scores and Ravik would not lose his bet. But there was no chance of that.

His hands were damp. The last thing he needed was the bow slipping in his grasp. He wiped his palms again and gripped the wood tightly as the catapult was readied for his turn.

As the tension in the bowstring released, the over-gripped bow twisted, kicking the arrow fractionally off-course. Given the size and speed of the targets, that slight adjustment was enough and the arrow flew past. Untouched, the target continued on its arc. For an instant, Fabiom was paralysed. Then, almost by instinct, he found a second arrow in his hand, an arrow that somehow found its way to his bow. One. He would hit one. How could he have been so stupid?

"*Not yet.*"

Time seemed to stand still. Tawr stood beside him, a steadying hand on his. "*Wait – and – now!*"

Two straw discs fell at Philon's feet, a single arrow skewering them through the centre.

The crowd came to its feet.

Ravik sat back in his seat with his arms folded and a broad grin on his face. Philon shook his head, then raised his hands in surrender.

After a restless night, during which he stopped missing Casandrina only to worry about the morrow; and managed to put thoughts of facing the Assembly from his mind only by wishing he was with his wife, Fabiom joined Masgor to prepare for the day ahead. They broke their fast as the sun coloured the sky, washing the white marble buildings beyond their balcony in cherry-blossom pink.

A servant had brought food while they slept. On the table was a basket of crusty bread and terra cotta bowls with rich, lemon-flavoured olive oil, fat black olives, dried figs, crumbly white cheese, honey and roasted sesame seeds.

Fabiom broke a piece of bread, dipped it into the olive oil, and ate it distractedly. He was to spend the day with the members of Morene's Assembly: the most influential men from the eleven holdings; currently numbering twenty-three, each hand-picked by the prince. One of them, he was aware, recently elevated to curator-holder of Riverplain, on account of the same disaster that had brought Fabiom to his position. The difference being that the new lord, Norgest, was a forty-something-year-old cousin to the late holder, and a member of the Assembly for some three years.

"I won't know what to say to them."

"That is not a problem I have ever known you suffer from." Masgor sipped his hot mulberry juice before coating a square of cheese in honey and sesame seeds. "Delicious." He licked his fingers.

Fabiom picked up his own beaker. "I suspect the quality of my words will matter more than the quantity in this instance."

"Meaning it doesn't normally? I haven't been *that* easy on you, Fabiom. Have you not had two of the best teachers in the land?" Masgor countered. "Your father taught you well. As have I; I trust you'll agree. You know far more than you realise. You are ready. Just don't do *anything else* rash."

"But what should I talk to them about?"

"Talk about what you know."

"I can talk about poetry –"

"If you must."

"It's a fine tunic," Masgor commented as he helped Fabiom pin and arrange the garment his mother had made for the occasion.

"It is, but why does she always have to complicate things? Where does this bit go?"

"Here." Masgor refastened a bronze pin shaped like a longbow. "Very appropriate. Over your shoulder. That's better."

Fabiom pushed a silver band through his hair, tied his sandals and chose a relatively plain armband to wear.

"If not my mind, my body is ready," he declared almost mournfully, making Masgor chuckle.

Belinda Mellor

The summons came shortly after, in the form of a short, wiry man with snow white hair.

"Lord Fabiom, I am Helund of Rushford, Scribe to the Assembly of Morene and your guide through today's proceedings. You must ask me for anything you need or if you have any concerns. I am entirely at your service."

"I appreciate that, Helund, thank you." Fabiom cast a desperate glance at Masgor, who could only pat him on the shoulder and wish him well.

The Assembly Hall was situated in the centre of the city, directly below the palace. Helund led him into a large, oak-lined room where, to his horror, the entire Assembly was waiting, standing in a three-quarter circle, all in silence.

He was bid stand before them, in the gap in the circle, as Helund went around and named each member and their holding. The little man had reached the third when Fabiom realised he had not taken in a single name.

"It is my honour to present Jarin of Greendell." The name jolted Fabiom out of his paralysis, for the extremely elderly Jarin was a poet whose work he had long admired; moreover, he was Silvana-born.

Delighted at the prospect of meeting Jarin properly, Fabiom listened intently to the remaining twenty names, committing them all to memory. As Helund finished his circuit, Fabiom apologised and asked him to repeat the first two.

Helund sighed quietly. "Elasus of Southernport and Lykas of Fairwater, then –"

"Jarin of Greendell," Fabiom smiled, and continued around the room, needing only one prompt on a name and two on holdings.

"Enough of the formalities." Kymon of Alderbridge stepped forward. Kymon was the only man there who Fabiom knew; the younger brother to the elderly lord of Deepvale's neighbouring holding, he had been a guest at Deepvale's hold-house on several occasions. "Come, Fabiom. Don't look so worried. You are welcome."

"Indeed, most welcome." A noticeably handsome man grasped his hand. Norgest, the new holder of Riverplain – Fabiom remembered. "We've not met, but I am well acquainted with your Uncle Tarison. He and I spent much of our service together. His humour kept me sane over a dismal winter in Gerik."

Much as Fabiom would have liked to engage Jarin in conversation, he was thwarted time and again as one or another of the Assembly members took him aside. As the prince had warned him, they were quick-witted and learned and he began to feel somewhat battered within a short space of time. Redemption came when Kymon brought the conversation around to Treelaw and the amendments that had been sent out some months previously.

"I read them," Fabiom said. "They were well considered. Though I was surprised at the suggestion that all woodlands should be mapped to five-hundred paces."

"Why would you not consider that necessary?" Elasus jumped on his statement.

"Of course it's necessary! I was simply surprised it needed to be stated, that there was a possibility that it's not common practice."

"Are Deepvale's woods so mapped, then?"

"To a thousand paces where they are anyway close to human habitation and to five hundred elsewhere. I would like to go further, though it's time-consuming. I intend to add a little more each year."

"But would you do the task yourself?" The question came from Jarin. Fabiom paused, wondering what the old man was actually asking.

"I would like to," he said at last. "There are other considerations to being a holder, other constraints on my time. But yes, it is a task I would relish, and one I would want to oversee."

"And the amendment to the penalties for unlicensed felling," Lykas of Fairwater asked.

"There were no such amendments," Fabiom said, frowning. "The last were made two years ago, possibly three. I will admit I took little notice at the time. Though I do know what they are, if that's what you're asking…."

"Leave the boy alone, Lykas," Jarin grumbled. "He obviously knows as much about Treelaw as you do, if not more. Come Fabiom. I cannot stand

Belinda Mellor

long. Help me set myself down somewhere comfortable and talk to me. I heard you were given a private viewing of the Silvanan frescoes in the palace."

There was a question in that statement in answer to which Fabiom pulled at the fine leather thong around his neck, revealing the two pieces of amber tied there that had been hidden beneath his tunic.

"Well, well." Jarin placed his hand on the amber and closed his eyes. "Ash, if I'm not mistaken."

"You are not mistaken."

"So, we hardly need discuss whether you are worthy to be a holder. That matter is settled. What would you rather talk about?"

So engrossed did Fabiom become in their conversation he forgot he had ever been nervous. Relaxed and confident, over the course of the day he so impressed the prince's advisors that, despite his lack of years, they not only recommended to Ravik that he should be recognised as holder, they also put forward that he would be appointed as a magistrate for Deepvale.

"I don't think that's a good idea," Fabiom argued when Ravik put the suggestion to him.

The prince raised his brows. "Are you questioning my Assembly, and not even appointed officially?"

"My lord, I –"

Ravik laughed. "Don't look so worried. Look, say yes. What you do when you get home is up to you. No one is suggesting you become chief magistrate. But you can cut your teeth on some smaller cases. A holder needs to be seen to wield that power, and it can't be learnt from books, or even from observation. Tarison is Deepvale's senior magistrate, is he not?"

"Yes. And I plan to keep him in that position permanently. I can do that, can't I?"

"You can, if you wish. If you don't want to hold all the power for yourself."

"I only want what's best for Deepvale, and Tarison is the right man for that task."

"And the fact that you know it makes you the right man for the tasks I will be commissioning you to tonight," Ravik said.

At day's end, in a formal ceremony attended by many of the capital's leading citizens, Masgor among them, Fabiom knelt before Ravik and made formal vows to care for and serve Deepvale to the best of his ability, and to serve as a magistrate for his holding:

"Friend and stranger, rich and poor, all are alike. It is an abomination towards all the Powers and all that is right and good to show partiality. The true mark of a ruler is to do justice."

He was presented with his scroll of office along with finely wrought armbands and rings in gold, silver and bronze. As he accepted the tokens from the prince, he wondered at Ravik's seemingly concerned expression and that of the Assembly members on the dais with him. Indeed Jarin and Kymon both looked almost sympathetic. For certain they were making him nervous.

"You have to speak now. You are aware? It's not easy – the first time. But remember, it is only a formality," Kymon of Alderbridge told him, one hand gently pressed between his shoulder blades, guiding him to the front and side of the dais so that he might be seen and heard by everyone present. Ravik sent him an encouraging smile.

After the day he had just had; meeting them individually, having no idea what questions they would throw at him or opinions they would put before him; this was by far the easiest part.

Masgor's grin and wink made him smile as he prepared to address the gathered dignitaries. They had been through this a dozen times and Masgor had summed it up perfectly that very morning:

"An overview of the holding, your hopes for both it and yourself as holder, your vision for the future. Finally how you see Deepvale's role in the country. When you are done, you present the gifts you have brought, and everyone cheers. And then it is over and you are free to go home."

Belinda Mellor

The speech went exactly as he had practiced it. As the cheers subsided, Fabiom presented the prince with a selection of the finest wines and silks produced in Deepvale. The look that passed between them acknowledged that, in the piece of amber from Casandrina's tree, the most precious of his gifts had already been presented.

"I am sorry you cannot stay longer, Fabiom," Ravik told him at their parting. "I would enjoy your company. I shall look forward to bettering our acquaintance."

"As shall I, my lord," Fabiom said sincerely.

His elevation, and the chance to test his archery skills against Fairwater's best, had pleased him. Walking home, coming close to the village of Watersmeet, where the rivers Minnow and Swan join with the Fairwater, and finding Casandrina waiting for him, delighted him even more. She ran to him and he caught her, lifting her off her feet and swinging her round in a laughing, crushing embrace.

"Oh, Casi! How did you get here? We're a half-day's walk from the house! Are you alone?" Kisses prevented any answer she might give him until he stopped to repeat, "How did you get here?"

"I asked Ramus to walk this far with me, and then I sent him home." Her hands caressed his neck and shoulders as her eyes held his. "I knew you were coming. I could feel you getting closer."

"Is this close enough?" he murmured, kissing her mouth again and her eyes and throat and neck. All of a sudden he stepped away from her. "Can you really *feel* where I am?"

"How far from me you are, not where." The roads stretched away, crossing the rivers, leading to their various destinations. She took one hand from the back of his neck and indicated north and south. "This means nothing to me, the roads, and names. Though I think I might be able to find you, if I had to. I do not know. The further from my tree I am, the harder it is. So please, may we go home?" A tiny, puzzled frown creased her brow. "Fabiom, where is Masgor? Where is your donkey?"

He had travelled from Fairwater alone and on foot, leaving Masgor and their transport in the city, where Masgor had been co-opted into helping with the latest stage of the treaty. There had even been mention of him travelling to Westmouth in Gerik to take part in the next round of talks. Casandrina shivered when Fabiom told her.

"He should not go there," she said vehemently. "Why talk with them? Their towns are built of nothing but timber. Simpler by far to burn them down, surely?"

An ancient anger flared in her eyes and, for the first time, he caught a glimpse of the strength and obduracy of the primeval forest that was as much a part of the lovely, lithe girl at his side as it was of the towering ash tree she sprang from. It would be too easy to be deceived by her outward form, to think the only threat she posed was through the haunting music at her command. But she laughed then as she caught sight of a fallow doe with a tiny fawn close by, moving among the shadows of the trees to the side of the road, and he did not have to argue the political case for reconciliation with Gerik. He was not sorry.

Belinda Mellor

Part
Three

Chapter One

Warmth came late to the fields and farms of Deepvale that spring, and many of the silkworm larvae hatched before the mulberry trees unfurled their leaf buds. Hatched and died for lack of food. Casandrina sang to the coppiced trees in the orchards and sent her woodmaids into the wildwood to look for wild mulberry. The diminished stocks of larvae were augmented by wild caterpillars and the crisis passed, though their troubles were not over. The chill spring eventually gave way to a summer of relentless rains that soaked the mulberry leaves. Every one had to be dried before the silkworms could be fed. They worked hard themselves, took on what extra help they could find, and watched for the weather to improve. It did not oblige until summer was all but done.

At regular intervals, after dusk fell and the day's work was complete, Fabiom and Kilm, his estate manager, pored over the accounts with a sense of despondency that matched the heavy skies. Meanwhile, the rains that soaked the mulberries bruised the young grapes on the vines and the grape harvest was poor. All over the holding, the story was the same, and Fabiom spent many hours he could ill afford in the municipal centre, reassuring worried farmers and traders, dealing with petty quarrels fuelled by fear and watching the holding's surplus food stores diminish. However, by the end of the season they realised that they had not lost as much as they had first feared. All the holding's mulberry orchards had flourished under Casandrina's care and, as the early part of the autumn had been as good as they could wish, even the grape harvest was not a complete failure. Providing they found a good market for their silk, they would avoid disaster.

As the days shortened into autumn, the market bustled with traders. They came to buy the holding's produce and to sell some of what they had already bought elsewhere. And it was not just foodstuffs they offered, for they knew this was the time when people were prepared to buy a few luxuries, even if they had not had an especially good summer season. It would soon be Festival.

Fabiom had more than the Harvest Festival on his mind as he wandered among the stalls set up in the market square. He had set all concerns aside and was in fine humour; cheerfully acknowledging the greetings from his people as he went and handing out honeyed fruit and tiny, sweet pastries to the children who came to say hello to him. Autumn had always seen the turning of his own year, with his birth anniversary falling two months past Harvest; now the season marked his marriage anniversary also, and he wanted to find something special for Casandrina. The quest was not easy: some stalls had fine clothing, but nothing that could compare to garments the woodmaids fashioned; others offered cosmetics and perfumes she had no need of, or trinkets that did not begin to express how he felt about her.

He had almost given up, and was thinking he would simply write her another poem, when a pair of finely wrought silver cloak clasps caught his eye. Even though they were oddly set with gaudy, rainbow-hued stones, the filigree silver-work was beautiful and like nothing he had seen before. The trader was asking a ridiculous price for the pieces, claiming the stones had marvellous properties for warding and protecting. When Fabiom

Belinda Mellor

questioned the price, the man glanced about before leaning across his stall to whisper, "Their last owner could listen to the songs of the Silvanii without being affected."

"Their last owner was deaf, I presume," Fabiom countered. "I'm not interested in the stones, take them out and keep them for your own protection. I would buy the mounts alone."

They argued for a while until Fabiom got what he wanted, at a price that was not entirely unreasonable; whereupon the trader deftly prised the stones from their setting.

"You don't know what you're missing out on. Such gems are very rare. What can you put in their place that will be of equal value?"

"What I have is of greater value by far," Fabiom informed him. "And I had thought to do it myself. However, I see you are as skilled with your hands as with your tongue. Will you reset them for me?"

Casandrina had brought a number of pieces of amber with her when she left the wildwood – pieces worth more than the combined value of everything for sale at the market that day. Not that he would dream of selling them, especially the two that had resulted from her altercation with Gracillia, over him. That they should be worn seemed a far better proposal.

"Well, I do have a small talent," the man acknowledged, beaming. "For a nominal consideration I shall gladly mount whatever you should choose."

The two pieces of amber Fabiom produced from the pouch on his belt made the trader's eyes widen in awe.

"Perfect," he whispered, though as he moved to take the amber from Fabiom's hand his look became suspicious. "Is this quite legal?"

Fabiom chuckled. "You are an honest man at heart. I'm glad to know it. I assure you, it's legal; I am not known for trading in contraband amber."

The trader's eyes darted from Fabiom's face to the amber in his hand and back again. "You have an honest face," he said gruffly. With that he took the golden spheres and chortled, "And a ring that declares you are likely telling the truth. I've not heard yet of a holder up before the Court of the

Assembly for involvement in damage to a Silvanan tree. My apologies, my lord."

The amber pieces were mounted into the brooches with the utmost care, then wrapped in a piece of raw silk before being handed back to Fabiom. It would be a fitting gift.

Fabiom left the market and headed home, wondering, as he climbed the hill that led to the hold-house, if he would be able to wait until their marriage anniversary to give Casandrina his gift. The soft leather pouch with its precious package bumped against his thigh as he walked. 'Silvana's tears' the poet Mahov called amber, though the historian Jerynn had favoured the term 'Silvanan blood' in his damning accounts of the destruction of the forests of Gerik.

Fabiom recalled the moment Casandrina had first shown him the other pieces. "Our gift and our curse," she had whispered. Apart from the two he had just had mounted and the larger piece he had found beneath her tree, there were a dozen or so that she had not explained, plus one for each of the nine Silvanan trees that had fallen in Deepvale since her own tree reached maturity. She could not tell him when that was in terms he would understand, for the Silvanii did not count the years, only noted the changing of the seasons.

"Lord Fabiom, Lord Fabiom!" A child's voice cut through his day-dreaming.

Fabiom grinned at the sandy-haired boy running down the hill towards him, Kilm's youngest. "What is it, Calbrin?"

"Father says can you come straight away. I know – I know you're on your way. He thought you were still at market. He sent me to fetch you."

Fabiom would have laughed had it not been apparent that something was amiss, though when he questioned the boy, Calbrin did not know what it was.

"Is your father at the mill?" Fabiom asked. He had been with Kilm there earlier and all had been well then, at least as well as it could be, given the season they had endured. What else could have gone wrong?

"No, sir, he's at your house."

Fabiom rinsed his hands absently as he passed through the heart room, his attention more on the woodmaid running across the courtyard than the ritual.

"What is it, Kir'h?" he asked, seeing her worried expression.

"Something terrible has happened, Fabiom. Casandrina is very angry!"

"Where is she?" A vision, not of his wife but of his mother, came unbidden to him. "Is it something I've done?"

"Someone must be responsible. It is hardly likely to be you!" Kir'h replied.

"Unless you have taken to trafficking sericulture secrets abroad, and that I seriously doubt," added a familiar voice behind him. Fabiom whirled around to see his uncle, and his farm manager – both of them grim-faced.

"What?" Fabiom almost choked. "Where?"

"Varlass," Kilm told him. "Or so we have been informed by the mercers from that land who are no longer interested in buying our silks, other than some velvets."

Two emotions strove for precedence in Fabiom's mind: fury at the betrayal of a sacred trust and fear at the certainty of financial ruin if they could not sell their produce. Varlass. He tried to remember what he had ever learnt of that land. He knew it to be larger than Morene, maybe twice the size, and away to the south, beyond Gerik.

"*Varlass measures its year by the movement of the stars through the heavens, not the greening and the turning of the trees,*" he quoted from some half-forgotten text of Masgor's.

"The lore of silk was a gift to those who swore to protect the wildwood, not to those who watch the night sky." Casandrina had joined them, her expression unreadable.

Fabiom took her hands in his. He had no words to offer her.

"Any silk mercers from Varlass must have passed through Southernport and several holdings between there and Deepvale. Even if they didn't go via Fairwater, word must have reached Prince Ravik by now," Tarison pointed out.

"What can he do? What can anyone do?" Fabiom asked helplessly.

That night, though Ramus had laid out a supper of truffled eggs and baked vegetables in the dining room, Casandrina did not sit down. She shook her head when Fabiom offered her a beaker of hot spiced wine.

"I have to go to the woods."

Fabiom put the beaker on the low table, beside his own. "No, you have to stay here. Casi, this is not just about the Silvanii. You knew when you accepted me as your husband you would not only be my wife but also Deepvale's Lady. Our holding is suffering already and now, with no sales for our silk, that will get worse."

"That is why I have to go. I am not avoiding you, I am not neglecting your people; I am trying to help."

"How? I don't understand. Talk to me. What's happening? What are the Silvanii saying?"

She turned her back to him and stared out of the small window that overlooked the fruit orchard. "They are afraid."

"I can understand that." He stepped up close to her and massaged her shoulders.

"Can you? This is what happened in Gerik: greed drove men there to think only of their own interests, to dishonour their commitments, to take more than had been offered. It is of no matter to us whether or not this Varlass profits from silk lore. What matters is that trust has been traded for money – something precious for something base. And those who thought to gain by doing this have no honour – such men would take amber from our trees with no qualms. That is why my sisters are afraid." She took his hands from her shoulders and placed them on her arms, so that his left

130

hand rested over the scars she still bore. "The wounded tree of a living Silvana yields far more amber than the same tree when it falls naturally."

"Enough, Casandrina! Don't talk like that!"

He only realised he had shaken her in the moment she twisted away from his anger and spun around to face him.

Horrified he reached for her again, pulling her towards him. "Casi, I'm so sorry. Forgive me."

"You, too, are afraid. I understand." She glanced disinterestedly at the food cooling on the table. "I have to go to the woods."

Over the next few days Casandrina was rarely at the house, spending her time instead in the wildwood. When she was at home she was quiet and barely spoke. Fear filled Fabiom, less intense than on his night in the Dancing Glade, yet darker and more chilling. Almost a year ago he had found happiness. He believed then that it would last his lifetime. Now he was less certain.

When Fabiom next went to Valehead he could not bring himself to tell his mother anything about his personal woes, and she was concerned enough about the silk sales not to notice anything was amiss. Not so Marid.

"Come to the stables and see how the foals are growing," his aunt suggested as Fabiom made ready to leave.

"I'll say goodbye," Vida said, touching his cheek. "I hear Marid's donkeys quite enough without having to look at them as well." She shook her head. "You look tired."

"I *am* tired." He kissed her. "Be well. I'll see you soon."

Marid linked her arm through Fabiom's as they made their way through one of the vine-covered pergolas that lined the terraces behind the house. Wasps buzzed lazily around the remaining grapes, competing with tiny silver-eyed birds for what was left of the fruit.

"You are worried. And don't say it's just about Deepvale and this silk business."

Fabiom plucked a bunch of deep pink grapes that appeared to be wasp free. "Isn't that enough?"

"It should be. You are not yet eighteen years and you've already had to deal with one of the worst harvests we've ever had, and now this news from Varlass. But I know there's something else. And I think it has to do with Casandrina."

"How –"

"There's a sadness about you I haven't seen since you married. It reminds me of the way your parents' arguments used to hurt you." She took some of the grapes from him. "Do you want to talk about it?"

"We haven't argued. Maybe it would be easier if we did. I don't know. It seems as if she wants to be in the woods with the other Silvanii."

"And you want her at your side?"

"Yes. Of course. It's not as if I'm not concerned for them. I'm not asking her to choose – we're all hurt by this."

They stepped out from the shade of the pergola. Before them were several steep, rock-strewn paddocks and the river, where Fabiom's barge waited to take him back to the municipal centre. They made their way down a set of stone steps that led to the first paddock. Four young donkeys wandered over to greet them.

Marid pulled handfuls of fresh grass and offered it across the fence. "A successful marriage needs to be based on more than just romance. I suspect it has all been rather easy until now."

"True," Fabiom admitted as he scratched the jaw of a tiny cream colt.

"So talk to her. More importantly, *listen* to her. Don't avoid each other. Good will come of this, if you let it. Strength comes from testing. You will grow closer – in ways you probably can't even imagine. Now go home to your wife. I will come and see you soon."

Word came from Fairwater two days later. Ravik sent envoys to all the major silk producers among the holdings. They came with letters from the prince, samples of the foreign silk, and the promise of help to find the best markets – from those that were left.

Fabiom called together all in Deepvale who had a direct interest in the matter, throwsters, dyers, mercers and farmers. For although most of the holding's silk was reeled at the one mill, silkworms were reared and cocoons produced by a number of families, some of whom made a small amount of their own thread too. Fabiom also invited Masgor to join them, given that most people were assuming their nearest neighbour had a hand in this treachery and Masgor was an expert on all matters pertaining to Gerik. Casandrina did not attend.

They met in the main hall of the municipal centre where the talk got louder and more aggravated as they awaited the arrival of the envoy who, when he came, turned out to be an intense young man, barely older than Fabiom himself. He greeted Fabiom warmly, though there was an anxious look in his eyes as he introduced himself.

"Lord Fabiom, I am Cleon of Southernport. I bring you Prince Ravik's felicitations and his assurance that he will do all he can to aid you, if aid is needed at this time."

Tarison had overheard. "How bad is it, Cleon?" he asked.

"Possibly not as bad as we first thought," Cleon replied with a lopsided grin. "The silk is poor. Here, see –"

He beckoned one of his assistants forwards and a bundle was unwrapped. A hush fell among those who had come together, as they gathered around.

"How can we be certain that this is their best?" Kilm asked, fraying the edge of the sea-green fabric. "And how can we be certain that they won't learn to do better than this?" The piece was in danger of falling apart in his hands as he passed it to another of the bystanders.

As questions were being fired at Cleon from all quarters of the room, Fabiom called the meeting to order.

A mercer at the back of the room stood. "Do we know who's behind this? Was it someone in Gerik? That's the one country which neither has need, nor use, for the knowledge of silk production. For now that no trees grow there such wisdom is redundant. They could gain more from imparting rather than safekeeping *their* knowledge."

"That was the first supposition," Cleon admitted against a background of muttering. "However, there has been some covert investigation and it seems the knowledge is no longer intact in Gerik."

"It isn't intact in Varlass either!" one of the dyers quipped as the fabric sample tore in two in someone else's hands. Grim smiles and brief, forced, laughter echoed his observation.

Masgor rose to his feet. "It would be comforting to think it was from Gerik, though word there has it that those with real knowledge all perished. The first settlers of Gerik *had* been gifted with the knowledge, just as those who made Morene their home were, but the Silvanii didn't give up that land so easily." Masgor caught Fabiom's eye and raised his brows meaningfully, except that Fabiom was not quite sure what his tutor was actually suggesting.

Whispers were being exchanged here and there, whispers from which a few words emerged. "They will be furious," Fabiom heard, and wondered what that actually meant. More than a few pairs of eyes turned towards him – the eyes of those who knew him best. It was true that Casandrina had seemed distracted since the crisis was brought to their attention. Worse, she refused to discuss the matter. Were they suggesting that *he* was in danger?

"That's how we learnt where it *was* from. Once we were certain the blame couldn't be laid on Gerik, we started looking elsewhere." Cleon's voice cut through his thoughts. "And so, when the Lord Holder of Rushford reported that his crops were failing, especially fruit trees and the like, we became suspicious. Through someone with access to the Silvanii, the perpetrator was discovered to be from there. The Silvanii of Rushford were already exacting their revenge.

"Since then, things have got worse – there's rumours of men gone into the woods who've not come out again."

"Have you discovered anything from Varlass, Cleon?" Tarison inquired, deftly changing the subject.

Cleon nodded. "It appears that, at the moment, we have less to fear in economic terms than we first thought. Their trees are not thriving: they are withering and dying almost as quickly as they're being planted."

"With no Silvanii, they cannot be growing the seedlings in Varlass. How are they getting the trees to plant?" Kilm demanded.

"That we don't know. But Prince Ravik has made stopping that trade a priority, and there are thorough checks now of all ships bound for Varlass."

"But how much silk have they made?" The question came from a man who had sold himself into a year of extra service to set his widowed mother up with her own small rearing and reeling business.

Cleon flicked through a sheaf of notes. "Little enough, it seems. What cocoons they produced were small and of poor quality. It seems the mercers are mainly concerned with trying to get our prices down. Varlass invested a lot in this project for little return. From what information we could glean it seems they are thinking of giving up altogether and looking to make peace with Prince Ravik. By next year things will, hopefully, be as they were."

"Next year!" someone grumbled. "That's a long time to go without."

"Meanwhile, the holder and inhabitants of Rushford will have to make peace with their Silvanii," Fabiom murmured.

Only Masgor and Kilm, standing close by him, heard.

After some light refreshments, Cleon and his companions left the municipal centre and went with Fabiom, Tarison and Kilm to one of the fabric workshops where hanks were made into thicker yarns by the throwsters; and then on to the dyeing and weaving rooms. They were impressed, though not surprised, by the standard of the work, which for generations had been renowned as among the best in Morene. However, they were amazed at the range and intensity of the colour they saw.

 Silvana

"I have never seen the like!" proclaimed the eldest of the four, whom Cleon had introduced as Obyn, a silk expert from Greendell. "No, once in my youth I saw something similar, it was in a holding where…." he paused as he caught sight of Lan'h who had come in with an armful of bark for one of the dyers. He offered no comment, but watched her for a while.

"Holly," Fabiom informed him.

"The bark?"

"Yes, that too."

Obyn chuckled with glee, his eyes twinkling with delight. "Quite beautiful," he declared. "We'll not find any to surpass this in Morene," he informed his companions as he picked up an armful of wine red satin.

"The prince gave orders to look out for the best silks," Cleon informed Fabiom. "I don't pretend to be an expert. How do you make this so – stiff – I suppose?"

Fabiom beckoned the master dyer over to explain the process.

"It's dyed as yarn, sir, not fabric. See?" the dyer said. He brought them to look into the vast dye vats, seething with colours wondrous to behold: greens the colours of moss, linden, olive, asparagus and pine needles; reds like sunsets, new wine and blood; the rich orange-yellow glow of amber. "We have improved our dyeing techniques recently. It gives us more scope." He flashed Fabiom a grin as Lan'h returned with a second armful of bark.

Cleon asked to speak with Fabiom privately while the others finished their tour.

"Ravik will go to Varlass himself," he informed Fabiom. "He will investigate the matter most thoroughly. If there is any threat remaining, he will discover it. This has caused much bad feeling between our two lands. The Varlassians would repair that. They have nothing to gain by making an enemy of Morene, and much to lose. The prince requests that you should accompany him…."

Fabiom frowned. "*Requests*? I don't understand. I owe him two years' service: he can command it of me."

"No. He was quite specific. If you can and if you are willing." Cleon's expression suggested that he did not approve of such laxity on the part of his royal master.

"I see," Fabiom hesitated. "I need to discuss this with my wife, I think."

"Should you go, your time away will of course count towards the service you owe his Highness," Cleon added.

Fabiom nodded. That was of little matter at present. The question was whether he was more use at home or in Varlass.

Before he left the mill for home, Fabiom arranged that Tarison should take care of their visitors. He did not extend any invitations and none were expected.

To Fabiom's chagrin, Casandrina was not reassured at all by the news that the mulberry trees in Varlass had failed.

They were in the day room. He, propped on the edge of a table by the window, while she stood beside the cold hearth, pulling the petals from the heads of blood-red roses.

"It is finished, Casandrina. Those who perpetrated the crime will be discovered. They will be punished and their lands confiscated. Varlass will make amends. It is finished."

"Would the rulers of Varlass be trying to make amends if their scheme had succeeded?" She crushed the remains of the roses and Fabiom flinched as the thorns pierced her skin.

"Probably not," he conceded. "Yet it could not succeed, could it? You knew that all along. The silkworms can thrive only on mulberry leaves, and mulberries grow only where the Silvanii dwell. No matter how much knowledge or experience the Varlassians gain, mulberry trees simply will not do well there. I don't understand that, I admit; still, I accept it. Won't you try to accept that this thing is over?"

"It is not over! Do you not see? Long before there was need or talk of a treaty between Morene and Gerik, there was a treaty between the Silvanii and mankind. That must be upheld also."

"It is probable that the Holder of Rushford knew nothing, nor the vast majority of the people there, yet if their crops fail all are punished."

Casandrina stared at her husband. "The holder is responsible. That is what his title means. If being responsible is *not* what he does, then what else does he do? What do *you* do?"

"So, if the perpetrators were here in Deepvale, you would hold *me* accountable? You do not readily distinguish between individuals where blame is to be laid, do you?"

"It is not something we are known for," she agreed.

Fabiom turned away without speaking. Maybe now was not the time to broach the idea of his travelling to Varlass. He fully expected to hear a door slam or the sound of breaking crockery, and it was with wonder that he felt the gentle pressure of her hand resting on his shoulder.

"Fabiom, I do not believe such a thing would happen here, for you would not let it. I have been trying to make my sisters understand that. So far, I have not succeeded."

Chapter Two

Rain drummed on the terra cotta tiles of the hold-house. Fabiom listened to their rhythm as he went through the ever-growing lists of people who had been forced to place themselves into service to pay off debts. He had been doing so since Ravik's envoys had left at first light, three hours ago – or so he estimated, for there was no light breaking through the clouds to illuminate the sundial in the courtyard. He had brought the papers home on the off-chance that Casandrina would be there. She was not.

Sighing, he reread one of the applications before stamping it as approved, noting his disquiet on a scroll. He would have liked to have refused, knowing the recipient of the service had misused others in the same position in past years, but the holding was not in a position to buy that service as well. He had already offered more positions than they could truly afford.

It was early afternoon by the time Casandrina came in. The rain had eased to a silent drizzle.

Fabiom put his work aside. "We need to talk."

She shook the rain from her hair. "Yes."

Surprised and relieved, he took her damp cloak from her and put another, lighter one, around her shoulders. "You do know you mean more to me than anyone or anything else? If I've given you reason to doubt that —"

"You have not! Why do you say so?"

"You've seemed distant – angry – with me."

"Afraid, not angry."

He pulled her close against his side. "I know you're afraid. But I promise I'll do everything in my power to keep you safe – to keep the wildwood safe."

With her head resting on his shoulder she traced the lines of his collarbone. "I am not talking of greedy men and what they might do, that is something vague and distant. My fear is much closer, much more real." She lifted her head. "I am afraid of being parted from you."

Wanting to both laugh and kiss her, he tried to do both, which managed to make her smile – something she had not done for several days. "I don't have to go to Varlass. I told you: Prince Ravik does not compel me, only asks if I am free to accompany him."

"It is not your prince whom I fear." As she spoke, her smile faded.

"Who then?"

She looked away from him, towards the window. "We have been summoned. The other Silvanii would meet with us."

"Summoned?"

She shrugged. "They cannot command either of us. Yet if we do not go, we will not be welcome in the wildwood."

"When?"

"Soon." She traced the shape of his mouth with her fingertips. "Though maybe not immediately."

Afternoon had turned to evening by the time they arrived in the Dancing Glade where Silvanii from all over Deepvale's wildwood had gathered, and that evening became night, lit by phosphorescent fungi and glow worms, while they talked. A cold wind blew, stripping leaves and seeds from the

Belinda Mellor

trees, toying with them before letting them fall. Casandrina shivered. Had he been able, Fabiom would have wrapped her in his arms, though he knew it was not the chill that affected her.

"You must choose, Fabiom – the town or the woods; your prince or your wife."

"It is not that simple!" he told them.

There were thirty or more Silvanii: ash, elm, beech, chestnut and oak. They had given him a draught of something bittersweet that had felled him to his knees and rendered him semiconscious yet able to see and hear them all clearly. He had drunk it willingly though now he was wondering whether coming here at all had not been a terrible mistake.

"It is simple enough: it is no longer safe for us to interact with mankind so closely. The bonds between Silvanii and men must be loosened; the bonds between men in authority and Silvanii especially so. If you wish to stay with Casandrina, you must renounce your holdership and dwell here, deep in the wildwood."

"Listen to me, please," Fabiom persisted. He could barely raise his head and his voice was weak. "Prince Ravik intends to go to Varlass. I will accompany him. We will discover what happened – exactly what happened – and what is happening now. At least give us time to do that!"

"You ask us to give you time? Have we not given you enough? We gave you silk, we gave you amber, we helped your crops grow, we gave you herbs for healing. All we asked in return was your protection and your respect."

"I know." Fabiom bowed his head. "And I'm sorry your trust has been repaid so poorly. I cannot promise all will be well; I am asking only that you give me a chance."

There was some muted discussion, Casandrina did not take part. In the past several days she had done all she could, said all she could, to sway her sisters. She knelt beside her husband and held his hand and waited.

"I am sorry, Fabiom." The Silvana who addressed him now was of an oak tree and her voice was deep and filled with sorrow. *"We are divided in the matter. However, those who would agree your proposal do not number enough."* It was clear she was one such. *"Will you accept ours?"*

"No," Casandrina said firmly before Fabiom could reply. "He cannot. Holdership of this land is more than mere title, as we all know. You cannot ask that of him."

"*Casandrina,*" another ash Silvana interjected, "*it is either that or renounce you. Surely you do not expect him to do that?*"

At that, another spoke. "*He will not have to. We can make him forget.*"

"Forget!" cried Fabiom, aghast.

"*Yes – forget – as if your marriage had never been. You will remember neither her face nor her name. There are songs that can strip a man's mind – either completely or in part.*"

There was whispered discussion among them, agreement, approval of the suggestion. Casandrina shivered again and a tear slipped down her cheek.

"You're crazy! I will never forget her! How could I?" Somehow, he struggled to his feet, though without Casandrina's support he would have fallen.

"*You do not know our powers – you may think you do. But no man does.*"

"No, I do not presume so much. You are powerful indeed, and mysterious. All I know for certain is that my love for Casandrina is as strong as your magic. I will prevail, or be broken in the trying."

"*Do not say so!*" another insisted. "*We wish you no harm. No, do not scorn, it is true. You are a good man, a fine holder and you were worthy of a Silvana's love. Casandrina was not the only one here who would have left this life for you. Yet now – it cannot be. You must renounce her. You can leave here unharmed, if you leave here alone.*"

"You ask of me the one thing I cannot do. I would sooner give up Deepvale!"

"*No. Casandrina is correct. That is not an option for you. The land is in your blood. For the sake of your people, for Deepvale – for all of us, human and Silvanii who dwell here – you must give her up.*"

"No!"

Casandrina turned to face him, held his face between her hands. Her eyes were pools of sorrow from which tears flowed unchecked. "My love,

142

Belinda Mellor

my sweet love, you must. What they are otherwise proposing carries far too much risk. You must leave me here, Fabiom; for it is the only way that I can be sure you will be safe."

"No! Casandrina, do not say so. I could no more stop loving you and live as I could stop breathing. I will always love you. And it will not destroy me." He had fallen to his knees again, as much in supplication as from the effect of the draught.

"*I truly hope you are right, Fabiom.*" It was not Casandrina who said so but another ash Silvana. Her beautiful eyes were filled with sorrow and compassion in equal measure.

And then the song began. It was like nothing Fabiom had ever heard before and it tore his mind apart. Yet, somewhere, there was a counterpoint, a gentler song, and it was not Casandrina who sang. Her voice was silenced.

She was gone.

Totally lost, totally bereft, Fabiom staggered home. He could not have said how he got there. Perhaps his feet were so used to the paths that they took him automatically; certainly he had no recollection of having made the decision to go back.

Exhausted, he fell asleep on a settle in the day room. When he awoke, the quality of light suggested it was mid-morning. He could not even say if it was the same day. He was alone. The house was silent.

Sitting, disorientated, he was aware of a terrible loss, yet he had no idea what it was he mourned. Eventually he slept again.

Some hours later, Fabiom heard a door shut, his name being called. He frowned and shook his head: *I know that voice.* It was his first coherent thought since waking. With some surprise he found that he was standing in his library, leafing through a book. He could not recall having gone there. He put the book down and regarded it curiously – Treelaw – something nearly remembered then lost.

"Fabiom! Fabiom! Are you here? Are you all right? Fabiom?"

"Uncle?"

Tarison had entered the library. "Ramus said you were behaving strangely…. By all that's sacred, what has happened? You look terrible!"

Fabiom stared at his uncle. "I don't know." He raked his hands through his hair. "I have no idea."

"What?"

"I think something has happened … something has gone. I remember singing, incredibly beautiful singing. I do not recall the words at all." He closed his eyes and began to rock backwards and forwards, a low moan issuing from his lips.

A look of horror crossed Tarison's face. "Come on," he managed. "Sit down. We need help."

Vida stroked Fabiom's face. "These moods come and go," she assured him. "Sometimes, like now, they affect you badly. Soon it will pass. It always does."

"And I really am all right – most of the time?" Fabiom asked, unconvinced.

"Of course you are! Do you think you would have been recognised as holder, or made a magistrate if you were not?" She studied the half-finished weaving beside her and shook her head. "It's this silk business. They are angry, you see. They are particularly angry with people in authority; and they already have – well – they have left their mark on you."

She had explained it to him, the day after Tarison had brought him home to Valehead: he had gone to the woods on his seventeenth birth eve and the Silvanii had rejected him, yet they had spared him because he was Deepvale's Holder. Bruised but not broken.

Belinda Mellor

Vida was speaking again; she was smiling. "We need to find you a wife. Yes. I should have thought of that before. Dala? She must be seventeen by now. No, not her. Someone less obvious, someone from the holding. Suva of Watersmeet? She would be most suitable. Or her cousin, Nona? Perhaps even better. A wife, children, a family of your own, that is exactly what you need. You can forget about the Silvanii then – apart from proper knowledge of Treelaw, as all holders should know."

"I have a daughter," Fabiom whispered. He shook his head, bewildered. "Why did I say that? Is it so?"

"No, Fabiom. Of course not. It is these dreams you are having. You are confused – for now. Soon you will be well."

Living in Tarison's house, cared for by his mother and aunt, Fabiom continued to function, after a fashion. No one except those closest to him knew of his condition and they did all they could to protect him. He even heard some simple cases in the magistrates' hall; straightforward ones. He was certainly not supposed to hear the case of the farm labourer charged with trafficking amber. However, the transcript only stated that the man had been accused of stealing from his master's land.

"Amber!" Fabiom sat forward in his seat, his eyes narrowing, jaw set.

"Yes, my lord. There are many trees on my land…."

"You said he stole from you – from your land. Are you claiming the amber?"

"No! Well yes – if it belongs to anyone it is mine."

"It does not belong to anyone," Fabiom stated. "Woodland with Silvanan trees does not belong to anyone either." His expression was dangerous and the farmer looked down, shoulders hunched.

Fabiom turned back to the labourer. "Where is this piece of amber you found?"

The man wet his lips and looked around nervously. "I gave them to, to a friend to mind."

"*Them?*"

The man pulled a face, furious with himself. "There were two pieces, my lord."

Fabiom regarded him for several very long minutes. "You lie. Produce this 'friend' and all the pieces of amber, and this court may yet be merciful; if I am satisfied that the amber was indeed 'found'."

"My lord! Are you suggesting I would harm a Silvanan tree? Never! I would never do such a thing!"

Fabiom glanced at the farmer. "How about you? Would you be tempted to procure a little more amber – a broken branch, say? Maybe an axe-stoke to a trunk – a glancing blow would do it, would it not?"

"No, Lord Fabiom! I did not mean to claim it. I never would. Just – he took it from my land. He profited while my family will go hungry if there is no silk market."

Fabiom closed his eyes for a moment – the man spoke truly. His first year as holder and what had been one of the most prosperous holdings in Morene was now teetering on the brink of disaster. No wonder the Silvanii had rejected him. He turned back to the labourer.

"And you. What actions do you think our present circumstances might justify?"

By this time Tarison had slipped into the courtroom, having been summoned by the physician, Namenn. The two men held a whispered, concerned conversation at the back of the chamber.

The labourer, defeated by Fabiom's furious tone and expression, looked towards the assembled witnesses and after a brief pause an older woman stepped forwards. She looked terrified.

"My lord," she whispered, holding a small cloth bundle out towards Fabiom whilst keeping as much distance from him as she possibly could. "He's my son. Please don't be too hard on him."

A court official took the package from her and began to open it.

Fabiom stopped him. "Give that to me."

146

The official glanced towards Tarison, who could only shrug and nod.

Fabiom took the package carefully and laid it on his lap. He unfolded the cloth until its contents were revealed: four pieces of amber. For a while he just stared at them, so long that Namenn began to make his way forward.

"Tears or blood? If only my wife were here, she would know."

He looked up, shocked at the words that had come from his mouth. His eyes widening with horror as memories came back.

"I, oh no —"

Namenn reached him.

"This hearing is adjourned. Take this man, and his mother. The case will resume shortly," Tarison ordered.

He was only one step behind Namenn by now and they shepherded Fabiom from the chamber into his private office as quickly as they could.

"What's happening to me?" Fabiom demanded. "I cannot tell dreams from waking. I have a wife, I have a daughter, I have heard the Silvanii sing. Tarison, Namenn — I can't live like this. Who am I?"

Tarison commandeered a river barge and brought Fabiom to Valehead. As Vida was out, Marid took care of him.

"Try to get him to rest," Tarison told her. "I must go back, briefly. I will be home as soon as I can."

Looks that Fabiom could not begin to interpret passed between them and then Tarison was gone, leaving Fabiom and Marid alone. She smiled at him encouragingly, her eyes bright with unshed tears.

"I'll fetch you something to eat."

Fabiom reached out and took her hands in his.

"No. Don't go. Marid, I trust you, more than anyone. You know that, don't you?"

"Thank you, Fabiom." She smiled, though her voice was guarded.

"I'm going to ask you a question. I beg you, please, answer it truthfully: how long have I been like this?"

Marid looked surprised and then relieved, which Fabiom failed to notice.

"If by 'this' you mean distracted and confused, I can tell you in honest truth that it has been exactly twelve days."

"So," he mused, "I am well, normally." Hope tinged his tone with urgency.

"You are well, dear one. Very well. This is horrible and I would do anything to help you. It breaks my heart to see you so."

"Thank you." He sighed. "Then I must listen to my mother. She is probably right. I don't know why – I thought she was lying to me. Though I don't know why she would."

Marid frowned. "What did she tell you?"

He shook his head. "I think I'll go and rest for a while, if you don't mind."

He seemed calmer after that and indeed he was resigned. The moment of clarity had passed and instead he believed his mother's tale and was prepared to go along with her plans for him. Anything to get better, he told himself. He had no thought of wanting a wife, just of trying to find a sense of normality, a rock he could cling to while his thoughts and memories and dreams and the song, always the song, crashed around in his head like so many broken branches adrift in a wild river.

Belinda Mellor

Chapter Three

When Prince Ravik eventually received a missive from Deepvale, it was not at all what he expected, nor hoped for. He immediately summoned Nalio from the School of Apothecary and charged him with conveying his reply and helping Fabiom in any way he could.

Nalio reached Deepvale three days later, arriving at his father's dispensary as the last patient of the day was leaving. He collapsed into a seat facing Namenn's desk. "How is he? Can I see him?"

"Patience! He is in Valehead. We can go there tonight." The physician mixed a spoonful of his favoured tonic into a cup of diluted wine which he passed to his son. "You travelled fast, I think. Have you brought word from the prince?"

Nalio nodded and handed his father the letter. "That's better," he said as he drained the cup.

"We need to take this to Tarison immediately. A final, short journey." Namenn seized his son's arm and helped him back to his feet.

As they hoped, they found Tarison at the municipal centre. Seeing the royal seal, and aware that Nalio was not due home for nearly a month, Tarison immediately guessed what they brought. He led them into a small ante-room where they would have privacy.

After brief pleasantries, the prince had written:

'I do not know how many Silvanii are corporeal. I suspect more men live entirely in the woods than Silvanii come out to dwell among humans. In fact I am only aware of nine, and of those, two of the husbands are very elderly. I do keep a record, of course. It is a useful contact and, as at such a time as this, when relations are strained, I think of such unions as a go-between, a source of contact and mediation. This is the list. I have named the trees, for that often makes a difference.'

Tarison sent for Masgor. Together they perused the list Ravik had sent. Eight names besides Fabiom's. Two extremely elderly, as Ravik had said, four too far distant to be useful except as a last resort. That left two.

"This one's a birch and this an alder," Tarison read.

"Birch," said three voices in unison.

"Fine – birch it is. She lives in Riverplain, this side of the Gallant. Her husband is in his fifties."

"Then they have a son," Masgor pointed out.

Tarison nodded. "Presumably. Is that a problem?"

"On the contrary, it might help. It is said the Silvana-born are gifted in Treelaw and we can use all the help we can get."

Tarison had to remain in Deepvale as surrogate holder, Namenn refused to go anywhere, insisting on staying close to Fabiom, and Masgor was busy researching Fabiom's dilemma; so it was Marid and Nalio who made the four-day journey to Riverplain to see the birch Silvana Taparaina and her family, and ask for their help.

After several inquiries, they eventually found the little house in the wood where the family lived, and where Taparaina's husband worked as a wood carver, creating beautiful and lovingly-crafted furniture, ornaments and utensils.

Belinda Mellor

When they arrived, he was oiling a large, leaf-patterned platter he had just completed. Seeing the well-to-do lady and the young physician, he set his work aside and greeted them cheerfully.

"Welcome." He indicated his rather chaotic workshop ruefully. "I am Truelan, the carver. I trust you will find my work more acceptable than the surroundings, please excuse."

"The work is excellent, and the surroundings are fine. Woodmaids do not make the best housekeepers, do they?" Marid said with a smile.

The man's eyes widened in surprise.

"We have come to ask your lady wife for her aid," Nalio explained.

Meanwhile, Vida was busy with her own plans for Fabiom. Nona, the girl she had chosen as her son's bride-to-be, was two years older than he. She was well-educated, pretty – though not overly so, serious to the point of being intense and already experienced at managing a home as, since an accident when Nona was only twelve years of age, her mother was often confined to bed. An ideal wife – as Vida had pointed out to Nona's parents – for a young, inexperienced man prone to daydreaming, who bore too much responsibility.

Fabiom was acquainted with Nona from his mother's soirees, and accepted that her qualities, as his mother listed them, were practical. However, he could not help but wonder if she had a good sense of humour, or cared much for poetry. When he voiced those questions Vida simply pointed out that it was a good thing she, not he, was choosing Deepvale's next Lady.

Had he been more aware of what was going on around him, he might have thought it strange that the arrangements were being made in Marid's absence; that the house was not decorated, nor was there any increase in the comings or goings; no one was making up new clothes or preparing food. Indeed all was going on as if nothing special was about to take place.

"Go and get yourself ready," Vida told him on the morning of his wedding, shortly after Tarison had left the house.

Fabiom went to his room and dressed himself in the garment his mother had laid out – wine red, bordered with amber and cream, far longer than he favoured and in a colour he considered more suited to furniture than clothing. Something bothered him: it was too ornate; the fastenings, armbands and rings she had chosen were overly decorous. They should be plain, simple. No – that was not right either. That was the other time – the time when he had gone to the woods and, and…. Perplexed, he tried to focus on the almost understood thought that nagged him: that he should not be doing this.

"Fabiom, hurry. Aren't you ready yet?" Vida was standing in the doorway; a determined though not particularly cheerful smile on her face.

He was ready, inasmuch as he was dressed. He was also heart-sick and dizzy with confusion. Then his mother was fussing around him, tidying and straightening.

"You'll do. Come on. We must hurry. There's not much time."

Her anxiety puzzled him. "Why the rush?"

They were half-way down the stairs when his answer came with the unexpected return of Marid.

His aunt entered her house to be confronted by a group of strangers in the day room, dressed in their finest clothes; Vida coming down the stairs, similarly attired; an elderly magistrate waiting below with a girl adorned for her wedding. She did not see Fabiom.

"Vida! Whatever is happening here!"

Vida hurried down the stairs and tried to lead her sister-by-marriage away.

Marid was not prepared to move. "What have you done?"

"What have I done? What does it look like? I have arranged a wedding for my son – a wedding to a nice human girl who will not try to destroy

152   *Belinda Mellor*

him. That's what I've done. I am helping him. This is what he needs and you know it as well as I." She spoke fast, and as quietly as she could.

Marid's voice, however, was not lowered and her words carried to the waiting bridal party, and up the stairs. "Fabiom is not free to marry: he already has a wife!"

He was down the stairs and beside her in a moment. "A wife? I have a wife?"

At Fabiom's exclamation, Marid's hands flew to her mouth, but the words were out.

He stumbled out of the house and away, towards the town and home, heedless of both women calling his name as he ran.

It was Tarison who found him in his darkened hold-house late that evening. It was Tarison who, reluctantly, told him the things he could not remember – as well as Tarison knew them, for there were things only Fabiom had been party to and no one could fill in those gaps for him, save the Silvanii.

For a long while, Fabiom sat in silence, his face buried in his hands; finally he faced his uncle. "I don't know which is harder – not knowing, or knowing yet not remembering. How can I not remember? If what you tell me is the truth, how can I have forgotten it? Forgotten her?" He stood and went to the window and stared out across to the wildwood, hidden by the night, like his memories. "My wife. A Silvana –" He turned back to his uncle. "And she has abandoned me because of the betrayal of silk-lore?"

Tarison made a yes-no gesture with his hands. "That I cannot tell you, Fabiom. All I know is, she has not been seen since the night you lost your memory; nor any of her woodmaids. We all hoped that you would remember, in time – by yourself. Namenn, especially, was against your being told these things. But after what happened earlier, the rest of us thought it best. If you choose to marry again, well – I don't know, to be honest. I just don't know."

Fabiom poured them both a glass of wine. "Marry – no, I do not choose that. I let my mother lead me. I just wanted the craziness to stop. No. If

I have a wife, even one I have no recollection of, I will be true to her. At least until I know what happened. But the girl – Nona – what about her? I cannot face her! Is that coward?"

Tarison laughed shortly. "Hardly! I suspect Marid dealt with her and her family. Anyhow, I will go to them on the morrow and see what needs to be done to smooth things over. As for your mother...."

Fabiom shook his head. "Indeed." He looked around the room and sighed. "I know I'm not entirely rational – and now I partly understand why. Yet I'd like to be here, I think, in my own house. Maybe it will be easier to get my thoughts together here – where she lived with me. What do you think? Could I come home?"

Tarison rested a hand on Fabiom's shoulder. "You are our Lord Holder, you may do as you please. And being apart from your mother is probably no bad thing. However, I have to say that I would rather you were not alone. Stay here if you will, but have someone stay with you. Nalio would be glad to, I should imagine. I'll stay tonight."

Though they sat up late, when his uncle retired, Fabiom did not go to his bedchamber. Instead the night saw him walk through his garden and cross over the bridge towards the wildwood.

One memory remained: a very little boy, lost and afraid, finding sanctuary in an ash grove. By virtue of concentrating on that, he eventually found his way to Casandrina's tree. For a long time he stood, searching for something, anything, that seemed like recent memory. There was nothing. Eventually, he lay down in the hollow formed by the tree's mighty roots and wept bitter tears.

"I cannot remember you. How can I not remember you? Am I mad?" He pressed his face and hands hard against the bark until the pattern was indented into his flesh. "I must be mad. Or are they all lying to me? This cannot be real."

Eventually, exhausted, he slept. At first, his dreams were terrible. Yet somehow, with him so close and in so much pain, she managed to reach

154

out to him, to touch his mind, to soothe his sleep as she had many years before. Instead of being dire, his dreams were sweet then – and all the more painful to wake from.

"Oh, Casi!" he murmured, halfway between waking and sleeping. Then full wakefulness was his and the overwhelming feeling of loss that had haunted him for the last twenty-five days.

He could not hear her as she wept and begged: "*Say my name, Fabiom, say my full name!*"

Chapter Four

Nalia strolled back to the day room where Fabiom sat reading. He had been into almost every room in the house.

"It feels so empty. I don't understand. Who came? Who took her things?"

Fabiom shrugged. "Maybe she did. I don't know. Apparently Ramus came home and found the place like this. He thought we had been robbed. He went to town to raise the alarm. I must have got back while he was out because when he came with some militia he found me here, though I have no recollection of speaking to him. The first person I remember is my uncle. Anyway, I was rambling – they thought I'd been attacked, hit on the head. They went for your father, as you probably know. I don't remember that either. He sent for Tarison.

"I have no idea what's missing. For certain there's no evidence of anything feminine around the place."

"It's not just that. There were animals, woodland creatures: martins, badgers, bats – that sort of thing."

"Truly?"

"Yes. And there was amber, a lot of it. Do you … no, I don't suppose you do."

156

Belinda Mellor

"Remember? No. When you say 'a lot', what exactly do you mean?"

Nalio considered. "Oh, I don't know. There were pieces in every room, and in the courtyard. And there were several necklaces. One, with twelve smallish beads, she wore often – so maybe she has that with her."

He rubbed his jaw and waited to see if Fabiom would react to his words but all Fabiom said was, "Go on."

"Well, of the most obvious, let's see: there were five in the day room, hanging in the window to catch the sun; there was a particularly fine piece in the heart room; and the largest of all I last noticed as a paperweight in the library."

Fabiom shook his head. "I haven't moved any." He sighed. "We could do with some amber right now, amber we could trade – the holding's stores are getting dangerously low. People will go hungry if the silk doesn't sell soon. One thing I do know for certain: the people of Deepvale have not gone without since this holding was first granted to Laurrus. I don't wish to go down in history as the holder who let Deepvale starve. It's enough that I'll be remembered for my addled wits."

Nalio laughed out loud at that and thumped Fabiom on the shoulder. "Bet your aim isn't addled. Let *us* not starve tonight – let's go hunting."

They brought down a fair-sized boar and three brace of partridge by the end of the day and sent for all the estate workers and their families to feast.

Kilm brought along his double flute and Nalio found a lyre in the house, and soon there was singing and dancing around a mighty bonfire.

For a while Fabiom was content to look on, more relaxed than he had been and yet not inclined to join in, until, persuaded by young Calbrin, he recalled a very old tune he had learnt from his father in the days when his mother played the lyre and Deepvale's hold-house was a happy family home. He took the lyre from Nalio and played that, followed by a well-known hunting song with a chorus everyone could join in:

The bow string, the lyre string; they play the same music.
The lyre sings of the hunt.
The arrow flies; the note strikes home.
The lyre, the bow, the chase, the song – are one.

Afterwards, when their guests had gone home, in high spirits and with food for the morrow, and Ramus had retired to his room, Fabiom sat by the dying embers of the bonfire.

"I won't be able to stay long, a few days at most," Nalio apologised, breaking into Fabiom's thoughts.

"I know. I'm grateful you could be here at all. Thank the prince for me – he's bound to call you to account for all this."

"Wine or morat?"

Fabiom nodded towards the fermented mulberry and honey and Nalio filled a large beaker almost to overflowing.

"What's the plan – get very drunk?" Fabiom asked, looking into the brimming amber liquid.

"If it would help."

"Is that your medical advice?" Fabiom asked with a half-laugh.

"Yes. It's all I have anyway. I know my father has considered giving you all sorts of things and has changed his mind as often. No doubt he'll come up with something eventually – meanwhile this is the best I can suggest." He raised his cup to his friend.

Fabiom stopped him. "No. Let's drink to you – to your success as a physician and the joy that will bring you. How is the lovely Eifa by the way?"

Nalio laughed. "Ah, lovely, as you say; and patient, fortunately."

Fabiom sat back and stared into the embers. "Does she know? About Casandrina? About me?"

"No," Nalio assured him. "No one has been told who does not need to know."

Belinda Mellor

"Tell her. I would not have you keep secrets from her. And, anyway, she deserves to be told; she and Casi had become close friends." He took another draught of morat, his eyes still on the remains of the fire. It took him a moment to realise that Nalio was looking at him intently, a broad grin on his face.

"I told you a decent drink was what you needed," Nalio said in a droll tone.

"What?" Then Fabiom gasped. "Did I...?"

"It's all there, my friend. Nothing is lost. And thank you – I shall tell Eifa. She will appreciate the confidence. In fact, I must leave you for a while tomorrow for I bought her a pearl anklet in Fairwater. I would show you before I give it to her – it's quite unusual." He paused and frowned, then sat up. "Gift! Fabiom. Do you – no – it doesn't matter if you remember or not. When you first heard of the silk disaster – that very day – you had bought a gift for Casandrina. You wrote me about it! You had found two brooches in the market and had them mounted with amber and planned to give them to her on your wedding anniversary. You must have hidden them away. Where are they?"

Fabiom had no idea, though, to Nalio's relief, he could recall both the marketplace and the vendor.

Finding the brooches was not difficult. Fabiom's favourite hiding place as a boy had been the cellars beneath the kitchen. Fond memories came to mind of hiding Festival gifts he had made for his parents, among them a wooden bird he once carved for his father and a shell necklace he made for his mother after a visit to the coast.

"Excellent!" Nalio exclaimed on seeing the pouch Fabiom retrieved and the two lovely brooches which he carefully removed. "Not that I'm suggesting you sell *that* amber. I believe they're the most precious of all the pieces she brought with her."

Despite Fabiom's insistence, Nalio would not elaborate, feigning no more knowledge than he had imparted. Fabiom did not entirely believe

159

him but let it go. One of the brooches he used to fasten his tunic, the other he placed beneath his pillow. It was enough to have something of hers, something real at last.

As Nalio had to return to his studies, Fabiom's aunt came to stay, leaving her son in Vida's care. Fabiom was glad of her cheerful company.

Ever practical, Marid brought several servants from Valehead, though none who had served in the hold-house before, and they bustled around, learning the lay-out of the house. Ramus immediately set them to work.

"I gave Nona most of the wedding gifts you'd put aside for her. I also gave her the cream colt you liked so well." Marid said as she arranged a vase of autumn foliage picked on her way up to the house. "There, that's better," she declared, setting the vase on a side table in the day room.

"Mother scoffed when I suggested giving her a donkey," Fabiom remembered.

"Your mother painted Nona as a very serious young woman, but in truth she's had little chance to be anything else. A frivolous gift will distract her from her circumstances, and a baby donkey is about as frivolous as you can get."

Fabiom chuckled. "So, she got the better bargain in the end – a wayward pet rather than a distracted husband."

A maid brought a pitcher of hot spiced wine and a platter of seed bread from the kitchen.

"We can be grateful your mother chose a bride for you from the holding. Had she decided to honour your betrothal to Dala, I don't know what would have happened," Marid said once the maid had left.

"You don't think we could have bought off Lord Herbis with a donkey and some jewellery?"

"Probably not." She turned to him with a smile. "But when Dala does marry, I shall give her one."

"I presume Mother chose a local girl over Dala because Herbis knew I married almost a year since. She would have had too much to explain."

Belinda Mellor

"I'm not sure –" Marid turned away and, for a moment, studied the arrangement of multi-hued foliage. "I suspect it was simply that she could hardly organise a wedding with my sister's daughter as bride if neither I nor my husband and son were present," she said at last.

Fabiom poured them each a beaker of fragrant wine. "Perhaps I should have married Dala. Life would have been a lot simpler, I suspect."

"True, it would," Marid allowed.

Fabiom frowned, "I thought … I had the feeling that you approved of what I –"

"Oh, I did. I do! Casandrina is the perfect partner for you." She squeezed his hand. "You said 'simpler', not 'better'."

Despite talking with Marid late into the night, Fabiom rose before dawn the following morning. His sleep was too troubled for his bed to keep him any longer than necessary. A heavy mist shrouded the garden, frustrating his hopes of doing some archery practice. Disconsolate, he was heading instead towards the bridge, thinking to collect some ferns to weave into a garland, when a tall figure stepped out of the mist, almost on top of him.

"My apologies," stammered the stranger. "I heard no one. I am seeking the master of this holding. Gwillon is my name. I come from Riverplain."

"You've found me," Fabiom replied, recovering his composure. "Which, given this mist, is quite remarkable. You've come a long way. Please, come inside."

In the heart room, Gwillon rinsed his hands with care; meanwhile Fabiom studied his visitor.

A couple of years older than Fabiom, with dark brown hair and eyes, and a ruddy complexion that appeared both natural and from spending time outdoors, there was an uncanny grace about Gwillon that would have marked him out in any company.

Fabiom knew who Gwillon was. Both Nalio and Marid had told him about their visit to the birch Silvana, Taparaina, and her family in Riverplain.

She had promised to consider his plight and send an answer as soon as she had one. Dare he hope that her son brought that answer?

"I have met one other Silvana-son," Fabiom said as Gwillon dried his hands. "The poet Jarin of Greendell. He was at my commissioning to holder. My memory of meeting him is blurred."

"Mine too," Gwillon said, "I believe he attended my birth presentation."

Fabiom chuckled. "Come on, let's find you something hot to eat. You must be chilled and hungry."

Needing little sleep and guessing how anxious Fabiom must be, Gwillon rested only briefly and barely refreshed himself before he suggested they go to Casandrina's grove. Fabiom was glad to do so. The mist had lifted as he led the way, knowing the path as well as he ever had.

"This is the one." Fabiom tenderly stroked a bough of his wife's tree.

Gwillon placed a hand on the trunk of the huge ash.

"She is here, trapped," he said after a long moment. "She is so unhappy it breaks my heart to feel it."

"Trapped?" Fabiom whispered. He closed his eyes and rested his face against the trunk, and though he wanted to weep, his heart felt lighter than it had for the past month. "Then she has not deserted me?"

"Not of her own will." Gwillon smiled at Fabiom's relief though, as his gaze returned to Casandrina's tree, his expression was one of concern.

That evening, although Ramus had prepared a fine meal and both Marid and Gwillon were excellent company, Fabiom had little appetite. He picked at his food for a while before pushing the plate away and pressing his fingers hard between his brows.

"I have to remember something – soon – else my head will crack from the effort of trying," he complained.

"This is what Physician Namenn fears," Marid reminded him. "You cannot force yourself to remember. The moments of clarity you've had came when you least expected – when you have not *tried* to think or remember."

Belinda Mellor

"I know," Fabiom agreed wearily. "It's hard, though – trying not to think."

"I think you should visit my mother. Maybe seeing a Silvana will help," Gwillon suggested.

In Truelan's workshop, five days later, Fabiom picked up a large turned bowl. "Hazel – it's lovely. Or maybe this one in larch? What do you think, Marid?"

"For yourself?"

"For my mother. A peace offering."

"Ah." Marid's brows creased in a tiny frown. "Your mother is not overly keen on wooden ornaments these days."

"Should I know that? It seems like something I should know."

She touched his arm. "It is of small matter. I think I should like to own this." She held up an intricately carved candlestick.

"Elm," said Fabiom without thinking. "Here is its twin. I shall buy them for you."

Realising they were being watched, he turned and saw a pretty dark-haired girl, nearer child than woman, who smiled mischievously at him.

"You know your woods. Do you know what I am?"

"*What* you are?" He frowned. "No, I'm afraid not."

For a moment she looked sad and then smiled again. "Would you like those?"

"Yes, thank you. The pair."

Marid watched the exchange before greeting Gwillon, who had entered the workshop.

"Seeing a woodmaid had no effect on him, though he recognises each type of wood in your father's pieces instantly. Maybe there is hope in that at least."

"Maybe." The Silvana's son seemed unconvinced.

However, a moment later, Fabiom smiled at a second woodmaid who entered with a tray of refreshments.

"I recognise your friend though – whitethorn. I'm right, am I not?"

"You are!" exclaimed the first woodmaid indignantly. "So why not me?"

Fabiom shook his head. "I cannot say. I'm sorry. Will you not tell?"

"Oh, very well," she agreed grumpily. "Mine is a bay tree."

"That would explain it," Fabiom said. "My lady has no bay woodmaids."

She caught the candlestick as it slipped from his hand.

The birch Silvana, Taparaina, welcomed them.

She was lovely – stately and gracious, with fine hair, shaded dark and silver-white, and bright green eyes – and Fabiom found himself staring. He wondered how he had ever dared believe he could win one such as she for his wife and was amazed by the sudden thought that not only had he dared, he had succeeded.

Meanwhile, Taparaina studied the pin he wore at his shoulder. "A potent symbol," she murmured. "I am surprised they left this with you."

"It was hidden," Fabiom explained, pulling himself together. "I have no recollection, though I am told I had two of them mounted as a gift, and that I put them away against," he paused and took a deep, steadying breath, "against our marriage anniversary."

She rested her hand over the piece of amber. "This is the result of an injury, not grief. A very recent injury."

They were invited to bathe and change their clothes and rest after their journey. Fabiom was glad of it. He guessed the Silvana had been hoping her words would stir a memory. An injury? Why would he choose to make an anniversary gift for his wife out of that piece of amber in particular? Taparaina knew, he was sure. It seemed important. Forcing memories was pointless so he went for a walk in the woods instead.

Nothing came to him as he walked, save a sense of peace, of wellbeing.

164

The wildwood was alive and welcoming and he belonged there. This was his world as much as any town or farm. He recalled a very similar feeling from long ago, when he was a small boy.

"The day I found your tree," he said aloud. "The day you first sang to me."

Marid and Fabiom joined the family for dinner that night, partaking in woodmaid-prepared dishes made from chestnuts, fungi, nettles, sloes, rose hips and bilberries; dishes that had once seemed as familiar to Fabiom as bread and wine yet now intrigued him. There was a lovely sense of contentment in the small house in the woods. It showed on Truelan's face; the woodcarver looked far younger than his fifty-five years. Fabiom wondered about his own life, what it had been like before she went away. He knew reaching for memories was counterproductive, yet it was hard not to do so. He found himself holding his amber brooch hard enough for the finding to cut into his hand. Nothing. He took a deep breath and tried to relax. That was almost as difficult. Instead he turned his attention to the easy conversation going on around him and began to enjoy the evening for its own sake.

Half-way through the meal they were interrupted by the arrival of a poorly-dressed woman with two little girls and a baby boy who was crying inconsolably. The exhausted mother was immediately guided into the house and given food and drink for herself and the children.

"He won't settle, my lady. Day and night. He barely sleeps. I'm sorry to trouble you – but if you could help. Anything. I'm at my wits end."

"You *can* help him, can't you?" the older girl said. "I told Mama you could."

Taparaina took the baby into her arms. "I think he just needs a tonic. Have you seen the physician?"

The woman shook her head. "We have no money. My husband has not had work this past month – since the silk mill closed."

Taparaina turned to her woodmaids and instructed them to make a drink that would soothe the child, with herbs, tree saps and honey.

While they waited for the mixture to arrive, the two little girls climbed onto Taparaina's lap, despite their mother's protestations. The Silvana was perfectly happy that they should do so and whispered things to them that made them laugh with glee and bury their faces in her flowing hair.

Watching them, Fabiom chuckled. "Children know, don't they? They always know. They would come to our house all the time. And Yan was delighted the first time he saw her. I remember! I can see his face, the way he looked at her. He gave her a gold lily. I can't remember anything else – just that. I can't see her. Why can't I see her?"

The mother and her eldest child both regarded him with puzzled expressions.

"I'm sorry. Excuse me." Rising, he made his way back out to Truelan's workshop where he attempted to calm the tumult in his mind by picking up random pieces of shavings and guessing – correctly – what wood each was; apart from one which he presumed was bay.

"My wife sang the child a lullaby," Truelan said when he went to call Fabiom back in to finish his meal. "You should have stayed." He regarded the younger man with compassion. "I've no words for you, lad. I can't begin to imagine how you're hurting. But trust me – if your lady's being kept from you, as my boy believes – it's a mercy you can't remember her. It would tear my heart out of my chest to be knowingly kept apart from Taparaina. Even the thought of such a thing happening to us knots my belly. Think on that before you try too hard to get your memories back."

"I can't just give up!"

"No, I'm not suggesting you do. I wouldn't either. But in all the talk I've heard, no one's mentioned how it could be worse for you. I think it's worth saying, that's all." The woodcarver picked up a small, lidded bowl he had crafted from a piece of ash. "I made this for you, when I heard you were coming. As I say, I've no words; this is the best I can do."

The grained timber was smooth beneath Fabiom's touch, light brown:

Belinda Mellor

the colour of her skin. "Thank you; it's beautiful."

Truelan nodded. "Come along. We're waited for."

Toying with a morsel of sweet elderflower cake when the meal was resumed, Fabiom admitted his true fears: "I think I cannot have been worthy of her if I've forgotten her face – her voice. If she is even half as lovely as you, my lady, what sort of husband was I? Maybe what has happened to me is fitting after all."

Appalled, Marid took his hand. "No, Fabiom – do not say so. That is further from the truth than you could possibly imagine."

Taparaina simply laughed. "That piece of amber you wear attests otherwise."

"I cannot remember."

"She fought for you, Fabiom. She adjudged you worthy of her love even if it cost her dearly."

Having never heard that part of Fabiom and Casandrina's tale before, Marid was as amazed as he to hear it.

"And these memories you have," Taparaina continued. "That you can remember anything at all is testimony to the depth of your feeling. The magic worked on you is strong, and should have been complete. These flashes of recall that haunt you prove your love. Do not despair, Fabiom, there is hope still." She reached out for her husband, who took her hand. "We are fortunate: with our quiet lives centred in the woods, my sisters were not concerned. There is a feeling that runs through the wildwood that the time has come to loose all bonds between Silvanii and humankind; the betrayal of the sericulture secrets cuts deep. We watched all trust lost in Gerik, and now this. There are Silvanii who fear Morene will go the same way as Gerik: that we will be valued for how we can be used, rather than for ourselves – silk first, and then what? Amber? Timber? There is fear, and where there is fear there is often cruelty. You have been cruelly hurt, Fabiom. Yet I believe it was not done out of spite. Furthermore, I do not believe that it was done with your wife's consent – unless to save you from deeper hurt."

With that small comfort, Fabiom settled down that night in a strange bed, a long way from home. Sleep would not come. Restless, he searched the deepest, most hidden recesses of his mind for some image of her face, some echo of her voice, until exhaustion overcame him and he slipped into a troubled sleep. At last, just before dawn, in that second between sleeping and waking, he saw her clearly just as she had appeared on their very first day and she was so beautiful to him that he wept.

The following morning, Fabiom and Gwillon hunted together. When they returned and began cleaning the catch – a brace of woodpigeon and a large hare – their talk turned to poetry, which Taparaina loved to hear.

"Whenever I go into town, I try to learn something new, to bring home for her. I listen to the poets on the street corners. I've a fair memory," Gwillon said.

"You write them out?"

Gwillon laughed. "I try. But it's a struggle. Writing's not my strong point; the letters tend to come out wrong. I can never read back what I've put down. That's why I developed a good memory, I guess. I read better than I write, though it took me a fair few years to get that right. My tutors weren't always understanding. When you…." He gave Fabiom a sympathetic look and shook his head.

"When I what?"

"It doesn't matter. We'll hang the hare and have the pigeons tonight." He gathered up the plucked birds and went inside.

That night, after an excellent pigeon supper, Fabiom wrote out several favourite poems, and two of his own that he hoped Taparaina would like. He did not need memories to know he would have spent a fair amount of time composing and reciting poetry for Casandrina. Was it surprising that the child of a Silvana, to whom written words meant nothing at all, would struggle with letters? With a painful jolt, he realised what Gwillon had nearly said: "When you have a son, be patient with him" – and why he had not said it.

168

On the second day, Gwillon, who was apprenticed to a master carpenter, had to return to work. Truelan took Fabiom to the birch grove where his daughter's tree grew beside his wife's. Fascinated, Fabiom watched the woodcarver talking – seemingly with no one.

He waited until they were away from the grove to ask, "You can see her, can't you? What does she look like?"

"She has my smile, and some of my mannerisms. But she is very like her mother, obviously. Her hair has more strands of black in it, but then so does the bark of her tree." He put his hand on Fabiom's shoulder. "That's why I brought you here, lad. It's small comfort, I know, but it's all I can offer you: whatever happens with you and Casandrina, in time you'll be able to see your daughter."

As they were taking their leave, Taparaina handed Fabiom a dried gourd.

"Inside this there is a potion I have prepared for you. Take it when you get home; close by Casandrina's tree may be best. When you drink it, you will sleep deeply, for a long time. Do not be afraid. Dreams will come to you – deep dreams. Some may disturb you, others may help you. I cannot promise they will reveal all you wish to know, only that they might give you a little more clarity and help you make the decisions you need to make." Smiling, she took his hand, "I believe we shall meet again, in happier times."

Chapter Five

All the way back to Deepvale, Fabiom and Marid speculated about Taparaina's gift: what effect it might have, what memories it might trigger, what it was made from. On the first evening, in a hostelry in a small town beside the River Gallant, Fabiom unstoppered the gourd. The pungent, earthy smell that wafted out hinted of fungi and burnt roots.

Having not seen her husband and son for many days, Marid was anxious to return to Valehead. Nevertheless, on their return to Deepvale, she stayed at the hold-house one more night, not willing to be too far from Fabiom when he took the potion, knowing he would not be able to wait for someone else to come and take her place.

"Come back safely," she told him, kissing his cheek as he made ready to go to the ash grove. She checked that he had enough covers to keep him comfortable overnight. "Be careful, and keep warm," she added as he left the house. He grinned at her over his shoulder and waved.

Once in the grove, Fabiom made himself a bed beneath Casandrina's tree. "Please let this work," he prayed as he unstoppered the gourd.

Wrapped in the extra blankets he had brought, Fabiom leant back against

Belinda Mellor

the tree. Taparaina had not said how much he should take. Unwilling to risk not drinking enough, he gulped down the entire contents. He barely had time to register the fact that the thick, pale liquid was quite pleasant before he fell into a state of awareness that was unlike either sleeping or waking.

Memories and imaginings tumbled through his mind: early childhood night terrors; the triumph of his first archery contest; awe at his first sight of Fairwater; his mother destroying a statue of a woodmaid he had given her; messengers coming with news of his father's death and the terrible grief he was barely allowed to acknowledge; waking beneath the great ash tree on the morning of his seventeenth birth-anniversary; watching the late frost destroy the holding's fruit blossoms; his first sight of the tender sapling growing beside Casandrina's tree in the grove; Casandrina weeping as she held onto him in the Dancing Glade that last time.

It was midday when Fabiom crawled from the tangle of blankets. His eyes could barely focus, his mouth was dry, his tongue swollen. As he made his way home, the sight that met him in the still water of the river's edge was testimony to exactly how he felt. After a brief moment of hesitation, he stripped off his clothes and threw himself into the biting water. Within minutes he was out again, shivering on the bank.

Slowly and painfully he made his way back to the house, where Marid and Ramus waited anxiously. Ramus immediately had two of the servants draw a steaming bath while Marid prepared a jug of hot morat. The scent and rich flavour of the fermented honey and mulberries soon revived him and he leant back in the shoulder-deep water, eyes closed, enjoying the simple pleasure of being warm.

"So, tell me – everything." Marid tucked her feet under her on the couch in the small bathing room.

He opened his eyes. "It tasted surprisingly nice...."

"I'm not certain the river was a good idea," Marid chided when he finished relating the night's events.

He ducked his head under the hot water before climbing out of the bath. "Maybe not. But it cleared my mind. I know now what I have to do."

She handed him a warmed towel then topped up their drinks. "I wish I could stay with you longer, and help you."

Fabiom kissed her cheek. "You've been wonderful – as always. I trust my uncle realises what a fortunate man he is. But, as I want to keep him on my side, and my cousin also, I must return you to them. I'll be fine. Truly."

When he had seen her off, in the company of her two handmaidens, he made his way to the library. There was a lot to prepare. He had seven days.

Fabiom's eighteenth birth eve drew to a close. He was bathed and dressed in his plainest clothes.

Imagine it is this time last year, he had told himself seven days before, as he scoured the library for the information he needed. *You are sixteen turning seventeen; imagine you have chosen this path, yet have no idea what the night will bring.* That was not hard. He had no recollection of having done this before. Yet he had. That much was certain. Even his mother's version of events supported that truth. So he read the books and relearnt what he needed to know. Barefooted and unarmed, he walked into the woods. He came, unerringly, to the Dancing Glade as dusk was settling over the land. A chill breeze blew fitfully among the autumn trees. He washed in the stream before settling down in the centre of the glade, knowing he must stay awake.

They came, as he knew they would. And when they did his heart beat fast with more than fear. He felt their shock and indignation as they realised who he was and that he was awake.

"I want her back."

"*Who?*"

He paused for just an instant, too long. A voice began to sing.

"No! Not again." He would not succumb, not this time. He fought against the urge to sleep. "I want my wife. I want Casandrina."

The singing continued. The song had changed.

He awoke to a pale, damp dawn, as he had on his last birth anniversary, in her grove, beneath her tree. And all that had been lost from his memory was restored. With a whoop of joy he leapt to his feet and threw his arms around the trunk as far as he could reach.

His elation was short lived. Beneath his feet, small, hard shapes shifted. He knelt and pushed aside fallen leaves and a layer of soil, jerking his hands back with a startled cry when he saw the mass of amber that had leached out of her tree's roots. With trepidation, he stood and studied the great ash: the golds and rich hues that last year gilded the leaves were muted; the leaves were dull and curled in on themselves; the seeds in their pods, small and withered.

Even as he tried to take in what he was seeing, he sensed the presence of a Silvana nearby. He recognised her voice as soon as she spoke.

"*I fear it is too late.*"

The Silvana's tone echoed the sorrow in his heart and Fabiom wondered at it.

"*She is my daughter,*" Narilina answered his unasked question.

"It was you – your song saved me!"

"*Saved you? I do not know. Time will tell.*"

Fabiom rested his hands against the trunk. How could it be too late? After all they had endured, she had to come back to him. They had a life to live together.

"Is this why they let me remember?"

"*In part. And also because they never intended you to suffer; only to forget. When you came back last night it was clear it had not been a wise path they had taken, so they relented.*"

Though he could not see her, and though she said little, Fabiom was aware of Narilina's presence. Bonded by a mutual sorrow, they stayed together throughout the day.

"*You should go home,*" Narilina told him eventually. "*There will be people concerned for you.*"

"Yes," he agreed, "I suppose so." Then he frowned. "How is it I can hear your voice?"

"*I was once as Casandrina. I can still make myself heard — by those who can hear. It helps too that you and I are related.*"

Fabiom frowned, "Related?"

"*My father was Laurrus, the first Holder of Deepvale.*"

"Laurrus!"

"*Yes — your many-times great grandfather. Sharaleima's tree grew just over there.*" A breeze that seemed to come from nowhere stirred the fallen leaves on the western edge of the grove, a short distance from where Fabiom sat. "*That was where Laurrus awoke on the dawn of his seventeenth year. Sharaleima's blood is in your veins, Fabiom. That is why you cannot renounce the Holdership of Deepvale — it was gifted to your line. You are dear to me. The connection is never broken.*"

She reached out an ethereal hand and brushed his face tenderly. "*Come back tonight and sleep here, and for the next six nights, just as before. Casandrina will come back to you in the morning of that final day — if she has the strength to do so.*"

There followed anxious days, which he could at least share with those he loved and trusted, and lonely nights which passed too slowly. On the final night, Fabiom could not sleep but sat against the trunk of Casandrina's tree, or paced around the grove, sick with worry.

She came with the dawn, and he could hardly breathe, let alone speak, for his heart was so full. She came to him but without words, and her eyes, her beautiful eyes, were less bright than they were wont to be. She was

174

Belinda Mellor

so weak, and so pale, and almost more lovely for it. He held her as if she might break or fade away, while he yearned to hold her tighter and closer than he ever had before.

At last she spoke, in a voice like the whisper of a breeze through autumn leaves, "You did not forget me. Oh, Fabiom – my love."

Narilina was insistent that Fabiom could not bring Casandrina back to the hold-house, that she had to stay in her grove; and he understood that, though it was hard to abide. Her next commission to him was harder still:

"There is nothing you can do here. You must go to – where was it? Varlass? Casandrina must stay close by her tree. Nowhere else will she be safe. Go and serve your prince and salvage the covenant between Silvanii and humankind. Come back before the Greening. We will not know until then how it will go with her."

"The Greening!" Fabiom was aghast. "That is over a quarter-year away."

Narilina was adamant. *"There is no restoration for Casandrina, or her tree, in the winter to come, only the chance to rest. Come the Greening she may, or may not, be restored to us. All we can do until then is wait, as must she."*

So taken aback with the news that it would be three months until he learnt if Casandrina was well, it was late into the night before he realised that he had been charged with resolving the conflict between men and Silvanii. He knew there would be nothing served in explaining, even to one as sympathetic as Narilina, that at barely eighteen years of age and a very junior member of Ravik's entourage he would have little or no influence on proceedings.

Whether Ravik wanted to include him because of his connection to the Silvanii or because of Deepvale's position as a leading silk producing holding he was not certain; possibly both, he reasoned. He had no illusions that the prince would require him to do more than be at hand to answer a few basic questions on either subject. Presumably there would be a large contingent of learned and wise counsellors along to advise and support the Ruling Prince on this venture. Yet Fabiom was determined that he would return to the Silvanii of Deepvale with some resolution they would accept – and not just for the sake of his marriage. They were right to be afraid and angry, and if he could do anything to allay that fear or assuage that anger he would.

He tried not to think about going away, not being there for Casandrina, not seeing her now that, against all hope, he had won her back. Instead he would go, for her sake and for all the Silvanii.

Belinda Mellor

Chapter Six

To travel by ship so late in the year, when winds whipped the sails, and waves crashed over the *Spikenard's* deck, took all of Fabiom's courage and brought home his double loss all too vividly. Though he was sick with worry for Casandrina, it was his father who occupied most of his thoughts on that first day of the voyage to Varlass.

That evening, in the galley, Prince Ravik sat down beside him to eat. "This cannot be easy for you, Fabiom."

"No, my lord. It's not. I can't help but wonder how it ended for them – for him. And I sorely miss him now."

"Yes. I'm sure you do. You carry heavy burdens, Fabiom. I am grateful that you consented to accompany me, after all you have recently endured."

Fabiom helped himself to some bread. "I'm not here solely of my own choosing – though if I can help in some small way I am glad of it."

"Whose choosing then, if not your own?"

Fabiom broke the bread and handed a piece to Ravik. "The Silvanii themselves. Though they did not say what it was they expected me to do."

"They still trust us?" Ravik sounded surprised and pleased in equal measure.

"Up to a point," Fabiom allowed. "And I sense that, for the most part, they have no more desire to loose the bonds between us than we have. They wish your venture well, my lord, though they will need to be satisfied that they are safe and that it's not to their detriment to trust us."

"Indeed. Well, I cannot fault them for that. One look across the Straits of Morena brings home how tenuous our relationship is."

Dead Silvanii; Gerik was washed with their blood. They were so strong and yet so vulnerable. When Fabiom closed his eyes he could see her, pale and wan – and in pain. She had not said it yet he knew it to be so.

That first night on board he dreamt of his father teaching him to swim when he was a small boy; of boating with Tawr on the River Swan in his early teens; of the day the messengers came with the news that Deepvale's Lord Holder had perished at sea.

"Father, why did you leave me? And if I should lose her too –" he whispered the words to the night. There was no reply.

The journey seemed long, though it lasted only five days. Even though he restricted himself to the plainest fare on board, whenever Fabiom managed to eat anything he regretted it soon after. He was not alone in his discomfort. Norgest of Riverplain was a terrible sailor and managed only dry bread and watered wine for the whole voyage, spending most of his time in his cabin. Every now and again they ran into rough patches where the *Spikenard* lurched and the waves towered above them. Fabiom tried not to show his fear, still it was none too soon when the pale cliffs of Varlass came into view on the horizon.

As they disembarked, the Morenian party were met by a contingent of ceremonial guards garbed in flowing robes of turquoise and orange who accompanied them from the dock, through the city, and up to the hilltop palace where Fwailan, the astrologer-king, dwelt. Fabiom would like to have

Belinda Mellor

lingered, for Varlass seemed very different from anywhere in Morene; even the sounds were different, and the ebb and flow of the Varlassian tongue had a musical lilt. However, their escort appeared anxious to bring them to the palace. Fabiom barely had time to notice more than the fact that the buildings were all very austere, and there was little by way of decoration anywhere. The most ornate things he saw were the costumes people wore, for the most humble made even Morene's Ruling Prince look plainly dressed. He could understand the attraction of silk here.

The palace had been visible from the dock, though its size had not been apparent. Up close, it revealed itself as an imposing, many-levelled building of dark grey stone shot through with crystals of mica. The levels rose above the city to the domed sky-chamber which, their escort informed them in solemn tones, was accessible to only the most learned astrologers.

The palace was also the centre of study and learning – which, besides astrology, were the things Varlassians apparently concerned themselves with most. It was reached via a spacious library and, as he walked through, it occurred to Fabiom that Masgor would have liked it. Once again, they were given no time to linger but led straight through. Beyond the library, corridors ran off in several directions and many of the corridors were narrow and gloomy. Straight ahead, however, was a wider passage which ended in a pair of high doors inset with crystals in the pattern of stellar constellations for which only the Varlassians had names. At their approach, these doors were thrown open to reveal the throne room and the king, in state, on an ornate seat of the same stone as the palace itself. Nodding and smiling, Fwailan rose unsteadily to greet them, gripping the arm of the throne with one hand, beckoning them in with his other. Apart from his heavy, elaborately embroidered clothing, that at first glance disguised his slight frame, the most noticeable thing about him was his bright red, braided hair and beard.

Mumbling apologies, and something about his health, he sat down once more on the great throne. It dwarfed him, for he was not a large man. Beside him, on a lesser throne, a young woman watched him somewhat anxiously. Like the king, the woman – who Fabiom guessed to be Fwailan's queen – was swathed in layers of brightly coloured clothing. The wide, high collar of the outer garment pushed her chin high, the multiple folds rendered her somewhat shapeless, and the patterns drew the eye to the costume, rather than the woman wearing them.

"Don't fuss so, child," Fwailan scolded as she reached out a hand to steady him. Fabiom amended his first assumption that she was the king's young wife and decided she must be a daughter; her colouring, once he noticed it, certainly suggested close kinship.

Before Fabiom had a chance to take in more than the enthroned couple, a formidable looking minister – his bare arms conspicuously muscled – stepped forward and bowed very low to Ravik and then to the rest of his entourage, which numbered a dozen.

"His Majesty bids you welcome, my lords. I am Seim, nephew to the king and astrologer-master of the house of Gliss. I am at your Royal Highness's command."

He would show the others around while Prince Ravik spoke with King Fwailan in private, he informed them in an accent almost as heavy as his clothing. There was some muttering among the Morenians and it occurred to Fabiom that he would find it impossible to carry out Narilina's request if he was in no way party to any discussions.

Ravik silenced the quiet revolt of his party with a glance and a barely audible, "There will be time later for serious business. Go, look, listen – learn what you may for now. I will join you later."

After small refreshments, Seim escorted the Morenians to the palace gardens which were considered a thing of wonder. Fabiom would have rather seen their silk mills and their mulberry groves but he knew enough about diplomacy to realise such matters would not be discussed today. *Patience*, Ravik had counselled before they disembarked. This was a game, with rules Fabiom was unsure of, for the Varlassian were quite different

Belinda Mellor

from his own people in their customs; he knew he should watch and learn, and tread warily.

As they went through the seemingly endless maze of palace corridors, Seim told them a little of the history of the island and its people. His accent was melodious, yet not always easy to understand, and Fabiom found himself listening more to the lilt of Seim's voice than his actual words. Despite telling himself to concentrate, his mind began wandering through Deepvale's woodland paths and it was not until they arrived at a high, arched door and paused, that Fabiom brought his attention fully back to where he was.

"Here we will be in the good care of Master Teibor, the foremost arborist of our land. Please, enjoy." With that, Seim opened the door with a flourish and they saw the gardens spread out before them.

Laid out in intricate patterns of colour and texture, the palace gardens truly were a delight. Seeming dead-ends revealed secret openings to unexpected areas of topiary; walkways that seemed to go on forever turned out to be polished metal panels reflecting paths back on themselves. Fabiom put other matters aside and allowed himself to enjoy the experience. He saw plants he had never seen before and others which he had come across in pictures only. Master Teibor, an elderly man with skin as weathered as tree-bark, noticed his pleasure and his understanding of growing things and commented on it.

"You seem to have an uncanny knowledge of these things, young lord," he said as Fabiom bruised a leaf of a tiny lemon-scented herb, releasing the bittersweet perfume.

Fabiom nodded. "I have some experience."

"Mulberries?" the arborist asked, quite unexpectedly.

"Among other things," Fabiom agreed, wondering if he dared pursue that line of conversation. The others had gone on ahead with Seim, so he could expect no help there.

"Disaster for us they were," Teibor told him.

Fabiom almost laughed. "For you? A disaster for us, rather."

"No, I mean – we razed several excellent cherry orchards to plant the wretched things. I've no idea how you get them to grow properly, and for me to admit that is something. I pride myself on my ability to grow anything – or rather I did."

Ravik's counsel to be patient warred with the realisation that he may not have as good an opportunity again. "Do you really want to know?"

The man looked at him, shocked. "You came here with your prince. Surely you would not betray him? I do not ask that!"

"I would never betray him, nor my country, be assured. But you would like to know, would you not?"

The man nodded nervously. "I have to admit it," he said eventually. "And what would you have in return?"

Fabiom looked around at the stunning gardens. He would like to have asked for an orchid for Casandrina, for none like these grew in Morene, as far as he knew, and they were quite exquisite. "I would see your silk mills; I would see for myself what you learnt, how large your production was – what the threat really was, in truth."

The gardener nodded. "I could arrange that," he allowed, "and it seems like a reasonable request. Though I still don't understand why you would tell me."

Fabiom shrugged. "I said I would give you the information; I did not say it would help you. Sometimes knowledge alone is not sufficient – you still won't be able to grow mulberry trees; not ones that will sustain silk moths, in any case. Do we have a deal nonetheless?"

They did. The man told him to meet him at dawn the next morning and that he was to bring no one with him. Fabiom agreed. Another of his party beckoned to him; they were returning inside.

Reunited with their prince, the Morenians were brought to a huge and gloomy dining room where an enormous banquet was laid out. The table was raised well off the ground and around it were many high-backed wooden chairs.

Belinda Mellor

"They sit at table to eat, as we sit at desks to write," Elasus of Southernport, one of Ravik's senior counsellors, told Fabiom, having noticed the young man's bemusement.

Seeing the unusual cutlery set at each place, Fabiom resolved simply to copy what the others did, guessing rightly that most of them had travelled to other lands before and were more used than he to foreign customs.

For the most part the food was good, though – between the preponderance of root vegetables and rich sauces – some of it sat heavily after a while.

"The food here is much like the women," Norgest confided to those closest to him, Fabiom and Ravik included. "Everything smothered and hidden under thick and elaborate layers – no clue as to what's underneath." On land he was a different man to the sea-sick bundle of misery he had been on board *Spikenard*.

Conversation with their hosts was somewhat strained and the wine was mediocre. Fabiom found his chair extremely uncomfortable and was glad when it was announced that the meal was over. Before they could rise from their seats, however, they were served a hot drink of water in which several herbs had been seeped, "To aid digestion," they were informed. Soon they were to be led up to one of the astronomy towers – the seven lesser towers which surrounded the sky-chamber, the largest three of which could accommodate many people. There they would view the night sky and have augerers read what the stars might foretell for their venture.

As they were leaving the dining room, and unnoticed by the others, the princess who had earlier sat beside the king – who, the Morenians had learnt from Seim, was the eldest of three sisters and whose name was Maedrim – beckoned Fabiom aside. Like her father, the princess was small in stature and seemed almost lost in the heavily embroidered robes she wore. Her bright red hair was coiled on top of her head, in the fashion of that land. Her eyes were an extraordinary shade of dark honey and her face was more freckle than skin. It took Fabiom a moment to realise that she was in fact very pretty.

"Lord Fabiom, spare me a moment if you would be so kind. I am sorry to detain you from the tower, though it is cloudy tonight and you will not see much," she said with a disparaging wave of her hand.

"You do not put much store in the star-lore of your people?" he wondered.

"Oh no, on the contrary – I have inherited the gift and read the skies myself. There is not much to see tonight, I have already looked. This is more for show; to let your prince know that we want things to be well between us – a gesture," she said bluntly.

"I see," he said; not at all sure that he did.

"I have been charged by my father to make certain your visit goes smoothly and that when you leave us it is on good terms. He and your prince will talk; yet very little of import will be said as is often the way with kings, is it not?"

Fabiom was even more taken aback. She smiled at his discomfiture.

"That is not how my father would have me say it, of course. However, it is the truth and I believe that, since we have gravely offended you, the least we can do now is be honest." She laid a hand on his arm. "I watched you at table and I saw that you have Prince Ravik's ear, so it is to you I shall speak."

Fabiom glanced over at some of the other Morenians who were starting up the long winding stairs that led to one of the open towers.

"It is you he trusts," Maedrim insisted.

Fabiom could think of nothing to say in reply. Fortunately she did not seem to expect him to.

"Go, join your countrymen for now. We shall speak later."

Maedrim was right. The night was cloudy and the stars were largely obscured, yet there was something both mysterious and peaceful about the high tower which thrust up into the sky way above the palace. Below them, lights burned across the city. Beyond that – indistinct shapes of hills and distant mountains. Between the city and the mountains – tiny

Belinda Mellor

pinpricks of light from outlying hamlets. A quarter turn to the left, the bobbing lanterns of boats and ships marked the sea. The distant sound of waves rose on the night breeze.

Later, they were shown to a circular sleeping room, with many curtained alcoves set into the wall, each with a hard narrow bed. All the Morenians, save Ravik and his two most senior advisers, were accommodated there, along with half-a-dozen other visitors to the palace and three serving men who were there should anyone need anything in the night. Fabiom was weary and glad to be on dry land, yet sleep eluded him. Eventually, fed up with twisting and turning on the strange, hard bed, worrying about Casandrina, he quietly took himself off to the library to see if he could find something to distract himself.

To his surprise, there were several people still in the library, all studying silently, intently. Maedrim was one. She glanced up from the text she had before her and smiled as she recognised him. At once she closed her book and rose to greet him, asking if she could be of help. Fabiom apologised for disturbing her, earning himself a scowl from the nearest reader. Maedrim giggled and led him away to a part that was not being used.

"I couldn't sleep. I just wanted something to divert me, nothing in particular," he explained.

"I was reading about Jano and Farran. Have you heard of them? It is an engrossing tale."

At his negative reply she explained, "Jano of Sakoy was husband to the sun-smith's daughter, Farran, who betrayed him for the king of Decorta. Jano came here to Varlass in his despair, to find aid in his search for his wife. He watched the stars and mapped their course across the skies and learnt how to read their dance, yet in doing so he fell under their spell and turned his eyes away from the world of daylight. Nothing pleased him save the darkness and the maps of the heavens so that even when Farran fled back to him, pursued by a ravenous sun-beast, he could not turn to her

Silvana

but continued to study the stars in their eternal round. It is a sad tale, and yet had Jano not come here we would not have the star knowledge we have today – sometimes good can come of bad. I trust that will be the same for the story we are all caught up in today."

Fabiom inclined his head in agreement. "I feel for your – Jano – was it? To lose the one you love is sad indeed," he said, then added ruefully, "and maybe I'd better not do too much star-gazing while I'm here; losing your reason once in a lifetime is surely enough."

She looked at him curiously but he did not elaborate.

"I trust your father is feeling better," he said, changing the subject.

She glanced around. "There is little wrong with him save wounded pride," she admitted. "This affair has given him dreadful indigestion; he does not like admitting his kingdom is badly at fault."

Fabiom laughed aloud before he could stop himself.

"I had better go before I get myself thrown out. Goodnight, your Highness."

"You have taken nothing to read," she pointed out.

He smiled and gave her a half-bow, "I think I shall sleep well now."

Back in the sleeping chamber he found he was indeed relaxed enough to sleep at last and, having arranged to be awoken just before dawn, he settled down and slept dreamlessly.

Master Teibor met Fabiom as the first grey streaks lightened the late autumn sky. They set off silently, out of the palace gardens, away from the city across farm tracks, towards what Fabiom could immediately make out was a mulberry grove even in the half-light of dawn. He shook his head when he saw the state of the trees, with their deformed limbs and stunted trunks. Stooping, he picked up a handful of fallen leaves, the dark pock-marks of disease still visible. There was no threat, nor ever had been. Of course, that did not take away from the enormity of the crime, nor undo the damage done to Silvanan-human relationships. Still, one thing at a time: at least his

Belinda Mellor

holding was financially safe; the talk of major silk production happening here had indeed been a ruse, as they had already guessed. It was reassuring to see it for himself.

The silk-mills lay just beyond the grove and what they found inside was in little better condition. Beside large copper vats, piles of undersized and misshaped cocoons waited to be boiled, the raw thread on the rows of bobbins looked dull, and the pervading smell in the building was rancid.

"I've seen enough, thank you," Fabiom said after a good look around.

The arborist led him back through the stunted trees, pausing in front of a particularly sad looking specimen.

"So, will you tell me, young lord – the secret for getting these damn things to grow strong and healthy?"

"As we agreed." Fabiom almost laid a hand on the cracked bark until he noticed the suppurating black mass of infection beneath. Unconsciously, he wiped his hands on his cloak. "Ours have songs sung to them," he said simply. "Our land is filled with music – it carries on the air, it flows in the water. The most fortunate – and productive – trees are sung to individually."

"By people, you mean?" Treibor asked uncertainly.

"Yes," Fabiom told him with a wistful smile, "though not humans."

The arborist's eyes widened. "I've heard – something. Tree spirits? Is that right? You have a name for them...."

"They have a name for themselves," Fabiom corrected him. "Silvanii. And the making of silk is their provenance; all our mulberry trees are in their care."

Over breakfast, Fabiom quietly imparted what he had discovered to Ravik.

The prince put down his knife. "So, let me get this straight: I make it quite clear that you are to be discreet and patient and you immediately offer to tell one of their senior arborists the secret of growing mulberries – in exchange for a chance to look around a silk mill. Is that correct?"

Taken aback, Fabiom could only stutter, "Yes, but – it wasn't – I didn't – "

"No. I'm sure you didn't. But I do have to wonder what your idea of patience actually is."

"My lord —"

Ravik chuckled. "It's all right. You made the right decision. I trust you, Fabiom. But you amuse me sometimes."

Fabiom frowned. "Is that a good thing or a bad thing?"

Smiling, Ravik sliced a chunk of meat from the cold joint of mutton in front of him, put it in his mouth, and did not reply.

"As you seem to have a knack for this sort of thing, I have a task for you," Ravik said as they were leaving the dining hall. "They have superb paper here; like nothing I've ever seen or touched before. I'd love to know what it's made from, and I'm loath to ask. I don't want them doing us any favours, not yet anyway. I am warming to Fwailan — he is not as obdurate as I first thought, yet he will not come around easily — he wants to make amends yet wants to save face at the same time. It's frustrating."

Having no idea how else to go about the task Ravik had set him, Fabiom simply mentioned it to the princess. Maedrim was happy enough to show him the paper, especially when he told her Ravik had been admiring it. He said nothing about wanting to know how it was made so he was not at all prepared for her revelation that it was a product of the mulberry trees.

"We cut some down. They were dying," she explained. "And some of our paper makers discovered that the inner bark is ideal to make the finest quality paper. We keep it for the most precious texts of course, and only the senior scribes and the master calligrapher are allowed to use it, there being so little of it; though I suspect we will soon have more trees to cut — they are good for little else, after all!"

On a whim, she offered to show him the copying room, where the scribes and calligraphers worked on transcribing and translating books and papers from far flung countries, and restoring old volumes from the library there in Varlass.

Belinda Mellor

"Prince Ravik would like to see that room," Fabiom ventured.

"Would he? Unfortunately he is engaged with my father once again." She sounded slightly frustrated, which Fabiom noted with interest.

The room was empty, to Maedrim's obvious annoyance, though there were some half-finished lesser works out on desks. However there were paper samples on a table and Fabiom had the chance to see what it was that had attracted Ravik's attention. The mulberry paper was quite unlike anything he had come across before, much finer than the reed paper he was used to; it felt strong and smooth.

Fabiom was engrossed in the paper when Maedrim said, "Your prince is a very handsome man."

"He would be very glad to know that you thought so."

"Oh no! You must not tell him I spoke of him to you. That would be quite unseemly," she protested.

"In Morene it would be not considered unseemly," Fabiom said lightly.

"Ah, I think we are less relaxed than you." She sighed. "Certainly your clothes and manners seem far more comfortable. Though I suspect that your women are not so. Prince Ravik's wife, for instance, I cannot believe she dresses much more comfortably than I."

Fabiom chuckled. "Prince Ravik is not married, your Highness. And as for the women of Morene generally, they too enjoy far more comfort than women in Varlass seem to."

As he said so he pictured Casandrina running barefoot across the dewy grass, loose hair flying in the breeze and he smiled so that the princess said, "You are thinking of someone special rather than women in general, I think."

He laughed self-consciously. "Apologies, my lady. I was thinking of my wife and how she would not take too kindly to the constraints of your court, marvellous though it is to see."

"Your wife? So, you are married. Yet you are some years younger than your prince, are you not?"

Fabiom chuckled again. "Indeed, your Highness. I am just eighteen; Prince Ravik is twenty-five years. By the standards of our people, I married early. But then I was fortunate – I had met the right woman."

Maedrim smiled at that. "Yet you are troubled," she said, serious again, "and not just by the economic problems our recent venture has visited upon you."

"You are perceptive, my lady." He regarded her for a moment and knew that, far more than her father, she would be sympathetic to their problem. "We stand to lose far more than wealth," he told her. "You do know how we first learnt about silk-making; how the Silvanii – denizens of the trees – entrusted to us their greatest secret, many generations ago?"

She had heard, though not in any detail, so he told her how the first human settlers in Morene had learnt sericulture from their Silvanan wives and had built the country's wealth on that knowledge.

"Thank you," she said when he was done. "For telling me all this. I understand far more now than I did. Yet I think there is much that you have not told me. The more I hear of your land, the more it intrigues me."

That afternoon, Ravik summoned Fabiom to his chamber. Before Fabiom had a chance to tell him about the mulberry-bark paper, Ravik said, "I want you to speak to the Varlassian court. Be open, be honest. We need to get to the truth of what happened here and a solemn undertaking that there will be no future forays into silk making, if we are to avoid disaster at home. I think you are the man to achieve that for us."

"Me? Why me?"

Ravik raised his brows.

"I'm sorry, my lord," Fabiom stammered. "It's just that you have some of the most senior members of your Assembly here. I presumed you would want one of them to address the Varlassians."

"You presumed wrongly. I heard you speak when you came to Fairwater to be conferred Holder. You addressed the Assembly then and were most

Belinda Mellor

impressive. I know you are good enough. And, as you are not prone to false modesty, I am certain you know it too. I have gambled on you before, Fabiom – and won. I'm prepared to do so again."

Fabiom might have said that the stakes were slightly higher this time, except he doubted it was necessary to remind Ravik of that.

"Consider, Fabiom," the prince continued, playing idly with a piece of Varlassian silk that had been hung over the back of a chair, "if the Silvanii abandon us, what have we left? We take the bonds between us for granted, yet if they unravel it will be like this silk –" without effort he tore the square apart, "there will be nothing left of any worth. Morene is theirs far more than it is ours. We will eke out a pathetic existence on the edge of civilisation without them. We will be nothing, have nothing."

"I know how that feels," Fabiom said quietly.

"Yes, you do. That's why I am asking you to do this. For the rest of us, losing the Silvanii won't be so personal, nor hurt so deeply, yet it will not be dissimilar: all that is wonderful suddenly stripped away, leaving a huge gaping wound and only the memory of the song remaining." He paused to let his words sink in. "You hold one of the most important parts of our land – and one of the most populous. What will Deepvale be like without their influence, do you think? There are holders who believe it hardly matters anymore. Their holdings are poorer – in more ways than one – for that attitude, for they are wrong. Even where there is no overt interaction between our two races, the Silvanii's influence is widespread and essential. Our crops, our water supplies, as well as our silk production, depend on them. You understand that far better than any of these august counsellors I have with me – however much wisdom they deem they have."

"Meaning they are not in favour of my speaking?"

"Of course they are not!" Ravik said with some asperity. "Each of them thinks himself the best choice, though some pretend otherwise. Luckily for me, I get the final say. You are my final say."

While Fabiom was mulling over Ravik's words, a manservant came into the room, bearing a tray of dried fruits, pungent cheeses and a bottle. He poured some thick, dark liquid into two tiny glasses and left.

"Apparently it is made from fermented figs. What do you make of it?" Ravik asked, handing one of the glasses over.

"It's horrible!" Fabiom gagged as he took a tentative sip. He put the glass to one side with a grimace.

The prince held his glass up to the window where the winter sun illuminated the etched patterns of flowers and leaves. "The glasses, on the other hand, are exquisite. It is rather like this land: a lot to dislike and a lot to admire."

"Princess Maedrim seems very sympathetic to our plight," Fabiom ventured, thinking of what was most admirable about Varlass.

"You have spoken with her?" Ravik asked in some surprise, and slightly piqued, Fabiom fancied, which made him smile – something he tried to hide by taking another mouthful of the fig liqueur and nearly choking.

"Here," Ravik produced a flask of Morenian wine from a satchel and took Fabiom's glass away from him, "luckily I brought something better from home. Tell me about the princess – I mean, what did she say to you?"

Fabiom looked at his prince for a long moment. "She told me the paper you admired so much is made from the inner bark of the mulberry tree; though she was really far more interested in finding out whatever she could about you," he said, and was well pleased with the look of delight that came over Ravik's face.

That evening, Fabiom addressed the Varlassian court as Ravik requested. In his hands, a fallen branch from a blighted mulberry tree. While he did not reveal his own relationship with the Silvanii specifically, he spoke with authority so that none doubted his words.

"Here in Varlass, I have seen beautiful trees, wonderful plants, and tasted water that is sweet and wholesome. But the song of the Silvanii does not

Belinda Mellor

mingle with the breeze, does not quicken the leafbuds on a mulberry tree or coax caterpillars to spin. Your land has its own power, its own magic. You find it in the stars. In Morene we look to the earth, to the cycle of growth and rest, to the seasons turning. In Morene, that cycle is accompanied by Silvana-song. From that cycle, and from that song, silk comes.

"Here in Varlass, I saw a stand of mulberry trees, deprived of the one thing they needed, dying from the inside, rotting. If Morene loses the trust of the Silvanii, it will be not only be our mulberry trees that wither and die, it will be our whole way of life. We have come here to ask you to help us restore relationships between humans and Silvanii and, in doing so, relationships between our two lands – relationships that need trust in exactly the same way mulberry trees need the Silvanii."

He paused and looked at the dead tree limb in his hands. "I have never been to Gerik, but I am told no trees grow there. I am told plants struggle and the water is bitter. There is no power. There is no song. There is no hope."

By the time he was done, no one in that great hall was in any doubt that sericulture was not a human undertaking but something mysterious that had been gifted to mankind; a treasure to be cherished and honoured. Norgest of Riverplain asked him how come he had such understanding, and Fabiom saw the Varlassian princess smile and shake her head.

"All will be well," she promised when no one else was close by. "I have seen it in the stars."

"For Morene?" he asked. "For our future?"

"Yes. For that too. Though it is not of that I speak."

"If not that, then what?" he asked quietly, wondering if he dared to hope.

"I speak of your wife, your Silvana," she said, smiling, and he saw in her eyes the truth behind her words and the pain in his heart lessened.

"Thank you," he whispered, fighting back tears.

Chapter Seven

The Morenians, once again without their prince, were being shown around the palace weaving room. Unlike cloth fashioned in Morene, there were no interlocking geometric borders, nor lengths of single colour. Fabiom wondered at the intricate detail being woven into the fabric. One piece, of silver diamonds and indigo spirals on a lavender field, especially caught his eye, and he paused to watch the work progress. Finally, conscious that their guide wanted to show them other things besides, he complimented the weaver and reluctantly prepared to move on.

The woman, who had been engrossed in her task, started at his voice. Shoulders hunching, head bowed, she mumbled a thanks but she had lost her rhythm and, as she resumed her work, her shuttle snagged. Then, as she fumbled with the tangled thread, she dropped the shuttle.

Apologising, Fabiom bent to retrieve it. She had no choice but to look at him then, and to thank him properly. Her accent was much more familiar to him than those he had been hearing over the past few days. And something about her face tugged at his mind. Memory stirred.

"This morning, in the weaving room, I saw someone I recognised: a woman from Morene. I couldn't remember her name then, but it came to me later, it's Cuivah. She and her husband used to run a prosperous silk mill – in Rushford."

"Are you certain?" Ravik said. They had finished their evening meal and were waiting to be entertained by a travelling poet brought in especially for their amusement.

Fabiom nodded. "I am. I met her there once when I was about twelve. She was very learned in all aspects of sericulture. My father introduced us; actually he threatened to leave me there for a while – thought I might learn something useful."

Ravik waited while a servant refilled their glasses with the customary bitter-sweet herbal infusion before asking, "What changed his mind?"

"To be honest, I don't know. I wasn't very keen, though that would hardly have persuaded him. I'm not sure he didn't have a falling out with her. I know we left quite suddenly in the end."

Ravik considered. "That would have been what, six years ago?" he reasoned. "I have seen the mulberry trees here; Fwailan finally showed me the mill and the groves. They are all about that age."

"But, if Tawr knew, or even suspected, he would have said something; done something!" Fabiom protested.

Ravik laid a reassuring hand on his shoulder. "Yes. He would. Still, if this woman Cuivah is behind our loss, her plans must have been afoot even then. If she truly is traitorous and wicked, she could easily have said something that upset him, without rousing his suspicions. After all, what would he have suspected? Who would have dreamt anyone could do such a thing as has been done here?"

Their conversation was curtailed by the arrival of the poet – who was far better than any of the Morenians had dared to hope – and the evening passed pleasantly, though Fabiom's mind kept wandering homewards.

That night, Fabiom hardly slept at all. He had come to Varlass to add the insight of someone who lived with a Silvana, who had more immediate understanding of what the betrayal of sericulture lore actually meant. It had not occurred to him that they – he – would discover the perpetrator. And now that he had spoken to Ravik, he had effectively signed the woman's death warrant. If anyone had ever deserved that most extreme penalty, surely it was one who risked their country and all its people for their own gain? Still, it sat uneasily with him. Twice, Tawr had made that hardest decision; both times it had sent him into a black depression for several days. Neither time did he involve Fabiom, although Fabiom knew that had his father lived and the situation arisen after he turned seventeen he would not have been spared the experience. What if he was wrong about Cuivah?

By first light he had come to the conclusion that there was nothing to do but speak openly with Princess Maedrim. She had been totally honest with him, he would deal with her the same way.

He found her in the weaving room, weaving star patterns into deep blue cloth.

He sat down on the floor beside her and asked her about the woman he had seen the previous day. Maedrim confirmed his suspicions.

"Cuivah came here to Varlass five years ago, with her husband. She came to bring us new spinning techniques, knowing that we value fine threads highly – for we weave stars and dreams and visions. Her services were not cheap. At first she said she needed to raise funds for her husband's business ventures. She began to teach us more and more wonderful things, tantalising things – until she was offered enough money to betray the secrets your people had been entrusted with by the Silvanii. Her price was high. I am sad to say there were those among our people who were prepared to pay it, though the knowledge was not hers to sell."

The cloth, thrice the span of her arms, was finished and she removed it from the loom, tying the edges deftly. "Give this to your wife, from me: an apology and a token of friendship, though we have never met," she said.

Belinda Mellor

"I hope you will, one day."

"I am certain of it," Maedrim informed him, her eyes shining with mischief.

"Thank you for this, it is quite beautiful."

"I must tell you, Cuivah's husband's 'business' was not quite what it seemed either: he has relatives in Gerik who would lay claim to lordship there, and it was to fund them that the money was raised." She began laying new warp threads onto her loom, sky blue this time. "Cuivah will be executed, won't she?"

"Yes." Fabiom twisted stray strands of blue silk around his fingers.

"Will her death satisfy the Silvanii?"

He looked up. "No. They tend not to worry too much about individuals. If she was to step into the wildwood, it might be a different matter. They can be deadly. But they'll be looking for assurances, not for legal penalties. Knowing she is dead will not be important to them."

"And is it important to you?"

"Yes. No. Why do you ask?"

"She is with child," Maedrim said.

Fabiom closed his eyes and exhaled forcibly. "And her husband?" he asked, eventually.

"He is not here at present. He comes and goes – visiting her maybe three times a year."

The day was ending before Fabiom had a chance to speak privately with his prince. When he informed Ravik that the Morenian weaver was indeed the one behind the betrayal, and had links to Gerik though her husband, the prince was less surprised than he.

"Yet we cannot lay the blame at the door of any in Gerik," Ravik said. "At the end of the day it was Morenians who did the deed. I am sorry for it – for more than one reason. Had it come purely from Gerik our Silvanii would more likely be mollified, would they not?"

Fabiom sighed and stared out at the gloomy sky where the first stars were showing faint and pale. "Maybe they yet will be," he said hopefully. He managed a slight smile as he added, "The princess seems certain all will be well in that regard. She is wise in ways I do not understand."

"Wise and lovely," Ravik murmured, then laughed at himself.

Fabiom chuckled. He would like to have added that Maedrim seemed to think she and Casandrina would be friends one day, but decided that could wait.

Late the following morning, Ravik gathered his party together in the ante-chamber he had been given.

"Fwailan is reluctant to give the traitor to me unless I agree to spare her life. Yet if I merely banish her, she'll turn around and return here to live in Varlass, in comfort and respect, which makes a mockery of our law."

"He is in no position to be making demands!" Elasus of Southernport insisted. "Your Highness – you must remind him that we are the injured party here!"

"I *could* do that. However, I am not inclined to." Ravik tapped the end of a stylus on the table and glared at Fabiom. "This impasse is your fault. And, to think, I once had high hopes for you."

"I only said –"

"I know exactly what you said. You said Princess Maedrim wished this woman's life spared, and that's why Fwailan was baulking at the idea of handing her over."

Elasus bridled. "The princess? What does a young woman like that know of politics? Is her father so besotted that she can persuade him that easily?"

"I know. Ridiculous, isn't it?" Ravik agreed, and Fabiom pretended a cough as the prince winked in his direction.

Ravik's advisors argued until Norgest of Riverplain suggested that, in return for her life, Fwailan should forbid Cuivah from ever returning to Varlass.

198

Belinda Mellor

"I should be able to talk him into that, without antagonising him," Ravik agreed. "I would rather he was an ally than an enemy."

Before they left, King Fwailan – his health much improved – signed a proclamation banishing the silk-maker Cuivah and her family from Varlass for all time; she would return to Morene to face justice there. The king gifted Ravik with books from his library, rare plants from the royal gardens and opals from the tiny isle of Patin off Varlass's south coast, and to Ravik's entourage he gave similar gifts. Furthermore he extended an invitation for the prince to return for the Varlassian New Year festivities, an invitation Ravik was quick to accept.

Fabiom hoped Princess Maedrim was right, and that relationships between humankind and Silvanii would be as easily restored.

Fabiom would have started for home immediately after disembarking in Fairwater, but Ravik insisted he attend the trial: he had identified Cuivah and would have to present that information to the Court of Assembly.

"Dine with me tonight," Ravik said. "You must speak with Deepvale's Silvanii when you get home. There are things still to be discussed regarding that."

That evening, they met, not in the prince's apartment but in the Silvanan Hall – now fully furnished.

"You have artichoke hearts. Of course, it's a full year since I was here for my inception as Deepvale's holder."

Ravik smiled. "Indeed. It is. A lot has happened in that year." He gestured toward the sideboard. "I didn't think you liked them."

"I like them. But they're messy to eat."

Ravik spooned a portion of the succulent vegetable into two dishes, along with some crumbly white cheese and golden olive oil. "Let's not stand on ceremony, Fabiom. Life is messy."

"So I've noticed."

Lounging on well-stuffed couches, admiring the peerless frescoes, they ate in companionable silence, until Fabiom wiped his hands on a damp cloth and asked, "So, you will spare her?"

"I have given my word."

"What about her husband."

Ravik sighed. "Indeed, what about him? I've made no promises there. And he has family in Gerik who, I presume, would take her in for the sake of his child. I have little stomach for executions though." He reached over to a side table and poured them each a goblet of deep red wine. "Life is sacred, and should never be taken lightly. There would be nothing gained by killing him."

Fabiom stared into his wine, relieved. "What do you use?"

"Fabiom?"

"Apologies, my lord. I was thinking. I didn't realise I'd spoken aloud."

"I can guess where your thoughts were. You were wondering what poison they would be offered if they *were* condemned. Hemlock is fast and relatively humane. And does not rob a man of his dignity."

"Older histories suggest yew –"

"Indeed. They were crueler times, I suspect." The prince raised his cup. "To health."

Servants brought platters of food.

"And now, to business. I have invited two others to join us. Jarin of Greendell for one."

Fabiom rose to his feet as the elderly poet made his way towards them. He was accompanied by another man, a decade or so younger, who, like Jarin – and Gwillon – had that air of grace and intensity of gaze that marked him as the offspring of a Silvana.

Belinda Mellor

"We get one chance to get this right. And then you, my friend, along with Jarin and Pellanus here, must be our ambassador."

Within four days of their return, and with Cuivah safely locked away, her husband was apprehended. He was brought from Rushford to Fairwater, where a trial was immediately convened. It did not last long. Having being found guilty – she of betraying the most sacred esoterica; he of smuggling hundreds of precious mulberry saplings – they were branded as traitors, exiled and forbidden from ever returning, and all their lands and property confiscated.

"I never want to hear of you or yours again. You have no place in Morene, now or ever in the future. Should any of you, or your descendants, step onto these shores again, there will be no mercy. Now that is an end to it," Ravik declared.

To which Fabiom added a fervent prayer that the prince would be proved right.

As they were being led away, Cuivah passed close by Fabiom. To his surprise, she inclined her head and touched her hand to her heart. "I owe you my child's life."

"You don't. I want nothing to do with you."

"What you want, what I want, doesn't matter. It is a debt that will be repaid."

Disquieted, Fabiom shook his head and turned away.

Two days later he was given leave to return home.

Chapter Eight

"*I shall* drink your draughts, if I must, and leave myself defenceless before you. But please, this time, do not take so much away from me, I implore you."

"*There is no need, Fabiom. I will speak for my sisters. They are here, as I am sure you are aware.*"

Narilina's presence helped allay his fears.

"Thank you," he said to her before addressing the unseen Silvanii, whom he could just about sense.

He sat cross-legged in the centre of the Dancing Glade and felt them gather about him – maybe even more than before. The air was drowsy with perfume and the winter sun felt warm. No, it was not the sun that warmed him: Fabiom felt compassion, and more – he was warmed by their love as he told them of Prince Ravik's resolution that all holders, and anyone else aspiring to positions of authority in Morene, would henceforth have to demonstrate a deep understanding of Treelaw, and an empathy with the uniqueness of their land before they could be elevated. And how the prince, though deeply contrite for the Silvanii's distress, knew the episode

202

had been a blessing, that through it he had grown and learnt and could be a far better leader of Morene's human population.

They sang him healing songs and brought him food from the wildwood before sending him home, weary yet elated. He found his house decked out in winter ferns, ivy, seed pods and nuts, both inside and out, and for one joyous moment he thought Casandrina was home; but the house was empty, save for a smiling Ramus.

"I missed those girls," Ramus said. "It was good to see them again. They've done a lovely job, haven't they? I shall be more than glad when they're home to stay – and your Lady, of course."

On the day of the Greening, when the Silvanii danced in the Dancing Glade, Casandrina danced too.

At last, a soft twilight fell and, as stars appeared between the filigree of bud-clad branches, the dance ended. The Silvanii dispersed. Casandrina, Narilina and their woodmaids returned to their grove. Fabiom was already there.

"Oh, I have rested too long!" Casandrina cried, throwing herself into his arms. "I think I shall never be tired again!"

Fabiom heard Narilina laugh.

"I have missed you so much, Casi."

"Good!"

There was a wildness about her, something primal. It caught his breath, made his pulse quicken and yet worried him too. He feared she would want to stay in the woods and no longer care to live in a house away from the trees.

She danced away from him, beckoning him to follow.

As he approached, she darted out of his reach, only to slip around her tree and catch him from behind. She wrapped her arms about his chest, kissing his neck and shoulders. "Now your people can miss *you* awhile. I am going to keep you to myself until they come looking for you!" Her eyes sparkled with delight as, laughing, he turned to face her.

Her scent was intoxicating and her touch was like fire on his skin. "Maybe they won't find me," he suggested, suddenly unperturbed by that thought.

Six days later, their friends did indeed come looking for them. Casandrina returned home, restored and more radiant than ever.

If Deepvale had once been prosperous, now it was the wealthiest of all the holdings, for the amber Casandrina brought home was plentiful indeed. She insisted that much of it go to replenish the holding's coffers and be traded to refill the food stores or used to compensate those who had suffered in the past poor seasons. There were also pieces for friends, which she gave to them as gifts.

"Silvana's tears." Fabiom held a particularly fine piece up to the light. They were relaxing with their closest friends and relatives on the terrace outside the hold-house, after a feast prepared by the woodmaids.

"That one is not for sale," Casandrina said taking it from him, "nor this one. These are for you, Nalio, Eifa. And these also," she picked out two rougher pieces, "which are to be traded; for soon you will need to make yourselves a nice home – so we can visit with you often."

Almost at a loss for words, they thanked her for the gift.

"Now all I have to do is pass my examinations." Nalio sighed ruefully. "No amount of riches will satisfy your father if I am not qualified."

"Ha!" Eifa exclaimed. "You think I should want to marry you if you fail to qualify?" She draped herself provocatively across the terrace. "I *suppose* I could support us if you cannot. After all, I do know all the sculptors in the holding; there's surely one to whom I could be muse and model –"

"Consider me qualified!" Nalio stated emphatically, hoisting her back to his side and pinning her there as Fabiom and Tarison laughed heartily.

"It is no wonder you were so weakened. I had no idea that one tree could produce so much amber." Marid let a handful of the precious stuff fall through her fingers.

Belinda Mellor

Fabiom reached over and stroked his wife's hair. "Only if that tree begins to die." And his voice caught as he said so.

Casandrina looked at him for a long moment. "I was missing you."

"I would rather we had gone hungry than that you should have suffered so," Eifa told her – a sentiment echoed by all their friends.

"These are not tears though." Fabiom touched the brooch Casandrina wore over her heart, and his own likewise.

She laughed at the memory. "No, indeed not. And I was right: you were worth fighting for."

Part
Four

Chapter One

Near to the start of winter, Fabiom succumbed to a mild fever and lay in bed listening to the hail beating a tattoo on the roof of the balcony outside their room. He dozed fitfully, then slipped into a deeper, troubled sleep. He was in the Dancing Glade, surrounded by innumerable Silvanii and they were laughing at him. The laughter faded as they went far away, leaving him alone. Forever.

He tossed in his sleep, pushing away the covers with desperate hands, crying out, "No, please, no!" and Casandrina, summoned by one of her woodmaids, came to him and held him close so that he awoke to the sound of her voice and her heartbeat, and the fear left him.

"He is all right now, Kir'h. I shall stay with him. Go, help the others attend our visitors."

"Visitors?" Fabiom murmured, still confused.

"Hush. Just Tarison and Marid. I thought your mother might have come too, with you being unwell." She sighed. "Never mind. Tell me what you were dreaming about."

He closed his eyes and shivered. "Nothing. It was foolish."

Silvana

"Tell me anyway. I shall not laugh at you."

"But you did. I dreamt you did anyway." He sat up and she pulled a bolster behind him. "Actually you did in reality, though it was not the same."

"Fabiom!"

"All right, I'll tell you. I dreamt it was my seventeenth birth eve, and you rejected me." He shook his head. "Maybe I still can't believe how fortunate I've been."

"I did laugh at you, I remember. I did not reject you. You know I always wanted you. If you had not come, well – you did come, just as I did not walk away from you."

"No, you didn't, for which I shall be ever grateful. I should get up if we have visitors."

She rested a cool hand on his brow and shook her head. "No, they say they will call back in the morning. They have business in one of the outlying villages, Dingle I believe, and they will stay there overnight. Tomorrow they shall have company and they wanted to know if you would be able to receive them. You are better than yesterday, tomorrow you should be well enough."

Fabiom did get up the next day, though he was not fully recovered. He knew he was lucky, others who had taken the fever were far worse affected than he, especially in the western holdings where they always bore the brunt of such infections. At least no one had died, this time. It had not always been so. Every few years Morene would fall prey to a contagious fever and fatalities were not uncommon. Now this latest was almost through. No new cases had been reported in Deepvale in four days. Elsewhere there was a similar tale and the country breathed a sigh of relief.

Fabiom learnt this from Nalio, who, home on a brief visit from the school of apothecary, called on him early that morning with a preparation his father had mixed to help him recover his strength.

"Don't try to do too much, Fabiom," Nalio warned.

Belinda Mellor

"My wife will make certain of that," Fabiom replied, at which Casandrina laughed lightly.

"I will, Nalio, be sure of it."

"You are having visitors, I believe," Nalio said, sealing the bottle. "Here you are, pellitory and tansy, grown in Riverplain. Sadly we cannot grow such things here in quantity, though Father tries. We have a garden of semi-withered and largely unidentifiable herbs to prove it. Take a few drops in the mornings and whenever you feel especially tired, but not more than three times in a day. This should be enough. Anyhow, I will call again in a few days to make certain. You can stop taking the purslane now the fever is passed."

Fabiom unstoppered the bottle, sniffed warily at the contents and pulled a face. "I suppose I must thank you for this though it smells disgusting. How do you know we will have visitors?"

Nalio sat on the edge of the stone parapet in the conservatory where he had discovered Fabiom upon his arrival, enjoying the pale winter sun. He took the cup of hot mulberry juice that Lan'h offered him.

"I was with my father and we had met with Masgor at the market. We saw your uncle and aunt there with four strangers. They were buying pomegranates. Masgor said he knew them, the Lord Holder of Windwood and his family, relations of your aunt's, I think he said, but a holder in Deepvale would visit with you, would he not?"

"Yes," Fabiom agreed absently. "Riann of Windwood is Marid's older sister," he explained to Casandrina. "Ah well."

"What is it, Fabiom?" Casandrina asked. "Is something wrong?"

"No." He smiled wryly. "No, but we had better be prepared. It's a great pity Ramus should be away right now."

Nalio departed soon after, with a promise from Casandrina that, come the spring, she would visit and see if she could improve things in his father's garden.

As soon as the young physician left, Fabiom went back to the suite he shared with Casandrina. There was a pleasant scent of pine resin from the fir cones in the hearth, though the fire was all but burnt out now. Reluctantly he stripped out of his comfortable day clothes and donned instead a longer tunic of saffron wool and raw silk mix, tied at the waist with a white goatskin belt from which hung an ochre-dyed silk sash. He removed the simple arm band and rings that he favoured and replaced them with the most ornate he possessed, pushed a bronze headband through his thick hair and, after a moment's indecision, decided against adding a dagger to his belt. More or less satisfied with his efforts, he glanced once into the silvered mirror he had brought back from Fairwater as a gift for Casandrina. "You'll do," he muttered grimly to his reflection.

He found Casandrina in the kitchen, with Lan'h and Kir'h, organising refreshments for the visitors. The woodmaids left their tasks and came to admire his appearance.

"He looks very handsome, Casandrina," Lan'h said archly. "These must be very important guests."

Kir'h hurried back to the food table. "We can prepare something special for them to eat, Fabiom. I have some new ideas."

"Kir'h, you always have ideas. However, on this occasion I'd be grateful if you could just do the things Ramus has shown you. Believe me, this is not the time to be experimenting."

Casandrina tilted her head to one side, and regarded him quizzically. "There is something you have not told me. Shall we talk?"

Fabiom glanced at the batch of honey cakes cooling on a rack. "We could, or else I could sample your cooking –"

Tarison and Marid returned before noon, as promised. The visitors they brought were, as Nalio had told them, Marid's sister and her husband, Herbis, Lord Holder of Windwood, a holding on the west coast that had suffered grievously from the recent sickness. With them was their son, Giar, who was some three years younger than Fabiom, too young to enjoy the adult company, too old to be good company for Yan and therefore bored

Belinda Mellor

and sullen. The wider span between Fabiom and Yan was easier to bridge and Yan was pleased to see that Fabiom was up, hopeful to find an excuse not to have to spend time with his other cousin.

"You remember Herbis and Riann, don't you, Fabiom?" Tarison inquired, as they paused in the heart room to rinse their hands before entering the house proper.

Fabiom nodded affably. "Indeed. Welcome to Deepvale." He included Giar in his welcome and looked around for a sign of anyone else.

"One of your serving girls is helping Dala mend her dress. She caught it on a rough stone by your gateway."

Lord Herbis's tone sounded accusing. Fabiom doubted if his rough wall was all the cause either. He trusted that whichever woodmaid was assisting Herbis's daughter would not object too strongly to being described as a 'serving girl' but he would not correct his visitor. Across the heart room Tarison raised his brows and Marid studied her hands with sudden interest.

"Please, come and rest from your travels," Fabiom suggested, leading them through the East door to sit in comfort in the day room.

Moments later, Nek'h came in through the courtyard door with an attractive young woman in a grey and mauve wool dress that showed no obvious signs of repair.

"Hello, Dala." Fabiom smiled, getting to his feet.

She returned his smile and kissed his cheek. "Are you better? You look rather pale."

"I am better, more or less. I'm sorry about your dress."

She laughed. "No harm done. It's really good to see you again, Fabiom. Oh, I brought you a present to help you feel well: pomegranates from the shores of Lake Minnow. My own favourite," she confided as she took the package from her mother and presented it to him.

"Casandrina has arranged for some refreshments to be served in the dining room," Kir'h told Fabiom, looking askance at Dala meanwhile.

"Good. Please –" He indicated back towards the heart room, off of which lay the dining area. "You are all welcome to whatever our home has to offer."

They reclined on velvet cushions and helped themselves from an array of wooden and pottery dishes set between them on a low table. In the dishes nearest to Herbis and Riann were chestnut and apple pasties, dates stuffed with spiced curds, and honey-soaked vine leaves wrapped around dried elderflowers mixed with cream. They tried them all and exchanged puzzled glances, nevertheless Herbis went back to the date dish twice more and Riann took a second vine leaf.

"We have couches in *our* dining area," Giar told Casandrina, "and bronze dishes. Don't we, Father?"

"This floor mosaic is quite exquisite," Riann commented to Fabiom. "I remember being very impressed the first time I came here. Wonderful workmanship."

Nek'h came in with a tray of glass goblets and Lan'h followed her with a large jug. Fabiom watched them, hardly daring to breathe, as they served everyone carefully and unerringly. He became aware of Riann watching him almost as intensely and he forced a casual smile. Herbis sniffed at the contents of the goblet and took a tentative sip. He puckered his brows and took another, then raised the goblet to Fabiom.

"I have no idea what this is, but it's very good." He sounded almost surprised, disappointed even.

"Morat," Fabiom said. "We make it ourselves. It is a mixture of fermented mulberry juice and honey."

"Do you produce much honey in Deepvale?" Riann's gaze took in the beeswax candles casting golden pools of light in the shadowy niches lining the walls where the wan afternoon sun could not reach.

"Hardly any," Tarison told her. "We don't grow the right plants. But the next holding, Alderbridge, has endless slopes where nothing but heather grows and there they produce what must be the finest honey in Morene."

Belinda Mellor

"And we have the mulberries," Fabiom added.

"Yes, of course, you produce much silk here, don't you?" Herbis said thoughtfully. "That is something I'm interested in."

"What's this?" Giar asked chewing on something he could neither identify nor decide if he liked.

"It's a type of mushroom, stuffed with herbs and almonds," Fabiom said. "I think," he added under his breath. Close beside him, Yan giggled quietly.

Though Tarison and Marid were quite used to the woodmaids' culinary efforts, unlike Fabiom they were not as used to seeing the effect those efforts had on visitors; consequently they derived much amusement from the meal, which necessitated a certain amount of camouflaging of expressions. Nalio's new potion had left Fabiom rather light-headed and that, combined with the suppressed mirth of Tarison and Marid, the coldly polite small-talk of Herbis and Riann, Giar's bad manners and Dala's embarrassment, resulted in him feeling quite bemused. Casandrina was not much help, concerned as she was with their guests' comfort and sitting well away from him, beside Herbis. His only anchor to normality was Yan, lying close beside him and half asleep.

"Why isn't there any meat? Don't you have any?" Giar asked.

Dala glared at him as Lan'h, who was refilling the goblets, replied, "Ramus does that and he is away today and Fabiom has been unwell and has not been out hunting and none of *us* like meat so we never prepare it."

With that, she left the room to refill her jug. Giar stared after her, open-mouthed, and Herbis turned on Fabiom.

"Surely you don't let a hired girl talk like that?"

"Have you tried these honey cakes? They are particularly good," Casandrina asked, passing the tray of cakes to Herbis who looked at her in amazement but took one nevertheless.

"Thank you," he muttered.

Shortly afterwards, they retired to the day room once more where Marid immediately took Fabiom aside.

"I'm sorry, Fabiom. When Riann and Herbis said they would visit you, what could I do?"

"But you hadn't told them! No one had told them about Casandrina and me. I thought –"

"I know, I know," she soothed. "It was never the right time. I'm so sorry. Am I forgiven?"

"Yes, I suppose so. But I don't understand why –"

Marid twisted a lock of hair around her fingers. "It's complicated."

Before she could think of anything else to say, there was a shriek as Giar leapt to his feet. "I saw a mouse! I'm going to squash it! Where'd it go?"

Fabiom watched as a small brown mouse skittered into Lan'h's outstretched hands and was whisked away to safety. "Inflicting your nephew on me, however, that's another matter!"

Marid laughed. "He's going through a phase. Unfortunately it seems to be lasting an inordinately long time, since he was born, if I recall aright. Uncharitable as it sounds, I confess that a few days of Giar's company once every few years is really enough for me."

It was Fabiom's turn to laugh. "And now you will have him every day for a full month. That should be very pleasant for you!"

"You may mock," Marid chided. "It's not you who has to live with him. And I was going to tell you how elegant I thought you looked, and how clever it was of you to take Herbis off his guard like that." She smiled fleetingly. "I should feel sorry for Giar, I suppose. He is not strong and it's well that he did not succumb to the fever. Windwood is likely to be the last place to be fully clear and if he has to stay here for his own safety, so be it. Ah well, he will learn a few social graces before he returns home."

Fabiom shook his head in mock sympathy. "Then I don't know whether I pity you or him most!" He watched Giar for a moment. The boy was sitting beside one of Ramus's cossetted house plants, shredding the leaves nearest him. "It's hard to believe he's Dala's brother."

216

Belinda Mellor

Reclining on a large couch and sharing a bowl of dates, Dala and Casandrina were talking quietly together. They seemed to be conversing easily, though Fabiom knew his wife well enough by now to see that she was taking in and analysing every detail of her companion, even as they talked and ate.

"I told Casandrina," he explained to Marid. "I thought it best. And I can guess what *they're* talking about." He nodded towards his uncle and Herbis, engaged in a seemingly heated discussion near the doorway, although Herbis's gaze kept lingering on Casandrina.

"But Tarison could not have forced you to honour the agreement!"

"I object to the term 'agreement'," Fabiom grumbled. "I never consented to be a part of any 'deal'. I am, and always was, very fond of Dala. But I never intended to marry her. Fortunately, as far as I know, she never had any wish to marry me either."

"That wasn't how Herbis saw it, nor Riann. I could never be certain about your parents' views. Your father was vague on the matter. Maybe he realised you would not be coerced." She gave a tiny shrug. "Wise man if he did."

Fabiom watched Casandrina. She and Dala were laughing quietly at some jest, heads close together. Marid followed his gaze.

"I think you would be unwise to ever consider being unfaithful."

Fabiom stiffened. "What do you mean? Why do you say so?"

"Oh, Fabiom. I didn't mean anything by it. I'm sorry. It was a silly thing to say. Forgive me? Fabiom?" She touched his arm. "Don't be cross with me. I really didn't mean…."

"Yes, you did. You meant that if I ever made Casandrina as angry as my father made my mother, she would do more than scream and break a few household items. And you're right, of course. If it came to it, she could probably choose from a dozen different ways to kill me. Whereas my mother could only threaten."

"I wasn't thinking, Fabiom. You know me – sometimes the words come out first and the thoughts follow."

"So it's true?" His voice was hollow. "He did betray her."

"I don't know. No, believe me – that's the truth. I really don't know. All I'm certain of is that Vida believes he did. She is so sure. Sometimes it's hard not to be swayed by that certainty."

Fabiom glanced toward his uncle. "Tarison knows, surely?"

"Maybe." Marid looked worried. "I have never pressed him. Vida has, of course. He is evasive."

"He would tell you," Fabiom insisted.

"If he knows; if I forced him. He would not lie to me."

"Yet you never did."

She did not answer that. Instead she said, "He would tell *you*, I think, if you really want to know."

Fabiom closed his eyes. He wanted to hear that his mother was wrong. Yet, if the truth was otherwise, *did* he really want to know?

"Fabiom?"

He took her hand off his arm and, for a moment, she looked worried, until he raised it to his face and rested his cheek against her palm.

"I'm not angry with *you*, Marid." He managed a smile. "Anyway, you mustn't apologise for speaking quickly. You have saved me with your words before today – were it not for you I'd have two wives now, and then I'd really have problems."

Marid turned away so that their visitors could not see her merriment. "Wicked boy!" she scolded. "You will get me into trouble!"

"I thought we'd established you didn't need my help for that."

Across the room, Riann, hearing her sister laugh, glanced in their direction. Fabiom met her eye and smiled.

The day had been damp, though not severely so. Evening brought heavy rains and howling winds that rattled the tiny glass panes in the conservatory and moaned under the terra cotta roof tiles. Ramus returned, windswept and exhausted from his journey, with news that the river was flooding.

Belinda Mellor

There was no question of anyone leaving that night and rooms were hastily made up for the guests. Fabiom, feeling the strain of his first day up from his sickbed, retired early and Casandrina went to him soon after. She did not speak but sang softly as she massaged his back and shoulders with a sweet oil pressed from the seeds of her own ash tree. He fell asleep before he could question her about her conversation with Dala.

The next morning dawned very bright and very cold. Fabiom woke early, took one look at the day and snuggled deeper into the bedclothes and closer to his wife.

"We have guests to attend to," she reminded him succinctly, which was not what he wanted to hear her say, especially when he awoke fully and remembered who their guests were. Soon he became aware of movement in the house, which sounded like neither Ramus nor any of the woodmaids.

"Indeed we do," he agreed ruefully.

When Fabiom and Casandrina joined their guests for breakfast, Riann asked after his health most solicitously; even Herbis spoke to him with less obvious antipathy, and regarded Casandrina with undisguised curiosity. Fabiom surmised that, since he retired last night, Dala had explained some truths to her family.

Giar evinced no particular interest in the Silvana, being totally preoccupied with her woodmaids and piqued that none of them would respond to his overtures in anything save the most casual way.

After all had eaten their fill, Fabiom went with Tarison and Herbis, and a reluctant Giar, to inspect the mulberry coppices and the mills. After visiting the orchards, Fabiom asked Kilm's eldest son, Darseus, to show the visitors around the silkworm rearing areas and the reeling rooms while he discussed the day's business with the boy's father. Giar would not stay to look around properly, objecting to the smell of the boiling cocoons.

Meanwhile, Dala and her mother wrapped themselves up and took a stroll through the still-wet garden. Casandrina accompanied them.

"Look, Mother –" Dala hurried through a trail of arches hung with the remnants of climbing roses. "You can barely see the hold-house from here. It's so clever this garden, full of secret areas, like a wild place. Yet it feels so safe, so secure."

"Thank you." Casandrina smiled. "I like it."

"Vida was very fond of her garden too, I recall," Riann said, looking through the lacework of bare branches to the pond and stream beyond.

"She grew lovely roses and lilies," Casandrina agreed. "I have taken nothing away, merely made some additions."

"What's that? I saw something white moving behind those bushes." Dala tried to see through the tangle of winter flowering shrubs. "Maybe I imagined it."

"I think not." Casandrina sighed. "Fabiom has a donkey that Marid gave him for his seventeenth birth anniversary. She likes the garden too. Excuse me for a moment."

"Did Aunt Marid give him a white donkey? Oh, isn't he lucky! They are supposed to bring good fortune, aren't they? So I've heard, anyway. May I help you?"

Casandrina laughed at her guest's enthusiasm. "Of course you may, thank you."

"I'll go back indoors, if you don't mind. Neither winter walks nor donkeys, white or otherwise, hold great appeal for me," Riann said.

"We will join you presently," Casandrina told her. "Meanwhile, maybe you would be so kind as to ask Ramus to warm some spiced wine; we shall need a hot drink after this."

"She's an indoor person," Dala giggled, watching her mother hurrying back to the hold-house. "Let's catch Fabiom's donkey before she eats too many of your plants."

They pursued Wish through the vegetable garden and finally caught her in the grove of fruit trees.

"She has a warm shelter and a fine meadow of her own; all she lacks

Belinda Mellor

is manners," Casandrina explained as they put Wish back where she belonged.

"You make her sound like my brother," Dala said, so seriously that Casandrina laughed. "No, Casandrina, truly I must apologise for him. Mother spoils him. He was sickly when he was a baby and now he can do no wrong in her eyes. Please forgive him for his rudeness." She sighed, then grinned wickedly. "A month with Aunt Marid will do him good, I think. Yan is a lovely boy, though I think it would take more than a month to transform Giar into the likes of Yan."

"A month can turn a garden from brown to green, or a tiny bud into a fragrant flower," Casandrina told her gently. "Come now, it is cold standing here, maybe Ramus will have the wine mulled and waiting for us."

"Are *you* cold?" Dala asked curiously. Then she blushed slightly at her temerity.

Casandrina fingered the short skirt of her sleeveless dress, fashioned from very fine grey silk. "I am. And I am still not used to the sensation, so sometimes I forget to put on the right clothes for the weather. It is very strange." She laughed lightly and Dala laughed with her.

Riann had used their absence to explore the house and, although she was not altogether impressed with the housekeeping, she was more than impressed with the hangings and ornaments that adorned the various rooms. When Herbis returned from his inspection of the silk mills she took him to look at the library.

"They have so many fine things."

"This always was a prosperous holding," he said, taking down an unusual portfolio of maps. "I came here first the year Giar was born, do you recall? Tawr was holder then, of course."

"Is it the silk?" Riann's glance swept the room. "Look at that wall hanging, that's silk. Have you ever seen the like?"

"No. Neither have I ever seen so much amber, there are pieces everywhere. Many are small, nevertheless...."

"That's because of what she is," Riann said quietly, glancing towards the door. She could hear Fabiom speaking, and a much younger voice replying. Moments later, the door opened and Yan came in.

"Fabiom says I can borrow one of his books about plants," he told his uncle and aunt as he went unerringly to the right shelf. "I'm learning all about them," he explained as he pulled down a small volume and checked the pages to be certain. He left again, leaving the door ajar.

"Come," Herbis muttered to his wife. She paused, looking again towards the silk hanging. "Riann, come. There will be hangings like that in Windwood before too long," he promised.

They left around midday, to Fabiom's relief.

"She seems very pleasant," Casandrina observed, not referring to Riann.

"Dala? Yes, she is," Fabiom replied casually. "But 'pleasant' is not enough, not for ever."

Casandrina pursed her lips. "It is not Dala who concerns me, nor her parents' anger. There is a darkness about her brother. I have seen it before and it bodes no good. Marid should not let Yan spend too much time with Giar. Yan is too precious. Speak to her, Fabiom."

"That won't be easy. I've promised Herbis we'll help him expand Windwood's silk production, and that includes Giar returning to Deepvale this summer to learn about sericulture. I cannot renege on that promise too! We must not antagonise Herbis further, if we can avoid it. Fortunately Deepvale does not border Windwood, else there might have been trouble before now. Despite his civility today, I suspect he's deeply insulted by my not being in a position to marry Dala. According to Tarison, that's what he'd come to Deepvale to discuss." He frowned slightly. "With Tarison, mainly. Apparently he was unaware that I had acceded to the holding, nor did he know that I already had a wife." He

Belinda Mellor

wrapped his arms about her at that. "I'm glad it was not to be, and not just for my own sake either. I doubt I could have made Dala really happy, and I truly hope she will be."

Chapter Two

It was a summer of unbroken skies, of sultry nights and languid days, when the woods afforded a cool respite from the unrelenting heat, and a haven from unwelcome interruptions. Fabiom lay on his belly on the damp moss of the stream's bank and dipped his arms into the clear water, trailing his fingers through fronds of silvery water weed. He felt a little guilty at having escaped, though not so guilty that he was inclined to leave the sanctuary of the woods and return to the hold-house. As for his office in the municipal centre, there was always tomorrow, or even the day after that.

"You are thinking too hard," Casandrina chided, dropping a single bluebell flower into the water upstream of him.

He caught it as it floated by.

"You are frowning," she said.

The next flower passed beyond his reach and he watched it disappear around the bend and out of sight.

"They'll be hammering on my door, 'What word from Fairwater, from Gerik, from Prince Ravik? The treaty, the treaty,' and I'm nowhere to be found."

Belinda Mellor

"And what would you tell them if you were there?"

He caught the next two flowers easily.

"Nothing. Ravik says 'be patient', as he did last month, last year. Gerik says 'no treaty except on our terms', as they did before and before that and will go on saying until the Frozen Lands thaw, no doubt."

"So, relax."

He laughed and rolled over onto his side. "It seems to me I've been relaxing for the best part of three years, ever since I married you." He sat up, dripping water, letting the last flower go by unheeded.

She wandered closer to him. "I think that is not true, even if it seems so to you. I have listened to people talking. You have earned the respect of the citizens of Deepvale. Tarison said –"

Laughing, he pulled her into his arms. "What? What did he say?"

"Nobody really minds that you are not always where they expect you to be."

Fabiom laughed heartily at that. "Did he indeed?"

"He did. Do you want to go home?" Casandrina inquired dubiously.

"Home? No! No…." He sighed. "Why do we always have so many visitors?"

'Visitors' was not exactly the right word for their latest house guests, Fabiom mused, in as much as his cousin Yan and Giar of Windwood were not staying entirely of their own free will. They would far rather have been with Tarison and Marid who were sojourning in Fairwater, attending the marriage celebration of Princess Jaymna, Prince Ravik's older sister, to Norgest of Riverplain.

Giar was back in Deepvale, not to avoid Windwood's notorious fever but to learn something about silk manufacturing, for Herbis had a notion to try to produce silk in Windwood after three consecutive years of disastrous peach and cherry harvests. The two boys were disappointed by their exclusion from the royal festivities, and the explanation that only personal friends of the couple were invited had done little to mollify them.

Dusk settled like a warm, scented mantle over the land.

"We'd better go back, see what they're up to." Fabiom climbed to his feet, holding out his hand for Casandrina.

"At sixteen you would not have thanked anyone for checking up on you," she reminded him as he helped her up.

"I was thinking of Yan, *he* is only eleven. Let's go by your grove though. There isn't that much urgency."

Casandrina smiled indulgently and led the way, finding paths where there were seemingly none, until they came out into the evening-decked clearing where her tree grew.

Fabiom dropped three crushed mauve blooms into the hollow between the roots, brushing the trunk tenderly as he did so; then, leaning his back against the deeply ridged bark, he tilted his head to look up through the widespread branches into the domed crown high above his head. Ripening clusters of winged seeds adorned the twigs, giving the tree a soft golden tint accentuated by the last glow of the day. He let his gaze drift around the grove then, until it settled on a slight ash sapling growing nearby, surrounded protectively by whitethorn, blackthorn and holly.

"Her tree is growing strong," he said, a fond smile shaping his mouth.

"Naturally," Casandrina agreed. "Now, home, Fabiom. I do not want to have to explain to Marid, less still to Lord Herbis, that our charges went astray whilst we were absent."

"Oh, I have no doubt Giar will be there when we get back, as cheerless as when we left, bored, needing to be entertained, as ever."

Back at the house, Fabiom took out a selection of bows. "There's an archery competition not too far distant, why don't you practice towards that in the morning," he suggested.

Belinda Mellor

"I'm too old," Giar said shortly.

Fabiom raised his brows and bit back on a comment that had come too easily to his tongue.

"I'm not," Yan pointed out.

"True, and there's a junior section. Help Yan then, Giar. You've a fair eye." Fabiom was fast running out of both ideas and patience.

Giar muttered something about having nothing better to do.

Yan had recovered from his initial disappointment and had decided that staying with Fabiom and Casandrina was actually preferable to going to Fairwater with his parents. He wished they had taken Giar though. "Mother and Father will be away ages yet, won't they, Fabiom?" he asked. "Mother says that Princess Jaymna always gave the biggest and best parties, and her weddings are the best of all."

Fabiom tried not to smile too broadly. "I believe that this is only her second wedding, Yan. You make it sound as if she gets married regularly! As for her parties, I wouldn't know. I've not had the honour of being invited to any."

"Your mother's gone though, hasn't she?" Giar asked Fabiom. "How come you weren't invited?"

Fabiom's smile faded as he glanced out at the darkening sky. "Lord Davin of Riverplain, Princess Jaymna's first husband, was a close friend of my father's. My mother was invited in acknowledgement of that friendship, I would imagine."

Vida had very nearly not gone, pleading all sorts of excuses, which Fabiom had thought strange. He would have expected her to be delighted at such an invitation. Eventually, ignoring claims of ill-health, Marid had persuaded her; concerned, apparently, that an invitation from the princess was not something anyone who valued their wellbeing or social standing should turn down.

"May we look in your library tonight?" Yan asked.

"Yes, of course," Fabiom replied, glad of another diversion for them, although the look on Giar's face suggested the idea held little appeal for him.

"*Viniculture; Seasons of fruit; Cirecca's ballads.*" Giar put the last down contemptuously. "This was a worse idea than offering to help Ramus repot the orchids."

"Well, I'm sorry," Yan said insincerely. He loved books as he loved plants and he was enjoying himself. "Listen: '*He would not say what he had heard or what he had beheld or what had befallen him, still it was plain to one and all that he had changed. "I am not sad," he would say again and again, whilst the tears fell down his cheeks. "Nothing can compare." Though with what he would not tell, instead he would sing and their hearts would be moved. Some merely pitied him, others so loved his songs that they, they . . .* ' What does that word say, Giar?"

"Let me see, where?"

Yan pointed to the word.

"Revered. '*. . . revered him as a wise man.*' What is this?" Giar closed the slim, well-used volume and turned it over to read the title. "*Tales of a Woodsman.* I remember this, I've read it before, years ago. It's an improvement on *The Poetry of Eryn's sons.*"

"You take it," Yan said. "I want to look at one about gardens."

"You have enough to choose from then," Giar scoffed as he propped himself on the window seat beside a bright oil lamp and opened the book at the beginning. "Fabiom looked a bit – I don't know – odd, when he spoke of the wedding, didn't he?"

"Princess Jaymna's first husband and my Uncle Tawr were drowned together," Yan said, raising his head from a beautifully illustrated book on water gardens.

"Well, I wasn't to know that," Giar muttered.

Casandrina found them both engrossed in their respective reading material much later, when she came to suggest that Yan, at least, should think about retiring for the night.

"You may borrow that if you wish, Giar."

So Giar took the book to his room and read until his eyes became too heavy and the words danced meaninglessly before him. In the morning he read again. Fabiom helped Yan with his archery practice.

'... *The summit was lost in dense mist that surrounded and enveloped and silenced, a silence so real that it was almost possible for him to touch it. Gulls, like phantoms, glided through the greyness, on wings as grey and as silent as the very mist. The air was thin and cold, ice cold, hard to breathe and yet, drawing impossible breaths, he began to sing and his voice reached out into the silence and transformed it into something entirely different. The wind blew sharp and chill, carrying the notes of his song away, through the crags and gullies, into the secret places only the wind knows. And the mountain heard his song, the song of the wildwood. Never before had it been heard there. Never again would it resound in those barren places high above the tree-line. Just that once, when the mountains became one with the forests, when the silence became one with the song. With that, the woodsman found his own peace and he came down from the high places, back to the plains of his youth, still singing his songs; now and again singing the echoes that the mountains had taught him.'*

Giar closed the book with a thoughtful sigh.

"*... He had heard them sing and he had seen them die and he could not say which was the most terrible....*" Giar recited as he sauntered over the bridge; for a moment he paused, then tentatively stepped into the wildwood beyond.

The shade was a welcome relief after the heat of the summer garden, drawing him in further than he had meant to go, beyond sight of the mulberry orchards and terraced vineyards that were Fabiom's estate. Despite the shade he was not happy. No one in Windwood went into the great woods from which that holding took its name, not unless they absolutely had to; certainly he never had. Now curiosity had got the better of him. He wanted to find Casandrina's tree. In truth he had very little idea where to begin his search though, like all Morenians, he knew enough Treelaw to understand that the Silvanii rarely dwelt at the very edge of their domain, so there was little point in looking seriously until he was well inside the wood. Having seen Fabiom's maps of his holding, he also knew that the woods covered a great deal, well over a quarter of the total area. Undaunted, he pressed on. From listening to Yan, who had several times been to the grove with Casandrina, he knew roughly how long it should take to get there from the bridge and a few landmarks to look out for on the way.

The main disadvantage he faced was that he did not know for certain what sort of tree he should be searching for. That was his own fault of course; he should have asked Yan. Anyway, he had narrowed it down to five possibilities: elm, beech, walnut, ash or birch. The book he had just finished re-reading made it clear that it had to be one of those whose Silvanii mature at seventeen years, given that Fabiom was twenty years of age and he and Casandrina had been together for three years. However, he was sure he would know the tree should he come across it, for Yan had told him that Fabiom brought tokens there regularly and, only yesterday, Giar had seen him braiding camomile flowers into a chain. He doubted that more than one tree in the woods would be bedecked with such a garland.

A pair of grey doves flew over his head, weaving between the branches of the woodland canopy on their way back to their nest with food for their young. He paid them no heed, intent as he was upon watching a column of big brown ants carrying the body of a dead beetle through the rotting leaf mould. It struck him as funny to think that there would be insects living in, and feeding upon, Casandrina's tree, especially as *Tales of a Woodsman* hardly differentiated between a Silvana and her abode. He walked on, not hesitating long to look at anything, though he paused briefly to watch two cock robins fighting. They separated and flew into the undergrowth when they noticed him, scattering bloodied feathers in their wake.

He chose the least overgrown pathways he could find, on the assumption that they were the most likely to lead him to his goal. It was with a certain

230

Belinda Mellor

amount of relief that he came upon the first of Yan's landmarks: a small waterfall where a narrow and fast flowing stream tumbled down a steep incline. Soon after that he was clambering over an oddly shaped outcrop of rock, crowned with a pair of rowans, and expecting at any moment to come across a stand of sweet chestnuts.

There was no sign of any chestnut tree. Giar cursed long and loud in frustration, and then again for the sheer luxury of being able to do so without anyone hearing and reprimanding him. He doubled back and tried another path, still swearing – and laughing at himself as he did so.

Just as he had decided that he had been walking long enough, he found himself in a wide clearing, bright with the sunlight which poured in through the spacious gap in the canopy onto short meadow grass scattered with periwinkles and heartsease flowers. His elation was short-lived. Across the clearing a shallow river splashed sluggishly over the rocks in its bed and told him he was in the wrong place. He kicked at some virulent yellow fungi growing from the bole of an ancient beech tree and turned back the way he had come, intent upon finding another path and reaching his goal. He was halfway back to the bridge when he realised that he had stumbled upon a Dancing Glade and with that he forgot all about finding Casandrina's tree.

Giar's absence had not been noticed. When he returned to the hold-house, he found Fabiom and Yan in the area of the garden set aside for archery practice, where Fabiom was showing Yan how to properly string a longbow. Lengths of waxed silk hung over the lower branches of a fig tree and a number of bows leant against the slim trunk. Giar sauntered over to join them as Fabiom handed a fine looking bow to Yan that he had previously measured against the boy's height.

"It'll last you a while," Fabiom said. "It stands a hand span taller than you, so don't put on a sudden spurt for a year or so, eh?"

Yan smoothed his hands along the polished length then gently touched the carved horn nocks which would hold the bowstring in place. He looked

Silvana

up at his oldest cousin adoringly; Fabiom merely grinned and passed him a bowstring.

"Now let's see you do this right."

"That's a fine bow," Giar commented, a touch enviously.

"It's Fabiom's old one," Yan told him with pride. "It suits me just right," he added.

"Not quite so tight," Fabiom warned. "See the bracing is too deep for you." He took Yan's arm. "Hold the bow please, Giar," he requested and held Yan's hand between the string and the bow's curved belly. "Now your other hand, see you've two palm widths there, not …"

"A palm and two fingers," Yan supplied as he took the bow back from Giar to loosen the string.

Fabiom nodded and picked up a plainer bow of elm wood. "If you want to do some shooting, Giar, you can use this one, though I think it may be a little too tall for you to handle comfortably. I'll borrow one that's a better length for you tomorrow or, if you like, we could make one – Anyway, we'll be eating soon so don't get too engrossed."

"We'll just shoot six arrows each, to get a feel for them," Yan suggested.

"You've been getting a feel for that bow all day," Fabiom reminded him.

Yan shook his head emphatically. "That was before you gave it to me to keep," he explained. "It feels different now."

The bows had been carefully put away, and the family was taking their evening meal in the shaded portico outside the dining room. Beyond the portico, the westerly sky was the palest shade of blue, shot through with strands of pink and mauve. The sky and the woods were the palettes for the fine silk fabrics for which the eastern holdings of Morene were justly famous, Deepvale especially so. A bolt dyed just the heavy purple that stained the eastern horizon that evening was the gift Marid had brought to Princess Jaymna for her wedding.

"May we sleep outside again? It's still too hot to sleep indoors," Yan asked.

Belinda Mellor

Giar, who had been coerced into sleeping in the garden the night before, shrugged as Fabiom glanced quizzically in his direction. "I don't mind."

"In that case, and so long as you promise to remain in the garden, yes," Fabiom agreed. "But don't stay up too late. Remember you are helping with the mulberry leaf harvest tomorrow. It'll be an early start; Kilm says he'll call for you at sunrise." He was pleasantly surprised when Giar said nothing derogatory about the prospects for the morrow.

"Giar, you have hardly eaten," Casandrina noticed with concern. "You are not sickening for something, I hope."

"It's too hot, I'm not really hungry." He toyed with a piece of bread.

"I know!" Yan exclaimed. "Let's have some food later, when it's dark. I'm too hot to be hungry as well. Later, though, it'll be cooler. It will be like being away on service."

"Camped out on the plains of Gerik: cold, miserable, forlorn," Fabiom added.

"No!" Yan laughed. Then he looked thoughtful. "Do you think Prince Ravik will send you to Gerik to do *all* your service, Fabiom?"

"I sincerely hope not. What have I ever done to Ravik to deserve that?" As he spoke, Fabiom felt Casandrina move closer to him and he covered her hand with his own.

"But you will have to go there?" Yan persisted.

"As will you – and Giar," Fabiom told him. "There are some disadvantages to high birth."

Giar seemed unusually thoughtful. "Eating later is a good idea, Yan. May we save some food for tonight, Casandrina?"

"Of course, Giar. You may have what you like from the kitchen."

She smiled as she said so and he regarded her quizzically from beneath lowered lids. She seemed so gentle, so benign. It was hard to imagine her in the grip of a terrible rage, as he had read about. Yet, according to '*Tales of a Woodsman*', she was quite capable of bringing about the destruction of another of her kind, even to uprooting a full-grown tree. Had she wanted

Fabiom so much that she would have killed to get him, or else risked her own demise in the attempt? If that were so, Giar was not really surprised that Fabiom had passed over the opportunity to marry his sister, Dala. Yet, had things gone awry, surely Fabiom too would have gone mad, like the woodsman. Apparently he had considered it worth the risk.

Unaware of Giar's musings, Fabiom was just glad the boy was not ill. His presence seemed a heavy responsibility. Giar's father had left Deepvale the previous year obviously convinced that he and his holding, let alone his daughter, had been grossly insulted. Fabiom was certain Herbis would like nothing better than to blame him for something else, anything, in order to demand satisfaction. It was bad enough to be reminded of the inevitability of having to go away for two years, without worrying about being involved in a feud with another holder.

Chapter Three

"**D**o you want some cheese, Giar?"

"No. You finish that, Yan. Let's sleep somewhere else tonight. The smell from the flowers here is so strong, it's sickening."

"That's the myrtle, I like it. Anyway, Fabiom said we were to stay in the garden."

"You're afraid of him, aren't you?" Giar scoffed. "Will he tell your parents if you don't do as he says?"

"I'm not afraid of him!"

"Prove it then."

"How?"

Leaning back on his elbow, Giar grinned knowingly.

"No!" Yan said at once. "Not the woods. Not without permission."

"Oh. You think you'd get permission to sleep in the woods do you, if you asked nicely. But you wouldn't ask anyway, would you? You're more afraid of the woods than you are of Fabiom."

"Am not!"

"*'And the woodsman stood at the edge of the forest and felt a shiver begin* at the back of his neck and work its way slowly along the length of his spine. *Cold he felt, though the night was warm enough. Cold with fear.'* Maybe the woodsman's name should have been Yan, huh?"

"I don't know what you're talking about," Yan said, feeling the conversation had gone beyond him. "But I'm not scared. I just don't want to sleep in the woods, that's all."

An owl hooted and Giar imitated its cry. "'fraid of the owls and the bats? I should have guessed you'd have no nerve. Or is it the shadows that frighten you. Boo!"

Yan said nothing, though in truth he was close to tears. Noises, shadows, disobeying Fabiom, all those were bad enough, but none compared with being humiliated by Giar. He packed up the leftover food and put his sandals on, awkward in the confined space of the makeshift tent.

"What are we waiting for?"

Night-shrouded, the woods were darker than either Giar or Yan had ever imagined. There was no need to be scared of shadows for there were none, just darkness layered upon darkness.

Only when he was certain that they were well out of sight did Giar uncover his lantern, by which time both of them had grazed and bruised legs and feet.

"This is far enough," Yan said, breathless.

"We need a clearing." Giar continued onwards, leaving the younger boy no choice but to follow or be left in utter blackness.

"Where are you going?" Yan had said nothing for some time, intent on keeping close to Giar, close to the light. Now he was becoming increasingly uneasy. "Why are we going so far?"

Giar seemed to know where he was headed, though he had turned back on his tracks once, muttering to himself.

"Nearly there."

"Nearly where?"

"Here!" Giar stopped, listening. "See, Yan, a good clearing. We'll set

Belinda Mellor

the tent here. In the morning the light will come in and we'll be back in the garden before anyone else is awake. It won't seem as far in the daylight. It wasn't really far, just seemed like it because we had to walk slowly. And I'm sorry – about before."

His light mood and good humour made Yan grin.

"That's all right. I was a bit scared. But I'm not now."

They set up the tent and Giar suggested they settle down at once, as the sun would wake them early in the morning.

Yan needed no more invitation than that, though he still wished they had stayed in the garden. He was tired after his anxious walk, glad enough to lie down in the darkness and let the night soothe him. He fell asleep almost immediately.

The whirr of the nightjar could not disturb him. The singing did.

"Giar?" Yan's voice whispered loud in the darkness, but elicited no response. "Giar, wake up!" He listened. There was no sound within the confines of the tent, other than the rapid beating of his own heart, the quick draw of his own breath. He needed no light to realise he had been left alone. Giar was gone.

Though Yan could not know it, Giar was not far away and he too stirred on his hard bed, moaning. The singing that had woken Yan – the rhythm of which had sounded deep within the earth – had stopped. The only sound, other than the melodies of the river and the breeze, was that of low voices. Giar strove to hear what they said but could make little sense of the words he caught. "… *cousin … guest … house … child …*" He wanted to hear the singing again, instead there was silence.

Finally a voice spoke up, "*Let him awake and go, for the child's sake. I can feel the young one's fear.*"

With that, the bonds of sleep were sloughed off and Giar sat up, shaking. His heart beat as if from great exertion; his brow was wet with perspiration. For a moment he had no idea where he was until, from nearby, Yan's quavering voice called out his name. Giar sat very still.

Silvana

"Where are you?" The terrified whisper sounded loud in the quiet night. "Where are you?"

Yan's sobbing and blundering exit from the Dancing Glade reverberated amid the trees and Giar chuckled softly to himself before laying his head down again. He closed his eyes and abandoned himself to the songs of the Silvanii.

Casandrina sat up with a startled cry, waking Fabiom, who caught her into his arms.

"I am all right. It is —" She put her head to one side, perplexed. "It is Yan. He is at my tree."

"*Your tree!* But, they're in the garden."

"No, Fabiom, Yan is...." She paused, remembering another time, another child. "He is curled up in the hollow by the roots." She felt the warmth of the boy's presence there, just as she felt the warm winds that moved the leaves in the high canopy. "He is afraid, very afraid. There are woodmaids with him. I do not know them."

Fabiom was already out of the bed and throwing a light wrap around himself. "Giar must be responsible. When I find him...."

Casandrina reached over and took his hand. "Do not jump too hastily to conclusions, we know nothing yet."

The woodmaids, aware of their mistress's concern, were ready to make their way to the grove almost before Fabiom and Casandrina were.

Halfway across the garden, Casandrina stopped and shivered.

"Fabiom —"

"What is it, my love?"

"I do not know for sure. Go on to the grove, Fabiom. You, too," she instructed her woodmaids. "Bring Yan home."

Belinda Mellor

"And you?" Fabiom asked.

"I shall be back as soon as I can."

She was gone before he could argue, running surefooted across the bridge into the gloom of the woods. He followed with the woodmaids, finding his way almost as surely as she, though headed in a different direction.

She was too late, as she knew she would be. Though Giar was still asleep, the grimace that contorted his features told her all she needed to know about his state of mind.

"*We gave him a chance*," Gracillia said. An ash Silvana like Casandrina; she had challenged Casandrina for Fabiom but had no interest in Giar, as had none of the others.

"*More chance than he deserved*," another added.

One of the Silvanii, standing a little apart from the others, regarded her sympathetically. "*This troubles you, Casandrina. I am sorry.*"

"It may well *bring* trouble," Casandrina replied, more to herself than the other, who inclined her head in mute acknowledgment then asked, "*Where is the child?*"

"He is by my tree, Narilina. Are they not your woodmaids with him?"

"*They are mine*," Gracillia told her. "*Is the child safe?*"

"Yes, and Fabiom has found him."

Despite her horror at Giar's circumstances, she smiled as Fabiom touched the tree tenderly. Yan was clinging to the trunk, obviously unaware of Fabiom's identity, then the hold loosened. Casandrina turned her attention back to Giar.

"How could I have been so unaware?"

Narilina brushed her arm gently. "*Do not blame yourself. To be as you are, you must be a little less than you were, so that by being less you can become more. It is called growing. It is what we do best.*"

Narilina knew. She had been as Casandrina was, once, long ago. The memory lingered in her gaze: joy and sorrow.

"Yes, I have grown."

"And will go on growing. You can do nothing for this one, though."

Herbis would blame Fabiom, of that Casandrina was certain. No matter that
Giar had acted of his own volition and had been of age. No matter that he
had knowingly and willingly risked Yan's wellbeing and had subjected the
boy to taunts and fear. It would all be laid on Fabiom's shoulders. Casandrina
felt powerless and in her powerlessness she felt angry. She quashed those
feelings as, with a swift and easy movement, she lifted Giar's supine body
from the earth to carry him home.

"The wind blew the song away, blew it away." Giar's eyes were vacant,
staring unseeing at the two men.

"That's all he says, over and over. It's been five days now." Fabiom met
Tarison's appalled gaze. "I didn't even know it was his birth anniversary. Not
that I would have guessed what he had in mind. He'd shown no interest
in the woods."

"Your not knowing is my fault," Tarison admitted. "I thought we were
imposing on you enough, without adding the burden of Giar's coming of
age as well. Marid told him to say nothing to you, that we'd have a grand
celebration as soon as she and I returned from Fairwater. Is there nothing
that can be done for him?"

A warm, summer rain was falling. Fabiom watched Marid and
Casandrina walk arm in arm across the moist garden.

"You know the answer to that as well as I," he said at last, his voice low,
tired.

Yan was sleeping on a couch in the shade of the portico, sung into
oblivion by Casandrina, attended constantly by one of her woodmaids.

Belinda Mellor

In the five days since Giar's misadventure, Yan had eaten almost nothing and his sleep had been beset by nightmares. Upon their return, his parents had sat with him for a while, but he had not woken and so they left him, to worry instead about Giar and what they would tell Herbis and Riann.

A letter was dispatched that evening.

The following day, Fabiom accompanied Tarison and his family back to Valehead. While his uncle and aunt tended to the two boys, Fabiom went to find his mother. She liked to weave on the roof surrounded by her fragrant roses, which trailed out of large terra cotta pots over wooden trellises.

He greeted her with a kiss, noticing she looked almost as weary as he felt.

"Are you well? You look tired," he asked as he helped himself to some mint-infused lemon and pear juice, and poured a cup for her.

She sighed. "It was a long journey."

"And the wedding?"

"It was elaborate – as was to be expected."

"Elaborate! The event of the year and that's all you have to say!"

"What more would you hear? I'm glad to be home."

With an effort, he held back what he wanted to say regarding her use of the word 'home'.

A refreshing breeze blew from the direction of the river, inviting him to climb up and sit astride the parapet, though he half expected his mother to chide him for his recklessness in doing so. Below, the gardens and terraces of grapes spread out towards the river, where – he noted with some satisfaction – a good quantity of grain was being unloaded from a barge. There had been talk of a shortage. That, at least, was one less problem.

"Something happened while you were away. Something bad –"

Vida glanced up. "Go on."

He gave her the briefest account of what had befallen Giar, prepared for her to make a point about the trouble they were in being due to his marriage to a Silvana, but Vida seemed distracted and said nothing other than: "It's a dangerous undertaking. Everyone knows that."

"Indeed," Fabiom agreed. "Well, we have grievously offended Herbis twice now. I intend to have nothing more to do with him. We can't afford a third time – that would cost us dear."

His mother sighed and put down her shuttle. "I'm afraid it's too late for that. I cannot contemplate what the price will be." She picked at the edge of her shawl with anxious fingers.

"What do you mean? What else have we done – save insult his daughter and cost him his son's sanity?"

Marid ascended the stairway as Vida said, "Your betrothal to Dala was payment for an earlier –" she hesitated and glanced towards her sister-by-marriage, "infraction, shall we say."

Fabiom shook his head. "I have no idea…."

"It's my fault, our fault." Marid included Tarison, behind her, in her admission. She came over to where Fabiom perched on the parapet and sat on a cushion by his feet. "Do you remember when I first came to Deepvale?"

"Yes, of course I do. I was delighted."

"You were. Your father was less happy. I don't know if…."

"I remember a row." Fabiom looked at his uncle. "I'd never heard the two of you argue before. I caught nothing of what you were talking about, only that he used some fairly strong language."

"He did," Tarison agreed. "As for the cause – it was about the position we'd put Deepvale in, and what he would have to do to appease Herbis."

Marid reached up and took Fabiom's hand in hers. "It was about me."

"I don't understand. What had you done?"

"Run away – with Tarison."

"Run away?"

She rested her forehead briefly against their joined hands before explaining. "When my parents died, I was only fourteen. Riann was already

242

married. She brought me to live in Herbis's hold-house. Within the year I was –" She took a deep breath. "I was betrothed to Nimo."

"Nimo! But that must have been around the time they came here," Fabiom realised. "He was a bully and an idiot!"

"Indeed," Marid agreed. "We were supposed to marry four years later, once he finished his service. It was not my choice."

"I can imagine." Fabiom looked back at his uncle.

"We eloped," Tarison admitted. "Your father had sent me to Windwood, on business. I met Marid." He shrugged. "They were due to marry while I was there. I couldn't let her –"

"No," Fabiom agreed quietly. He leant down and kissed his aunt's brow. "And I'm glad of it, whatever the outcome."

Twelve days later, Fabiom walked in on Tarison and Masgor arguing in his office in the municipal centre.

"Gentlemen?" He tried to sound surprised, pretending no idea of the cause of contention between them, though for thirteen days, since his messengers had set out for Windwood, speculation had been rife throughout Deepvale.

"Are they back?" Tarison demanded.

Fabiom shook his head and poured himself a beaker of morat.

"Herbis will demand retribution…." Masgor began, to be cut off by Tarison.

"Retribution, pah! He will seek revenge. There is a world of difference, Masgor. It's called bloodletting!"

"There will be no revenge," Fabiom said wearily, putting down his beaker and throwing himself onto a settle. He looked older than his twenty years, and the easy smile that had been his trait for most of the last three of those years had deserted him. He raised his hand to ward off his uncle's question.

"I won't be here. He can do nothing against Deepvale in my absence." From inside his tunic he withdrew a folded sheath of papers clearly marked with the Royal seal.

"Two years?" Masgor asked and, at Fabiom's nod, added, "It should be long enough."

"Herbis will honour that I suppose," Tarison muttered darkly.

Masgor shook his head. "What choice? Ravik will see that he does. Never in Morene's history has a holding moved against another whose holder was absent." He looked towards Fabiom. "It will be hard on you though."

"I could have wished for better circumstances, but I expected to be called soon, anyway. Get it done with. Let this blow over. I should be able to get home briefly, now and again." Fabiom shrugged. He was refusing to actually consider what two years meant, in terms of days and nights, of months or seasons. He was duty bound, and Prince Ravik had stepped in to rescue him from a situation that could have developed into something serious.

"And?"

Fabiom looked at his uncle, momentarily puzzled. "Oh," he muttered at last. "Yes, there will be more –"

"A son for a son," Masgor supplied.

Fabiom raised his brows, surprised by his old tutor's perception.

"There is nothing new in Morene," Masgor said by way of explanation.

"He'll have to serve two years' service in Windwood," Fabiom added, for Tarison's benefit.

"It could be Yan. It should be Yan," Tarison offered reluctantly, catching up with the discussion.

Fabiom shook his head. "No. He's been through enough. And, given your history in Windwood, I'm not sure he would be welcome."

"Either that or misused. I doubt Nimo would be gentle with him," Tarison agreed.

"Indeed. Anyway, Ravik's missive is quite specific on that point. Apparently, Herbis went to Fairwater to speak with him – to ask for a lot more than that; he must have gone as soon as he heard what had happened."

"But you don't yet have a son."

"And won't have for another fourteen years. Hence I cannot be too concerned about the demand. It *is* somewhat premature."

"So where is Ravik sending you?" Tarison asked after a moment's pause, glancing at the papers thrown onto Fabiom's desk.

Fabiom smiled at last. "Just as far as Fairwater, for now – with its bath houses and theatres, libraries and gardens. All comfort, and every convenience. Under the circumstances, I can hardly complain."

Chapter Four

Fabiom surveyed the muddy expanse of the Gerik marshland and sighed. It was supposed to be summer, though the only discernible difference in the weather since their arrival half a year ago was that it was no longer actually freezing. He was tired beyond words of the cold, wet, treeless monotony of the place. 'A peace keeping mission,' the Prince of Morene termed it. It was more correctly an intimidation exercise: the continued presence of a large contingent of Morenian troops within Gerik.

Fabiom's two years' service were done. Now he was just waiting on word regarding the treaty and he could go home. He had only got back to Deepvale on three occassions during those two years, ten days in all. The most memorable of those had been when Nalio qualified from the school of apothecary. They travelled home together and Fabiom officiated at his friend's wedding, as he had always promised he would.

On each of his visits home, he left Casandrina with poetry too intimate to send by courier for others to read to her. After just a few days together and months apart, each time he left was more painful than the last.

Despite missing home, Fabiom made the most of his time away. The

Belinda Mellor

first year in the capital had seen him rise to a position of trust: both as a diplomat and the prince's constant hunting companion. In the process he earned himself a place in the royal escort when Ravik accepted an invitation from the astrologer-king of Varlass to return to that land – to join the month-long celebrations of the Varlassian New Year and watch the rising of Caruth, the so-called 'Dream Star'.

They had returned to Morene to find the situation regarding the treaty critical, with minor leaders vying for power, eager to succeed in breaking Morene's resolve in the absence of her ruler and thereby verify their particular claim to sovereignty.

Three days after their return, Ravik summoned Fabiom. "It's time for you to go to Gerik."

Initially Ravik wanted him to be a part of the negotiation team, for he had proved himself an able diplomat. Reluctantly the prince yielded to the opinion of senior advisers that their Gerish counterparts were known to place more value on age than on oratory skills, and so it was that Fabiom found himself as a commander in the 'peace-keeping' force, exercising his other particular talent and responsible for the entire complement of archers in liege to Ravik.

As the ice-bound winter sullenly gave way to a sodden spring, information filtered through to the field units that there was a real possibility of the talks collapsing and the 'peace-keeping' force becoming a fighting outfit.

Mercifully, and almost at the last minute, an acceptable treaty had been hammered out. Now it was a matter of getting the appropriate rulers of Gerik to sign. Ravik was not about to let the opportunity slip – they would be here until the ink was on the parchment and the seals had been stamped. Fabiom thought of the woods and hills of his homeland, especially the woods. He had not expected to be away from Morene for so long.

Beyond the field of pitched tents, the plateau stretched away as far as he could see, relentlessly dull. Less than a hundred years ago Gerik had been as

Morene, lush and green. That was before the trees had been hacked down, to bleed them of their amber and to provide building materials. At night, Fabiom dreamt of falling trees and awoke startled and afraid.

"Cheer up, Fabiom. They say they'll sign this damned treaty within the next few days."

Fabiom dropped the tent flap, blocking out the view. He looked sourly at his commanding officer. "That's what they said last year."

Philon of Alderbridge, erstwhile commander of the palace-guard was now Strategos of the Morenian army in Gerik. Fabiom had been pleased, and somewhat relieved, to be serving with someone he had met before, if only briefly. More pleased still when he had discovered that Philon had requested him especially, to command Morene's archers.

Philon laughed. "Probably next year too. However, I have to remain optimistic, otherwise I'd go mad."

"They'll send someone to relieve us if it's not signed soon, won't they?" Seric of Southernport, the third officer present, massaged his brow. "I am so bored!" A renowned spearman, Seric had been stationed with his unit on the western edge of the marshland, near to the town of Stonehaven and had only recently joined the bulk of Ravik's force, now gathering together in a show of strength. Seric was only a few years older than Fabiom and, like Fabiom, it was his first time in Gerik. Now he turned anxious grey eyes on Philon. "I don't know how much more of this I can stand – mud and dirt; awful food and worse weather."

Philon was older, a veteran soldier and commander. He cheerfully assured them that it never got any easier. "You lads need something to take your minds off all this. There's a good supply of wine and some pretty girls in the village beyond –" He waved an arm vaguely in the direction of the nearest habitation.

"Count me out," Fabiom chuckled. "Someone ought to be here when word comes that we can all go home."

"You're no fun," Philon complained. "If that's what marriage does for you I'm glad I never bothered."

Belinda Mellor

"I didn't know you were married!" Seric said. "How come I didn't know you were married?"

Fabiom grinned self-consciously.

Philon nodded at Seric. "Neither did I, until a couple of days ago. Half a year here together and he tells me nothing. Huh!"

Fabiom was used to Philon's badinage by now. "Go on, if you will. Just don't get too drunk, else you might find the rest of us packed up and gone in the morning."

As they were leaving the tent to go out into the wet evening, Philon looked curiously at Fabiom who had settled as comfortably as he could beside a hot brazier.

"How old are you?"

"I'm twenty-two, as you well know," Fabiom told him.

"Twenty-two, eh? And away from home for two years."

"And your point is?"

"Just that after this long I don't think I could be so constant. At your age, I'm certain I couldn't – speaking for myself."

Fabiom shrugged. "Maybe you would surprise yourself."

"Is she pretty?"

"My wife? Pretty's not quite the word I would use. But yes, I suppose you might say she is."

Seric called from outside, "Are you coming, Philon?"

"Goodnight," Fabiom said pointedly.

Philon grinned and turned to follow the sound of Seric's voice. "Goodnight," he called back over his shoulder.

Fabiom turned his attention to an equipment inventory from one of the unit officers, then, satisfied with that, began his regular nightly check of his own accoutrements and discovered that the crisscrossed leather binding on his short bow needed replacing. Everything else was in good order. Still, they had to be careful. Arrows were no problem, the marshes provided reeds for shafts, fish skins to boil down for glue, flight feathers from water fowl, even flint for arrowheads, should their supply of iron heads not be sufficient.

Bows were a different matter. What he had been told was true: not a single tree remained in Gerik. There was no wood left. He chose not to dwell on that thought. The thongs he was winding needed his attention. It was hard to concentrate. The burning peat made strange shadows appear on the canvas of the tent, picture shapes that reminded a homesick man of leafed branches moving in the wind. Fabiom left his seat to rummage in his pack for the bunch of ash keys that had accompanied him since he left Deepvale nearly two years ago. He let the winged seedpods drop, and watched them spin towards the ground, round and around, catching them deftly before they landed.

"Goodnight, Casandrina," he murmured.

Word came just eight days later: the treaty had been signed. Gerik at last recognising Morene's autonomy, abandoning her old demands for tributes in the process, reluctantly acceding the right of Morenian vessels to free use of the Straits and accepting a reciprocal harbouring clause in case of adverse weather. They could go home.

Home. No word was sweeter to Fabiom's ears. He had discharged his obligation to Prince Ravik and had done so with honour. Now his duties lay in Deepvale and he could hardly wait to be there.

They sailed across the Straits of Morena under a blue sky. The *Galingale* rode the swell with ease, though Fabiom watched each wave that broke upon the prow with misgiving. It was five years since Tawr, his companions and their vessel had been lost in those waters. To Fabiom it seemed only days ago. Even now, it was hard to believe that when he arrived home his father would not be there to greet him.

He pushed aside such thoughts. Tawr might not be there but he was not going home to an empty house. As the coast of Morene came close

Belinda Mellor

enough for him to make out the wharves and buildings of Southernport, his heart lifted and soared with the gulls riding the currents of air in the wake of their ship.

"To think I'll sleep in my own bed again tonight." Seric raised his hand to shield his eyes from the glare of the sun as he tried to make out the road leading to his house, just out of sight, beyond a low hill. A small boat nudged Galingale's stern as he spoke; messages to and from shore were exchanged over the deck railing.

Fabiom sighed. "It will take me three days to get home from here."

"Three days! You'd have to travel fast to manage that!"

"Believe me – I intend to."

"As it happens, you're both wrong," Philon told them, clapping each on a shoulder. "It will be four days before you see your hold-house, Fabiom, and your beloved wife of course. And you, Seric, are not going home today. That pleasure will have to wait until tomorrow."

"What?" Fabiom scowled in a rare show of anger, whilst Seric meekly asked: "Why, what's happening?"

"An 'invitation' was just delivered, for us all to attend Princess Jaymna's birth anniversary celebrations. You can see her villa from here." Philon pointed to a barely discernible pale shape high in the hills overlooking the bay where they were making landing preparations.

"I was not aware that joining the prince's service included the necessity of obeying the whims of his many relations," Fabiom muttered.

"Not all of them, no. But his sister is married to his chief advisor and wealthiest subject. An exception is *always* made for her."

"She's spoilt?" Fabiom suggested, frowning. The reminder of Jaymna and Norgest's marriage brought back uneasy memories.

"Utterly. *Her every* whim must be satisfied. It's probably written somewhere."

"In blood, by the sounds of things."

"Hush!" Seric glanced around. Fortunately, Fabiom's caustic comment had not been overheard. "I've met her," he said quietly. "I live nearby, and would like to continue to do so. It's no joke, Fabiom. She's a very powerful woman. Southernport is her own holding."

"I've met her, too," Fabiom remembered. "I must have been, oh, twelve, thirteen maybe. She came to Deepvale with Davin, her first husband. They stayed with us – Lord Davin and my father were friends." The memory was vague, but he remembered it was about the time things started to fall apart at home.

"Excellent," said Philon. "You'll be able to renew your acquaintance. And, as long as you are on your very best behaviour, you'll be off home before you know it."

Fabiom ran chapped hands through battle-cropped hair and groaned. "I'll come and I'll be tactful," he promised. "What's one more day?"

To stand with both feet upon Morene's soil was a splendid sensation. To see trees, vital, majestic trees – it was impossible to feel anything but light-hearted at that moment.

"Come on, lads, we've a party to go to," Philon urged.

They made their way up through the lively port town to the pale villa. As the road climbed, cabbage trees and date palms gave way to olives and figs, and the scent of flowering myrtle filled the air. On both sides of the final stretch, almond groves lined the road, their fuzzy fruits beginning to darken and split, revealing the sweet nuts within. Fabiom touched the trunk of every tree he walked close to. He was not alone in doing so.

Even before they entered under the high stone archway, they could see that the gardens of the royal villa were extraordinary. Laid out in goemetric patterns, with narrow canals dividing them and bridges linking each area to the next, their absolute orderliness and neatness was their most noticeable feature. A dozen or more gardeners toiled there, despite the heat, but rushed out of sight with the arrival of *Galingale's* contingent.

"We surprised them. We must be early," Philon said with a chuckle.

Belinda Mellor

A gong sounded from nearby and within moments they were surrounded by a flock of brightly dressed hand-maidens and led into the villa. They barely had a chance to take in the bronze statuary that filled the portico, and the marble friezes in the heart room beyond, before they were invited to wash in vast, ornate baths; a luxury they were all keen to accept. Afterwards they were given rich robes to wear. All the while they were being greeted as heroes, their praises sung, their comfort promised. Nothing could have been in greater contrast to the last half-year.

There were singers and instrumentalists and flamboyant dancers for their entertainment, and wines and rich foods for their indulgence. Seric had recovered completely from his initial disappointment at not going directly to his home and was mingling with the crowd, a young woman on each arm, renewing old acquaintances as he went. Philon, even further from home than Fabiom, was unconcerned. His philosophy was never to waste an opportunity and he was determined to enjoy himself, no matter what.

Fabiom decided Philon was right. He would have liked to be on his way home; as that was impossible, he would make the most of what was offered. At least he was in his own country.

The gathering had been complete for some time before the hostess made her appearance. Jaymna swept into the banqueting room like some fantastic, rainbow-hued bird: a gown of feathers and multicoloured silk trailing out behind her, her copper-bright hair, entwined with strands of pearls, in a braid over her left shoulder, almost to her waist. Silence fell for a moment and then the assembled guests applauded loudly. She bestowed a radiant smile and held out her arms in welcome.

Seric had managed to find Fabiom in the melee and together they observed the royal entrance.

"Isn't she lovely?" Seric whispered.

Fabiom watched the shimmering woman moving among her guests, bequeathing a smile here, a touch there. She looked younger than her thirty-one years.

Silvana

"Lovely? No," he replied after some consideration. "But she *is* very pretty."

"Lord Fabiom."

"Princess Jaymna." His voice betrayed his surprise. She could hardly have recognised him from the time when she came to Deepvale's house, ten years before. Trails of pink feathers and the scent of jasmine blossoms wafted about his face as he inclined his head towards her.

"My brother has spoken very highly of you. I've been looking forward to meeting you." Her gaze held his as she spoke.

"I am flattered. You have a charming home. Thank you for the invitation."

"You are most welcome." She smiled as she took his arm and guided him towards a long-table groaning under the weight of the delicacies piled upon it. "You must eat. You must enjoy yourself," she insisted. "So long away from Morene, this is the least I can offer you, Fabiom."

He took some candied fruit to please her and his curiosity made him inquire, "How did you know me, among so many guests?"

"I asked," she said. "Ravik goes on and on about that last trip you made to Varlass. How much he enjoyed your company, how you wooed the Varlassians with peerless silks so that they allowed you both into their most hallowed sky-chamber to view the rising of the Dream-Star. How you so impressed other visiting dignitaries that we now have trade links with, where is it? Malandel? Yes? I should remember that name. A country which apparently is huge and fabulously rich. And how you pressed his suit with some pretty little Varlassian princess. After such tales, of course I wanted to meet you for myself." She sounded petulant and he was instantly wary.

"I am sorry if you have been bored by the retelling of our exploits," he ventured. Apart from himself, the prince's other travelling companions had been much older counsellors and it was true that Ravik and he had made the most of the time on board ship and their stay in Varlass. He could not

254

Belinda Mellor

deny that. Though it had been the gift of three pieces of unflawed amber, linked with bronze to form an exquisite neckband, that had particularly moved Fwailan, the Varlassian astronomer-king.

"Not bored!" she insisted, a flicker of irritation giving way to an apologetic smile. "Merely put out that I was not included." She rested one hand lightly on his chest. "That would have been fun, don't you think, Fabiom?"

He was immediately very glad she had not come, though he knew that would be the wrong thing to say.

"I am sure you would have enjoyed the journey," he said instead.

"Oh I would have, believe me, especially as Norgest *hates* ships. He only travels when he absolutely has to. *He* wouldn't have come –"

Lord Norgest of Riverplain – most influential holder of Morene, even before he married his cousin's widow, the elder sister of Prince Ravik. His wife sounded less than devoted.

"Lord Norgest is well, I trust," Fabiom said casually. She shrugged, feathers fluttering around her shoulders with the movement.

"Last time I saw him he was well enough. He's always off somewhere. Ravik sees to that for me."

Her eyes dared him to believe her and he allowed himself a slight smile which he hoped was the right response. He recalled that Norgest had been leaving for Malandel to finalise those proposed trade agreements at the same time that he himself was setting off for Gerik. He also recalled hearing that Jaymna had given birth to her second daughter just previous to then, so she would not have been able to accompany Norgest either.

She let go of his arm and bade him mingle, promising to introduce him to other 'special' guests later, instructed him not to leave. Fabiom was relieved when she moved away to exchange pleasantries with another favoured visitor. He felt weary. The day had already been too long and the journey across the Straits had unsettled him. If she had not made him promise to stay he might have made his exit then.

"You seem to have made a good impression," Philon observed, making no excuse for having watched the exchange with interest. "I tell you, you wouldn't have done so a few years back, when I first met you – you were a scrawny lad, weren't you? All arms and legs. I was amazed you could even pull a bow string. You're already twice the man you were back then." He gave Fabiom a playful and non-too-gentle punch on his upper arm.

"How much wine have you had?"

"Plenty. Not enough. A bit of muscle isn't enough though. I reckon it must be those blue eyes of yours, and those thick, dark curls of course. What's left of them. I'm told certain women find such features irresistible."

Fabiom made a dismissive gesture and helped himself to another drink.

"Don't be so modest. I understand her Highness is very particular about the company she keeps."

Fabiom looked around the vast crowd gathered to celebrate the royal birth anniversary.

"I wouldn't have said so."

"Not general company, specific company," Philon leered. "You know what I mean."

Fabiom was only too afraid that he did, but he shook his head emphatically.

"All a figment of your overworked imagination. The princess is a married woman, I am a married man and, as we are not married to each other, our *relationship* will go no further than a casual talk in a public place."

"Provided Jaymna is happy with that arrangement," Philon reminded him. "Constancy may be your trait, I hear it's not hers."

"That, then, is her problem," Fabiom said firmly.

Philon regarded him for a long moment, uncertain whether to take him seriously.

"You mean it, don't you?" he said at last. "You really would reject her. You walk very dangerous paths, my friend."

The musicians were grinding out some loud, discordant sound. The air in the room was growing stale.

Belinda Mellor

"Ridiculous talk!" Fabiom replied with some asperity, wishing he was anywhere except where he was. This was not how he had envisioned spending his first night back in Morene. "She's not interested in me."

Shortly after midnight, he discovered exactly how mistaken he had been. Summoned to a private chamber, he stood transfixed as the princess emerged in a flimsy dressing-robe of lavender gauze that left few of her charms to the imagination.

"Your Highness, there must be some mistake."

"I don't make mistakes, Fabiom."

"You do. You have," he stammered, retreating toward the door. "I can't … won't … I'm married."

"Really? And your wife – is she here?"

"No – "

"So she need never know."

"I'd know! I'll not betray my vows – or my lady. I must go."

"Go! How dare you? How *dare* you?"

He ducked as a large ceramic bowl shattered into a myriad of glistening shards against the wall behind him.

"Your Highness, I do not mean to offend you," he said, backing away.

"No one … no one … dares! Who do you think you are?" She was not so pretty with her face contorted in rage.

"Madame, I'm sorry. Please, I must leave now. Let me go home. I cannot stay with you."

"You will pay for this insult," she hissed. "I will make you pay. Don't think that your acquaintance with my brother will help you."

"I must go," Fabiom repeated, not trusting himself to say anything else.

"Go then," she spat.

With a slight bow, he turned towards the door of the ornate chamber.

Unexpectedly Jaymna laughed. "She's probably tired of waiting for you by now, this precious wife of yours. She might not even be home when you hurry in like some love-sick boy." Her voice was relaxed, casual, as she adjusted the robe, by now in danger of slipping completely from one perfumed shoulder.

"She will be there," Fabiom said, with no more emotion, "of that I can be certain."

Jaymna's eyes narrowed dangerously. "You think your wife better than I. Is that what you are saying? Another insult, Fabiom?"

"It was not intended so, Highness," he said wearily. "May I go?"

"You inherited much of your father's look. He was a very handsome man too. You have that in full measure; it's just a pity you didn't inherit the same good judgement as he, or taste, for that matter."

Her words made no sense, not unless.... He pushed that thought aside. "May I go?" he repeated.

"For now." She turned away, surveying her reflection in her mirror, tidying a strand of bright hair that had fallen free of its pearl bonds.

He left before she could change her mind, berating himself for a naive fool.

Seric was across the banqueting room, conversing amiably with a group of young men. Philon was lost somewhere in the throng. Fabiom decided against pushing through to take his leave of them. Instead he asked Philon's lieutenant, who was standing nearby, to extend his apologies to his friends. Ralfus went off to do his bidding, after a look that suggested he too would like to be away. Fabiom did not wait to see the message delivered, instead he slipped out of a side entrance and across a courtyard, breathing in the fresh night air with relief.

He persuaded the gatekeeper to give him a lantern and retraced the winding path down to the harbour, to collect his belongings from the berthed ship. If the watch officer was surprised to see him at that hour he made no comment on it, merely asking if the party had been a success, to which Fabiom replied that if the number of guests and the level of noise

Belinda Mellor

were any indication he was sure it had been. The watch officer chuckled, bade him good night and a safe journey, and Fabiom was on his way.

In the morning he would no doubt get a lift on a merchant cart travelling the well-used trade roads that connected all the holdings of Morene. For now he would walk, putting some distance between himself and Southernport, striding out towards his own home. Away to the east, the first roseate tinge of dawn coloured the horizon.

Chapter Five

Casandrina met him at the standing stone marking the point where Alderbridge became Deepvale, far further from her tree than he had ever known her to travel. The scent of new grass, leaf buds and blossoms surrounded him and the sound of laughter like a stream babbled in his ears, but in his arms, unmistakably, was a real woman.

"I missed you so much, Casi," he said as he buried his face in her hair.

Eventually she freed herself from his embrace and took his hand.

"Come on to Watersmeet," she urged. "Calbrin drove me that far and is waiting for us there with the donkey cart. And tell me of your travels as we walk. Or would you rather hear tell of your holding and the wildwood since you have been away?"

He saw in her eyes the glimmer of starlight on secret glades deep in the heart of the woods; heard, in the lilt of her voice, the sweep of warm winds through leafy branches.

"Tell me your tales, Casi. There'll be time enough to remember where I've been for the past half year." He hoisted his pack onto the back of his

260

Belinda Mellor

white donkey, whom Casandrina had brought along. "Anyway, I would rather hear the sound of your voice than my own," he added as, arm around her waist, they started along the road to Watersmeet, with Wish the donkey ambling along behind without being led.

To their right, the shallow waters of the Swan tributary glinted beneath the hanging branches of alders and willows. To their left, the steep vineyard terraces carried the promise of a fine harvest. Overhead, swallows darted after midges, their high pitched voices filling the air with the excitement of the chase. Fabiom saw and heard none of these things, caught up as he was in her magical telling of the seasons of the trees and the Silvanii. The dismal plains of Gerik suddenly seemed a long way away.

It was nearing midday when Calbrin turned in through the gates leading to the hold-house. At once they were surrounded by woodmaids and Fabiom was festooned with garlands of flowers. In a kaleidoscope of multi-hued silks, the woodmaids danced a complicated measure around the donkey cart as, slowly, Wish made her way up the hill to the house. So eager were the woodmaids to greet him that he was almost lifted from the cart. Usually only three or four stayed around the house at any time, though those few might change from day to day. Now, from the mass of hair in every shade of brown, and cavorting limbs from palest cream to richest red, it appeared that every woodmaid whose tree grew near Casandrina's had come from the grove to be near him on this special occasion. To Fabiom, caught up in their dance, it certainly seemed so.

"Welcome home, Lord Fabiom!" Ramus said with obvious relief as they came up to the door.

Casandrina shooed the woodmaids around to the garden, to let Fabiom enter the house alone. The doors were open and he went through to the heart room – savouring the moment of coming home. Standing by the basin, he made himself pause and draw a deep breath to compose his thoughts and relax before washing. All four sets of double doors leading from the heart room were wide open, and, starting at the East, facing the day room, he turned slowly sunwise, ending by facing the front of the house where he had entered. Having been away for so long, and given where he had been and everything that had occurred, he was not content to merely rinse his hands.

"That bad?" Ramus enquired, handing him a towel.

"Worse," Fabiom answered with a grimace.

Water was still dripping from his arms and hair and he towelled himself absently as through the open doors he noticed how the woodmaids had decorated every room of the house with sprigs from their own trees: holly and whitethorn, hazel and blackthorn, rowan and cherry.

"Now you are truly home," Casandrina said as she came into the heart room from the courtyard. She regarded him mischievously. "I am sure you have brought me presents."

"I might have done."

"You always bring me lovely things, and this time I have a gift for you." She held out her hand and he went to her.

"What gift?" he asked as she led him across the courtyard.

"Something I think you will like," she replied.

To his surprise, she pushed open the door of the bathing room. He could see nothing amiss though he heard muted giggling, a telltale sign that some of the woodmaids were nearby, and waiting for his reaction to whatever was in store for him.

"Close your eyes," Casandrina instructed. He did as he was bidden, hearing a door open as he did so and what sounded like a dressing screen being moved out of the way. "Walk forwards now."

He would have opened his eyes then but her hands were over them so he complied, though tentatively, expecting to come to the far wall at any

Belinda Mellor

moment. Suddenly he was stepping onto a differently textured floor, a floor he did not recognise. He reached up to his face to take her hands from his eyes and found himself looking at a new room that had not been there before. A room with two sunken swimming baths, one of them gently steaming.

"Casandrina!" He whispered her name in amazement.

"Is this the luxury you enjoyed so much in Fairwater?" she asked, standing behind him still, though her hands rested on his shoulders now.

"Luxury indeed." Fabiom shook his head in disbelief. He reached across his chest to take her hand and lead her round to face him.

"Tarison helped me. He too remembers the swimming baths in Fairwater with pleasure," she explained, her eyes shining at his obvious delight in her gift. "And I invited Gwillon to come and build the frame for the room – he is a master carpenter now."

"You parted with more amber for this, didn't you?"

"It was a fair exchange, if it pleases you."

"It pleases me very much." He kissed her. "And being with you pleases me even more."

Escorted by singing, laughing woodmaids, Fabiom wandered from room to room, admiring the floral decorations and enjoying the feeling of *home*. In the day room, he scooped a sleepy owlet off his favourite couch, and stretched out with a contented sigh.

"We are going to have a party!" Lan'h exclaimed, moving the baby bird from the floor cushion to a perch above the hearth.

Fabiom looked at her askance.

"It was Zin'h's idea," she added.

"It would be." He had been looking forward to an afternoon alone with Casandrina and a long, relaxing soak in his new baths, not another party.

"Not a *party*," Zin'h corrected, coming into the room with a jug of morat and some goblets and hearing the end of the conversation. "More of a *gathering*, just people you like, or used to like before you went away."

"In that case, it will be nothing like the last party I attended," Fabiom chuckled. "Thank you, Zin'h," he added, not wanting her to think him ungrateful.

She smiled as she put down the jug and tripped out of the room again, singing.

"Your mother would not come," Lan'h told him sadly. "Casandrina asked her to." She touched his hand. "You should go and see her tomorrow."

"Yes, I will. Don't worry, Lan'h. I didn't expect things to have changed that much." Thoughts of his mother made Jaymna's parting words come back to him. He wanted to believe she was lying, yet it made some sort of horrible sense: that was the summer the fights began, and the deathly silences.

"Tarison and Marid will be here though," the woodmaid said more cheerfully, breaking into his thoughts. "And Yan, and the new baby. Tarison was silly to think they could not have another child. They should have spoken to Casandrina before. I like babies. It will be nice when we have our own baby here." With that she skipped out of the room to help with the preparations.

"What had Casandrina to do with Tarison and Marid having a baby?" he asked, but she was already gone.

Fabiom and Casandrina took advantage of the time it took for word to get around that he was home. She sang to him softly, enticingly, as hand in hand they traversed summer-decked pathways to her grove and Fabiom rejoiced as all his senses responded to the vitality of the wildwood and to her closeness. Undisturbed, they lay together in the grove until the day slipped into dusk. Warm breezes whispered endearments amid the grey-green foliage which moved above them in gentle rhythms. Love and dancing leaves. Fabiom knew for certain that he had come home. Very gently he brushed stray strands of hair from Casandrina's face and kissed her eyes and lips and could not bring himself to tell her about Princess Jaymna's birth anniversary celebrations.

He regretted not seeing the spring, the soft flowering of the ash, the months when Casandrina, like her tree, dressed in pale mauves and sang of beginnings. But he was glad that he could at least share the remainder of the summer with her, listen to her songs of fulfillment and being, watch the ripening of the tree and the gilding of its boughs as the seedpods swelled and quickened.

"So, Tarison and Marid have a new baby at last," he murmured sleepily.

"Yes, a beautiful daughter."

A red and black butterfly briefly alighted on her shoulder then spiralled up through a beam of sunlight into the crown of the tree. They watched it go.

"I thought there was a problem after Yan was born. Marid lost several babies long before their time...."

"You think that the art of making fine fabric from moth cocoons is the only knowledge the Silvanii possess?" she challenged lightly, sitting up and tossing her flimsy gold stole over his face. He pushed the soft silk aside, his eyes laughing, belying his otherwise serious expression.

"No, I would never presume to guess the depths of your wisdom, my sweet."

"That is good, and wise also," she replied equally seriously, equally betrayed by the glimmer of laughter in her eyes. "There are plants with properties mankind hardly begins to understand, and songs with power beyond telling. And there are times for everything, for planting, for growing, for ripening, for resting. These are the things we know best." She bent her head and kissed him, her hair falling soft around his face. "Among the things we know best," she amended indistinctly.

The gathering Zin'h had arranged turned out to be a success. Just a small group of close friends and family invited to celebrate his safe return. Much of the evening was passed in the new bathing extension, with everyone revelling in the waters or resting on the towel-draped couches set out around the baths.

Tarison and Marid introduced Fabiom to their new baby daughter, so long hoped for and almost despaired of. Tarison was still in a state of delighted incredulity and told Fabiom as much. Marid and Casandrina exchanged knowing looks.

"Her name's Kita," Yan said as Fabiom bent over the cradle and tenderly stroked the baby's brow. Yan had quite grown since Fabiom had last seen him and he had changed in other ways, having become quiet and somewhat pensive. His mood seemed to have little to do with the arrival of his infant sister, whom he gazed upon with undisguised adoration.

Kita was not the only newcomer at the house that evening. Nalio and Eifa, his childhood sweetheart, were there with their eight-month-old son, Nissus, whom Fabiom had also met for the first time that evening.

"Only another twelve years and it will be your turn," quipped Nalio.

"I can wait," Fabiom replied easily. "After all, there are proper times and right seasons for everything."

Across the cradle, Casandrina smiled.

There was so much news to catch up on, so much to talk about, that the events of four nights ago went, briefly, out of Fabiom's mind. However, late in the evening when he was conversing with his old tutor and no one else was within hearing, on an impulse Fabiom vouchsafed the episode of Jaymna's party. Masgor was worried by the tale. He knew the princess only by reputation and what he had heard did not lead him to believe the matter would be either forgotten or forgiven.

"What could I do?" Fabiom groaned when Masgor expressed his concern.

"Nothing, other than what you did. Offending even the princess is a small matter compared with betraying the trust of a Silvana."

That was certain, Fabiom knew; though fear of Casandrina's wrath had little to do with his refusal to be untrue to her. Since the eve of his seventeenth birth anniversary she had been the pivot of his life. He would no sooner betray her than himself.

Belinda Mellor

As they had hoped, there had been no further developments in the situation between Deepvale and Windwood. Herbis had far more immediate problems on his hands that summer, for the unseasonable weather that had swept Gerik while Fabiom was camped there had come also to Morene's west coast, devastating much of Windwood's vulnerable soft-fruit crop.

Deepvale, along with the other eastern holdings, had suffered none of the adverse weather that had beset the western regions. There had been just enough sun, just enough rain and the spring floods, that yearly burst the banks of the River Minnow on its journey from Greendell to Minnowlake, had covered the north-west plains of the holding in rich alluvium. At his homecoming party, Fabiom and his guests had sampled the wines of the previous year and pronounced them the best in memory, and the silk harvests were as good as they had ever been in recorded history.

Fabiom recalled Herbis's interest in silk production and, though it was that interest that had led to Giar's predicament, he took the risk of dispatching two hundred mulberry seedlings – not as a personal gift from himself to Herbis, rather as a gesture of solidarity in the face of grim weather – from one holding to another.

Tarison approved that decision. There had been no official communication between the two holdings since Fabiom had begun his service but Marid and Riann corresponded with each other and, from what Marid could glean from her sister's letters, they had come to terms with Giar's condition. Riann had even visited once, shortly after baby Kita was born, and she had brought some good news of her own: Dala was soon to be married to an Assembly elder's son, Lambrose. Fabiom was glad at the news, glad too that he could put the matter of Giar behind him for the foreseeable future.

Tarison had looked after the holding and his nephew's business interests most ably in the interim. Nevertheless, as he had expected,

Fabiom had plenty of catching up to do on his return. He was busy and he was contented.

So it was that the matter of Jaymna's party slipped further and further back in his mind, until he arrived home from the municipal court one afternoon near summer's end and found his erstwhile service companions, Philon and Seric, awaiting him in the inner courtyard. Casandrina was nowhere to be seen, neither were any of her woodmaids. The two men had beakers of wine, there were dishes of sweetmeats and dried fruits on the low table and, across the courtyard, the door to the wash room was open. Ramus was obviously in attendance.

"Gentlemen," Fabiom said warmly.

As they rose to greet him, Philon shook his head, his expression grim. "Don't say I didn't warn you."

Fabiom looked from one to the other. "You are not Jaymna's errand boys, surely?"

"No, they'll be here tomorrow," Seric said. "We thought you had better be forewarned."

Ramus returned with a basket of bread. Fabiom told him that his guests would be staying overnight. "Unless you would rather be gone when the storm breaks?"

"I've no intention of going anywhere," Philon said firmly. "You need friends around you right now!"

Fabiom suspected that the Strategos was secretly enjoying himself.

"When do we meet your lady wife?" Seric asked, glancing about. "I do hope she's worth all this."

"Soon; and yes, she is," Fabiom replied.

That evening, Casandrina relaxed, curled up on a large cushion, her hair unbraided, her robe unadorned, her feet bare. She ate grapes and listened to her husband talking with his two friends. After a while she took her leave of them, promising Fabiom that she would not be gone long. She slipped

Belinda Mellor

out of the open garden door and ran across the damp lawn, towards the distant woods.

"All right, you win," Philon conceded. "I, too, would die for her."

"I have no intention of dying just yet, even for Casandrina," Fabiom assured him.

Seric grunted scornfully at that. "I doubt your intentions are uppermost in Jaymna's mind right now."

"Thank you for your reassurance," Fabiom said, helping them all to more wine.

Philon was studying the remains of the meal. Without Casandrina there to distract him, he was able to see what an odd assortment of food they had been served.

"An interesting repast. I don't think I've ever eaten wild strawberries with garlic before," he remarked.

"What did Casandrina say when you told her about Jaymna's, er, *suggestion*?" Seric asked.

Philon shook his head. "He hasn't told her. You haven't, have you? I can see it in your face."

"No. I haven't. And don't say I should have. I know I should have! If going to Jaymna's room was a mistake, not telling Casandrina was a far bigger one. And yet – how could I tell her and risk her not believing me?"

Philon chuckled. "Glad I never married."

"So you've said."

Jaymna's emissaries arrived around midday, while Casandrina was away tending a new crop of mulberry seedlings. Fabiom was relieved. It had not been necessary to justify Philon and Seric's presence. They were friends, and friends were forever calling by. However, the advent of Jaymna's couriers would need some explanation, unless they could be dealt with before her return. It was a hope he had very little faith in.

As soon as the three men came up to the house, Ramus ushered them into the heart room, where Fabiom waited to greet them. One, thin and slightly balding, Fabiom recognised as the man who had summoned him to the princess's private apartment on the night of the party, a fact that did nothing to ease his apprehension.

They barely acknowledged his presence before washing their hands with great precision and care. That done, they turned to face and bow deeply towards the four doorways in turn, all closed now, including the way they had come in. Fabiom stood watching them, arms folded across his chest, wondering if he was meant to be impressed or intimidated by the performance. Eventually they were done.

The thin, balding man squared his shoulders. "Lord Fabiom. I am Wrill of Southernport. My companions are Targin and Faldor, both of Riverplain, of the household of the Princess Jaymna and the Lord Norgest. We bring you … *greetings*, from her Highness."

"Please be seated, all of you. You have travelled far. You must be weary. May I offer you refreshments?" He directed his comments towards Wrill, who was obviously senior among the three emissaries.

Wrill seemed taken aback at Fabiom's convivial tone. "I have a missive from her Highness," he said quietly.

"As I expected."

Fabiom indicated towards the west wall where Ramus had arranged a number of carved wooden seats around an elaborate table set with a jug of wine and a tray of goblets. The furniture was beautiful, although barely comfortable. The three sat down.

Fabiom wondered which of them was carrying Jaymna's letter. He wanted nothing more than to simply take it, go into the privacy of his study and read it, alone. He knew that was a luxury he could not afford. Every word, every reaction, would be reported back to Southernport, and it was essential he appeared as unconcerned yet as polite and hospitable as possible. As Philon had succinctly pointed out to him earlier, he was walking a very narrow bridge over a very deep ravine.

"You will excuse me for a moment. I have two companions whose advice I value. I wish them to be present when I read what you have brought me."

Although Seric had been initially reluctant to play the role, Philon had persuaded him, pointing out that having witnesses was essential. The two men were now waiting in the courtyard and Fabiom went out to tell them what had transpired thus far.

Seric sighed. "Yes, I know Wrill and no, I would not entirely trust him. But you are my friend, Fabiom. Come on, go back in, before I change my mind."

Fabiom did not sit, neither did Philon nor Seric, who stood slightly apart from Jaymna's men. Wrill and Faldor had obviously recognised Seric, though nothing had been said.

"I will see your mistress's letter now," Fabiom said tersely.

Wrill turned to Targin, who slowly and deliberately opened the leather satchel he was wearing under his cloak. He took out a cream scroll, tied with scarlet cords and sealed with gold wax. The scroll was handed first to Wrill and from him to Fabiom, who split the seal unceremoniously and scanned the words within as rapidly as he could.

Fabiom had already considered every retribution he thought Jaymna might be in a position to visit upon him. He was in no way prepared for the import of the message he did receive.

"A contest!" he choked, unbelieving. He turned to Seric and Philon, who came closer at his beckoning to read over his shoulder. "She demands that she is judged against my wife. This is preposterous!" The last sentence was directed at Wrill.

"*Over several days and in diverse ways,*" Seric read. "What does that even mean?"

"I don't understand," Philon said to Wrill. "What does your mistress hope to gain? Will she publicly admit to trying – and failing – to seduce one of her guests while her husband was absent?"

Silvana

Wrill stood and coughed, embarrassed. He moved a few paces away from his two companions.

"No," he admitted, speaking very quietly. "She will give the reason to none but a small number of most trusted confidants. No one else need know the reason behind the contest. They must think it a fancy of the princess's. She is quite adamant, though the idea was not her own. She had some, er, other plans for you. The ratification of the Gerik treaty means that a number of our people will be in that land henceforth…."

"Exile," Fabiom stated bluntly. "Then whose idea was this alternative?" Had she given Tawr a similar ultimatum, he wondered, or had his father been seduced by the beautiful young woman she must have been?

Wrill shifted his weight from one foot to the other, glancing again at his companions who contrived to look uninterested in the discussion being conducted beside them.

"I believe Prince Ravik himself first mooted the suggestion."

So, Fabiom mused, Jaymna had gone to her brother with some tale. Would she have told him the truth? Possibly she would. However, Ravik was one of the few people who knew the nature of Fabiom's marriage. Could Fabiom hope the prince had gambled on Casandrina, whom he had never met, bettering the princess simply by virtue of her being what she was? Or was the prince taking his sister's part? Jaymna must think so, but Fabiom felt that unlikely. Ravik's 'solution' surely favoured Casandrina, unless –

"How fair will this *judging* be?" he demanded. Who would dare to choose another over the vindictive princess?

"It will be fair," Wrill promised. "No one but the judges themselves know who they are; the prince himself has selected them."

"Will the prince be attending?" Seric asked.

"No, that would not be – appropriate."

"Pity. *That* would be a contest worth a wager," Philon muttered into Fabiom's ear.

Belinda Mellor

"And Lord Norgest?" Fabiom asked, ignoring the Strategos, who was enjoying this far too much.

"Her Highness's husband is currently employed in a judicial capacity in the northern holdings. He is not due to return for some while."

Fabiom sighed. He was trapped. The letter he had been handed gave a date for ten days hence and Jaymna's villa as the venue. How could he ask Casandrina to travel so far from her tree? Would she go, even if he asked? More importantly, would she ever trust him again?

"Here," he said, pushing that last thought aside. "It would have to be here."

Wrill shook his head. "I have the strictest orders regarding this matter. I'm sorry."

Fabiom asked for some time to think. He ordered food and more drink to be brought for the three men and asked Philon and Seric to wait with them.

He walked across the garden towards the river, thinking, though of nothing sensible, only wishing he had said something to Casandrina before now. He wondered how he could have been so stupid, and how he had failed to learn anything from the mess his parents' marriage had become.

On the bridge, he stood and watched the dark waters lapping at the stones below, wearing away even the hardest rock to pebbles, gravel, finally to sand. To nothing.

"I will go."

Fabiom started at the sound of Casandrina's voice. She was watching him from the far side of the bridge, her expression unreadable.

"You overheard!"

"No, Nek'h did. I will go with you. Foolish man! Why did you not tell me of this?"

"I didn't know how," he admitted. "I wanted to. No, that's not true. I knew I ought to —" He shrugged, for once at a loss for the right words.

Silvana

"But nothing happened, Casandrina. I swear to you, on all I hold dear. Nothing happened."

She came up close to him and took his hands, intertwining her fingers in his.

"Still, you should have told me."

"Told you what?" He lifted her hands to his lips and kissed them tenderly. "That I am a more fortunate man than Norgest, whose wife drinks too much and flirts with strangers at her parties?"

"Yes, even that. Or, more importantly, that you spurned a woman who has the power and authority to command us so." She frowned, puzzled. "A contest – what a strange fancy."

"I cannot ask you to go through with such a charade, Casi. And it's so far away."

Letting go of his hands she slipped her arms around his waist and rested her head on his shoulder.

"I have said I will go, and I will. We shall get through this thing. She might contrive to have you sent off to Gerik, otherwise. I would rather we took this path." She managed to imbue that one word, 'Gerik', with loathsomeness; conjuring up the abomination of forests laid waste, of Silvanii murdered. And, as easily, she dispelled the horror as she murmured, "I do not want you to go away from me again, Fabiom."

She began to sing, softly; weaving a spell he was only too happy to fall under. The river below seemed less menacing, the waters less dark and quickened with the play of sunlight. Nevertheless, not all his misgivings were banished.

"Jaymna may be even less forgiving afterwards. She would not do this if she did not feel confident."

Casandrina sang on.

Belinda Mellor

Chapter Six

Midnight had long since passed. Fabiom sat alone in his study. He was tired but could not contemplate trying to sleep. He kept reliving the audience with Jaymna – and thinking about his father.

As the eastern horizon began to pale towards dawn, it occurred to him that some small good might come of the mess he had created for himself.

In the morning, he took Philon and Seric to meet Masgor, swearing his erstwhile tutor to secrecy. He left his visitors to explore the town in Masgor's company, and took the river-barge to Valehead, an hour away.

The house was quiet when he went in. He listened for a moment, until he heard a muted sound from the family room. When he looked in, his mother was there on the floor, playing with baby Kita's toes while the infant gurgled and waved her legs in delight.

Fabiom watched, leaning against the frame of the archway into the room. "No wonder I have ticklish feet," he observed eventually.

"Fabiom! You surprised me. Tarison isn't here. Do you need him?"

"No. I came to see you."

"That's lovely, dear one, but you were here just two days ago. Is something amiss?" She looked at him properly then. "It is. Isn't it?"

"Yes." He looked around as a servant entered with clean cloths for the baby. "I need to talk to you – in private."

Leaving Kita in a nursemaid's care, they went to the roof garden.

"Is this private enough?" Vida asked as she settled herself on a couch, leaving room for Fabiom beside her. He did not take the offered seat but instead sat at her feet and rested his head against her knee.

"Fabiom. What's wrong? What's happened."

"I did something stupid. Princess Jaymna –" He felt the sudden tension in his mother's posture. "I offended her."

"How so?" she asked carefully.

"The day of our return from Gerik, she threw a party. At it, I – She invited me to spend the night with her."

Vida's hand, which had been stroking his hair, stilled. "And?"

"I refused."

"My good boy. You did the right thing."

He raised his head and looked at her. "I'm not so sure it *was* the right thing at all."

"Of course it was!"

"I rejected her. She wants to punish me."

"Punish you! How? What can she do?"

Fabiom dropped his head to her knee again. "She wants me exiled to Gerik."

"No! No! Ravik would not countenance that. You did nothing wrong."

"She only has to say I did! I have to go back to Southernport."

"Whatever for? To try to persuade her? Surely not?"

"No." He sighed and sat back on his heels. "She has devised a contest. Casandrina has to come with me and 'prove herself'. I don't know how exactly. Apparently there are various tests."

"Tests! That's ridiculous!"

"Mama – the whole thing is ridiculous. But, I have no choice. And

Belinda Mellor

I'm so afraid that, whatever happens, it will not be the end of the matter."

Tears were forming in Vida's eyes. "You will not go alone?"

"Masgor will accompany us. I need one of the holding's elders with me, just in case. I trust him totally."

"Good. That's good."

"I should have let her have her way. One night! Would it have been so bad – to save so much grief and hurt?"

She looked away from him and wiped her eyes. "You did what you thought was right. That's what matters. Perhaps…. Perhaps there are times when there are no easy choices; people will get hurt whatever you decide."

A distant gong sounded. The barge was getting ready to make the return journey.

Fabiom got to his feet. "I need to be on that. I must go. I wanted you to know; someone had to know. But please, don't say anything unless –"

"I won't, Fabiom, I promise." She embraced him fiercely.

As he made his way down the stairs, her voice called after him, "Be safe, my sweet boy." And he heard her sobbing.

Fabiom and Casandrina travelled by donkey-cart from Deepvale to Southernport with four woodmaids. With them were Philon, Seric and Masgor. The journey took four days, a day longer than it had taken Fabiom travelling alone.

Casandrina would not stay in the public hostelries along the way, so at night they made camp: in the familiar woods of Deepvale; in the rain on the heather-strewn moors of Alderbridge, where the beekeepers keep their hives during the flowering season; in the rocky hills between Fairwater and Riverplain, where the bilberries were just ripening and the wild goats fought; and finally on the rolling hills of Southernport, from

Silvana

where they could see the creamy-white buildings of the harbour town away in the distance.

Once inside the town walls, they parted company. Philon and Seric headed to Seric's homeplace while Fabiom, Casandrina, Masgor and the woodmaids went on up to Jaymna's house. There they were met by one of her ladies and given a choice of staying in the villa itself or in a small lodge within its confines. Fabiom and Casandrina chose the lodge, which consisted of just two highly decorated rooms and a verandah overlooking an ornate water garden.

Until they were alone, Casandrina said nothing and kept her visage hidden within the cowl of her deep grey cloak. It had been Masgor's suggestion, and they had agreed, that it would be best if she was not seen by anyone until the formal gathering. There could be no telling who might be reporting back to the princess.

While Fabiom was politely but firmly rejecting the offer of servants, Casandrina wandered out onto the verandah. In the garden, a maze of bridges and footpaths – overarced by ornate pergolas smothered in white jasmine and pale gold hibiscus – connected the fountains and lily ponds. Across a sea of pink and green lilies, the wall of Jaymna's house rose stark and tall. Casandrina paid the view scant heed. In Deepvale the rain that had been falling for the past two days had stopped; now the wind was blowing, drying the autumn fruits of field and wood and stripping the leaves from her tree. She could barely feel it.

Masgor left them as soon as he had seen them settled. He had elected to accept the alternative accommodation that had been offered. Indeed, there was little enough room in the lodge as it was; still, the presence of the woodmaids was welcome and their singing and unabated high spirits kept Fabiom from brooding.

Casandrina eventually ceased her appraisal of the view and came into the main room. "Jaymna has a truly magnificent garden," she said unexpectedly as she threw her cape down onto the azure deerskin seat of a three-legged, filigreed bronze stool.

At her words, two of the woodmaids burst into fits of giggles. Fabiom was immediately on the alert.

"Please don't antagonise her further. I just want this over, so we can all go home – and stay there."

"What do you think I would do?" she asked as she took a golden lily from a vase and began to strip every petal from it.

"Exactly what you are doing right now, perhaps?"

She let the last petal fall to the floor and sighed. "Very well, my beloved. I make you a promise – I shall kill nothing in the princess's garden. Not one single plant shall wither while we are here, nor after we are gone; not even those which are failing now. Are you satisfied?"

He might have said yes, had he not seen the expression on Nek'h's face.

Having destroyed each of the lilies in turn, and with nothing left to distract her save the frescoes that adorned the walls: palms and citrus fruits – none native to Morene – at which she gazed listlessly for a while, Casandrina began to pace up and down within the confines of the room.

Fabiom watched her until he could bear it no more. Leaning back on the soft, wide couch, which doubled as a bed and took up a good proportion of the small room, he held his arms out to her.

"Just a few days, Casi," he said solicitously as she nestled into his arms. "I'm so sorry to have got you into this," he added, stroking her hair.

"As the only way out would have been for you to indulge her desire, I am not at all sorry," she retorted.

He laughed shortly. "You have a point."

From the second, smaller room the sound of merriment reached their ears. "They seem little concerned anyway," Fabiom observed.

"Casandrina! Zin'h has an idea. It is wonderful," Kir'h announced.

Fabiom groaned.

"Really, Fabiom, it is a good idea," Zin'h assured him. She was of a whitethorn tree, delicate and innocent looking, and forever coming up with outrageous schemes.

Silvana

Casandrina sat up. "Tell us."

"First, Fabiom must answer a question. Am I prettier than this Princess Jaymna?"

Though Casandrina's attendants looked very young, none of them more than fifteen, they were all quite beautiful, and Zin'h was undoubtedly the most attractive, as she well knew. Fabiom smiled at the question and called an image of the princess to mind, though he tended to remember her in her fury and that was not the face she would be judged on tonight.

"Yes," he said. "You are prettier than she."

A feast and a gathering, almost as large as the fateful event which had brought Fabiom to this pass, had been arranged for that night. No one would know who among the many guests were the judges Ravik had appointed. Even they would not know who their fellows were. Indeed, most of the other guests were unaware that a contest was in progress. Jaymna threw too many parties, with little or no reason, for anyone to question the purpose of this one.

For much of the afternoon they could hear the muted sounds of guests arriving, on foot, by donkey and goat carts, and in litters borne by beasts and men. They saw little, apart from distant figures of the few people who wandered into the water gardens. Time passed slowly. Eventually a very young page arrived, breathless and flustered, to announce that the banquet would begin shortly and their presence was requested. As soon as his message was delivered he ran off again, towards the house and his next task.

Fabiom's jaw tightened. "So, it's time to play her games."

Dressed well, though not ostentatiously, Fabiom entered the hall alone. Guests were seated in groups of about ten, around low, square tables, and positioned so that they each had some sort of view of the dais that ran part way along the length of the hall and where a group of musicians were playing an assortment of rousing tunes that relied heavily on tambourines

Belinda Mellor

and cymbals. Close by the dais, and somewhat to one side, were a number of couches, some already occupied by elderly or particularly distinguished guests. One, ornate and draped with heavily embroidered silks, stood slightly apart and vacant, presumably for Jaymna herself.

As Holder of Deepvale, Fabiom was offered a couch. He refused, preferring the slight anonymity afforded by mingling with the other guests who lounged on bright floor cushions, waiting for their hostess to make an appearance. Fabiom suspected that making an appearance was something Jaymna would be very good at. Having declined the couch, he was shown to a central area with many empty places around him. Music played, bright, lively music that contrasted with his mood and jarred on his nerves. The thought of the meal to come unsettled him even more. Even the cornucopias, the woven reed horns overflowing with fresh fruit, within easy reach of everyone, were too much for him to contemplate. He wished he had been seated in a less conspicuous spot, somewhere near the periphery of the hall, from where he could observe yet not be observed. Though wherever he had been seated there would be little chance of that, he realised. Just then two servants began setting lighted tapers to a multitude of candle sconces hung on the walls and columns, to impart further brilliance to a room already illuminated by numerous oil-filled lamps suspended from the frescoed ceiling.

Anxious for any diversion to distract himself from the events to come, Fabiom studied the images depicted over his head until his neck ached, then turned his attention to the niches and alcoves which lined the walls, some housing exquisite marble statues and fine ornaments, others with flower vases filled with elaborate arrangements of rare blooms or tender potted plants. Meanwhile the hall filled to capacity. He felt sick.

Having been briefed beforehand about the procedure, he did not expect to be surprised by anything that transpired, so it was with some amazement that he saw Philon and Seric come into the hall and head towards him. Philon had a broad grin on his face while Seric kept glancing about nervously. They had given no indication they would be attending.

Silvana

"Don't ask!" Philon chortled as he lowered himself down onto the cushion on Fabiom's left.

"From the expression on Seric's face, I don't think I need to."

"Well, he did take some persuading," Philon allowed.

"Given the proximity of my family's abode to this house," Seric elaborated. "But Philon convinced me to come – and to get him in. I must be mad!"

Masgor arrived shortly afterwards. He had been accommodated in the villa, along with a number of other guests, and had barely settled into his room when a procession of musicians through the courtyard signalled to all house-guests that it was time to make their way to the hall to join the rest of the assembly.

The stream of guests being welcomed into the banqueting area had slowed to a trickle. Those who came in late, hurried to find a place for themselves, talking and laughing excitedly. As far as the other guests knew, they were waiting only for their hostess, they could not know that she was waiting for word that Casandrina had arrived before she would make her own entrance.

Whispers ran excitedly through the gathering and all heads turned towards the top of the stairs. Yet it was not Jaymna who had caused the appreciative murmurs from the crowd but a stunning apparition in white who stood there, smiling gently at the faces turned towards her. She waited a moment to be certain she had made the desired impression, then glided down the four wide, curved steps and over to Fabiom's side. He reached up and took her hand as he made room for her on the velvet cushions between himself and Masgor. Philon, on his other side, shot him a puzzled glance. All around people were staring.

"You look lovely, Zin'h," Fabiom said appreciatively. Whoever the judges were, they would think so too, he was sure.

At that moment the musicians stopped playing, as if on some signal. Even as the implication registered, and heads turned once more towards

Belinda Mellor

the stairway, they burst into a new tune that heralded the arrival of the hostess. On a crescendo, Jaymna, even more flamboyant than the first time Fabiom had seen her, swept in. She was dressed in reds and oranges, flame hues that complemented her bright hair, accentuated her pale skin. Ribbons of flimsy material floated from her sleeves and she shimmered as she walked.

As she paused and smiled at Fabiom, and at the young woman at his side, he fancied a slightly disconcerted look came to her eyes, though he could not be sure. She turned away then and spoke with a smiling man, then with an elderly couple. She seemed unperturbed. However, before she could finish greeting her favoured guests and making her way to her place, another ripple of surprise swept through the assembly, fading into a moment's silence when even the musicians forgot to play as Casandrina stepped through the entrance.

She had donned a sleeveless, floor-length gown, multi-hued gold and grey, sunlight and shadow in a forest glade. At her throat, Fabiom's first anniversary gift to her, the clasp of amber set in silver, held the fabric. Her hair was loose, flowing like a cascade of sunlit water over the fine silk of her gown and the bare skin of her arms.

Fabiom had meant to watch Jaymna's expression as Casandrina made her entrance but, as usual, he had eyes only for his wife. Beside him, Philon chuckled.

Casandrina's green gaze embraced the assembly. A half-smile played about her mouth, widening as she caught sight of Fabiom. She swept down the steps, gold and grey silk furling about her legs, accentuating her graceful limbs. Fabiom watched her for a long moment, then he stood up. Philon did likewise. Casandrina slipped into the place between them. Philon was still chuckling away.

No one was looking at Jaymna, of that Fabiom was certain, unless it was to see how she was taking the fact that she had just been completely upstaged. Casandrina brushed a strand of unruly hair from her cheek and smiled at her husband. A young man, sitting opposite, sighed audibly as she did so.

"Was that satisfactory?" she inquired archly.

"Perfect," he told her. "For once, Zin'h, I must congratulate you," he added, turning to address the white-garbed woodmaid reclining on his left. "Your idea was excellent."

She smiled and bowed her head slightly, then laughed. "I thought so."

"You remember Zin'h, don't you, Philon?" Fabiom inquired.

Philon nodded and wiped his eyes. "I do indeed."

"She just wanted an excuse to come to the gathering," Casandrina said. She shook her head as a servant offered wine. "May I have some water please?" she asked.

Zin'h made the same request.

"What happens now?" Seric inquired. He was sitting on the far side of Masgor, disinclined to be amused by what had just transpired, still wondering if he really should have come.

Masgor studied his interlaced fingers for a moment before replying. "Apparently Casandrina will be 'invited' to entertain the gathering. Jaymna is reputed to be an accomplished musician and a talented dancer. She too will perform. The judges, whoever they are, will assess the performance of each."

"And, if Casandrina wins, Fabiom gets to go home – forgiven?" Seric asked derisively.

"That is the theory," Masgor replied. "If his wife can prove herself the more desirable of the two women, his refusal of the princess cannot be adjudged an insult."

Seric groaned.

"Exactly," Masgor agreed.

A sumptuous feast was served, course after course of the best the fertile and bountiful land of Morene could provide. Fabiom played with his

284   Belinda Mellor

food, wishing the whole debacle was over and done with. Casandrina ate nothing.

She rested her hand on his. "Do not worry, Fabiom," she whispered.

Yet he *was* worried.

At last the dishes and platters were cleared away and a voice called for silence. The man who stepped up onto the dais was Wrill, who had delivered Jaymna's ultimatum.

"Honoured guests – we are indeed fortunate tonight. We are to be most splendidly entertained. Some ladies present have agreed to dance for us, including her Highness, Princess Jaymna!"

Exclamations of delight greeted his announcement.

Jaymna elected to give the final act. She invited four other guests, besides Casandrina, to perform before her and, laughing self-consciously, they agreed. Casandrina was given the choice of whether she went first. She told Jaymna's master of ceremonies that she would.

Fabiom frowned. "Is that wise?" he asked her as she rose from her place.

Raising her hands, she gave a tiny shrug. "Who can say?"

Before stepping up onto the dais, she unfastened the amber clasp at her throat and let her gown drift to the floor. Under it she wore a short dress of wild silk, seemingly dyed in every shade of green that grew in the woodlands. Several strands of amber beads hung about her neck. Fabiom felt his palms grow hot, his heart beat a little faster. She was dressed as she had been on the night she had first come to him in her grove.

Zin'h left her place too. She would play for her mistress, along with the three other woodmaids, who had been waiting near the door. As the first notes of music sounded, Fabiom found himself digging his nails into the palms of his hands. Surely she did not intend to perform one of the high measures of the forest? It would certainly win the judges' approval, but it would be singularly inappropriate for the sight of, what was by now, a rather drunken rabble. His worries were unfounded. The music was evocative though not spell-binding. It was composed of the tunes they played daily around his house. He had almost learnt to take such music for granted and was surprised to see the effect it had on Jaymna's guests.

Casandrina was dancing, just. The slightest movements, yet so expressive. Fabiom felt his throat constrict. She was dancing for him alone, he could see that in her expression. She moved as the branches of her ash tree moved to the rhythms of the breeze and, as she danced, he was transported back to the nights he had spent beneath her tree, hoping she would come to him.

"I am enthralled, and ever will be, until my dying breath."

On a sudden flurry of a lively refrain, she spun off the stage, stepping lightly through astonished diners, back to Fabiom's side on the last notes of music. He caught her as she fell, laughing, into his arms.

"I quite enjoyed that." She sounded rather surprised.

He kept his arms around her as her audience, realising she was finished, burst into great applause.

Seric no longer looked as if he desired to be elsewhere, though neither he nor Philon offered any comment. They had not seen Casandrina dance before.

The four other ladies took their turns. One was older and elegant, though no longer as lithe as she once had been, another was portly and jolly, the other two were sisters, both hoping to attract the attentions of some eligible young man and consequently resentful of the impact Casandrina had made on the assembly, especially the male element. All danced well, if not spectacularly, lamplight flickering off jewels and bright fabrics.

When it came to Jaymna's turn, Fabiom began to grow uneasy again. His words, spoken to Casandrina on the bridge in their own garden, half in jest, had come back to haunt him: Jaymna would never forgive Casandrina for humiliating her.

The princess obviously had no intention of capitulating easily. Around the room, the oil lamps were turned low, some extinguished, leaving only an aura of pale illumination surrounding the stage. Jaymna stepped up into the light. She had changed her gown and had donned a creation

Belinda Mellor

of vivid purple, tight fitting and revealing. Over that she was swathed in lengths of almost transparent shell-pink gauze. Her hair was bound with amethysts and in her hands she carried two tiny candles, burning with mauve fire.

Her dancing was flawless, each step perfectly in time with the music. The light of the candle flames accentuated every slight tilt of her head as the jewels in her hair twinkled and shone. Fabiom was not moved. It was a show. Casandrina danced with the same grace with which she walked or ran or stood still. Jaymna danced as she had been taught; it was not part of her being.

Whatever Fabiom's views, the princess's confidence had evidently been restored by her performance. When she was done, she bade her guests goodnight, telling them they were expected early the next evening and that they were to enjoy themselves during the day. Those who were staying at the villa drifted towards the apartments prepared for them.

Casandrina made a hasty exit with her woodmaids, leaving Fabiom with his friends in the banqueting room.

"She must not win at everything," Masgor said urgently.

"We don't know that she has," Fabiom pointed out. "I cannot judge. I am too biased."

"So is every man in this room, since the moment Casandrina walked through the door," Seric muttered. "You are getting in deeper and deeper, Fabiom."

Philon sighed. "Could you not have explained to Jaymna? You are married to a Silvana. Even she would understand why you would not be unfaithful."

"Would she? I suspect she would not have believed me and, even if she had…. Well, my mother was not comforted by those sorts of arguments. She resented the fact that Casandrina was lovelier than she, and would not live in the house with her. The fact that Casandrina was a Silvana made no difference."

"She came around, surely?" Philon persisted.

"No, she did not. Has not done so *yet*, anyway. It's five years since she left the hold-house. She has not been back since."

"Talk to Casandrina," Masgor urged, as he rose to his feet and prepared to leave.

Fabiom frowned, then nodded. "If they are to be judged on the playing of a musical instrument, perhaps Casandrina could make less effort." He shrugged. "Just so long as they don't expect her to sing."

Masgor flinched. "She must not be asked to sing!"

Making his way back to the little house that had been lent them, Fabiom was surprised to see a number of gardeners working by torchlight. They were tending the beds alongside the pathways, and beside each was a heap of greenery he had already cut back. An overseer was urging them on, a hint of panic in his voice. Fabiom recalled Casandrina's promise and the woodmaids' amusement.

In the lodge, Casandrina refused to be drawn on the matter of the garden, but when Fabiom told her of the worries that his friends shared regarding the contest, she promised not to upset Jaymna on the morrow.

"So you will stop encouraging her garden to overgrow quite so alarmingly?" he asked, unconvinced.

"Well, perhaps none of her vines will actually grow into her chamber and strangle her in her bed," she returned.

"Were you...? No, I'm not even going to ask you that," he decided. Instead he picked up the lyre he had brought with him and played a tune for her, and made her smile.

"They have set more tests than you know, Fabiom." He had finished playing and now lay with his head in her lap, listening to the woodmaids' soft voices raised in song. Deep night had settled in the room.

"More?" he mumbled, sleepily.

Belinda Mellor

She ran gentle fingers through his hair. "As I returned here a man spoke with me, very flattering. He had a silly jewel necklace he wanted me to have in return for a little affection, he said. I do not think he came by just on chance. Neither was he intoxicated."

"And you think Jaymna might be 'tested' in that way too? She will fail, miserably, then."

"Perhaps she will be astute enough to realise. You must not underestimate her."

He sighed and closed his eyes. "Believe me, I do not."

They passed the next day quietly. Casandrina would not go out of the lodge, neither would she eat. She had eaten nothing since they had passed the borders of Deepvale into Alderbridge. Fabiom would have stayed with her but, at midday, she sent him away to find his own entertainment. As he went, he could not help but notice that the garden was running wild; trees sported buds, fruit and new leaves all out of season, while flowerbeds merged one into another, despite the efforts of the gardeners whose number had seemingly doubled since last night.

He met with Seric and some of his acquaintances and they spent part of the afternoon at archery. Fabiom had not brought a bow of his own but a borrowed juniper longbow served him well, once he got used to the pull and weight of it.

Afterwards they took some food together, though Fabiom was anxious to get back to Casandrina, and as soon as he had eaten he returned to the lodge. He found her sitting by the window, playing a simple tune on the lyre. The four woodmaids sat nearby, regarding her forlornly.

"This will serve the purpose tonight; I play it neither too well nor too poorly." She put the lyre aside and held out her hands to him. There was a dullness in her gaze that made his heart ache.

"We can go back, Casi, right now. I'll not have you suffer so." He took her hands in his, pressing them to his lips as he knelt beside her.

Silvana

289

"Hush; we cannot go," she whispered. "And there is no need for you to worry. It is just that I can hardly feel my tree from here, it is as though I barely exist."

That evening, Casandrina went in with Fabiom and was at her place long before Jaymna arrived. She attracted no less attention despite that. She had recovered from her earlier morose mood and was in fair spirits. Nevertheless, her attendant woodmaids were concerned. They had all four come to the gathering and were staying close by her.

Jaymna's appearance as she entered was startling. Her right hand was strapped tightly with material, as if she had injured herself. This evening she was supposed to play for her guests on a kithara, an instrument for which she was quite renowned and for which she needed full use of her apparently injured hand. Furthermore, she was dressed in woodland shades, with a cape of the darkest green over a gown of pale gold. Emeralds glinted in her hair and at her throat. The colours did not become her.

Casandrina observed the princess silently and for a long moment before leaning over to Fabiom and whispering, "I have seen that necklace before."

Around Jaymna's neck was a rope of twisted gold links, encrusted with jewels.

"The one you were offered?"

She smiled and raised her brows, eyes glittering with green fire. "The very same." She rested her head on his shoulder and hummed a lilting tune only he could hear.

"We are not out of this yet," he told her sternly, yet he could not help but smile.

Seric tapped Fabiom's arm. "That fellow is trying to attract your attention." He indicated a recess at the back of the hall.

The recess partially concealed a side door, from where someone was beckoning urgently. Casandrina gave him a questioning look but Fabiom

Belinda Mellor

had no more idea than she what was going on. He kissed her cheek and excused himself.

Fabiom had only just reached the recess when he was pulled aside, out of view of the dining area, by a middle-aged man he had never seen before.

"I thought you ought to know: there is a change of plan. Prince Ravik set me in charge of seeing that all fairness was adhered to, so I must tell you." The stranger looked anxiously over Fabiom's shoulder but they were unobserved.

"This has something to do with the princess's bandaged hand," Fabiom guessed.

"Precisely," his informant agreed. "In truth she is not hurt, yet that will be her excuse for not playing tonight. She will sing instead." He paused, obviously waiting for the impact of his words to sink in.

Fabiom was confused. "I'm sorry. I don't understand. Why the change?"

The other coughed uncomfortably. "One of her ladies overheard a conversation between your three companions while they were on their way to their sleeping quarters last night. Her Highness understood, from what she was told, that your wife was, how shall we say – not competent – as a singer. The princess herself is quite accomplished, you see."

Fabiom looked at him intently. There was no doubt Ravik's agent was telling the truth. "Do you know, precisely, what was overheard?" Fabiom guessed from his discomfiture that he knew exactly what was said. "I shall not be offended," he insisted.

"I gather that the oldest of the three said to the other two how it was as well there was no singing contest. That no one could bear to listen to your wife sing, save perhaps yourself."

Fabiom bit his lip to stop himself laughing aloud. Still his shoulders shook with suppressed mirth. "Indeed. Thank you for the warning," he said after he had composed himself somewhat.

He rejoined his party at their board.

"Whatever happens to me will be on your conscience," he informed Masgor, and repeated the warning he had received. He raised his hand and beckoned a steward over.

"Please give our apologies and tell your mistress that my wife will *not* be singing tonight."

"Eavesdropping is such a bad habit," Philon said sombrely once the man had gone to deliver his message. It was he who had questioned Masgor as to why he had given Fabiom strict instructions not to let Casandrina sing.

Masgor shook his head slowly. "Obviously the princess's informant either did not hear, or thought it unnecessary, to report the rest of the conversation, during which I explained my stricture."

The steward returned with a folded parchment:

I understand Gerik is not so pleasant in the winter. Or would you rather negotiate with me privately? I might yet be persuaded to forgive you.

Casandrina touched his arm. "If the princess demands, I will comply," she said.

"You cannot!"

"I do not need to be able to read the words to know what that says. I can read your face. I will sing."

When it was announced that Princess Jaymna had decided that the night's entertainment should be singing, there was much applause. Tonight the invitation for other guests to take part in the proceedings was open, and many came forward. Ballads and bawdy rounds followed each other carelessly. Music, songs and rich wines flowed in abundance. Spirits were high, talents were varied.

Every now and then someone would ask Jaymna when she might sing for them.

"Later, be patient," she replied each time.

Belinda Mellor

Casandrina did not volunteer. She told Fabiom she would only sing if she was asked, not otherwise. He was certain Jaymna would ask her.

The night wore on. The number of guests coming forward was dwindling. Fabiom guessed Jaymna intended to give the final performance again, but he was wrong. A young couple stepped off the stage after their rendition of *The Ballad of Tibbeau and Droshean* and it was clear that no one else was waiting their turn. Jaymna, still applauding the duet, stepped up onto the dais and surveyed her audience. The emeralds at her throat cast a strange green light onto her skin.

Masgor leant closer to Casandrina. "What tree do you think she favours, my lady? An alder?"

Casandrina smiled briefly, then her smile faded. "Not at all. Alders are foolish but harmless. No, this one would be at home among the yews."

Her tone was light but Fabiom shuddered nevertheless. Damning words indeed, yet true enough. Jaymna was dangerous, of that there could be no doubt.

"Friends, thank you. The night is drawing on and soon we must retire. Some of you have come a long way to be with us. We even have friends from the eastern holdings, including Lord Fabiom and Lady Casandrina from Deepvale.

"Last night we were fortunate that we could admire Lady Casandrina's dancing. This is the first time that I have been able to welcome her to my home and tomorrow, alas, she will be leaving, so tonight I will ask her to bring our little party to a close. I will sing for you next and then, Casandrina, if you will be so kind?" Jaymna smiled her ravishing smile and Casandrina bowed her head minutely in agreement.

"Just play the lyre! We'll take our chances," Fabiom hissed.

"I have fought for you before. I will do so now!"

He had no answer to that.

"Who is that man, just entered?" Casandrina indicated the elegant, well built man standing near the foot of the stairway, his fair complexion and

293

rich, copper brown hair suggesting he was kin to Jaymna.

"Ravik!" Fabiom replied, amazed. "Whatever is he doing here?" Relief washed over him; Ravik would end this debacle.

The same thought had obviously occurred to Masgor, who squeezed his shoulder. "You should eat something. This will soon be over."

Jaymna sang well. She was indeed talented. Prince Ravik, meanwhile, had taken a seat, unobserved by most of the guests – they were too engrossed in the entertainment. Only when Jaymna finished, amid much applause, did he make his presence known, moving forward to take her hand as she stepped down from the dais.

"I wish I could hear what they were saying!" Philon complained.

Ravik was shaking his head, Jaymna was smiling innocently. She patted his arm as if in reassurance. He did not look well pleased. He said something quietly, close by her ear and Jaymna's face changed: a look of horror, mingled with rage, replacing the benign smile. Had her brother not a firm hold on her arm she may well have fled the room.

"He has told her," Masgor said to Fabiom.

Fabiom nodded. "It would seem so."

"I do hope we're not going to be deprived of a chance to hear you sing," Philon whispered to Casandrina. "As a soldier, I have learnt to tolerate the unbearable." He was rather drunk.

It appeared that Ravik and Jaymna were arguing, a spectacle that clearly delighted the majority of the onlookers. Finally Ravik shrugged and let the princess go. She went to her place and sat down sulkily.

"Kind guests," the prince addressed the assembly. "Friends, I am sorry to have missed what has obviously been a fascinating party. I believe you are looking forward to one final, momentous, event." His eyes briefly met Fabiom's across the room as he said so.

Puzzled, Fabiom wondered what the prince could be referring to, other than Casandrina singing. He thought Ravik seemed amused, though, at this distance, he could not be certain.

294

Belinda Mellor

"Lady Casandrina." Ravik bowed in her direction and she acknowledged him with a slight bow of her own.

"Will you do us the honour of singing something – gentle?"

With another slight inclination of her head, she acquiesced.

"Surely not…." Fabiom whispered to her urgently.

Casandrina turned to him with a mischievous smile. "Your prince is a wise man, my love. Trust him. Trust me."

"I do. Of course I do," he protested.

"Lady Casandrina is to sing for us. I am delighted I arrived in time." Once again, Ravik bowed courteously towards Casandrina.

Casandrina did not take the stage. Instead, she moved closer to Fabiom, resting her head against his shoulder. Her song began as a murmur: the susurrant whisper of a summer breeze. All movement in the room ceased. Guests and servants alike were rooted in their places. On a lilting note, her voice rose, echoing the undulating ripple of water over rocks; and then more lavish still: the exquisite notes of a bellbird at dawn. And her words, beguiling, mesmerising, told of seeds bursting with abundant life and mighty trees long dead, of love and loss, of the force of nature and the wonder of life.

Afterwards, when everyone else had left the hall wordlessly, Fabiom and Casandrina remained alone. Still leaning against his side, encircled by his arm, she was silent now. He held her close, his other shoulder resting against one of the carved marble columns that supported the ceiling.

Finally, when the lights had burnt low, she stirred. "Shall we go?"

He moved, as if rising from a deep sleep. "I didn't know that song."

She smiled. "Like the alders, it is harmless."

Maybe her understanding of the word 'harmless' was different to his, he reflected. Yet, even though all the other guests and the servants had left bemused and seemingly disorientated, there was no remnant of the song left in the room, or in his mind. He got to his feet and offered her his hand.

"Maybe we should start for home?" he wondered aloud. But they could not, for they had not yet been given leave.

Early the next morning, Prince Ravik was admitted into the lodge by two laughing woodmaids, who were keenly anticipating their return to Deepvale, for they too missed their trees. He looked from one to the other in wonderment, before cordially greeting Fabiom who had stood up upon the prince's entrance.

Fabiom had lain awake most of the night dreading this moment.

"My lord, I am truly sorry."

"No, Fabiom, I should be the one apologising – for my sister's lack of grace if nothing else. Your telling of your wife's charms was somewhat understated. Is she here?"

"She is walking, down among the almond trees I think. Now that the, er, party, is over, she feels able to go out more freely."

"Oh," Ravik breathed. "Well, I never was too fond of almonds anyway. Though they are Jaymna's favourites."

"Exactly." Fabiom gazed out at the once neat gardens, now riotous with bright flowers and trailing greenery, and wished with all his heart that things had not come to this pass. "What happens now?"

"You return to Deepvale, immediately. Should Jaymna invite you to Southernport again, think of a reason not to attend."

Fabiom smiled wistfully. Fond recollections of their travels together were revived now that they were face to face once more. He deeply regretted that events had conspired to sour those memories.

"Casandrina had been judged most favourably before last night." Ravik propped himself on the edge of the couch and motioned for Fabiom to be seated. "Even if Jaymna had been correct in her assumption about their relative singing skills, it would have made no difference. She is put out of course. No, she is furious – with me as much as with you and Casandrina. Still, she will have little time to dwell on it. Norgest is arriving home today,

Belinda Mellor

much earlier than she expected. He will not be going away again for some time. Maybe Jaymna will settle down." He looked squarely at Fabiom. "She came to me with a very different story."

"That's what I was most afraid of."

"I know you to be rash and impetuous at times, but not a fool. Not to that extent anyway. Though the very fact that you got yourself into this situation suggests you didn't utilise as much common sense as you might have done.

"She pushed me. Exile was her compromise, if I was determined to spare your life –"

Fabiom closed his eyes.

"Once she realised I didn't believe her, she told me the truth, or at least a version of it. One that still painted you in a poor light. I could have told her to go home and let it be – and how I knew her story was false. I deliberately chose not to tell her you were married to a Silvana. Jaymna has been vexing me for far too many years; this situation presented me with a perfect opportunity. But I would not have let it go any further."

"That's why you came," Fabiom realised. "I'm glad of it, my lord. I was more worried about the consequences of winning than losing."

Casandrina came into the room at that moment and the prince, suddenly less poised than usual, stood to take her hand and raise it to his lips.

"I have looked forward to meeting you, Prince Ravik," Casandrina said with a smile that brightened the morning and would have melted far harder men than Ravik.

"And I you," he managed to reply. "I came to tell you how sorry I am that my sister should have caused you such grief, and that the only solution I could think of was so bizarre and so base. I can only hope that you can find it in your heart to forgive me."

He let go of her hand, rather reluctantly, and she linked her arm through her husband's. "Fabiom only speaks well of you. Perhaps one day soon you will honour us and be a guest in our home?" she suggested.

"I would be delighted to do so," Ravik agreed hurriedly, and Fabiom breathed an inaudible sigh of relief. Jaymna's antagonism was not going to drive a wedge between Ravik and himself. Casandrina had won over the prince effortlessly.

They sat then and the woodmaids brought food and drink for Fabiom and Ravik. Once again, Casandrina accepted only water.

"I think you worried my husband, Prince Ravik, when you invited me to sing." She threw Fabiom a teasing glance.

"I understand Sulmarita used to sing for her husband's guests from time to time – without ill effect. Indeed, Lincius used that ploy once to prevent a treacherous rebellion among some would-be holders who thought they were to be pleasantly entertained by her singing and were instead utterly subdued."

"I must have skipped that chapter of the Chronicles," Fabiom admitted ruefully.

Ravik chuckled. Then, more seriously, "Lady, will you permit me to take your husband away for a short while, later this year?"

Fabiom raised his brows in question.

"I must return to Varlass," the prince explained. "I have a bride to bring home."

Casandrina clapped her hands in delight, and all the misery of the past few days faded from her face. Through the window came a sudden waft of perfume as the daphne growing there burst into new flower, and the prince started as a tendril of hibiscus undulated into the room, heavy with blooms. Casandrina's hand flew to her mouth to cover her laughter.

"Oh my! I am sorry," she said, sounding far from contrite, "but it is such happy news!" Fabiom had told her how Ravik had been besotted by the petite, flame-haired daughter of the astrologer-king of that land since their first sojourn in Varlass.

Composing himself, Ravik laughed self-consciously. "I had thought to take Norgest with me, despite his aversion to sea journeys. Now I think

Belinda Mellor

he might be better employed here in Southernport. I would value your company once more, Fabiom, if you are willing."

"Has Jaymna reduced her husband's status with her foolishness?" Casandrina wondered, once Ravik had taken his leave of them.

"She has probably reduced his wealth considerably, and the two often go hand in hand," Fabiom replied. "Maybe he has less influence than he once had, and more creditors."

Casandrina laughed softly.

Masgor was coming along the pathway, pushing his way between overgrown shoots while around him anxious gardeners pruned and cut, to little avail. He was accompanied by Lan'h, who had gone to tell him they were ready to be on their way, and Philon and Seric, who had come to see them off and wish them safe home.

Casandrina took Fabiom's hand and urged him towards the door.

"Come, Fabiom, let us go home. We do not belong here; not one of us."

Part
Five

Chapter One

Fabiom and Casandrina had been married sixteen years when Casandrina announced that she was going to visit Vida.

It was barely dawn and the sun was only beginning to light the morning mist. Fabiom, up earlier than he would have liked, was reading through some notes from the last Assembly meeting that he had to present to the holding's elders later that morning, and thought he had misheard her. He glanced up from his papers.

"You did not say – *my mother*?"

"I did. Soon it will be the Greening. She will undoubtedly have a present for you. I thought I would save her the trouble of sending it over by going to see her myself. Calbrin will drive me."

"Let things be, Casi," he said wearily, laying the sheets aside. "She resented you when I brought you home, simply because you were younger than she. She would have objected to any woman I married on those grounds. Now she feels she truly has cause for complaint – you are as young as the day you first came here. It was one thing to know that would be so, another for her to see it." He leant back in his chair, stretching long legs beneath the desk. "For my part I have no objections of course."

Laughing, she dodged as he reached to catch hold of her. "I want to try to make peace with her," she told him sternly. "It is important."

He sighed. "If you insist."

She tousled his hair then left before he could raise further objections.

Vida would have refused to see Casandrina had not her brother-by-marriage insisted. Casandrina had made it quite clear to Tarison that, having exchanged gifts and enjoyed a pleasant visit with Marid and Kita, she intended to have this audience however long she might have to wait.

"I made her a gift. It is a herbal essence for bathing. Though I do not know if she will accept it."

When Vida came into the vestibule where the Silvana was waiting, she made a point of looking at the flames engulfing the wood in the narrow hearth rather than looking at her son's wife. Casandrina had expected nothing else and took no notice.

"The seasons turn. The morrow marks the first day of another spring. It is now well into his thirty-third year...." Casandrina began.

Vida stiffened, though she did not look away from the burning wood.

"Do you presume to remind me of the age of my own son?"

"I presume nothing. I merely bring up the fact. Shall I leave you to draw your own inferences?"

"You may certainly leave me."

Casandrina hesitated. "Lady Vida —"

"Was there anything else?"

Casandrina toyed with the flask of herbal oil she had prepared for her mother-by-marriage, then set it down gently on a side table. "No, nothing else."

Evening had closed in around Deepvale's hold-house. The aroma of baking

Belinda Mellor

pastries wafted from the kitchen into the family room where a blazing fire crackled in the hearth. Fabiom lounged on a settle reading from *The Poetry of Eryn's Sons*, yet he was not content. Casandrina's absence for the past two days had been extremely convenient: while he was busy in town and hunting with Kilm and his sons for the traditional Greening feast, the best artists of the holding had fulfilled their service duties, as he had been planning for several years. Nevertheless, the house simply did not feel right with her away and it was with relief that he heard her greet Ramus.

"Did you see her?" he asked as soon as she came into the room.

"I saw her. I thought you were going out."

"That was yesterday," he said. "Tell me what happened."

She slipped her arms about his waist and brushed his lips with hers.

"Ah, you have been drinking spiced wine. I think I should like some of that."

"Tell me," he repeated.

"There is little to tell. I saw her. She seems well. I said what I went there to say. I hope she listened with her heart. Now I am home with you." She kissed him again.

He took the hint and dropped the subject.

The following day, the eve of the Spring Festival, which the Silvanii call the Greening, Fabiom rose early. Taking his outdoor clothes from the press, he dressed, seemingly oblivious to Casandrina watching him from their bed.

"Are you working in the orchards today?" she inquired after a while.

"Yes. There's a lot to do," he answered offhandedly, looking for his knife to go into his belt.

"It is Festival. Will you not stay with me?" She pushed back the silken bed sheet, inviting him close to her.

"Sorry." He bent and kissed her forehead, tucking the covers back around her as he did so. "I promised Kilm I'd be there early. I should be finished by midday, in time for the Festival party."

"Fabiom! Are you really going?"

"Why, what else would I be doing?"

"I do not want you to go. It is the Greening. I want...."

Silencing her mid-sentence with a kiss, he whispered, "I *know* what you want. You want a present."

"That as well. Yes." She regarded him serenely.

He had intended to make her wait, to pretend he had overlooked the occasion. He should have known better. Laughing and shaking his head, he threw back the covers and swept her out of the bed onto her feet.

"Very well. I do have a little something for you," he admitted. "Come with me. But no looking until I say."

With his hands over her eyes and accompanied by giggling woodmaids, he guided her into the guest room beside their bedroom, through a door which Lan'h held wide.

"I hope you like it," he murmured into her ear as he removed his hands from her eyes to let her see her gift, finished only yesterday while she was away.

"Oh, Fabiom – this is wonderful!"

Four walls, four ash trees, four seasons, all perfectly painted. She tilted her head back against his shoulder to gaze up at the ceiling, at the intertwined branches of the trees depicted there.

"I like it very much. And he will like it, I know."

With gentle care, Fabiom rested his hands over their child, growing now within her.

"*The seasons turn, the time approaches when there will be born a son for this house, an heir for this holding,*" he quoted, from *the Poetry of Eryn's Sons.*

Casandrina turned her head towards him, her eyes sparkling with pleasure.

"A son, yes. But there is more besides," she said. "So much of the lore of my people has been forgotten. Even you, who care so deeply, know less than your ancestors knew."

306

Belinda Mellor

"Will you not tell me?" Fabiom implored.

"Were you really going to the farm this morning?"

"No." He kissed her. "I was just teasing." And again. "So will you tell me?"

She smiled as she shook her head. "I think not. The knowledge is not lost. You will find it if you want to. Now, come back to bed with me."

Well did Fabiom know there was more besides, and berated himself that he did not know what. Yet he had been a boy when he first searched out all he could find pertaining to the Silvanii and their woodlands, and he had been selective in what he took to heart. Since he gained Casandrina as his wife, he had largely neglected the heavier treatises concerned with such study, and much of what he had skimmed over in those far away days was almost forgotten. He realised that some of the dry, historical passages he had taken little interest in then might have stood him in good stead now.

'Knowledge is power, Fabiom.' Masgor had told him so often. Belatedly, Fabiom understood how right his old tutor was.

That night, after the Festival-eve feast, when all their workers had gone home satisfied, Fabiom sat beside the dying fire in the courtyard. The wine and amber sunset had darkened to deepest blue and the spring stars glimmered bright above him. Almost remembered snippets of information teased his mind and he struggled to grasp hold of them but they slipped from his reach each time. Casandrina regarded him sympathetically, but would not answer the questions he did not ask.

Festival was busy, as always. Throughout the day there were athletic competitions and foot races in the arena, magic acts, recitals and plays in the town squares and marketplaces, and entertainment wherever there was space for a small crowd to gather. Casandrina distributed small gifts to the children, and officiated at a music and dance competition, before leaving at midday to join the other Silvanii in the wildwood. Fabiom conferred two new court officials, granted licences for a new school and a new hostelry, and blessed three new fishing boats. Late in the afternoon, he went with Nalio to watch the final athletic contests, and award the victors their wreaths and prizes.

Although his mother and many of his close friends were attending a new play, as soon as the daylight began to fade, Fabiom left the town. He strolled through the woods to the grove, where he sat with his back against Casandrina's tree, staring up into the still leafless crown, through smoke-grey branches bedecked with tiny purple flowers that had burst from the fat black buds of winter. Eventually his gaze moved across the grove to the young tree growing nearby, around which the protective cordon of shrubs and small trees was bursting into flower for the first time. He smiled and closed his eyes. Casandrina would return to her grove soon, and the wildness of the Greening would still be on her. They would not go home for several days.

Spring and Casandrina blossomed together into summer.

One morning, when Fabiom was supposed to be at an important municipal meeting, Casandrina found him sprawled out, asleep, in the ash grove, a look of deep peace on his face. Reluctantly she sang him to wakefulness. He arrived late at the meeting, but the untroubled rest had cleared his mind and his lapse was overlooked in deference to his incisive comments regarding the rights and responsibilities of land-holders. Afterwards, Tarison returned to the hold-house with him, pleased with the outcome of the meeting – especially decisions made with regards to gleaning rights, which were being eroded in some areas by land-owners who let pigs clean up harvested fields so there was nothing left for the needy, while in others they were being abused by people taking a share before farmers had a chance to harvest. As chief magistrate for the holding, Tarison frequently of late had cause to be concerned about the matter, which in some places had resulted in outbreaks of violence.

While Fabiom and his uncle were at the meeting, Marid and Kita had gone up to the hold-house to help Casandrina and her woodmaids prepare the nursery and to enjoy the bathing pools. They did more, and Fabiom and Tarison arrived to find the portico festooned with garlands of summer flowers, and four more strings made and waiting to be transported back to Valehead.

Over a meal of tarts, made from salmon Fabiom had caught the previous day with an arrow line and apricots Kita had picked that very morning, they discussed their expectations for that year's harvest. After the meal, they sampled a wine of two years since, which had matured nicely, and Tarison declared himself delighted with the current year's grape crop. He seemed distracted nevertheless.

"He's disappointed that Yan is not interested in viniculture." Marid shook her head in despair for both her husband and her son. "Fortunately for family harmony, he knows it's not fair to *make* him be involved."

"I wouldn't say that sending him off to the rather inferior vineyards of Alderbridge to study new grape varieties was not coercion," Fabiom said, grinning.

Tarison guffawed. "He volunteered!"

"So did I," Kita said petulantly.

"I know, little one," her father agreed. "You will be able to do such things soon, but not just yet."

"I'm almost twelve. I'm old enough. Yan would have looked after me. I know as much about grapes as he does!"

"More, probably," Tarison allowed. "But that doesn't change the fact that you are too young to be going off like that."

"If you would like to, you can come back here in a day or two and help me collect foliage and flowers to dry, so that we can make garlands and decorations for Festival," Casandrina suggested.

The child's face broke into a wide grin. "Oh yes, please," she said. "May I, Mama? Please say I may."

"Of course," Marid agreed. "Thank you, Casandrina. At least we have one child who will gladly take over the family business. There is nothing that grows that does not interest this one. And I have no worries about Yan. He has chosen his own path and he's doing very well. The fact that his interests do not include grapes...."

"Is largely down to what happened here, with Giar," Fabiom said.

"No! Well – yes. But that doesn't matter. You don't think we blame you?" Tarison asked, horrified.

"No, I know you don't," Fabiom reassured him. "Nevertheless, it is a fact."

Marid patted his hand. "Yan is a scholar. Masgor thinks he should go to Fairwater to study in the school of philosophy there. He will do very well for himself. Now let's get back to the matter in hand and talk about this year's Harvest Festival. Summer is already well advanced."

They discussed arrangements for the celebrations in both the silk mills and the vineyards, until talk of the harvest led to the municipality meeting and the subject of gleaning.

"Our lord holder seems to have the matter in hand," Tarison said in droll tones. "He was very decisive and very fair in his considerations. I was impressed."

"As it happens, your lord holder had little choice," Fabiom retorted. "He has had his chief magistrate hounding him for a month now on the subject."

"I understand you slept out under the stars last night," Marid said, laughing with them. "Obviously all that fresh air is good for blowing cobwebs away from the mind."

"That may well be true," Fabiom agreed as he poured more wine for them all.

"In that case, you might consider sleeping in the woods rather than the house before any important meeting," Tarison suggested, helping himself to another honey cake. "Especially now that Ravik has appointed you a

Belinda Mellor

member of the Assembly. A clear mind will be essential on those days when the full Assembly sits in Fairwater."

"Yes." Fabiom sighed, resigned. "I am honoured, of course...."

"And so you should be – as one of the youngest ever in Morene's history to hold such a position," his uncle reminded him.

"Even privileges make demands on your time," Fabiom pointed out.

"Privileges especially," Tarison agreed. He grinned across at Casandrina. "For instance, fatherhood – that's a privilege. You are soon to be amazed at the demands on your time *that* will make. Being a favourite of our Ruling Prince will in no way compare, believe me!"

They stayed, enjoying the company, and talking about nothing consequential, until the evening sun dipped behind the hills away to the west. Then, reluctantly, they took their leave. They would not get home until well after midnight but Marid had promised Vida that they would go to the market first thing in the morning, and Vida did not like to be disappointed.

Although Tarison's suggestion had been made in jest, Casandrina chose to take it seriously. That night they made their bed beneath the branches, and Fabiom did indeed sleep better for it. Still the answers he sought remained elusive.

The day after midsummer, Prince Ravik sent for Fabiom to accompany his family to Varlass and meet again the leading citizens of that land, while the prince and princess introduced their fifth son, Raidan, to his maternal grandparents.

Summer ripened into autumn.

Chapter Two

The linden trees were bare as Fabiom strolled down the road. It was early in the morning and few people were about. Those that were hailed him but he acknowledged the greetings absently, his mind back in distant days when he had walked that path almost daily. Age, and some awareness of his position, forbade him to meander in and out of the pale trees as he had been wont to do as a boy, still he idly brushed each with his hand as he passed.

The lime wash had worn away from Masgor's garden wall almost completely, exposing the pale yellow stone beneath. At the far end, the gates hung somewhat awry and protested loudly as Fabiom forced them open. Oddly, a small white donkey grazed the overgrown flower beds. Fabiom stood, puzzled by some almost perceived lack, until he realised that never before had he stood in that place and not heard the gushing flow of the fountains. They were still now, clogged with fallen leaves. What little water remained was stagnant.

He knocked on the door, surprised that the voice that bade him, "Come in," was not Masgor's but one he knew quite as well, that of his cousin Yan.

Belinda Mellor

Yan was scowling, though his expression softened when he saw Fabiom enter.

"How is it with you, cousin?" Fabiom asked.

Yan did not reply, putting his finger against his lips instead and indicating with his head towards a closed door at the far side of the hallway.

"Masgor is unwell. Has been so for days, it seems; still he won't rest. I've been away these past days. I had to return to Alderbridge, to make a final decision on the new strain of disease resistant vines they are developing." He grimaced. "Anyway, I called in here on my way back this morning and found him pale and coughing badly. So I stayed, and have been turning visitors away ever since. Now I think he's sleeping. People keep coming, and he would receive them all. You know what he's like."

"What's wrong with him? I've had no word of fever."

"No, it's nothing like that. He's seventy years old, Fabiom. His chest is bothering him and he has pains. He hasn't eaten for a while. I'm heating some gruel that was prepared earlier. It smells good – he may take some."

"Has his physician attended him yet?" Fabiom asked, keeping his voice as low as possible.

Yan opened the door to the living room, where they could talk without fear of disturbing the patient.

"No, Masgor refused to let anyone call for help. I sent a servant to fetch Namenn though, despite his protestations."

"Who is it? Who's there?" a weak voice called.

Yan and Fabiom looked at each other helplessly. Yan shrugged, "You, I think, he'd be pleased to see. Go to him if you will. I'll see if the gruel is ready."

Fabiom knocked lightly and opened the door to Masgor's bedroom. The old tutor's eyes crinkled in pleasure when he saw who his visitor was, until his attempts to raise himself from his semi-recumbent position resulted in a racking fit of coughing, which left him breathless and limp. He beckoned

Fabiom over to his side, indicating a carafe of honey-gold wine on the oak cabinet beside the bed. Fabiom poured a small amount into a glass beaker and held it to Masgor's lips.

"Yan tells me you've been overdoing it," he remarked lightly.

"Yan worries too much," Masgor replied, and would have said more had he not begun coughing again.

Fabiom helped him sit up higher in the bed, pulling the covers up to Masgor's chest, only for Masgor to push them away again.

"Don't fuss so!"

Fabiom grinned. "Yan is right to worry," he told his old tutor. "You don't take proper care of yourself."

"You didn't come here to fuss around me like a nanny," Masgor guessed, ignoring Fabiom's admonitions. "Do you have a problem?"

Fabiom pulled a stool over to Masgor's bedside and sat down. "Nothing that can't wait."

"Nonsense! If it's to do with your public role then it shouldn't have to wait, and if it's personal, well – I'm bored – it will give me something to think about besides myself."

"It's personal, and it *can* wait."

At that moment, Yan came in with a steaming bowl of gruel.

Fabiom stood up. "I'll call back later, to see how you are. Are you able to stay, Yan?"

"Of course I'll stay, I've nothing urgent to do, other than sort out how many new vines we need to order for the next planting," the younger man replied. "We'll see you later."

Fabiom returned home, wondering what he should do. Had this happened any other year, he would simply have asked Masgor to come and live with him and Casandrina, at least for the winter.

Unlike Fabiom, Casandrina was unperturbed. As soon as she heard that Masgor was ill she insisted he must be persuaded to move in with them

Belinda Mellor

until he was quite recovered. Since the day they first met, she had held the tutor in high regard.

"And he will give you something else to worry about, besides me," she told Fabiom, as if that were good reason enough.

The woodmaids were excited at the prospect of having a house-guest who needed looking after, and immediately set about persuading Ramus to let them help with the preparations. Fabiom's efforts to dissuade them, on the grounds that he had not yet suggested the idea to Masgor, let alone had Masgor agreed, went unheeded. Ramus himself merely smiled. He had become very pragmatic with the passing of the years since Fabiom's marriage, being well used to the ways of the woodmaids. He also accepted that, as Casandrina had not the slightest interest in matters such as the buying of food or the repairs to the house that were sometimes necessary, such things were his responsibility for the most part. At least that burden was lessened now that he had the full-time help of Calbrin, the youngest son of Fabiom's farm manager, who had been taken on in the house, in deference to Ramus's advancing years.

With his household behind him, Fabiom returned to Masgor's home later that evening. Yan let him in, reporting that, despite his best efforts, he had not been able to prevent all of Masgor's would-be visitors from disturbing the sick man. Consequently, Yan was more than pleased when Fabiom told him what he had in mind.

They wondered if they might have difficulty convincing their old tutor, who valued his privacy and independence, but when they went through and mooted the suggestion, Masgor agreed immediately, providing he could bring some of his books with him – for he was engaged in research he was not prepared to abandon merely because he was unwell.

"You'll have your books. But it might not be the most restful convalescence anyone could wish for," Fabiom warned, though he knew Masgor, like most other frequent visitors, had long since learnt to take the sometimes oddly prepared meals and occasional lapses of etiquette in his stride.

Yan promised to keep an eye on the tutor's house in his absence, delighted to have free and undisturbed access to the library there. He thought he might even use the opportunity to act on Masgor's long held assertion that he should take on some junior pupils.

It turned out to be quite a performance to get Masgor ready to go, for he was hardly well enough to dress himself yet forbade them assist him. Instead, he sent them off to collect the books and papers he required, along with his writing accoutrements, his money box and a few personal treasures he wanted to have near him. The books he wanted were obscure and scattered throughout his house so that, by the time they were all gathered together, Masgor had managed to get himself washed and dressed to travel, although he then needed to rest from the exertion. After that, there were instructions for Yan, about locking the doors and minding the fires and reminders of where he would find things, should he need them.

Fabiom had arranged for Calbrin to drive the donkey-cart to the tutor's residence. When Yan had promised, for the third time, that he would mind everything and do exactly what was required, they loaded the boxes and trunks and, finally, Masgor himself and the vehicle set off for the hold-house, leaving Yan behind to lock up in accordance with Masgor's instructions.

The first thing Fabiom did, after seeing Masgor settled into the most comfortable guest room, was to send a message to Nalio.

Nalio came with a supply of hellebore root and scabious, picked from his father's garden which had, for many years now, produced an abundance of the finest medicinal herbs. With him came Nissus, his thirteen-year-old son, already an apt student of his father's and grandfather's profession.

Nissus bruised the scabious leaves as Nalio needed them and carefully poured boiling water on to make an aromatic inhalant for the invalid. As he did so, he chatted amiably with Masgor and Fabiom, telling them how he was about to start classes in mathematics, but that he really wanted to learn about history and science. He told them too, about the music lessons he was taking with his great aunt, who had also taught his father music when he was younger. Fabiom was well acquainted with Nissus's great aunt, for the formidable lady had been his music teacher also, though Nissus seemed to be no more daunted by her than he was by anyone else. He held the iron dish while his father carefully measured out the powdered hellebore root and, despite Nalio's protestations, explained to them how it was good for killing rats, and how sorry he was that Masgor was no longer taking on pupils as he would like to have gone to him for tutoring, as his father had. Nalio sent him off to fetch more water at that point, for Masgor had begun coughing badly – an attack brought on by trying not to laugh at the boy's frank honesty.

"I apologise. I shall leave him at home tomorrow," the physician sighed in exasperation.

"You will do no such thing!" Masgor told him. "He's good for me, I'm sure. I'm tired of you, and Fabiom here, and Yan – three people who should know better – treating me like some old fool in my dotage. I have a chill on me, that's all."

"Yes, sir," replied Nalio meekly, with a sideways glance at Fabiom who would have laughed, had he dared.

"Speaking of Yan," Masgor said, "that's who you should speak to, Nalio. He'd tutor the boy, I'm sure, for a year or so anyway. With luck he'll be away in Fairwater soon after; still it would be a start." He lay back then and almost immediately fell asleep.

"Pity I didn't know more about the properties of such plants when we were younger, eh, Fabiom? Could have saved us all a few sore knuckles," Nalio joked as he put away his vials and pots in a sturdy leather satchel.

Only three days had passed and Masgor had barely begun to recover when he commented on how Fabiom appeared troubled when he saw him first thing in the morning. When he questioned his erstwhile pupil, Fabiom had to admit he did not exactly know what it was that was preying on his mind. He felt as if he was searching for something but, just as he was about to find it, he seemed to forget what it was he was looking for.

Masgor considered Fabiom's predicament. "And you are certain that it's not simply the natural concerns of impending fatherhood?"

Fabiom shook his head. For certain, the child would bring great changes to his life and a deal more personal responsibility than he was used to, yet he felt he was ready and was keenly, if rather nervously, looking forward to his son's arrival. He was sure that what was eluding him had to do with something else altogether. And yet, maybe not. In some way it seemed that it was not entirely unconnected.

"Then all I can suggest is that you try to concentrate on something quite different. That's a ruse that often brings errant thoughts to mind, is it not?" was all the advice Masgor could offer. "I too have been looking for something," he remembered. "I've had young Calbrin searching for a particular book and some papers, but now I think they must have been left behind in my study. The papers are quite rare and I would rather not entrust the task to anyone else, so I must ask you to put aside your high office and become my errand boy, Fabiom."

With that, Masgor gave him his ring of keys, the book title and a list of papers, many of which Fabiom knew from long, if not enthusiastic, association. He promised Masgor he would fetch them that very day.

Yan was not at Masgor's house when Fabiom arrived. There was, however, much evidence that he had been. The gates had been oiled and the fountain was clear of leaves and scum, though the rest of the garden was untouched and Fabiom knew it would remain so. He resolved to send Calbrin along to help tidy the garden against Masgor's return, for Yan's childhood love of growing things, a love Fabiom had fostered and encouraged, had been badly eroded by the incident in the Dancing Glade fourteen years ago.

Belinda Mellor

When Fabiom opened the front door, the house smelt fresh and clean, yet not familiar and comfortable as it should. It was almost a relief to find that inside Masgor's study were the same smells of old books and leather as always, though it was cold enough without the fire lit.

Beside the dead hearth, Masgor's desk was piled high with papers. Across from that, beneath the window, the autumn sun shone weakly onto the low, barely padded seats where the tutor's pupils, Fabiom among them, had sat – sunlight pouring over their shoulders, illuminating their books and their writing boards. Fabiom smiled at the memories that flowed from the wellspring of his mind, though the chill draught gusting through the open door soon brought him out of his reverie and reminded him of his purpose there.

He located the book and papers Masgor wanted easily enough. They were on the far side of the hearth, piled onto one of the smaller tables in the room and had obviously been missed amid the confusion of packing. As he collected them together, he looked up at the shelves reaching from the floor to the high ceiling. Like those behind the desk, they were still laden with reading matter, for Masgor had only brought his most prized books, and those he referred to most often, to the hold-house.

Despite the pervading chill, Fabiom could not resist spending some time looking through the library, selecting a weighty tome or a slim pamphlet at random to glance through. He smiled wryly as he came across a well thumbed version of the *Chronicles of Lincius, Prince of Morene*. It had been heavy going and he had been glad when Masgor decided that he could put it aside and proceed on to other histories. That had been in the days before he and Lincius had something in common – a Silvanan wife. On a whim he took the book and added it to the pile he was bringing home.

'*The Prince Lincius, upon reaching his thirty-fourth year, presented his son Tibbeau, heir to the bountiful land of Morene, to the people of that land. They rejoiced greatly. Later (gentle reader understand that your chronicler cannot be*

Silvana

certain of these things) the child was presented to the people of the woods, as is the way; brother and sister, as is told....'

'Brother and sister', Fabiom cast the book aside. That was it! The half-known facts tantalising his mind came back. Awake he could at last begin to make sense of them. If he understood the quotation from the *Chronicles* aright, within the month he would have a grown daughter as well as an infant son.

On his way through the garden he paused to pluck a sprig of hibiscus flowers.

Fabiom was not surprised to find Casandrina waiting for him when he arrived at the grove. He kissed her before he laid the sprig of wine red flowers in a hollow formed by two crossed branches of her tree. She acknowledged his gift with a smile.

"I think I've been rather stupid," he apologised as he walked over to the slender replica of Casandrina's tree. "Almost seventeen years has this grown here," he murmured, almost to himself, and he caressed the branches of the young ash as he said so.

Casandrina was singing so quietly he could barely hear her, yet her song filled his heart – as did the knowledge that the denizen of the young tree, the seed of which had been sown on the night of their marriage, would emerge on the day he achieved his thirty-fourth year, a Silvana. The smaller trees surrounding it rustled and grasped at his clothing, their woodmaids sentient already.

"Now soon I will meet my daughter," he added, as he disentangled the fabric of his tunic from the clutch of the blackthorn.

A drop of bright blood stained his thumb.

Belinda Mellor

Chapter Three

*O*n Fabiom's birth eve, all of Casandrina's woodmaids gathered and sang about the house. Casandrina rested in their bed chamber and smiled her most encouraging smile for her husband.

"I am weary, nothing else. And he is strong."

"I know," he muttered. "Still I can't help worrying about you, both of you."

"And I love you for it," she told him.

Just then, Zin'h and Kir'h slipped into the room, wide-eyed with wonder.

"Fabiom – your mother has arrived," Kir'h whispered.

Vida took charge of the woodmaids, of Ramus and Calbrin, and of Casandrina. Nalio, whom Fabiom had insisted should be in attendance, she dismissed.

"You can go now, physician Nalio. I don't think you'll be needed here, do you?"

"Er, no, probably not." Nalio looked at Fabiom, who could only shrug.

"Thank you, Nalio." Casandrina shifted position on the daybed. "Perhaps you and Eifa will visit tomorrow, in the morning? I should like that."

Silvana

He kissed her hand, bowed slightly to Vida and grinned at Fabiom. "I'll take my leave then, if there's nothing I can do –"

"There is something you could help me with, if you've time," Fabiom remembered. He glanced at his mother and his wife. "I presume I'm not wanted, either?"

They both smiled, though as he and Nalio left the chamber, Casandrina said: "Do not go far."

"What are we doing?" Nalio asked as Fabiom led the way out of the house towards a stone outbuilding.

"The yew tree at the edge of the garden is almost as big as when we were children."

"True, I noticed it has a good crop of berries too. Brings back memories."

Inside the building, Fabiom rummaged around until he found two axes, one of which he handed to Nalio. "We were lucky that my father caught us when he did, before we swallowed any. I'd rather not rely on luck. Let's deal with it today, before my son is born."

The axes were sharp and both men were strong. Before long the tree was down, the golden heartwood bright against the creamy-white sapwood.

Fabiom regarded the fallen yew. "I never like cutting a healthy tree, of any sort."

"There is some beautiful timber there," Nalio pointed out.

"Indeed. Father had a garden seat made from the trunk and boughs of the last one. Maybe I'll do the same." He smiled wistfully. "I'll ask Kilm to take it away and dry the timber. But I want to get the branches burnt straight away." He flexed his hand and Nalio noticed a red line across the heel of his thumb.

"Idiot. You've cut yourself. No – don't touch it! The tree can wait."

Leaving the axes, they went back to the house, where Nalio tended the cut. "You do realise the berries are the least poisonous part of a yew?" he scolded. "Keep an eye on that; if you got any sap in there, you'll know about it. Your wife won't be impressed with either of us if you get sick! As for your mother…."

Belinda Mellor

Lan'h, who had brought them each a beaker of cold water, giggled. "I shall look after him, Nalio," she promised. "I shall make him a tonic. Casandrina will know if any of the poison has got into his system."

"Except, I'd rather you didn't mention this to her, not now," Fabiom said.

The woodmaid scowled. "I would not need to mention it! I told you – she will know."

Nalio chuckled. "I'll see you tomorrow, Fabiom, and your new son. Go back to your wife now. I'll be thinking of you."

In their room, Casandrina examined his hand, but merely shook her head and kissed the wound. "You are fortunate," she told him.

He gathered her into his embrace. "For certain I am," he agreed.

As Casandrina's time drew near, and having nearly tripped over her son for the third time, Vida found the simplest way of dealing with him was to send him to attend the needs of the still frail Masgor.

Taking pity on him, one or other of the woodmaids ran along the corridor every few minutes to let Fabiom know what was happening. Invariably they would tell him that the baby would come soon and that Casandrina was in good spirits. Sometimes they would add that his mother had held her hand. Then no one came for what seemed like a very long time, and Fabiom paced around Masgor's room, every now and again mumbling apologies to his tutor, who was sitting by the window in an overstuffed chair, wrapped in several blankets.

"Fabiom, sit down. She's a Silvana; 'strong' seems a totally inadequate word. What can happen to her?"

Trying to humour him, Fabiom sat down. He fidgeted, raking his hands through his hair, biting his lip.

Masgor cleared his throat. "Walk around, Fabiom. You'll drive me to distraction otherwise."

He had only begun his first length of the spacious room when the door opened. Sweet singing drifted through the doorway, along with Kir'h, whose smile told him all he needed to know. Urged on by Masgor, he followed the woodmaid and the trail of song along the corridor, to his own rooms.

All the woodmaids were singing and somewhere, just beyond his hearing, Fabiom could sense the grander song of the Silvanii, as his mother placed his new-born son in his arms for the first time.

The following morning, Fabiom's birth anniversary, Vida rose with the sun, checked on Masgor, then went to take her leave of her son and his family.

"Mother," Fabiom said in some surprise. She had never been an early riser.

Reclining on the bed, Casandrina cuddled her tiny babe and took in Vida's attire. "You are leaving."

"Will you not stay longer?" Fabiom asked.

"Masgor was coughing when I looked in on him. I believe he needs some medication," Vida suggested.

"Poor Masgor. He *has* been rather neglected," Casandrina murmured, gazing at Fabiom anxiously.

Throwing a dressing robe about himself, Fabiom flashed the two of them a lopsided grin and left them alone.

At Casandrina's invitation, Vida picked up the baby. He yawned, waking, but did not cry.

"He has Fabiom's eyes, Tawr's too. My grandson." She looked at her son's wife then. "I have been foolish. It has taken this new child to show me that. I am a grandmother now, and I am content."

Casandrina accepted her son back. "Then you will come home – to stay?"

"No, I'll not do that. Though not because of you. I shall visit often. But I have a home in Valehead now and well, I like to live – differently."

Casandrina laughed softly at that. "I understand. And thank you for everything. I am glad you came."

"As am I. Have you decided what you will name him?"

Belinda Mellor

'*Lesandor*', the name whispered in the breezes that played in the branches and sent the drying leaves pirouetting to the earth. The river that ran through the Dancing Glade chattered '*Lesandor, Lesandor,*' as it tripped over the stones in its bed.

They had brought the infant here to be greeted by his mother's people and to meet his sister.

The rich scent of mushrooms and humus rose all about, as the rotted leaves of past years were disturbed by dancing feet. Casandrina nursed Lesandor and looked with pleasure on the rejoicing and gaiety that filled the glade. Silvanii had come from all over the wildwood, most of them barely visible; a few, like herself, temporarily substantial – including the birch Silvana, Taparaina, who had come all the way from Riverplain with her family. The woods were decked in russets and golds, bright autumn colours that glowed in the warm sunlight. Rowan, whitethorn and holly were hung with glistening berries, while hazel and almond sported ripe seed cases, so that the glade appeared to have been decorated like some great hall for a high ceremony, with living tree trunks supporting a canopy of bright boughs, as carved columns would uphold a vaulted ceiling. Brighter even than their trees, the woodmaids were there in great number and their laughter and playfulness lent a still more festive air to the occasion.

Despite his life-long association with the woods and his seventeen years of marriage to Casandrina, Fabiom found it an awe-inspiring experience, for a far less potent draught than he had once imbibed had rendered him sensible to every Silvana and woodmaid there. They were dancing high measures and singing songs that filled his mind and made his heart ache with their beauty. Never before had he witnessed anything like it.

Among the numerous Silvanii were some he recognised; Narilina of course and another, who said to Casandrina,

"*So, no regrets?*"

"Are you still jealous, Gracillia?" she replied. "He was ever mine and I would have striven hard for him. You do know that?"

There was no rancour in her voice and Gracillia merely laughed as she rejoined the dance.

Fabiom's smile faded. 'Ever mine.' He should have been pleased to hear her say so and was, in a way, but he shuddered nevertheless. He had reread *Tales of a Woodsman* recently, in his quest for his elusive answers, and the conversation between the two ash Silvanii recalled a passage to his mind:

'The woodsman accepted that he had not been chosen by the Silvanii, for so he thought. And in a way he learnt to be content in that knowledge, listening to little but the music that sang in his mind. His haunted life was nearing its end before he learnt the truth.

"You think that you were not loved enough? Rather you were loved too well," she told him. "They destroyed each other rather than give up their claim on you."

And he brought garlands of fresh flowers and lay down beside one of the blighted trees, many years dead. Four days he spent there and four beside the other tree, similarly bedecked with bright blooms, and he wept onto the earth. But there was no life there and his tears were lost in the barren soil.'

Fabiom remembered the angry welts on Casandrina's arm and could not help but wonder if a similar doom might have befallen her, had she not prevailed. He had no thoughts for what might have happened to himself; it was enough to know that she would still have wanted him. Suddenly filled with an urgent need to hold her, to be certain she was really his, he turned towards her – to discover she had moved away across the glade, dancing now with the other Silvanii, and he found himself watching her, almost fearful that she would fade away.

Eventually he was distracted from his musings by the exodus of Silvanii and woodmaids dancing in and out of the trees, voices echoing, as they made their way from the Dancing Glade to the grove where Casandrina's

Belinda Mellor

tree grew. She returned to him, singing as she did so, and he put aside his fears.

They had not been long in the ash grove when the sun reached its zenith. Silence fell. Casandrina moved closer to Fabiom, Lesandor asleep in her arms.

"Father."

Fabiom turned and found himself looking into the eyes of a girl so like Casandrina and yet so different, in ways that hinted of his own parents, he knew her at once to be his child. She held her hands out to him and he took them tenderly in his own.

"I did not expect to be able to touch you," he marvelled.

Casandrina told him gently: "Only for today, Fabiom, unless she takes a husband in your lifetime; though you will always be able to see her clearly."

He held her hands more firmly at that. "Elzandria, welcome," he said formally. And the voices took up that chorus and welcomed the new Silvana into the wildwood.

Reluctantly, Fabiom released her. Elzandria turned to Casandrina and held out her arms to take her baby brother. She kissed him lightly and he gazed up at her serenely, with eyes as blue as the bright autumn sky.

"All happiness," she whispered.

All was hushed once more as Elzandria began to sing, a hymn of blessing for the child and for her parents. Slowly, other voices took up the theme, each apparently singing something quite different, yet there was only one voice to be heard – it was the voice of the wildwood and it sang until the sun began to slip beyond the horizon, burnishing the clouds visible through the depleted foliage of the autumn trees.

"Now I must go," Elzandria told Fabiom as she kissed his cheek. "Come and visit me often."

She was gone before he had the chance to promise that he would. She did not need to hear him say it. The other Silvanii and the woodmaids had faded into the shadows, leaving Casandrina and Fabiom alone with Lesandor.

Fabiom put his arms around his wife and baby son.

"It's mild. Do you want to stay here tonight?" he suggested.

She looked down at the sleeping child in her arms, then up to the crown of the ash tree high above them.

"No, not tonight. He will spend enough time here of his own volition, no doubt. And he is, after all, heir to a Grand Holding, there are likely to be other visitors to greet him. Let us go back to the house tonight. Maybe we will stay tomorrow."

Since Jaymna's invidious party and Casandrina's subsequent invitation, Prince Ravik had been a frequent guest in Deepvale's hold-house. He arrived the very next day, accompanied by his eldest son, the nine-year-old Prince Romarus. Yet though they came bearing splendid gifts for the new baby, Ravik was clearly more interested in Elzandria.

"Did you see her, Fabiom? Is she beautiful?" He sighed enviously. "She may be grown, but at least you *have* a daughter. One son is perfect, two, even three, fine. But five! Is it really too much to ask for – to have just one daughter as well?"

"Your poor wife!" Casandrina scolded. "I am sorry she could not travel with you this time, it is too long since I have seen her. How many children do you plan to have dear Maedrim bear you before you concede that sons are to be your lot?"

"Oh, since Raidan was born we've abandoned hope!" Ravik chuckled. "We can now only wait for the boys to grow up and trust that one of them gives us a grand-daughter to cherish and indulge." He grinned as Romarus, astride a rather elderly white donkey, rode into view in the garden.

"You have a niece," Casandrina reminded him, a hint of old antipathy in her eyes. "Your sister had a daughter, as I recall."

Belinda Mellor

"Two, but I see them rarely." His expression was pained. "The oldest is twenty, no, twenty-one and to be married next year. In truth, she has grown too much like her mother. As for the younger girl, she's twelve and already spoilt enough, without any help from me."

Fabiom rocked his son's cradle.

"As you've given up your quest for a girl child, does this mean we won't be making any more trips to Varlass for a while?"

Ravik laughed heartily at that. Over the past nine years he and Fabiom had visited Varlass on five occasions since they had gone there to bring home Ravik's new bride, each time to introduce Maedrim's parents to their latest grandson.

"I'm sorry. I do keep dragging you away from home. But it's your own fault – you make a splendid travelling companion. No, no more visits to Varlass for a while."

"I do not mind your taking him to Varlass," Casandrina said quietly.

Ravik inclined his head. "And no more trips to Gerik either. We've done all we need to do there, at least for the foreseeable future."

They had gone twice more to Gerik, though only briefly, and just as Varlass had been as pleasurable as Fabiom remembered it, Gerik was as depressing. Ravik enjoyed his company and appreciated his talents and that meant he demanded his time.

"I am glad," Casandrina smiled. "Now, why not go with Fabiom to the grove and meet his daughter? She will be pleased, I think. You will be her first visitor."

Ravik's eyes narrowed, unsure whether she was being serious. Across the room, Fabiom smiled broadly.

"You mean it, don't you?" Ravik breathed. "I, I don't know … may I?"

Lesandor whimpered and Casandrina lifted him from his cradle.

"Yes. Bring her a flower."

The courier arrived from Southernport while Ravik and Fabiom were in the woods.

Lesandor was drifting into a contented sleep in his mother's arms when Calbrin brought the package through to the day room, carrying it with ease, though it was large enough.

"Another gift for the little one," he said with a grin.

Casandrina regarded the package curiously.

"Open it for me please, Calbrin. As you can see, my hands are full."

"It's some sort of musical instrument," he muttered as he removed the leather casing. "It'll be a while before he's big enough for this. It's an old one too, a real beauty. My lady, is something the matter?"

Casandrina had moved towards him and was staring at the ornate kithara Calbrin was holding in his hands, fashioned from sycamore, inlaid with amber, detailed in copper. Copper. Only in Gerik was that metal found. And the amber.... As her fingers brushed the inlay and then the wood, she felt what she had most feared: the amber and the wood had come from the same tree: a Silvanan tree.

Her voice was barely audible as she asked him, "Who sent it?" Yet she knew. She already knew.

"The Princess Jaymna, my lady."

"Oh, Calbrin – take it from me, please. Burn it, burn it at once."

Seeing her distress, he hurried from the room to do her bidding.

For only the second time since she had come to Fabiom's house, Casandrina wept.

the end

Belinda Mellor

The story continues...

Silvana

The Turning

Available 2014

Fabiom travelled on foot, for he could make better speed than with the donkey cart, yet Fairwater had never seemed so far away. It rained incessantly. He passed the two nights it took to make the journey in roadside taverns, pausing only long enough to get some sleep and dry his clothes. He ate on the move; walked, ran, walked, ran. Eventually the river widened into the estuary that led into the sea.

Set atop the highest hill, built of white marble, the royal palace overlooked the shining city – though Fabiom had neither time, nor inclination to be awed by the splendour. He went up to the palace immediately and requested an audience with Prince Ravik even as he rinsed his hands in the red marble basin of the palace heart room.

"Fabiom! This is a pleasant surprise. More pleasant than the other surprises I've had sprung on me today, for certain! There's new trouble brewing in Gerik, I fear, or so my sources tell me. But – something's wrong. What is it, my friend?"

"What sort of trouble?" Fabiom demanded. "I'm sorry, my lord, I forget myself. It's just … no, I must know. What trouble?"

"Rebel forces are massing, even in the towns. Robstrom's name is being spoken openly once more. There's talk of a new order, even if it must be achieved by civil war. That is what I've heard. Now, tell me what has brought you here."

Ravik watched Fabiom pace towards the window to stare down onto the city and out to the ocean beyond.

"Lesandor is in Gerik. I can't believe, no, I *don't* believe you sent him there. Yet, he was given no option. He sailed from Windwood, with your youngest son." Fabiom turned to look at his prince. "His mother fears for his safety. Gerik – Gerik could destroy him."

The colour had drained from Ravik's face and briefly he covered his eyes. "I know that!" he hissed. "It isn't even my venture. Norgest has organised it. Larse his son – step-son – is in command. It's a trading voyage. Believe me, Fabiom, there is no way I would have sent Lesandor to Gerik. He was meant to have been on board the *Spikenard*, which sailed for Varlass six days ago. Raidan *should* be with him, I had intended them both to go to Varlass. Raidan was away in Rushford on my behalf. I sent a message to him there to go to Southernport and take ship; I told him they should go together. But why would he think that meant to Gerik?" He muttered the last, almost to himself.

Fabiom slumped down on a settle. "You may not have sent them, but please – bring Lesandor home. My lord, I will do anything…."

"No." Ravik held up his hand. "You need offer me nothing, Fabiom. You're my friend. Even if you were not, I do know enough about the people of this land not to send such a one as Lesandor to Gerik." He paused and shook his head. "Just as Jaymna knows it."

about the author

Belinda Mellor lives with her husband and daughter and far too many animals on a lifestyle block in the Top of the South Island of New Zealand; a place the family came to on holiday some years back and forgot to leave. A background in theology and applied spirituality make her eminently suited to a life of goat milking and egg collecting.

At the age of five she won a school award for 'free expression' and has not stopped writing since. She was an inaugural winner of an Ian St James literary award for her fantasy story *Bronwen's Dowry* (published with the eleven other finalists in the Collins anthology *At the Stroke of Twelve*). Since then she has been awarded a literary bursary and an award for a character-driven story, had numerous non-fiction and occasional fiction pieces published in magazines and local newspapers and a play for children performed by a theatre-in-education company.

acknowledgments

Silvana has been a long time in the making. And I do mean a long time. Twenty years ago, the basic story came to me and I wrote a 40,000 word novella. A decade later, it came out of a drawer and over time became a fully-fledged novel, and then two. Now three.

Over the years, a lot of wonderful people have come into my life. Many of them have had a positive impact that has contributed to this project finally reaching fruition.

So, I would like to thank my family, especially Peter, Iona and Alison, and many friends, especially Emma, whose beautiful painting 'Wildwood' adorns the front cover of this edition, Vonnie, Karen, Katherine, and Anne (the very first reader), for encouragement, inspiration and motivation.

My parents, Ann and Albert Raine, always supported my writing. I have fond memories of my father overwriting my penciled poems and stories in ink when I was six or seven, so that they wouldn't fade, and I will never forget dancing around our house in Ireland with my mother, celebrating the announcement that my story *Bronwen's Dowry* was an Ian St James Award winner and we were off to London for the awards ceremony. That was in 1989. Sorry it's taken so long to get to this stage and neither of you are here to enjoy the publication of *Silvana* with me.

I can hardly begin to express my gratitude to *Scribophile* writers and readers for all their help, nagging, good humour and common sense. I must mention Allison, Aubrey, Brett, Cheryl, Chris, Helen, Jim, Kirsty, Margaret, Pat and Rebekah; as well as being so encouraging, you have brightened my on-line hours! Extra special thanks to Teresa for sharing the journey and for editorial services above and beyond.

I also owe a debt of gratitude to several professional writers who have kindly given their time to help me: Vincent Banville, David Corbett and Katherine Kurtz.

Finally, to the wonderful publishing team at The Copy Press, especially Dave and Suzanne, a huge 'thank you'. You are brilliant.